STARGAZY

PIE

By the same author:

STARGAZY PIE

PIE

Greenwing & Dart
Book One

VICTORIA GODDARD

Underhill
Books

Grandview, PEI

2016

ISBN: 978-0993752278

First published by Underhill Books in 2016.

Underhill Books
4183 Murray Harbour Road
Grandview, PEI C0A 1A0
www.underhillbooks.com

To my family, for all their support this year.
Thank you.

Chapter One

THE MARKET TOWN of Ragnor Bella in south Fiellan is generally considered a bucolic backwards sort of place, the sort of hometown you leave as soon as possible.

I left at eighteen to go to university; I hadn't been planning on ever coming back.

Ragnor Bella's major claims to fame, in the views of the one travel writer who discusses it, are the house of Chief Magistrate Talgarth, which is one of the finer examples of Late Bastard Decadent Imperial architecture in Northwest Oriole; the unparalleled and undefeated racehorse Jemis Swiftfoot, which was personally commended by Emperor Artorin; and the strange and disturbing history of Major Jakory Greenwing, who was also personally commended by Emperor Artorin, and subsequently arraigned as one of the worst traitors in Astandalan history.

As a result of a lost bet I was named Jemis after the racehorse, and the late Jakory Greenwing was my father, but I'd never had much to do with either the Talgarths or their house until I returned from university and, against all plans, preferences, and public advice, promptly acquired a job in the local bookstore. It probably tells you all you need to know about Ragnor Bella that we only have one. It's run by one Mrs. Etaris, the Chief Constable's wife.

It had been a beautiful summer, but by the time I got to Fiellan in September the autumn rains had set in in earnest. Friday morning, my first day of work, was no different, and although there were a few customers, none of whom I knew and all of whom ignored me, not very many people were havering for books.

"There'll be more tomorrow," Mrs. Etaris said to me, when I peered out the window at the rain and lack of custom in the square. At my blank look she added, "Market day."

I dropped the curtain aside and petted the cat absently. "Oh, of course."

"I generally close early on Friday, and open during the market."

"I see."

"Tomorrow should be quite busy, as certainly people will be interested to see you back in town."

Since returning to town on Tuesday, I hadn't seen anyone to speak of besides my family. Stepfamily. Stepfamily's inlaws. "Mm."

Mrs. Etaris smiled. "Why don't you get us some coffee and nibbles from the bakery, Mr. Greenwing? Here's a bee."

It was raining when I left the bookstore, so I turned up the collar of my old coat, put on my new hat (bought in Leaveringham when seeing off Hal—or rather, since in Fiellan, as Mrs. Etaris informed me that morning, we do not follow the *radical southern fashions* of Morrowlea—his Grace the Right Honourable Duke of Fillering Pool), and dashed across the square with only a sideways glance at the pigeons pecking disconsolately at the ground outside the bakery.

I'd begun my studies at Morrowlea reading the History of Magic, and always liked the idea of haruspexy, divination by way of birds. That was a magic system that entered the Empire from somewhere far away from Northwest Oriole, and if it ever worked at all, it certainly didn't now.

Not that it would be a good idea to try it, since my reputation was on shaky enough grounds as it was and magic was even more out of fashion in Ragnor Bella than first names. Not to mention that I had no gift at magic. Or that I changed subjects after that first course on divination. Or that—

Anyhow.

The pigeons were ruffled and damp, and fluttered away as if glad for the excuse when I neared them. I sneezed at a gust of wind full of woodsmoke, an even surer sign of autumn than the rain, and hastened inside the bakery.

Mr. Inglesides was just putting out a tray of cinnamon buns. I'd known him since my mother married Mr. Buchance and we came to live in town, and then got to know him better after my stepfather remarried, since the second Mrs. Buchance was his sister.

By the Emperor, my family confounds me sometimes. Three years at Morrowlea ignoring it hasn't helped much.

"Mr. Inglesides," I said, sketching an elaborate bow complete with heel-click I'd invented during the summer.

He stopped, tray held aloft.

After a moment wondering if he didn't recognize me, I realized that probably young gentlemen oughtn't make elaborate bows to bakers, convoluted relationship or not, but even if the summer had stripped away a number of my illusions, I wasn't prepared to abandon all my principles just yet.

He set down the tray on the counter. "My sister mentioned you were back in town. I'm sorry about your stepfather."

No one had made a hurry to offer me condolences, six weeks after the event, not when I'd been so gauche as to miss the funeral. I nodded awkwardly. "Thank you."

"I hear you're going to be working at Elderflower Books now. Mrs. Etaris sent you out for coffee?"

"And cinnamon buns, if you please." I put the bee on the counter and he counted out a handful of silver pennies in change. A couple were shiny-new, but when I looked at them they had Emperor Artorin's bald and benevolent head on them.

"He's still High King, at least until we hear otherwise," Mr. Inglesides said.

I looked up at him, startled. He smiled with a slow and sly pleasure, as one realizing that I'd gone to Morrowlea, famously the most radical of the Circle Schools—possibly the most radical of all the continent's universities—and ready to show me he was a kindred spirit.

I would *never* have suspected that.

He waggled his eyebrows. "Not that some people don't want a bit of change."

"I'll just take this for now," I said with a grin, for the door had opened again. I turned to see who it was, half-expecting a total stranger (for it *had* been three years since I was last in town), and was quite astonished to see Dame Talgarth sailing in.

If ever there were people who don't want a bit of change in Ragnor Bella, the Talgarths were them. They were famous for keeping to pre-Fall standards in their country house, which must cost a pretty penny in these days without magic—as must their house,

Late Bastard Decadent Imperial architecture not being noted for its efficiency. Dame Talgarth comes from money in middle Fiellan, or so they used to say, and as Chief Magistrate of Ragnor Bella, Justice Talgarth must make a good income to add to his rents—which are probably extortionate.

"Dame Talgarth," I said politely, with a bow. She looked me once up and down, and I saw puzzlement change to astonishment, and then she gave me the cut direct.

Well, that answered the question of whether a scholarship to Morrowlea might have changed the local gentry's views on me, I thought, and smiled pointedly at the woman with her. She was dressed in a Scholar's black robes, the trim on her hood proclaiming her a professor, at Kilromby probably from the plaid.

She ignored me without, however, any of the venom displayed by Dame Talgarth; she appeared to be ignoring everything but some invisible specks floating in the air in front of her.

Dame Talgarth spoke with an air of superb condescension she must have been practicing for years, keeping her gaze fixed well above Mr. Inglesides' head. "Half a dozen loaves of the best white. The maid will pick it up on her way home from her half day."

"Of course, Dame Talgarth. Good morning, Domina Ringley." Mr. Inglesides smiled at the strange woman. She was wandering vaguely around the store, taking slow, deep breaths. She looked around the same age as Dame Talgarth, fifty or thereabouts, though where Dame Talgarth was stout and corseted under her old-fashioned cloak, she was all bones and angles under the black robes, the skin on her face drawn tight as a drum.

I hovered near the end of the counter, watching the coffee drip into the clay jug the baker had placed under the percolator. A waft of flowery perfume from one of the women made me sneeze. I fumbled for a handkerchief while Dame Talgarth gave me a look of cold dismissal.

Mr. Inglesides seemed to be speaking at random while he collected the loaves. "It's lovely you've been able to have your sister's company all summer while Justice Talgarth has been in Ormington. Will he be returning soon?"

Dame Talgarth glanced impatiently at her sister, who continued to stare myopically at the air. "Any time now. Perhaps even this weekend."

"Will you want anything else for your dinner party on market-day, then, ma'am? I've a lovely pear-and-walnut cake. The coffee'll just be a moment, Mr. Greenwing."

Dame Talgarth looked as if she wished to complain at the impertinence of addressing me, but since that would have required acknowledging my existence, she contented herself with a pointed withdrawal to the other end of the counter and a bored tone of voice. "The buns are more than sufficient."

"It's stopping raining," Domina Ringley said suddenly, pointing out the window.

Her voice was high and breathy, and she began to cough immediately. Being prone to sneezing fits myself, I was sympathetic, and I guided her to the bench Mr. Inglesides had placed along the side wall.

The baker fetched her a glass of water. Domina Ringley batted away the water and fumbled instead in the sleeves of her robe. She pulled out a narrow black bottle and took a large sip.

A sudden overabundance of intense lilac perfume made me to sneeze vigorously. With some difficulty I fetched out another handkerchief for her from my coat pocket. She made a face and stoppered the bottle tightly again, and accepted the handkerchief.

"Are you all right, Domina?" I asked between sneezes, drinking the water myself. Both Mr. Inglesides and Dame Talgarth stared at me as if this were quite the rudest thing ever. I sneezed one last time and sighed with aggravation.

"This cough," she said carefully, rubbing her throat with one hand. She glanced up at her sister, who was frowning in concern. "I shall have to talk to my attendant physicker about it. I am sorry to trouble you, Mr. —?"

"Mr. Greenwing, lately of Morrowlea," I replied, with my little bow.

She smiled in approval. "Morrowlea, indeed? Are you connected to the Arguty Greenwings?"

"No," said Dame Talgarth, a lie so blatant my breath caught.

I lowered my handkerchief, about to retort, when Mr. Inglesides caught my eye. He hastily put my packet of cinnamon buns on the counter and set the coffee jug beside it. "Here you go, lad."

I can take a hint when it hits me over the head, so I shut my mouth, bowed to Mr. Inglesides and Domina Ringley, ignored Dame Talgarth (and no doubt that would come back to haunt me), and went out into the square, furious and embarrassed.

I had—or had had, anyway—friends who would have been able to correct her with devastating aplomb, but all I could think of was blunt crudities.

No connection to the Arguty Greenwings. Indeed. The *bitch*.

I paused a moment in the middle of the square to let the fresh air cool my face. Domina Ringley had been entirely wrong about the rain stopping.

I covered coffee and cinnamon buns with my hat, and stood with my head tipped back and eyes shut to the rain, hoping no one was looking, knowing that my family situation was never going to become less complicated, and that I would have to make the best of things as I found them.

And I was grateful to Mrs. Buchance for arranging and Mrs. Etaris for giving me a job—truly I was. There was little enough work elsewhere in the kingdom, and rumours of war outside of it. I'd seen that over the summer. And after the spring term—and my stepfather's death—I was going to have to reassess everything, and having a bit of extra money would help, and surely I could stand this for a season. It was just—

"Seeing visions, young sir?"

I opened my eyes and jumped back. There, very much too close in front of me, was a thin predatory figure dressed in a shabby Scholar's robe, the orange and blue trim proclaiming Fiella-by-the-Sea. I recognized Dominus Gleason after a moment, and bowed to make up for my instinctive recoil. "I beg your pardon?"

He watched me shake out my hat and put it back on, the package of cinnamon buns slipping as I did so. He reached out and caught the parcel, but then as he resettled it into my grasp he let his own hand linger far too long on mine.

"Come now, Mr. Greenwing," he said, smiling oddly, "I do believe you heard me."

Dominus Gleason was known for several things: a scholarly interest in the Good Neighbours, a former career as a professor of magic, and an easily-accessible library full of illicit books where most of the boys of Ragnor Bella had first learned about sex and treason.

(It was where I'd first learned about sex: my father's career had already taught me about treason, and not of the picturesque kind.)

Dominus Gleason smelled of aniseed and glue. I swallowed and pressed my lips together, trying to step back. His grip tightened around my hand. I stopped moving, unable to think clearly through the desperate need not to sneeze in his face.

"There are benefits, you know," he said softly, pale eyes boring into mine, "to being considered not quite the thing."

"I'm not sure I follow," I said stupidly.

Still holding my right hand with his, he turned my hand over to run a horny yellow fingernail up and down the old scar on my palm. I shivered, and he smiled with disquieting satisfaction. "And here I'd always thought you were a most *gifted* young man."

The tingling triggered my sneezes, and as I lost control I turned instinctively, reaching for a handkerchief. Behind the Scholar I saw a figure in a grey cloak huddled over the fountain.

"Hoy!" I exclaimed, as much to break free of Dominus Gleason as out of any concern.

The person in grey half-turned, saw us, and after a moment of hesitation picked up its long skirts and fled. It was quite androgynous: the hood had covered the face, and the dark skirts could as easily have been a woman's dress, a Scholar's robe, or a physicker's gown.

I crossed to the fountain, wondering if the person had made a mess in the water. He, she, or it hadn't. Where the figure had been bending, however, there was a pie.

Well, I supposed it was a pie. It had a crust, at any rate.

And fish heads.

Chapter Two

WHEN I CAME back in, Mrs. Etaris had just put another piece of wood into the stove that heated the bookstore. Her welcoming smile didn't falter when I sprinkled water into the middle of the store when removing my coat; instead she took the jug of coffee so I could put the cinnamon buns down on the parcel table. She did blink twice at the pie.

"Thank you, Mrs. Etaris," I said when I'd sorted myself.

"Thank *you*, Mr. Greenwing."

At times that day I'd thought she must be the person behind the "Etiquette Questions Answered" column in the *New Salon*. It was not that she was so excessively starchy—she was not, thank the Lady, Dame Talgarth—but she was so very devastatingly polite.

To my considerable relief, since I did need to keep the job until the Winterturn Assizes at least, she went on. "I hadn't realized Mr. Inglesides had started making, ah, savoury pies."

We both stared at the pie. I sneezed twice, and fished in my pocket for a clean handkerchief. Sniffles had become the background of my days after a bad cold last winter and a worse relapse in the spring, and I'd taken to carrying spares.

There were seven fish heads sticking out of the pie. The fish seemed to be grinning at our discomfiture.

"I didn't get it at the bakery," I responded after a moment. *Fish heads!* "Someone left it on the side of the fountain."

"Indeed? Whyever did you bring it in?"

I started sneezing again out of sheer embarrassment. I felt beet-red at the mere thought of Dominus Gleason. And Dame Talgarth putting me in my place—my new place. I supposed I'd have to get used to it.

I shook my head vigorously and returned to my purpose in going out, and set the cinnamon buns onto the counter beside her. "I'm afraid I sneezed on it. Here's your change, Mrs. Etaris."

She accepted the coins with a sudden air of distraction. "Did you indeed, Mr. Greenwing?"

"I thought I shouldn't leave it there," I muttered, "and I didn't know what the person bending over it was doing."

"Oh? Oh!" She laughed, obviously entirely unconcerned about possible random acts of poisoning. "How curious!" Mrs. Etaris poured out the coffee, but just as I joined her in the comfy chairs she jumped up again and strode over to the shelf of cookbooks. "I'm sure I've read about this sort of pie. You didn't see who left it there, did you?"

I glanced at the pie. The crust was a rich burnished gold, as beautiful a pie as I'd ever seen—except for the fish heads sticking up out of the pastry. And tails. There were tail fins sticking out, too. I swallowed. "No ... Dominus Gleason was crossing the square, and a stranger in a grey cloak ... Dame Talgarth and her sister were in the bakery, but I left before them."

"Well, no matter." She cocked her head at the bookcase tucked beside the door to the back room. "I don't think you've had a chance to look through the cookery shelves yet, have you?"

I might as well do the thing properly, I thought, and brought her coffee over. "No, Mrs. Etaris. How are they arranged?"

"Badly," she sighed, pulling out *Household Hints of Mont-Brisou-of-the-Snows* and replacing it next to *Fanciful Dishes of the Lesser Arcady*. "At one point I had them by region, but people kept asking for them by type of food, and then I received half the library of the Honourable Mrs. Waverley, who collected cookbooks for fifty years, and my previous assistant put them on the shelves all higgedly-piggedly, and everything got even worse out of order."

She considered the shelves for a moment. This was the first I'd heard about a previous assistant. I wondered who it had been and what had happened for him not to be there any longer, apart from being bad at sorting books.

"Perhaps you might spend some time next week re-arranging them."

"Yes, Mrs. Etaris."

She sipped her coffee, then sneezed delicately as a soft cloud of dust rose up out of *Vegetable Entrées of the Farry March*.

"The Lady preserve you," I said solemnly, backing up a step, but the dust didn't set me off again. In Morrowlea we'd started to say ... well. Not that little piety. During my first episode of nasal congestion (as the physicker called it), my friends had instituted a kind of competition for what to say, which rather took off, as the sensitivity to whatever-it-was, alas, continued.

One particular young lady had led the teasing, arm wrapped fondly around mine, laughing over books and ideas and the endless witty conversation that followed them both—

I winced away from the thought. I'd promised myself I'd stop thinking about that—about *her*—when I returned to Ragnor Bella, once I finally got the spring's horrible influenza out of my system and was able to think straight.

Apart, that is, from the lingering sniffles and propensity for sneezing ... and companion headaches, aching bones, lack of appetite, and occasional disconcerting fits of trembling ...

Sometimes I felt I hadn't been able to think straight since long before leaving Morrowlea.

"Thank you, Mr. Greenwing. Now ... let me think ... well, we might as well use this as an example of doing research for a customer. Who would have fish pies?"

I forced my thoughts back to the matter at hand. "Coastal regions? Fiella-by-the-Sea?"

"I was raised there, I'm sure I should have heard of a pie like this." Then she stopped and smiled ruefully. "Not that that helps with our hypothetical researcher, does it?"

"Ghilousette, perhaps?"

"Good thinking. Could you step on the ladder and see what's on that higher shelf, please? I believe there are several Ghilousetten works out of Harktree there. Next to the one with the orange cover."

I climbed up the brass ladder and reached up for the top-shelf cookbooks. While I was lunging after one on the far side of the shelf the shop door opened.

I jerked in surprise at someone crying, "Halloo the house!" in a huge voice, and toppled off the ladder nearly onto Mrs. Etaris, only to be caught by someone with strong hands amidst a gust of air smelling like wet wool and stable muck.

A big buoyant laugh followed.

"Steady there, man! You'll crush the bookmistress if you light on her!"

I caught my breath and relaxed my death grip on the cookbooks, which Mrs. Etaris probably cared for more than whether or not she'd be crushed if I fell on her, given the consideration with which she took them from me. In the middle of the store, filling the space between the main shelves and the inglenook, stood a large young man.

About my age—twenty-one—he was tall and broad-shouldered and had dark blond hair done up in the curling Beaufort style that in Morrowlea said *dandy* and in Ragnor Bella *old money*. He wore hunting breeches in a scarlet that must have been bought before the Fall, since I'd not seen anything that splendid a colour in the haberdashers of the Rondelan duchies on my tour. He had quite tremendously muscular thighs.

I blinked up from his mud-spattered boots, which raised enormous envy in me—I'd never be able to afford riding boots of that quality, any more than the horse or the groom or the valet that would go with them—past the hunting dagger at his belt with its gold hilt inset with red carbuncles, and up to where he was beaming at Mrs. Etaris with an expression between affable pleasure and amused befuddlement.

"Now, what did I come in here for?" he demanded to himself, and belatedly I recognized him. The expression had not been anything like I remembered from three years past, nor the clothes, and he seemed to have put on about fifty pounds of musculature. I supposed I'd grown some while away at university, too, though nowhere near that much. "Gadsbrook! It's gone straight out of me head."

Mrs. Etaris smiled at him. "Would you like a cup of coffee while you consider, Master Ragnor? Mr. Greenwing, would you fetch another cup, please?"

There was a pause; I was obviously going to have to get re-accustomed to them. And then: "Mr. Greenwing!" said the Honourable Master Roald Ragnor, heir to the barony, with hearty amazement. "I didn't see your face as you toppled off the ladder! When did you get back from Morrowlea?"

"Earlier this week," I replied, and, at a glance from Mrs. Etaris, added, "sir." Then I did my little bow and went into the back room.

I returned to find him lounging in my chair (well, all right, it was the chair for customers) and poking at the pie with the tip of his dagger. Mrs. Etaris was flipping through the indices of cookbooks, looking, I supposed, for a recipe for fish pie. I passed the Honourable Master the cup and started through another pile of them.

"You found this on the lip of the fountain, I hear?" he said, with another booming laugh. "Just laying there?"

I wondered what he'd ended up taking at Tara. I could perhaps have asked ... but we were neither friends nor social equals any longer. Even if I had gone to Morrowlea. The University of Tara vaunted itself the oldest and best university of the Nine Worlds, and did not look kindly on other contenders, even the other Circle Schools.

I shrugged. "Someone was leaning over it. I couldn't see whether they'd left it there or were just curious."

"Didn't think to ask? Pretty girl, was it?"

"Someone in a cloak. Sir."

"Now that's an old-fashioned style." He patted his exceedingly to-the-mode riding coat, which was as beautifully tailored as the rest of his clothing, sleek and slimming and black as a beetle.

A jewelled gold ring he wore on his signet finger caught the light in the facets of its red stones. The little flower wasn't a sigil of Ragnor, and I wondered what it signified to him. A token of affection from a lady?

"Not much use out riding in a wind, cloaks," he went on. "What did you get up to at Morrowlea? Hunt much?"

There was a whole history in that question, one I'd have preferred not to bring up. I tried to keep my voice level. "We preferred other activities. Sir."

"It was all falconry or fishing around Tara," he said, "but up in the mountain estates there was better game—"

Mrs. Etaris made a soft exclamation, and we both looked at her. "My apologies for interrupting, Master Roald. I've found a Ghilousetten recipe for a fish pie of this description."

"Heads and all?" said the baron's honourable son, sticking the tip of his knife into one of the eyes and drawing it out. He considered it for a moment. The eye was a horrible white orb with a squamous glitter. I could smell eggs and bitter saffron under the fishiness, which didn't help my stomach any. Nor my nose.

Though I probably shouldn't admit it, I wasn't altogether unhappy that the attack of sneezes prevented me from explaining why he might not want to eat any of it.

Master Ragnor popped the eye into his mouth and crunched down on it happily before plucking out the next. "Want one?"

"No, thank you," I managed.

"Gone squeamish, have you?"

"Stargazy Pie," Mrs. Etaris said. "Calling for pilchards, saffron, hard-boiled eggs, potatoes ..."

I swallowed another mouthful of coffee. Master Ragnor had muck on his fancy boots and had tracked it all over the floor of the bookstore and onto the rug laid before the wood stove. I'm sure it never once would occur to him to worry about such things. I probably wouldn't have, either, before Morrowlea.

He swallowed another fish eye with every evidence of pleasure. "These ain't pilchards, Mrs. E. Any fisherman could tell you they're herring—Oh! I remember, I wanted that book on coursing by that Scholar from Birckhall, whatsisname. Merganser. No, that's a duck. Merkleman?"

Mrs. Etaris said, "Mr. Greenwing, I think you were looking at the sporting titles earlier this morning. Did you come across *The Art of the Greyhound?*"

I'd already gotten up. I had to edge behind Master Ragnor, who'd shoved his chair well back towards the wall. He was leaning forward and jabbing at the fish heads with his knife again. "Look here, Mrs. E., the size of this jaw—that's no half-grown sardine!"

"Is it a north coast herring?"

"Either that or Fultoney red—open 'er up and we'll see the shape of the fins. Am I in your way, Mr. Greenwing? You're working here, are you, now?"

"Yes, sir," I said, having squeezed past his chair to the bookcase between it and the window.

"'S a good job to get, eh? Good lad!"

I bit my tongue. "I believe I see your book. Melanger's *Art of the Greyhound.* We also have his *Otter and Badger Hounds of the Rondelan*

Duchies, if you should be interested. Sir."

"Otter hounds! Gadsbrook, I haven't hunted otters in ages. Bung it over, Mr. Greenwing, and I'll see if I can roust up a few men to bring some dogs up from the Erlingale bottomlands. We've otters in the Rag. I'll bet Sir Ham—" He stopped there, whether because he'd been about to voice an illegal wager or because he was about to name my father's cousin, I didn't know.

He covered the moment by jerking his chair forward. Since I didn't have to suck in my gut to avoid catching the buttons of my waistcoat on the back of the chair this time, I decided not to push for the rest of the sentence. Instead I went over to the counter to wrap the books in brown paper, the second thing Mrs. Etaris had shown me that morning, the location of the coffee cups having taken priority.

Mrs. Etaris, with a slight air of condescension that made me rather like her, asked, "Do you think it's a Fultoney or a north coastal, Master Ragnor?"

"Oh, Fultoney red," he said, "You can tell by which of the dorsal fins is foremost. And what a colour in the scales! Like Crastor kippers." He started to point out something else about the fish, but the door to the shop opened and his sister walked in, and I didn't hear what he was burbling on about.

She glanced around with a slightly pained-looking frown. The Honourable Miss Jullanar Ragnor—or so she had been; I didn't know her married name—was older than the Honourable Master Ragnor and me, in her late twenties, and as superbly beautiful as I remembered, like an incarnation of the Lady of Summer.

"Sister!" cried Master Ragnor, with a grin. "Am I so very late?"

"Nearly," she said, with near perfect disinterest. "The Baron has called for luncheon at the hotel, and Dame Talgarth and her sister are returned."

"I was distracted from my mission by a little mystery our lad here's discovered."

After a moment I realized I didn't warrant an introduction, but something seemed required, so I bowed silently. She didn't look at me; didn't look at the pie; barely looked at her brother, instead keeping her attention focussed on her kid-leather gloves. "Come along, Roald, we are due at noon."

He winked at me as he got up. "It's good you've a suitable hobby, Mr. Greenwing. I'll be most eager to hear what you discover of your herring pie's origin, purpose, and point."

I cut the string on the honourable master's books with an unnecessarily extravagant motion. This unfortunately sent the scissors flying out of my hand.

Mrs. Etaris caught them with a quick gesture before they walloped her on the head, and shot me a sharp glance. I tried not to sigh. She said, "Master Roald, the books will be two bees and a silvertun."

He tossed her a wheatear from out of his waistcoat pocket and grinned at his sister's obvious disapproval. "To get Mr. Greenwing hobnails on his boots," he said, laughing. "Keep him from falling off any more ladders."

And still laughing, he slung on his coat with an easy motion, thrust the parcel of books into one vast pocket with another, licked his knife clean and re-sheathed it with a third, and took his sister's arm with a gracious gesture that caused her annoyance to melt into a fond smile, though it didn't stop her from a sharp comment about the muck on his boots as they went back out into square.

Mrs. Etaris passed me the scissors. "Beg pardon," I said belatedly. "My grip was loose."

She began putting the cookery books back on the shelves. "I seem to recall hearing you and the Honourable Master Ragnor and Mr. Dart of Dartington kept each other's company quite often, before you went to Morrowlea."

"And they went to Tara and Stoneybridge," I said, and let the schools' rivalry stand in for any further need of explanation, such as the fact that the Honourable Master Ragnor and I had parted ways a good few months before we left the barony, the result of one too many arguments about what it was reasonable to gamble and with whom.

I picked up the rug and shook it out the front door, Mrs. Etaris watching me with a bright interest I found disconcerting. After I placed the rug back in its position before the wood stove I stopped, staring at the pie.

Half-mangled so that we could examine the fish—excuse me, *Fultoney herring*—it looked even less appetizing. "What would you like me to do with the pie, Mrs. Etaris?"

"Oh, you're the one who brought it in, Mr. Greenwing. Will you have it for lunch?"

She was laughing, eyes dancing with amusement. I took a deep breath. I knew better than to let people rile me up. I smiled back and kept my voice light. "Not when the baron's son has asked me to find out its nature and history."

"Ah! In that case, then, you might wish to take some time over your lunch hour to ask the fishmonger who bought herring. It may well be the beginning of great things for you, Mr. Greenwing."

I bowed to her with all solemnity. "I had not thought of asking you advice on derring-do."

Mrs. Etaris laughed and gestured at the crowded shelves of her bookstore. "My dear Mr. Greenwing, if there is anything I know about, it is how to have an adventure."

Chapter Three

I JAMMED MY hat on as I went out the bookshop door, and slammed straight into someone walking along minding his own business.

I swallowed half of a Morrowlea curse. "My apologies, sir. I wasn't looking where I was going."

"Jemis! Mr. Greenwing!" said the man, grabbing my arm and embracing me roughly. "You're back!"

I took a step sideways to get back underneath the store awning. Before me was a young man in clothes as well-tailored as the Honourable Master Roald's, if less brilliant in colour: dark grey wool coat, plum breeches, high polished riding boots. Silver buttons engraved with a family crest showed wealth and breeding. Snapping brown eyes under thick eyebrows suggested a temper, belied by the wide grin; the trim auburn beard startled me into blurting, "Good Laurre of the Summer, man, face fur!"

He rubbed his beard with great solemnity. "Mr. Greenwing, I shall have you to know that this is all the rage in Stoneybridge. Or was," he added, starting to laugh, "four months ago when I left.

They might well be on to something else by now, fickle feckless fools of undergraduates as they are. What about you? Your stepmother said you'd gone off on a walking tour of Rondé with the Count of Westmoor. You haven't written me in months."

"Mrs. Buchance isn't really my stepmother, Mr. Dart," I said, and caught a glimpse of Mrs. Etaris looking at us through the shop window. She made no gesture, merely continued on moving books around.

I didn't remember writing to tell Mrs. Buchance who my walking companions were—though I didn't remember much of the first part of the summer, to be honest, between the influenza and the headaches and the drinking parties that had undoubtedly contributed to both.

I coughed. "And Marcan—ugh! His Grace the Count—only came as far as the top end of Erlingale before he had to go back to Lind."

"And the dearth of letters? The sad state of the post, I assume?"

"Well—"

"Or perhaps you were preoccupied sauntering around Rondé looking for revolutions, is that it?" said Mr. Dart. "Before coming back ... when did you get back to Ragnor Bella?"

"Tuesday."

"Tuesday! You sent no word. And I've heard nothing of late from the good gossips." He made a face. "Not that I *would*. I've been thoroughly occupied with the harvest—I'm land agent for my brother, have you heard? I couldn't well write when you were off a-wandering. He was finally able to dismiss that ogre of a steward when I came back."

"That's wonderful news," I said heartily, knowing that though

Mr. Dart had a strong academic calling, he was also his much older brother's heir, and he'd been hoping the Squire would find a position for him.

Perhaps I spoke too heartily, for he gave me a sardonic glance. "And what do you here, barrelling out of the bookstore with that positively fetching hat from a foreign haberdasher?"

"It's an Ronderell tricorner from Fillering Pool," I replied, then decided I had best get it over with quickly. "I've got a job."

"What, for wages?"

I raised my eyebrows at Mr. Dart to cover my embarrassment. "We don't all have brothers needing land agents."

We hadn't discussed wages in the interview. My stepfather would have been terribly ashamed of my lack of business sense.

"Where? O where, o where, o where, billy-my-boy?"

I glanced around hastily to make sure no one could hear him quoting Fitzroy Angursell, but the square was empty—not another pie in sight, nor even anyone looking for the one they'd misplaced. "Here. Elderflower Books."

"What, for the Poker herself!"

"Shh!" I said. "She'll hear you."

"I'm sure she knows that's her nickname. I well believe she knows everything. Come, come, are you on your lunch?" He laughed. "How funny to think you have a lunching hour! Jemis, Mr. Greenwing, come with me to dine, I must hear about how you went from a walking tour of Rondé with the Count of Westmoor to working in Elderflower Books!"

"I neglected to return before the end of the Midsomer Assizes," I said dryly, and he made a face.

"Ah. The reading of the will."

"I was in Ghilousette, and missed the funeral," I said. My step-father had died ignominiously and without warning, stung to death by a hive of wasps just after Midsomer. Having seen the last of my friends home the month before, I'd been dallying more and more in my travels, and writing less and less frequently as I found my life petering into solitude.

I'd ended up eventually in Ghilousette, drifting to Newbury to see the Hall of Marvels, and stayed there in a mood not much improved by the duchy seat, half-crazed as it was with political ferment and scientific invention and raving enthusiasm for *Three Years Gone*, the hot new play from Kingsford.

The letters forwarded from staging inn to post office had eventually found me, three weeks after the death, two weeks after the funeral, a week after the end of the Assizes, and guilty as anything that I hadn't written a word to anyone since crossing the duchy border.

"I should have thought someone would have mentioned you were home," Mr. Dart said, "though—I suppose—my brother's friends don't really mingle with—" He stopped as abruptly as had the Honourable Master Ragnor, but then tucked his arm into mine. "Will you come to dine with me?"

I tried to tug my arm out of his grip. "Will you regret tomorrow asking a shopkeeper's assistant to dine with you today?"

"Shopkeeper's assistant, my foot. Mrs. Etaris is the hinge-pin of Ragnor Bella, and *you* went to Morrowlea on merits. Come tell me what revolutions the good folk of Erlingale have been fomenting, and I will tell you the gossip of the barony."

"Not the hotel," I said, having visions of being humiliated in an even more public situation by the Baron and his guests.

"Don't be a fool! If I am dining with a radical, I must take him to the starchiest place in town."

"And that's not the hotel?" I asked, as he was dragging me the other direction.

"No; it's Mrs. Landry's front parlour. Come, if we're lucky she'll be hosting a séance."

"I do beg your pardon?"

Mr. Dart burst out laughing. "It's all the rage in Chare, you know."

"Strangely enough, I didn't."

"She's set up a café; haven't you seen it? Or hasn't the Poker mentioned her sister's enterprise?"

"Strangely enough, she hasn't. But I've only been working there since this morning."

"A whole morning for honest coin! More than I've ever managed." He grinned at me. "It's just past Fogerty the Fish. What is it? Have I offended your sensibilities again with my cavalier use of nicknames, Mr. Greenwing? I shouldn't have expected that from a Morrowlea man."

"No, Mr. Dart. I have merely remembered that I was intending to enquire of the fishmonger whether he might inform me—"

"Yes?" he asked, when I paused in trying to disentangle the rest of my sentence.

"Whether he might inform me which of his customers had bought Fultoney herring from him."

"And why, by the Emperor and all his gods, do you want to know who bought Fultoney herring?"

"I found a fish pie on the town fountain, and wanted to know about it."

"The Emperor! That must be the most exciting thing to have happened in Ragnor Bella since your father came back after the Fall. By all means, let us find out who is abandoning their dinner in the square. There can't be many people who want herring." He waggled his eyebrows his eyebrows at me. "There might well be secret meanings behind it."

"Bearding people used to involve a tug, did you know that? If the beards have returned to favour ..."

"I'm taking you to lunch, you ingrate."

Fogerty the Fish had a couple of customers, middle-aged women dressed in housekeepers' aprons whom I didn't recognize by sight. I bowed slightly to them upon opening the door for their exit. Mr. Dart shook his head and murmured, "You shall have to tell me all about Morrowlea's experimental politics, Mr. Greenwing. We heard such things in Stoneybridge ... and the rumours here in town ... Is it true you served each other at mealtimes?"

"Well, yes," I began, and faltered at his genuine shock.

"Now, what can I get you two young gentlemen?" asked the fishmonger, wiping a sprig of parsley across the counter. "You'd surely be catching your own trout, Mr. Dart, and—well, well, well, if it isn't young Mr. Greenwing. Back in town at last, are you? That explains why Mrs. Buchance was buying a jiggot of lamb when Mrs. Fogerty saw her in the butcher's this morning."

"A jiggot of lamb!" said Mr. Dart, with a great sigh; when I looked at him he grinned. "Mrs. Buchance is said to be a very fine cook, Mr. Greenwing. The reputation of her table has increased rapidly since you went away."

I bowed again in acknowledgement of the compliment to my stepfather's second wife, who was only about five years older than us but had dropped into housewifery like a duck into water. If she had been twenty years older I might possibly have been able to refer to her as my stepmother; as it was, she remained Mrs. Buchance. We hadn't even *had* a conversation about first names.

I realized I hadn't prepared any sort of a story for the fishmonger, and felt unable to prevaricate on the spot. My father would have been ashamed at that inability. I coughed awkwardly. "I was wondering, Mr. Fogerty, whether you had any herring in."

Mr. Fogerty pointed at a row of glass jars sitting beside the mustard and horseradish pickles. "I've some Kingsford roll-tops, but that's all today. I sold out of my fresh catch, oh, the day before last."

"Who buys fresh herring this far from the sea?" asked Mr. Dart.

The fishmonger smiled. "My fish is kept perfectly cool," he said, "I've an ice house and all." He waved vaguely towards the back door of the shop. I wandered over to look at the glass-fronted casement of the fresh fish, and had to back away again at the strong odour of parsley and hay that wafted up from it. It didn't smell fishy, for which I was grateful as I sneezed into my handkerchief.

"I meant no imputation, Mr. Fogerty," Mr. Dart protested happily. "I am merely curious. Herring is not a fish one expects to find in Ragnor Bella. Up on the coast, down in Ghilousette, over in Kingsford in Ronderell, all those places indeed. But Ragnor Bella down by the Farry Marches? I am astonished."

"We've been getting a handful of Ghilousetten exiles, ones who don't agree with their duke's ban on magic. Let's see ... Mr. Shipston the physicker was homesick—" Mr. Fogerty chuckled a little at the pun— "and asked me if I mightn't be able to bring in some herring. D'ye know him, Mr. Dart? He came about five months ago, took up the old Millhouse along the Raggle. When he asked, I got them jars in, then had the opportunity to order a fresh catch when I was down at Ragmouth Tuesday last. He took a dozen. Then Mrs. Landry's cook was in same time as Mr. Shipston's man was a-picking his up, and said the mistress was from Fiella-by-the-Sea and might like a taste of home, so we had a parcel made up for her. And then Dominus Gleason took some because we'd sold clean out of trout."

Dominus Gleason, I thought, and shivered again at the thought of him running his fingernails up and down my hand. *Gifted*, indeed. Smart enough to get into Morrowlea on merits; and foolish enough to fail out of it on heartache and injured pride.

Mr. Dart was nodding judiciously. "Just those three, then? Not a huge order of herring."

"I only had the one small barrel down from Ragmouth. I wanted to see whether there was a market—something you're learning the use of, I hear."

"Duck confit is very popular in Chare, Mr. Fogerty."

"You need to introduce a new food gently, Mr. Dart. People don't like change to come too quickly. Especially not in Fiellan. Too much changed in the Fall, people are careful about liking delicacies that might disappear again."

"Well," said Mr. Dart, with a shrug and a slightly shamefaced smile at me. "I'll bear your advice in mind next year."

"Get Mr. Greenwing here to suggest the food, he's got the Morrowlea fashions well in style."

"What, already? He's new come home—of course! He's still in the intriguing stage. You'll see, Morrowlea's behind Stoneybridge— unless it's ahead? You'd probably say ahead—but where are the beards? Where are the moustaches? Where, I ask you, are the Beaufort curls?"

"In Tara," I said, "judging by the Honourable Master Ragnor's sartorial choices. How many herring fit in a barrel, Mr. Fogerty? Three dozen?"

"Depends on the size of the fish," the fishmonger said with a wink. Both Mr. Dart and I groaned at my walking straight into the old joke. "About two peck ... uh, five dozen of the Fultoney herring, six or seven of the north coastals."

"I thought you said you'd sold out?"

"Out of the shop. The barrow-boy took the rest around the country houses when he was delivering the week's orders, in case anyone had a sudden hankering for them. I didn't want to keep them too long here—scarcity, my lads, make people think they're special. Kim'll be back this afternoon if you want to know where you can invite yourself over for to try them."

"We may be back, if we decide we're willing to be second-run adopters ... except perhaps Mrs. Landry will have them on her table this noontide. Come along, Mr. Greenwing, let us see whether she does. Thank you kindly, Mr. Fogerty. Are you sure I can't interest you in duck confit?"

"No, nor your miniature purple cabbages either, Mr. Dart. I'll stick with my fish and potatoes, thank'ye kindly."

Mr. Dart led me at a plunging speed out of the store and along the lane. "This investigating gig is a lark! What fun it is to have a reason to gossip. Makes me see why people go into sociology. Mr. Greenwing, you dog, when did you see the Honourable Rag?"

"He came into the store this morning."

"And?"

"And what?"

Mr. Dart stopped before a puddle caused by a blockage in the sewer. "Would you look at this gutter? Shameful."

He pulled out a stick from the mass and poked at the leaves.

"I see you had the same thought I did. Poor fellow—he'd have been far better for going off to be a radical with you at Morrowlea. Tara seems to have made him over into the mould of a grand young nobleman. He'll be a member of parliament before the decade's out, I reckon, if he doesn't break his neck hunting or his fortune gambling before then. I suppose that's why you thought I was going to disown our friendship when I found you working in Elderflower Books? Pisspoor friend I'd be in that case. Oh, my apologies, misses, I didn't see you there."

A couple of fine young women accompanied by a stately matron had heard his last few words and paused with identical expressions of disapproval. I didn't recognize any of them, but they were years younger than we were, still in school, and the matron's garb had a north Fiellanese cut. She was probably someone's aunt or spinster cousin given a position as companion or chaperone out of charity, or a new teacher at the kingschool on the west road.

Mr. Dart dropped his stick into the now-gurgling gutter and bowed with southern flourishes. Chare seemed to run to curlicue gestures—unless he was just making them up, too. I bowed to hide my grin at the thought, clicking my heels with as much aplomb as I could muster. "Please, do accept our earnest apologies."

The matron sniffed, but the young women giggled as they were led past us. I looked after them, thinking they were far too young for me—and nothing like the firebrands of Morrowlea—and saw a figure in a grey cloak scuttle out across the road behind them. I grabbed Mr. Dart's arm. "There! Did you see? It's the same person

I saw over the pie."

But he had turned to open the door of Mrs. Landry's café, and by the time he looked over his shoulder the figure had disappeared, and I had missed which of the side streets it had taken. I thought this time it was almost certainly a woman.

"It's not that big of a mystery," Mr. Dart said practically.

I shrugged, pretending to a mild interest. "Aren't you curious?"

He laughed. "What, are you?"

"It's better than nothing to do over the weekend." Though actually I was probably supposed to be working.

"That is very true. Which reminds me, now that you're home I needn't go alone."

I hesitated before giving in. "To do what?"

He waggled his eyebrows again. "Will you come mushroom gathering with me this evening?"

Chapter Four

MRS. LANDRY'S FRONT parlour contained five small tables, a large quantity of natty linen doilies, and no other men. A young woman stood near the door. She was dressed in a pale pink gown with white lace ruching and a finely embroidered apron over it, and was very pretty: brown hair, brown eyes, rosy cheeks, a bright smile. I thought I half-recognized her but didn't recall her name, and then realized I didn't know her when Mr. Dart greeted her. "Miss Featherhaugh, I believe Cartwright reserved a table for me?"

"Mr. Dart," said Miss Featherhaugh, with a smile for him and a doubtful but pleasant glance at me. "I thought you were dining alone?"

"I hadn't realized my friend was back in town," he said, "and entreated him to join me. Please will you rustle up another setting for him?"

"I expect I could do that," she said, smiling, and guided us to the only unoccupied table, which was snugged into the window bay.

"Mr. Dart," I said in a low voice once we'd seated ourselves, with him on the side facing the room and me facing the window, "this seems a rather feminine sort of lunching-spot."

"Precisely," he said placidly, picking up the vase on the table to sniff the red carnation in it. It didn't smell very strongly, I thought, nothing the ones Mrs. Etaris had had in the front room before I had sneezed so hard on encountering them she'd had to remove them from her premises. "Did you find a sweetheart in Morrowlea?"

My thoughts flashed to the glorious winter—and the disastrous spring. "No."

"Well, then," he said. "Nor I in Stoneybridge. All the smart women are going for parliament instead of husbands. Oh—unless you've come to realize you prefer—" I shook my head at the suggestion and he shrugged. "Nor I. My brother is well enough in that line."

Master Torquin Dart, Squire of Dartington, was well known for his long-standing relationship with my father's cousin Sir Hamish. Though not scandalous in the least, this relationship was much to the distress of the wider Greenwing family's dynastic ambitions—and also figured largely in the calculations of every mother in the barony for the young brother and heir Mr. Perry Dart's high eligibility and apparently obstinate bachelorhood. Four months out of university and still disengaged was considered most obstinate, as I'd already learned from Mrs. Buchance.

Mr. Dart smiled at Miss Featherhaugh as she brought over a linen napkin and silverware for me. It didn't strike me as anything more than mild admiration, but then, it had been two years since I'd spent a month at Stoneybridge with him, and he was surely feeling the pressure at dinner parties and assembly balls.

Not that Miss Featherhaugh would ever be considered *eligible*.

Mr. Dart said, "Miss Featherhaugh, what is on the bill of fare this wet autumnal day?"

"Tenderloin of pork with apple, a cheese soufflé, a mixed salad, and a pear tart."

"No fish today? I'd heard Mrs. Landry was experimenting with herring—I even heard rumours of a Ghilousetten pie?"

Miss Featherhaugh giggled and clapped her hand to her face to hide her amusement. "Mr. Dart, you are a card! The herring went the way of your duck confit: the only one who et it was Mr. Landry, and he complained it was too foreign by half."

"There was nothing wrong with my duck confit," Mr. Dart said loftily, "you shall see, Miss Featherhaugh, I shall succeed in guiding the taste of the good folk of Ragnor Bella into the heights of gastronomic sophistication one of these days."

"You'd do better to sell good honest goose grease for fried potatoes, and leave the sophistication to the men-about-town." She smiled interestedly at me. Mr. Dart made an exclamation and stood up; I followed hastily at his gesture. "My apologies, Miss Featherhaugh. May I present Mr. Greenwing? Mr. Greenwing, Miss Featherhaugh is Mr. Landry's second cousin once—or is it twice?— removed. Mr. Greenwing has just returned from Morrowlea, Miss Featherhaugh."

There was a distinct pause in the conversation behind Miss Featherhaugh when Mr. Dart said my name. More than one person glanced over at us. I kept my attention firmly on Miss Featherhaugh as I bowed politely. Miss Featherhaugh did not appear to know quite what to say, except to smile awkwardly and bob in return.

One of the older women in the café, a fearsomely proud matriarch in Astandalan-era black silks, made a vague gesture, which distracted my attention. Miss Featherhaugh looked around, bit her lip, and said, "Oh, I must return to my work. Saya Etaris will want some coffee with her tart."

When she had bustled off (Mr. Dart and I both observing her thoughtfully, at least until I realized that half the room was observing us in turn), we sat down again. "I begin to see why you come here."

He made a vague gesture, stroked his beard again. "Mrs. Landry opened her parlour for lunches and afternoon teas in the spring. My brother sent me in to enquire whether she wanted duck eggs, and, well, I've made a point of dropping in occasionally, on my visits to town."

"What is all this about ducks?"

He chuckled. "Even less interesting than your mysterious pie, I'm afraid. My brother—I said he asked me to be his land agent? Well, when I came back in the spring, I thought we could introduce some Charese specialties here. I loved the duck confit we'd get in Stoneybridge—I think I took you to Malcor's when you visited, didn't I?—and I brought back a dozen ducks and as handsome a pair of drakes as ever you saw of the right breed, and started hatching them out."

"Sounds reasonable."

"It is. Except as you've heard, my skills at making the confit aren't quite ... well, I think I might head back down to Chare this winter and see if I can't find an artisan to come up with me and show me how to make it properly. It can't be that hard, dammit! but by the Emperor! You'd think I'd suggested pies with fish heads sticking out of them, the way people carry on about my ducks."

"Perhaps you need to try abandoning them in the middle of

town, and let mystery make them popular."

"I don't think stealth abandonment would make *me* eat something—who'd know how old it was? Or what was in it? Besides, everyone knows I'm the one with the ducks."

Miss Featherhaugh eventually returned with two glasses full of sparkling perry. I sipped mine experimentally. It was made from Arguty pears, the bittersweet flavour as complex as my relationship to my family estate. Mr. Dart said, "It was a good year for pears out on the easter side of town. Hagwood said he expected this year's vintage to be the best since the Fall."

"Good to hear," I said. Hagwood was the Arguty Greenwing estate's factor. I'd met him often as a boy, when my father was alive, and liked him well enough, though naturally hadn't had much to do with him after my mother's remarriage, and certainly not after my mother died.

The pork arrived and we ate in silence for a while. The women in the room chattered softly, genteelly, in voices too low for me to make out the topics of conversation. Clothes and husbands and business, probably, and gossip masquerading as news—unless it were the other way around.

Judging by the glances across at us, most of them were talking about how I'd had the nerve to return to town after missing my stepfather's funeral and how very interesting it was that Mr. Dart wasn't shunning me. I finished before him and looked out the window to see if it had stopped raining.

It hadn't. Baron Ragnor was coming down the street with his party, which had swelled to include a tall and skeletally thin Scholar unknown to me. They were all bundled in coats and capes and picking their way through puddles.

I felt a savage pleasure that they did not appear to have had a very satisfactory meal. Dame Talgarth's sister seemed to have an even more tenuous grasp on her surroundings than in the bakery, judging by how glassily she was smiling at the Honourable Miss, whose own expression was petulant and angry. The Baron was speaking earnestly with the Scholar, who was frowning, and Dame Talgarth's shoulders were set in a furious rigidity. Only the Honourable Master seemed to be enjoying himself, as genially boisterous in his saunter as he'd been inside the bookstore.

Mr. Dart said, "I say, Mr. Greenwing, you've gone quite still. What's the matter? Another pie?"

I shook my head and quickly attended to the soufflé that had been placed before me. "Just woolgathering, Mr. Dart. The Baron and his party are coming down the street. They've a Scholar with them and I was wondering who he might be."

Mr. Dart twisted around to look. "Oh, that's Dominus Alvestone. He's from ... oh, I forget. Either Inchpoint or Inkpoil."

"One's in Ronderell and the other's halfway to Pfaschen."

"And one is known for anthropology and the other for alchemy, I know. I just forget which it is. I met him at a ball the Baron held a couple of months ago, and again at one of the Talgarths' dinner parties. The Emperor, those are even more boring with the Justice away."

"Oh? Where is he?"

"Teaching a class in Ormington. Makes a big difference to the dinner parties, not having a host to lead us astray to the back room with the port."

I chuckled, pleased at the thought that Dame Talgarth's cutting me meant that I would be able to avoid her infamously dull dinner parties, at least. "Has the Scholar been here all summer?"

"I think so. He's researching something in someone's library. Or all of them. I think my brother mentioned seeing him at the Woodhills'."

"You're a fount of information, Mr. Dart."

"I do try, Mr. Greenwing. Oh, look, there's Mrs. Landry come out to make her courtesy to Saya Etaris. I bet she's glad *she's* not her mother-in-law."

"Shh," I said, but he'd already lowered his voice.

"Not much of a radical at home, are you?"

"Shh," I said again, embarrassed, and he winked.

"Of course! You're undercover."

Saya was the old Astandalan honorific, which used to be widely applied—every adult gentleman or woman was *Sayo* or *Saya* when I was a boy—but after the Fall the fashion for that changed, too, and people started going with Mr. or Mrs., and only the starchiest of the old guard still went by the Astandalan title. Saya Etaris, Mrs. Etaris' mother-in-law, was one of these. As soon as Miss Featherhaugh had mentioned her name I recognized her, though I'd never had more than a nodding acquaintance with her as a boy.

"I've always wondered what she was like in her salad days," Mr. Dart said. "I bet she was a right beauty."

I gave a surprised snort and hastily drank perry to cover it up. Saya Etaris had risen and was making her majestic way through the room to the door, trailed by her silent cousin-companion, a woman of such extreme propriety I could barely hold her in my mind's eye a moment after looking at her.

Saya Etaris herself wore black silks and a hat of exquisite featheriness, and had an ebony cane from Zunidh that must have been expensive even in Astandalan days, and though she was short and plump and wore too many rings on her fingers, you just knew that if she'd decided that something was so it was, well, so.

She stopped before our table. Mr. Dart and I rose with alacrity. "Mr. Dart," she said, and then, with a rather cooler tone of voice, "Mr. Greenwing." We bowed; Mr. Dart clicked his heels a moment after I did. Saya Etaris smiled slightly, so that her piercing blue eyes glittered. She wore small pince-nez with gold frames. "Miss Featherhaugh tells me you are intrigued with new things, Mr. Dart."

Mr. Dart glanced at Miss Featherhaugh, who was hovering behind with Saya Etaris' cloak in her hands and a pained expression on her face. He bowed again. "Saya Etaris, one of the joys of travelling is discovering new things. I merely wished to share the pleasanter traditions of Chare with my own countryfolk."

"Not bad," she said, and then gazed gimlet-like at me. I met her stare as composedly as I could manage. "We did not think to see you back in town again, Mr. Greenwing, but then that is something of a specialty of your family, is it not? I hope you do not take after your father in too many other particulars."

There was a playwright in Erlingale who'd written a tragedi-comedy called *Three Years Gone*. It had been a smash hit in Kingsford in the spring, and continued to be wildly popular throughout most of the kingdom.

It was, ostensibly, about my father. My friend Hal's mother, to whom I had not told my surname—there never seeming quite the right moment, after a sneezing fit in the middle of my first effort had made Hal himself think it was "Greene" *simpliciter*—had taken us to see it when I was in Fillering Pool, thinking it would be a pleasant diversion.

They had, thankfully, been willing to attribute my morose silence to a relapse of my illness.

One of the more popular catchphrases was "Welcome as a Greenwing come home."

It infuriated me to admit even the smallest grain of truth in the play: but the world did not bend to my will, alas. I swallowed several times, and finally I said, "It's true, I can hardly hope to win commendation from the Emperor himself for my bravery, Saya Etaris."

Someone on the far side of the room dropped her fork; it chimed loudly against a plate. Saya Etaris didn't even blink. Everyone in the room knew—everyone who'd seen *Three Years Gone* knew, everyone who'd read Tadeo Toynbee's *Guide to the Kingdom of Rondé* knew, everyone who'd been in Ragnor Bella when my father came home three years after he'd been twice reported dead knew—what I wasn't adding.

Treason, cowardice, perjury, bigamy, suicide.

I kept my back and my face straight.

Saya Etaris' smile was a humourless twitch of her lips. "I cannot think what possessed my daughter-in-law to give you a job. But then she always was more than a bit contrary."

I swallowed again. "I'm very grateful to Mrs. Etaris for giving me the opportunity."

"Good," she said, and swept off with her cloak half-on her shoulders. The room suddenly frothed with chatter. I slumped back into my seat and earnestly regarded the remnants of my salad.

Mr. Dart said, "I am actually growing curious about this pie of yours." I looked up at him; he grinned. "Whom do we interrogate next?"

"I have to go back to work," I said, hearing the bells from the town clock ring the hour in the gust of damp wind that came in the wake of Saya Etaris' exit.

"All the better, we can ask Mrs. Etaris what she thinks, she's always putting her nose into things. Are you done? Miss Feather-haugh, will this cover it?"

"You haven't had the pear tart," she said, taking the coins he offered her with a hint of disappointment.

"I know—but Mr. Greenwing is a working man these days, and I mustn't keep him from his honest labour." I started to protest, until he winked at me. "I invited you, gosling. Come—where's your hat gone? Such a fine tricorner it is, too. I hope Fogerty the Fish is correct and the local haberdashers have taken note. Please mark the plural: we have graduated to two now, you know. Mr. Jack Pepper had a fight with Mr. Ben, and set up as a rival."

I stared wordlessly at him. He took my hat, stuck it on his own head, and banged out the door. After a stunned moment I has-tened after him, to find he'd stopped to light a pipe.

"You smoke?" I said in astonishment. "First the beard, now the pipe—how far back in time has Stoneybridge gone? It sounds like something out of a Ystharian novel."

"Fewer orgies than in a Ystharian novel," he said sadly, blowing a smoke ring with the evidence of much practice. "Though even more unprovoked and unsubstantiated gossip. How degenerate we've become since Astandalan days."

Chapter Five

MRS. ETARIS HAD left a note on the door for me:

> Mr. Greenwing: I have been called to receive a shipment at
> the post office. Please carry on with your duties. I should
> return by half past two. Mrs. Etaris.

"The Poker in writing," Mr. Dart said, blowing another smoke
ring as I fumbled for the key under the flowerpot. "Like something
out of a calligraphy book. D'you know where she went to university, Mr. Greenwing?"

"No, I don't," I said, a bit surprised; it was usually what one
first found out about someone, after their family. "If you want to
come in, will you put out the pipe? I shouldn't think Mrs. Etaris
would want her store to smell like pipe smoke." Though I was more
concerned about being unable to breathe in the enclosed space.

"You never know, she might consider it a mark of distinction,"
he replied, but he took a few last puffs and then proceeded to tamp
down the bowl and close it off with a small cork while I took off
my coat. "I have the cork from before I got the windcap, which I've

got somewhere in my pockets, but—curses! I must have left it in my saddlebags. I'll have to ask Cartwright when I meet him. Huh. I don't think I've been in here since the last assistant left."

"Who was the last assistant?" I asked, ignoring the nonsense and plucking my hat from Mr. Dart's head to put on the coat tree. The fire was banked and the room still smelled strongly of fish, though I found the saffron undertone increasing. I sneezed. "Excuse me."

"If you insist. Is this the famous pie?" Mr. Dart went forward to lean over it. "That's revolting. I don't remember the assistant—a stranger to these parts, I believe. Possibly another second cousin or the like out of Fiella-by-the-Sea. There was some small difficulty a month or two ago ... he's no longer in town, anyway. Is there a book about the stargazing?"

"Stargazy pie out of Ghilousette. I think ... yes, Mrs. Etaris left the cookery book there." I stirred up the fire, then looked awkwardly around the store. There didn't seem much to do. Mrs. Etaris had tidied all the paperwork away, leaving only *The New Salon* and *Traditional Dishes of the Wardrider Coast* next to the pie. Mr. Dart took *Traditional Dishes* and sank meditatively into the chair.

"This is when a pipe is a doddle," he said, looking at the smoothly polished wood of his and sucking on the end, then making a face and putting it back in his pocket. "For thinking."

"I thought it was a dottle?"

"Oh, very good! But you don't smoke yourself?"

I shrugged, and decided I might as well organize the cookery books while we were talking. "No. I tried it once in Morrowlea, but I found it a bit queasy-making."

"What on earth were you smoking?"

I decided not to describe the night spent retching helplessly in a vile post-Astandalan outhouse after I'd tried what had turned out to be wireweed-laced tobacco, and which had put me quite definitively off all forms of both drugs, legal and not. "Do you think cookery books should be organized by food or by region?"

Mr. Dart looked up at where I was pulling them down from the shelf. "What striking covers they have. Why not by colour?"

"People don't usually come in and ask for books by jacket colour."

"Don't they? The aesthetics of bookcases are probably as satisfying as anything else. I know my brother only cares about his Collian scrolls. Everything else is ordered by the yard from the publishers."

"If you send me a list of colours his library his lacking, I'll keep out a selection."

He laughed, and flipped through the book in his hand. I decided to go by type of food, which was how cookbooks were arranged in the Morrowlea library, and worked silently for a while, the noise of the rain on the window and the sound of turning pages soothing. Mrs. Etaris' cat Gingersnap jumped up onto Mr. Dart's lap and started to purr. Some wave of tension started to ebb, and I thought that maybe it wouldn't be so bad to work in Elderflower Books in Ragnor Bella, after all.

"Hullo!" said Mr. Dart suddenly. "This is odd."

I blinked up from trying to decide whether *Fifth Imperial Decadent Style Dinner Parties* should go under Cookery, History, Ethnology, or Etiquette.

There was an entire chapter, I noted with some astonishment, on how to host an orgy. With diagrams for partner placements based on rank. Dame Talgarth's dinner parties would probably be better attended if she included—I tore my gaze away with difficulty. "Odder than fish-head pie?"

"I thought I'd look in the *Encyclopedicon*," he said, and I saw that at some point while I'd been focused on the shelves in front of me, he'd found the reference section. Gingersnap was kneading her claws on the arm of the chair, her ears flattened to protest that no one was petting her. "And look what I found. This is the new edition, by the way, the one that came out of Tara this spring, so it's got post-Astandalan references in it."

I took the volume. "I hadn't realized it was out. I'm impressed she has a copy already."

"She's the hinge-pin of town, I told you. The person who controls access to books—and the newspaper—" He gestured at the stack of *New Salons* on the counter—"controls information."

"You should have come to Morrowlea."

"I should have enjoyed running riot with you, but my tutor was spectacular," he said. "Actually—no, I'll tell you later. I have a paper I want to show you, but I'll have to fetch it next time I come to town."

I felt a pang at the reminder that he lived six miles out—not so far for a gentleman of leisure with a horse, nor if I had the time to walk—or the courage to continue flouting social mores and run—but— "Do you come into town often?"

His gaze strayed out the window. "I might come more often now that you're home. Go to, Mrs. Etaris is coming down the street."

"She said it might be the beginning of adventures," I said, in portentous tone, and we both laughed.

I rifled through the *Encyclopedicon* until I found the S entries. There was no entry for *Stargazy Pie* itself, but *Stargazing* warranted one—or rather two. The first entry was dedicated to the normal meaning, with cross-references to Astronomy, Astrology, Navigation, and the Astandalan Court, but the second ... "It's slang for hobnobbing with hobgoblins?"

"What a way with words you've got," Mr. Dart said with mock admiration. "Hallo, Mrs. Etaris! Let me take that from you." He jumped up to relieve her of a well-wrapped parcel while she dripped on the front mat. "We've been probing the mysteries of herring pie. Read the passage aloud, Mr. Greenwing, if you would."

I cleared my throat, a little embarrassed by how Mrs. Etaris was smiling with a polite, sardonic kind of expression. She hung up her coat to dry. Mr. Dart came over beside me to lounge against the counter. "'*Stargazing*, in the parlance of eastern Ghilousette (*quod vide*) and western Fiellan'—"

"We get the idea of cross-references," Mr. Dart said.

I refrained from rolling my eyes. "'Stargazing, in the parlance of eastern Ghilousette and western Fiellan (*quod vide*)'—"

"Go to."

"—'means an unattainable yearning for impossible things, taken so far as to become a detriment to all society and custom, and particularly the ill-advised formation of attachments to the Good Neighbours'—"

"That is, the Fair Folk," Mr. Dart said helpfully. "*Quod vide.*"

"We should avoid naming them," Mrs. Etaris said placidly. Mr. Dart and I both looked at her; she smiled and shrugged, still sardonically. "They tend to leave South Fiellan alone, except for the Woods Noirell. But then the Woods Noirell—"

"*Quod vide*," I murmured.

"—Are just down the highway," Mr. Dart finished for her. Then he frowned at me. "Isn't your grandmother the marchioness of the Woods Noirell? Shouldn't she be—"

"She disowned my mother after she married Mr. Buchance. I haven't heard from her since I wrote to tell her mother had died. Shall we continue?" At my frown he was quelled, and shrugged amiably. I continued, "—'And the druggery use of magic. Since the Fall of Astandalas'—"

"*Quod vide*," said Mr. Dart.

"I think we're all adequately well acquainted with that," Mrs. Etaris said, when I paused to raise my eyebrows at him.

Mr. Dart and I both grinned, the destruction the Empire of Astandalas being, obviously, by far the most important thing in anyone's life who lived on any of the five worlds that it had covered (or, presumably, the other four, since a magical cataclysm of that magnitude affected everything). Each of the five worlds had experienced a different sort of disastrous consequence. We on Alinor called the period immediately following the Fall the Interim, it having been a time of strange fogginess in all respects, temporally, magically, physically, and emotionally, between the concrete one-day-follows-another normal periods before and after.

I returned to the *Encyclopedicon*. "—'It'—that is, Stargazing, 'has expanded its meaning to denote the lingering effects of the Interim (*quod vide*)'—"

"Let us not," said Mr. Dart.

"—'The lingering effects of the Interim on both people and places, the desire to recreate the hallucinations and euphoria experienced by some during the Interim, and, in Ghilousette, has moreover the additional connotation that one who *stargazes* is not only insane but also treasonous."

Mrs. Etaris paused in the moment of taking off her bonnet, the long hatpin in her hand catching the light with a wicked flare. "Now, doesn't that put an interesting complexion on the sudden appearance of a stargazy pie in the centre of Ragnor Bella."

"*Quod vide,*" I murmured, but I did not turn back the page to find out what was under that heading in the new edition.

"I am astonished," said Mr. Dart: "there might be secret meanings after all. And here I thought you just wanted to give the good gossips something else to talk about besides your belated return when we went into the fishmonger's."

Mrs. Etaris seemed to be trying not to smirk. "What did you find out from Mr. Fogerty, Mr. Greenwing?"

"He brought a barrel of Fultoney herring down from Ragmouth on Tuesday," Mr. Dart said eagerly, while I was still trying to digest the implication that there *was* something interesting going on. "Half the barrelsworth was divided between Mrs. Landry, Mr. Shipston, and Dominus Gleason, and the other half sent on the country rounds with the barrow-boy."

"I shall have to speak with my sister."

"We had lunch at her parlour," I said, "and Miss Featherhaugh said Mr. Landry hadn't liked the fish, so it wasn't like to be on the menu any time soon." I felt there was no need to mention Saya Etaris' comments. Mrs. Etaris would surely hear them all, and more besides, the next time she met her mother-in-law.

"Well, well, well," said Mrs. Etaris, and jabbed the hatpin back in. "Have there been any customers this afternoon?"

"Nary a one so far," I replied, but she seemed neither surprised nor annoyed.

"It's nearly time to close, anyhow. Let us go speak to Mr. Shipston. This order is for him, so we have a perfect excuse to call. Mr. Dart, would you care to join us?"

"I should be delighted, but actually I'm supposed to be calling on my aunt, and she'll be wondering what in the world I've done with myself today." He got up with a hand held out to me. I looked at it stupidly and he chuckled. "Not shaking hands in Morrowlea, either? Silly fashions."

He punched me lightly on the shoulder instead. "I'll tell her I met Mr. Greenwing and found a mystery, and she'll be wholly delighted at the invitation to gossip, and no doubt tell me every mystery there has ever been in town back to before the Fall—not that there are many, Ragnor Bella's known for being the dullest town in the four duchies. They mocked me in Stoneybridge for it, I tell you. Will you meet me at seven for mushrooms, Mr. Greenwing?"

"It's rather wet," I objected, before the penny dropped.

He winked under the cover of helping Mrs. Etaris back into her coat. "All the better for finding truffles. You've always had the knack—or is it the nose?—for it. Meet me at the walnut tree by the Little Church."

And out he bounced with a cheery whistle, leaving me and Mrs. Etaris to look at each other with surmise. I thought about how close the Green Dragon was to the Little Church crossroads. The tavern had always had a more than slightly raffish reputation. The Lady knew what they did on a Friday night that Mr. Dart might have developed a taste for.

"Mr. Dart was very enthusiastic about the pie," I said, with a vague attempt at misdirecting Mrs. Etaris' possible thoughts, as I put on my coat. "I think he enjoyed the excuse for asking questions."

"I had an aunt who was a sociologist," Mrs. Etaris said, smiling, as I picked up the box of books and followed her out into the square, where it had once again ceased raining, though the wind was picking up.

Mrs. Etaris carefully locked the door behind us. "I always remember her saying to me, 'My dear, do remember that gossip when well organized is sociology, and when ill regulated, slander.'"

I looked at her. She stuck the key under the flowerpot again and smiled at me.

"But I'm sure you already know all about that, Mr. Greenwing."

Chapter Six

I WAS SO preoccupied with preventing the box of books from slipping out of my grasp that I didn't realize until we were well on our way that Mrs. Etaris was carrying the pie. Despite her flashes of humour, I didn't feel I knew her anywhere near well enough to ask impertinent questions about it, and was rather disappointed she didn't say anything as we walked, beyond a comment about someone's potted flowers.

"Outer Reaches asters," I identified, pleased to show I knew something. I'm not an expert on plants by any means, but my roommate and closest friend at Morrowlea, Hal, had studied—and talked my ear off about—botany, and been particularly enthusiastic about the plants coming from explorers re-opening the trade routes after the Fall of Astandalas.

Sadly, Mrs. Etaris only gave me a thoughtful glance and said nothing more.

Mr. Shipston lived on the outskirts of town, in a squat stone house with a large and untended garden. I noticed a few chickens pecking down the bottom, and smiled at the thought of Mr. Dart trying to import Charese duck recipes.

A manservant answered the door. He did not betray surprise at seeing us there, but merely bowed when I announced: "Mrs. Etaris and Mr. Greenwing, with a parcel of books for Mr. Shipston."

"I shall inform the master," said the manservant, with a thick Ghilousetten accent. Mrs. Etaris had covered the pie with a cloth against threat of rain, so he didn't raise an eyebrow at it, nor at my name. They must not have been in Ragnor Bella very long, I thought.

He led us into the drawing room, and I caught my breath against a series of sneezes.

Mrs. Etaris gave me a curious glance as I wiped my nose and streaming eyes with one of my fresh handkerchiefs, glad I'd thought to replace the dirty ones from my stash in the store before we left. "Excuse me," I said. "I'm afraid I am sensitive to smells."

"I've noticed," she said mildly. "What is it in here, may I ask?"

I got my sneezes under control with a series of shallow breaths. "The metalwork. Strange. That doesn't usually raise it in me."

"Hay fever, I expect."

"Something like that. It comes and goes." I looked around the room. "I've never been in here before. Very modern Ghilousetten décor, isn't it?"

"Is it? I've never been to Ghilousette, I'm afraid."

"I went to Newbury on my way home."

She smiled sardonically again. I flushed at the thought of what she must be thinking, that I had chosen that over my stepfather's funeral. "That was why I was delayed getting back. I hadn't written with proper directions for where I was staying before Mr. Buchance had—had passed away."

"Indeed."

I swallowed. "I visited the Hall of Marvels. They've banned magic, as I'm sure you've heard, put all their efforts into mechanical devices and contrivances. The Hall of Marvels is for educating people about the best and newest inventions."

"And this?"

I gestured at the elaborate clockwork mechanism on the inside wall, all turning cogs in brass and copper and gold wire. "Isn't it curious? The cogs turn from ... well, I'm not sure what the source of power for this one would be. Often it's water or wind ... I didn't see whether Mr. Shipston had a windmill, did you, Mrs. Etaris?"

"This is the old millhouse, so I expect he has a waterwheel. What is the mechanism for? Purely the beauty of motion?"

I hadn't thought of it as being beautiful, although I supposed it was, all gleaming surfaces and whirring movement. "I believe this is ... let me think of what I saw ..." I closed my eyes and tried to retrieve what I'd learned in the Hall of Marvels. "I think it's a time-piece," I said, looking at how some of the pieces were connected to enamelled spheres and plates. "Yes ... here's a clock for the daily hours, and this one would be the moon's phases, and here ... is it possibly a year's count?"

"You know your cogswork, young sir," said a dry elderly voice, and I jumped.

Mrs. Etaris rose with a smile and a hand outstretched to the owner of the voice. Mr. Shipston wore the long black gown of a physicker. His grey hair was cut short in the style popular in Ghilousette. He bowed over Mrs. Etaris' hand, and kissed it with a gesture I thought both affected and rather fine. Pity I hadn't thought of introducing *that* as a Morrowlea fashion.

"I had the opportunity to visit the Hall of Marvels in Newbury this summer, sir," I said.

"Mr. Greenwing made a walking tour of Rondé on his way back from Morrowlea, Mr. Shipston," said Mrs. Etaris, sitting back down on the sofa when he released her hand.

"Indeed?" he asked. "I went to Avalen, myself."

Avalen in Tifou, the kingdom south of Chare, was one of the Circle Schools, but like Stoneybridge kept itself mostly aloof from the rivalries between Tara and Morrowlea. I nodded awkwardly. "I've not travelled that far south, I'm afraid, sir."

"Sensible young man. You're quite correct, Mr. Greenwing. This is a year's count." He showed me a series of elaborately carved figures on rings arcing across the face of the wall. "Not though it is all that accurate, since the Fall. It used to tell the Emperor's Years and so on, but now ..." He chuckled sadly. "It is something of a marvel it tells the Moon's phases correctly. Can you reckon it?"

I studied the notches and figures and symbols until I found the silver and black-lacquer image of the Moon sandwiched between a sun-in-glory for the Emperor's Years, the main annual calendar used throughout the Empire (and which did appear to be more than a little off, since it read the 954th year of the Emperor Artorin's reign; I wondered briefly why the maker had felt the need to include such high numerals in the first place), and the white unicorn symbol of Lady Jessamine of Alinor.

I cleared my throat. "It is ... the third of the Autumn Ember Days; the New Moon will be ... oh, tonight, yes. She's in the House of the Dragon, which is really of interest to students of the old religion."

"And are you one such?" Mr. Shipston asked.

I sneezed at a whiff of copper—perhaps it was the polish Mr. Shipston's domestics used that was doing it for me? I hadn't sneezed so much in all the Hall of Marvels. "No," I managed, wiping my nose. "I've read some accounts in the History of Magic."

"I'd forgotten about the Zodiac houses," Mrs. Etaris murmured, setting the still-wrapped pie on the coffee table as the manservant came forward with a tray of coffee and biscuits. "Well done, Mr. Greenwing."

I could tell right enough that this was a veiled request for me to explain what I had taken at Morrowlea, but I didn't feel like explaining why I'd moved from History of Magic to Classical Literature via Architecture, or how poorly that choice had worked out for me in the end.

I had discovered a great appreciation for the complex coded architectural poetry of the Fourth Calligraphic Horizontal School, and I had lost my heart, and neither was really any of their business, any more than my paltry efforts to figure out how long exactly it had been between my father's death and the Fall of Astandalas.

Except, of course, my father hadn't died then after all, and it hadn't mattered a whit to anybody but me. *Three Years Gone* ... or five ... or none at all ...

But I didn't feel like explaining that, no matter how pleasant Mrs. Etaris was and how bright an eye old Mr. Shipston turned on me, so all I did was bow to acknowledge the compliment and do my best to turn the conversation. "It is a beautiful piece of cogswork, Mr. Shipston."

"My hobby," he said, a bit bashfully. "I am a physicker by trade, you know, but I've always enjoyed the complications of the Astandalan calendar. I understand the one used in the Collian portion of the Empire was even more complex than our Alinorel calendar, since Colhélhé has several moons and no strong agreement between the cultures, and half of them live below the surface of the sea and do not reckon with human measurements at all. I have always regretted I did not travel to Colhélhé when I was a young man, and the Empire made passage between the worlds possible. But I was ambitious in my trade." He shrugged. "By the time I had thought I might retire, the Fall came upon us, and I was hard put to put my training to use in the Interim. I moved from Ghilousette five months ago, but came no farther than Ragnor Bella."

"There were rumours of war in the southern lands," Mrs. Etaris said. "Or indeed, I should say there are rumours of war. Even Chare's borders are not secure."

"We are very fortunate in Rondé, and particularly here in Fiellan," Mr. Shipston agreed. "The young might wish for more prospect of adventure—don't look at me like that, Mr. Greenwing, you are a young man and a red-blooded one I am certain!—But to those of us who have travelled farther afield, or recall the stories of those who joined the Astandalan army, the peacefulness of Ragnor Bella is a balm."

"My father was in the Astandalan army," I said quietly. "He fought in the campaigns of East Orkaty and the Seven Valleys." One to the greatest acclaim; the other ... not.

Mr. Shipston opened his mouth and then closed it again, and then bowed slightly. "Jakory Greenwing, of course. I apologize, Mr. Greenwing. You of all in this town would know the cost of adventure."

"Or of war," said Mrs. Etaris, with a smile to remind us not to talk of gruesome things in her presence (or so I interpreted it). "But we do have a very small mystery to relate to you, Mr. Shipston."

"I did not order novels in this shipment of books!" he said, chuckling.

"To be sure, no." Mrs. Etaris pulled forward the pie and unwrapped the cloth covering. "Does this mean anything to you?"

There was a ghastly pause. Mr. Shipston stared at the pie and I stared at him. His face contracted in an expression of horror so frank I felt an answering fear rise up in me like a distant echo.

Then he called his manservant to have us thrown out of the house.

Chapter Seven

THE MANSERVANT WENT rigid and grey when he saw the pie.

"Mrs. Etaris and Mr. Greenwing are leaving," Mr. Shipston said abruptly. "Tell Miranda—" he stopped even more abruptly. "No; I will come up myself."

Mrs. Etaris gestured at me and stood, putting her gloves back on as she did so. I hesitated a moment and then picked up the pie. Mr. Shipston made a strangled noise. I turned, and, astonished at my own insolence, said, "Was there something else, Mr. Shipston?"

He didn't lift his gaze from the pie. "Seven," he said in a tight voice. "That's fourteen ..."

"Two are gone," the manservant replied brusquely.

"Twelve ... twelve ... O Lady, they know. They *know*."

"Learned—" said the manservant, his voice cracking. Mr. Shipston swayed and sat down. The manservant glared in anguish from him to us. I hesitated, staring, as Mr. Shipston seemed about to faint, but Mrs. Etaris took me by the arm and led me firmly to the door.

As it shut behind us, she said cheerfully, "Now, wasn't that an interesting reaction! What do you think, Mr. Greenwing?"

I thought Mrs. Etaris sounded insanely cheerful, to be honest, and was irresistibly reminded of my friend Violet, who had always sounded happiest in the thick of things.

Former friend Violet. That was one of many things ruined in the spring examinations.

I didn't even try to match Mrs. Etaris' insouciance as I gathered my fragmenting thoughts.

(My tutor's voice came to mind: *You must discipline your thoughts, young man, or you will never be a scholar of note.* Of course, ending one's university career with one's tutor ripping one's final paper in half would do it, too, disciplined thoughts or no.)

I swallowed. "One, the number of eyes seemed important, and two, who is Miranda?"

She beamed at me. "Very good, Mr. Greenwing. And there is also three: what has Mr. Shipston done for someone to accuse him of treason in such a roundabout manner?"

I waited, but she merely took my arm for balance as we picked our way across slick cobblestones and between the puddles in the close. I glanced at the sky and hoped the lighter colour meant that the clouds were clearing, or that Mr. Dart just wanted to gamble or carouse and not poach salmon (or, Lady forbid, actually go truffle-hunting) in a storm.

"Yes, very intriguing indeed," Mrs. Etaris murmured as we turned the corner. "Now, shall we see Dominus Gleason before we call it the end of the day?"

I wanted to demur, for I had no desire to speak to Dominus Gleason again today (or, really, ever), but before I could formulate an excuse, Mrs. Etaris had turned down a narrow lane I hadn't even noticed and led me up to the old wizard's door. I resigned myself to yet another uncomfortable conversation and rang the bell.

Dominus Gleason's house smelled of old things: dust, books, corruption. I remembered the odour from those illicit library visits, though it seemed far stronger than I recalled. While Mrs. Etaris enquired of the butler whether the Scholar was in, I backed down the close until I stopped sneezing.

I was still wiping my face when Mrs. Etaris returned to my side. She frowned, then started to sneeze herself at a sudden gust of wind that threw a handful of leaves and small particulate matter in our faces. I pulled out my third handkerchief and passed it to her with a little bow.

She used it without comment, then looked briefly disconcerted. I grinned. "I always carry several spares with me, Mrs. Etaris. One never knows."

"How foresighted of you," she replied. "Dominus Gleason is not at home today, and his butler does not expect him to be so this evening, tomorrow, or the next day ..."

"I saw him this morning in the square."

"Did you? Oh, yes, you mentioned. Hmm. Well, there are several reasons he might not be at home to us."

I was the source of at least one of those reasons, I suspected. Mrs. Etaris took my arm to negotiate another large puddle at the bottom of the close. As we turned the corner, me thinking dispiritedly of how wet it was going to be tonight, we came face to face with Mrs. Etaris' husband, the Chief Constable of Ragnor Bella.

And my uncle.

While the Chief Constable greeted his wife, my uncle and I studied each other. He wouldn't have liked what he saw regardless of circumstances, but I knew that after the summer I wasn't at my best, being too thin from the influenza, red-nosed from the sniffles, and a bit bloodshot in the eyes from the lingering hay fever; only the tan I'd acquired from being so much out-of-doors in the summer ameliorated the winter's pallor.

He looked more like my father than I did. I'd inherited the long Greenwing nose and dark hair, but otherwise took after my maternal grandfather, or so people said, being short and lean and prone to freckles. Sir Vorel Greenwing was tall, with dark curly hair, broad shoulders, and naturally browner skin.

He also had a growing embonpoint, as Mr. Dart might say (I myself would be more inclined, with regards to my uncle at least, to call it a paunch), and had developed another chin since I'd seen him last, which the older fashion of narrow cravats still popular in Ragnor Bella did not flatter. The thought that the foamier cravats and higher collars that Mr. Dart and I both were wearing would suit him physically much better, if psychologically be deeply aggravating, made me rather more cheerful, and so I was able to smile almost sincerely when I bowed and said, "Sir Vorel. Chief Constable Etaris."

The Chief Constable nodded shortly. My uncle's nostrils flared as he pinched his lips together. I still felt a bit light-headed from all the sneezing at the door to Dominus Gleason's house, and not very politic at all, so I added with the most exaggeratedly polite tone I could muster, "I hope Lady Flora is well?"

"She was grievously disappointed to hear you'd come back to town," he growled.

I tried not to let my smile twist into a mortified grimace, which I fear it very probably looked like. "I'm sorry to hear that."

He stared at me, hard, for a good long moment before sneering. "You would do better to remedy the cause, but I'm sure that's too much to ask for."

I stared back, unable to believe he'd just said that outright. I had no idea what to say. Mrs. Etaris was still holding my elbow, and now her hand tightened on my arm, hard enough that I reflexively glanced at her. She was smiling placidly, but spoke with a noticeable edge to her voice. "I do hope you don't mean that, Sir Vorel, as your nephew returned at an ideal moment to help me, and I shouldn't want to lose another assistant so soon. People would begin to think me very careless indeed."

Sir Vorel flushed angrily, as I was interested to see, while the Chief Constable frowned hard. Mrs. Etaris gave my elbow another squeeze and stepped forward between Sir Vorel and me to take her husband's arm. Her movement swung us all around so that the Etarises formed a pair between the Greenwings.

She went on amiably. "It's Friday, so the store's closed early, Sir Vorel. Mr. Greenwing was just helping me carry Mr. Shipston's order. Are you finished with your day, my dear?"

Her husband looked at Sir Vorel, obviously awaiting permission.

My uncle shook his head, jowls wobbling a bit, as I was distressingly glad to see. "Mr. Greenwing, eh. Go home with your wife, Etaris, there's nothing more to be done about it tonight, since you were so late finding the news."

"Sir Vorel," began the Chief Constable, but Sir Vorel made an abrupt angry gesture that silenced him and was, evidently, his only farewell, for he brushed past us with a deliberate shove against me with his shoulder.

I swallowed and looked (about as plaintively as the Chief Constable) at Mrs. Etaris. She gave me an encouraging smile. "I will see you tomorrow at the market-bell, Mr. Greenwing."

And thus ended my first day of honest work.

***

I STOPPED OUTSIDE the house gate to gird myself before entering, and a young woman picking flowers in the garden next door straightened and said, "Mr. Greenwing! You're back in town! Did you want my mother?"

I started and looked around wildly, before remembering that while I was away at Morrowlea the Buchances had moved houses, and I'd gone unthinking to the old one. "Oh ... no," I said, and cursed myself for blushing. "To be honest, Miss Kulfield, I was woolgathering and forgot where I was going."

She grinned, with a blessed lack of anything besides honest curiosity in her expression. The family of the town blacksmith, the Kulfields had been good friends to us after we'd moved to town. Miss Kulfield in particular had been captivated by my mother's stories of growing up in the Woods Noirell.

The highway to Astandalas the Golden had run down the centre of that enchanted wood, right through my mother's people's land, and my mother had wonderful tales of seeing knights and lords and high princes and all sorts of people riding down the road in procession. She had once even seen the Red Company go a-riding two by two one midnight by the light of the moon, the year the companions had crashed the Imperial Heir's birthday party in the Palace of Stars itself, and had never forgotten the sight—nor the secret pleasure that she had warranted a verse in one of Fitzroy

Angursell's song as a result.

"Understandable, Mr. Greenwing. You've only been back, what, a week?"

"Only since Tuesday."

"Not enough time to get accustomed to a new house."

"No ..."

Mrs. Kulfield came to the door, wiping floury hands on her apron, no doubt wondering what strange man was speaking to her daughter. She looked me up and down. "Mr. Greenwing. Come back at last, are you." Her tone was uncharacteristically cool. "You look as if you've been unwell."

"I have," I admitted. Miss Kulfield made a concerned noise; her mother still was frowning. "Although it's not exactly a good excuse for writing so little this summer, and not giving good directions."

"A terrible reason," she agreed, but her voice was warmer.

I bowed to her with a flourish like Mr. Dart's curlicues, which made her smile. Mrs. Kulfield flapped her apron at me. "I've known you far too long for that, Mr. Greenwing. Will you come in for a drink?"

"I should be delighted," I said, "but I've been invited out later this evening, and really must get back to Mrs. Buchance before it gets any later. I was going—" I faltered on saying, *home*, and lamely finished up with, "I was thinking of other things, and forgot where I was going."

Mrs. Kulfield gave me a penetrating glance. "You do know that you will always be welcome here."

I bowed again, gravely. For all that I might prefer Morrowlea's egalitarianism, it has to be said a bow is a very good response when you can't think of anything else to say.

***

THE ROUTE TO the new house took me back along the high street. As I passed along the shops I saw Mr. Kim, the fishmonger's assistant, turning into Mrs. Jarnem's sweet shop. Filled with a vague sense of guilt about Mrs. Buchance—and a vague curiosity about the pie, which for lack of a better idea of what to do with it I was still carrying—I followed him in.

Mr. Buchance had been something of an inventor in the Ghilousetten model (he'd gone to Newbury and studied containers: "Somebody has to," he always used to say, with an abrupt chuckle; "somebody has to"), and had made quite a lot of money in the Interim and subsequently by his inventions for preserving food without the use of magic.

The roll-top herrings in jars at Mr. Fogerty's were from a Kingsford recipe, but the jars were Mr. Buchance's. So too were the jars containing mustard and pickles, jams and conserves, fermented cabbage and pickled capers from down south that ranged in every Fiellanese housewife's pantry.

So were the bungs on the barrels of beer, the corks and wine hoods in the bottles of perry and cider, the special lids on the bottles of vinegar and verjuice.

So were the canisters of liquorice and candied angelica in the confectioners, and the tins of cocoa, the jars of clarified cocoa butter and clotted cream from Ronderell; all of them bore the little double B sigil that stood for Benneret Buchance.

Mrs. Jarnem was doing brisk business in the few minutes left before closing, selling chocolates and sugared violets and butterscotches and all that jazz to the other young folk who were just finishing their day's work and heading home.

I made sure the pie was still covered in its cloth and slid into the crowd, exchanging heel-click bows with half a dozen people, most of whose names I half-knew at best. Their faces were vaguely familiar from their shops—the haberdasher's, the grocer's, the rival grocer's—or from the kingschool from before I went to university. I sidled up to Mr. Kim, who had been in the year above me in the kingschool.

"Back from your round, are you, Mr. Kim?"

He was choosing four chocolate truffles with exquisite concentration, and scowled at me for interrupting. After a shocked moment, he smiled in cautious welcome. "Mr. Greenwing! Which should I get, do you think?"

"Who are they for? Your mother?"

He blushed. "No ... I'm meeting ... do you know Alisoun Artquist, sir?"

I considered. Three years away from Ragnor Bella, but everyone seemed fair set to assume I remembered everyone who'd ever passed through town. Artquist was a Kilromby name, not Fiellanese at all. I vaguely remembered reading, in one of Mrs. Buchance's chatty letters, that several families from north Kilromby had sought refuge from the island wars. I tried to concentrate. "Is her father the one who grows the prize marrows?"

Mr. Kim gave me an impressed glance. "Yes. Miss Artquist is in service with the Talgarths, and she and I ... well, it's her half day today, and she gave me permission to call on her after my work was through. I wanted to bring her something as sweet as she is ... but I'm not sure what I should get."

I looked at the array on offer. Dark chocolate, milk chocolate,

cream; mint, violet, liquorice, lavender; hazelnut, walnut, pistachio.
I shifted the pie in my arms and suppressed a sneeze. Each square
of chocolate had a few grains of the flower or nut on the top in a
decorative little pile. "She might appreciate a pattern," I said; "and
if her family are gardeners—"

Mr. Kim nodded eagerly. "The marrows."

"Well then. I should choose the violet and lavender, one dark
and one white chocolate of each type, and arrange them kitty-
corner in the box."

"How clever you are," said Mr. Kim. Mrs. Jarnem made up the
order without even waiting for his agreement. "I should still be
hemming and hawing over it, as if I were a housekeeper deciding
what fish to buy."

"Do you often have people debating long?" I asked, pointing
out the sweets I wanted. Mrs. Jarnem passed across the glass jars
of bright candies like a round smiling planet, rather like one of
the year-counters across the face of Mr. Shipston's cogswork wall.
"Mr. Fogerty likes to introduce new fish every once in a while, so
I suppose people dither about that? He had herring this week, I
thought he said?"

Mr. Kim was counting out his pennies carefully, and did not
look down at the wrapped object in my hands. I hoped its fishy
smell was overwhelmed by all the chocolate and sugar and the
crush of people behind us. Hopefully he would think any lingering
fishiness was from himself.

"Oh, yes, that herring. Mind, herring's not *new*—we just don't
get it in often. Not like them foreign ducks Mr. Dart was trying to
make believe were all the rage."

"Really? I shouldn't have thought herring would be so popular here. Who bought it?"

I paid for my sweets and accepted the paper bag Mrs. Jarnem handed me in return. Mr. Kim, clutching his precious box of chocolates, said, "What? Oh, there wasn't much. The Baron and the Talgarths took all I had—the Figheldeans were sore put out that the Talgarths had their tally first, but what can I tell you? Fashions. Mr. Fogerty'll get in another barrel in a month or so, if you think Mrs. Buchance will want some? Reckon you brought a recipe or twain home from your travels, eh?"

"I'll be after Mr. Dart to make some Charese delicacies, just you wait and see," I returned, and Mr. Kim laughed and went his way.

The Baron and the Talgarths: neither of them had connections to Ghilousette that I knew of, though perhaps the Baron ... but the Honourable Master Ragnor had disclaimed all—

Well, no, I thought, cutting down side streets, nodding to people as I passed them, bowing to a few of the grander folk. He hadn't, had he? He'd identified the fish as Fultoney herring, and then eaten two eyeballs (ugh!), and then his sister had come in and interrupted his discourse before he'd said whether or not he'd had anything to do with it.

I would have expected him to say something—or I would have expected the Roald who'd gone runabout with Perry Dart and me to say something. The Honourable Master Roald Ragnor was something of a stranger.

Still, I wasn't sure that I could possibly credit the Honourable Rag (yes, I liked Mr. Dart's term) having anything to do with a Ghilousetten accusation of treason being passed on to Mr. Shipston.

***

MY SISTERS WERE playing in the front hall when their mother opened the door for me. Mrs. Buchance was young and plain and had married Mr. Buchance for the opportunity to mother his two small children (my half-sisters Lauren and Sela, now seven and six) and have her own (my three stepsisters, Elinor, Zangora, and Lamissa—the latter two names the result of both Mr. Buchance and the second Mrs. Buchance being ardent imperialists), rather than for the money that Mr. Buchance was already accumulating.

She had blossomed: still not beautiful, she'd become gracious and warm and motherly, all of which I found deeply strange because she was, after all, only five years older than I, and had come back from university in Fiella-by-the-Sea the spring of the year my mother died to assist her brother in his bakery. When my mother died, Mr. Buchance had desperately needed help with the children. Miss Inglesides had been hired as a nursemaid to Lauren and Sela in the early summer, and by the autumn was the second Mrs. Buchance.

By the spring of the next year Elinor had made her appearance, and I was studying harder than I've ever done anything in my life to get good enough marks on the Entrance Examination to have my pick of the continent's universities.

I'd done well enough to make Morrowlea: only one Miss Alvorline of Yellton, over in the next barony (and no doubt as desperate to get out of Yellem as I was to get out of Ragnor), had done better in all of Fiellan. Miss Alvorline had chosen Tara, and so with a full scholarship to any other university in Northwest Oriole open to me, I had ignored all questions of academic specialization and gone for the only one that required the abdication of one's surname upon matriculation.

"Mrs. Buchance," I said, with another bow and a smile.

"Mr. Greenwing," she replied, with a curtsey and a giggle, scooping up Lamissa, who had just learned to crawl and was scooting around the polished tile floor like a water strider. "How was your first day of—No, Sela, I don't know what your brother brought home. Ask him nicely and perhaps he'll tell you."

Sela came running up to me before slamming to a halt and performing a wobbly curtsey. I set my hat down on top of the pie while I took off my coat, but once it was off I made her as fine and florid a heel-click bow as for anyone else. "How can I help you, Miss Sela?"

"Did you bring anything for us, Jemis? You've been gone ages and *ages*. We thought you'd be back at half of four!"

"And here it is almost a quarter after five!" I said apologetically, hanging my coat on the hooks beside the door. "However can I make up for it, Miss Sela?"

She began to grin. I smiled and shooed them towards the kitchen. Mrs. Buchance might be a very wealthy woman, at least in theory, but my stepfather's sudden death had left his paperwork in such disarray that no one knew exactly where to find anything, including most of his fortune, which was in any case tied up until the Assizes. Moreover, she liked housekeeping and felt uncomfortable with live-in servants, and contented herself (as she had immediately informed me on my arrival, with just a hint of defiance) with a bit of help with the charing and the girls during the day.

I glanced sideways down at Sela, who was tugging at a handkerchief hanging out of my pocket. It was in my clean-handkerchief pocket, so I let her. "I did happen to stop by Mrs. Jarnem's, but I'm

not sure ... you shall have to ask your mother whether you might
have a piece of candy now or must wait until tomorrow."

"Oh, please, Mama, *please!*"

"They've eaten their supper already, so they can have one each,"
Mrs. Buchance said, giving me a grateful look as Lamissa emitted a
frightful fart and started to cry, as if she'd surprised herself. I par-
celled out a piece of liquorice to each of the girls, made sure that
Zangora was sucking at hers rather than choking, and had been
roped into a game of ride-the-horse (me being the horse) before
Mrs. Buchance had finished changing Lamissa's garments.

I eventually managed to get upstairs to bathe and change my
clothes for supper. My room still felt entirely a stranger's, decorated
in Mrs. Buchance's very conventional taste. The three small chests
from my mother were arrayed under the window to one side; my
childhood books, romances and adventure tales for the most part,
filled one small bookcase, and otherwise ... I had the clothes and
books I'd acquired in the summer, and that was it.

It wouldn't take too much to leave this behind, I thought.

I sat on the edge of my bed, looking at the small portrait I had
of my mother and father. It was an exquisite miniature, painted by
Sir Hamish, who had once been their good friend as well as cousin.

My father was in his dress uniform; gleaming bravely on his
chest was the great golden pectoral showing the Emperor's favour,
which he'd earned by saving the life of General Halioren in the
Battle of Loqui in East Orkaty. He was smiling, as if about to laugh.

All my childhood memories seemed to involve him laughing,
especially those from that wonderful long summer when I was nine
and he was between wars, and against my mother's token protests
kept me out of the kingschool so we could spend as much time as

possible together.

My mother, chestnut-haired and beautiful and barefoot like a Traveller, in a flaring dress in a fine bright blue, with a hat full of flowers, smiling up at my father. Sir Hamish had captured love in their expression, and a fierce pride; but I thought, for the first time, how very young they had been. My age. She'd been barely nineteen when they met one summer between her university terms, and he one-and-twenty and on his way to take up his first commission in the Imperial Army.

This picture must have been painted a year or two later, after their marriage but before the crowded week in which my father received his second commission and my mother found out she was increasing. Before the Fall, but still a time of propriety: neither her family nor his had liked that they'd eloped, despite him being the second son of a marquis and the hero of Orkaty and her heiress to the Woods Noirell.

And one-and-twenty years from this portrait, they were both dead, the Empire was fallen, and their only child had at the very end of his degree failed out of Morrowlea, failed abysmally to win the lady he'd been courting, and was sliding inexorably down the social classes to—

A crash from downstairs interrupted my meditations, and I hastened down to find that one or other of my sisters had let her curiosity get the better of her, and the stargazy pie had broken across the entry hall floor.

Mrs. Buchance, coming out of the kitchen, said, "Oh, Jemis, I'm so sorry—it was such a—an *extraordinary* pie—"

"It was at that," I agreed, trying not to laugh, and starting to sneeze instead when my breath caught.

"I ... it was a kind thought, though we have lamb for supper," she added, bending over to begin picking up the pieces of egg and fish and potato and clay, and then, in a changed voice, while I attempted to say why it had not been intended as a gift for her: "Oh! Is this yours, Mr. Greenwing?"

And she held out a ring.

Chapter Eight

AS A RESULT of my sisters' insistence that I read a story to them
before bedtime, I was a bit late leaving. I hoped that since the new
house was on the eastern (or *easter*, as Dartington folk said) side
of town and therefore the right direction for heading towards the
Little Church, the Green Dragon, and the walnut tree, I would be
able to make up the time.

I had not, however, reckoned with the effect of a week's heavy
rain on the Raggle. The usually placid little river was boiling and
grey, well over the old bridge footings that provided stepping-stones,
and so I was obliged to pick my way along the backs of houses to get
to the new bridge.

For the most part, the houses had long gardens running down
to the stream, with shrubberies, chicken coops, and post-Astandalan outhouses tucked here and there. The slow rebuilding of magic, along with the cleverness of artificers out of Ghilousette and
further afield (the Lady of Alinor herself had put forth an award
for engineers who could recreate clean water indoors without the
constant flow of magic that had provided it previously), had meant

that the wealthiest folk in Ragnor Bella were no longer using their outhouses ... but everyone still had them, covered over with shrubs and vines, just in case. Mr. Fogerty's comment about people being afraid of becoming too fond of new things after the Fall extended to a fear of other things going missing again.

It was starting to get dark as I made my way along the footpath. I'd thought to provide myself with a candle-lantern, but I didn't it need it for the footpath, even the bit beyond the old bridge pilings.

I'd gotten in the habit of extended daily exercise while at Morrowlea, long-distance running for a while seeming the only thing I could focus on through the hay fever, and continued even while on my walking tour. Marcan and Hal hadn't been inclined to go more than a handful of miles a day afoot, wanting to spend the rest of the time lounging about in country pubs talking to people. To be honest, I'd enjoyed that, too, but had felt the need for more exercise—and solitude—than either of them.

No wonder I was feeling a bit out-of-sorts, I thought. I had only gone for a run once since I got back to Ragnor Bella, and that was on Wednesday. And I was very much with other people. Mrs. Buchance had been very curious about where I'd gone so early in the morning, and more confused when I told her, and it had seemed easier not to go on Thursday ... and then this morning I'd been worried about work ... I'll go tomorrow, I promised myself.

I passed by Mrs. Etaris' house just as she was drawing the curtains against the evening. In the glow of the oil lamps her mousy hair looked auburn, and I saw the inner chamber like a play set: the lady of the house in a pale blue dress, the heavy white wool curtains with their geometric embroideries in black and red folding around her as if she were the goddess coming into her aspect as the White

Lady of Winter. A table set with copper and pewter and white porcelain dishes. And stepping in to this scene, like the White Lady's own hunter, the Chief Constable still in his official uniform of green and yellow.

Mrs. Etaris paused a moment at a word from her husband, her eyebrows drawing down in a grimace, turned towards the night; he looked briefly smug; and then she smiled and let the curtains swing shut as she turned to take the hand he'd stretched towards her.

I felt inexplicably as if I'd just witnessed a secret, and picked up my pace, rather glad that the other houses on that stretch had all already drawn their drapes close and guarded against passers-by. The water rushing away on my left sounded like it was chewing the ground. After a moment I thought, *the Lady's hell with it*, and began to run.

Over the new bridge, nodding at a pair of men fishing there, the same pair I'd seen Wednesday morning, though I had yet to learn their names. Or they mine, obviously: one flicked his finger across his cap, the other nodded. Both had pipes clamped in their mouths, sending billows of smoke across my path as I dropped to a walk to stride past them. I felt in my pocket to make sure I had replaced my handkerchiefs safely, but the whiff of tobacco didn't make me sneeze.

The road bent after a row of cottages and the Ragglebridge public house, which had a swinging sign and a candle lantern in a glass chimney. The light formed a cone in the fine drizzle. No one was sitting on the bench tonight, though there were a couple of horses tied up to the railing. Both horses and tack were of a good quality, and a groom stood beside them. He was hooded in a closely-fitting coat; he turned as I walked past the light, and I saw that he wore a sword.

That was no strange thing in the Farry March or in south Erlin-gale, where the wars past the borders of Rondé threatened to pour up into our kingdom, but it was highly unusual in most of Fiellan, and very unusual indeed in peaceful out-of-the-way Ragnor Bella.

He might have been guarding a Scholar going to—or from—one of those more conflicted regions, but in that case why spend the night at the Ragglebridge, when the far better inns of the town were visible across the bridge? And why go through Ragnor Bella at all, which wasn't really on the road anywhere? There were easier ways to get to the Farry March than across the Green Mountains.

I spun out a handful of possibilities to amuse myself once I was around the bend and it seemed safe to start running again. He was a spy—they sought adventure—they were looking for the Border between worlds, which used to pass south of town—he'd heard ru-mour of a dragon in the Gorbelow Hills or the Woods Noirell—he was an addlepated wannabe knight of a chivalric order—he was a Fairy prince passing as human for his own nefarious and enigmatic reasons.

No doubt, I thought.

I rather wished any of those things might be true, for any of them at all (well, except perhaps the first one) would be something of more interest in Ragnor Bella than my return home. Social disrepute is trumped by actual physical danger any day; even the starchiest of the old guard would bend the rules if it meant their continued survival.

I thought of my uncle. Well, probably.

The tower of the Little Church caught low streamers of clouds ahead of me, barely visible in the gloom and rain. Somewhere behind the clouds the sun had set, and the light was draining out of the sky. A fine old poem about the building of a church in Rondelan came to mind, but as I tried to recite its lines to myself the words failed and faded.

No, I wouldn't be going on to higher studies, not when I couldn't even remember the words of a poem I'd written a paper on. I couldn't remember what the essay had been about—something to do with how the imagery in the poem was structured according to the symmetry of the White Lady of Winter (and war) and the Green Lady of Summer (and peace), running counter to the description of the church as an expression of—what was it?

I frowned at the darkness. My head hurt. That had been the last paper I'd written before the start of my illness. It was one of my better papers—better than my final paper, anyway. At least only Violet and my tutor had read that one.

I kicked viciously at a rock in the path before me, then hugged my summer coat closer about me as a gust of wind blew cold rain in my face.

The goddess' churches were always built on hillocks in Fiellan, and always fairly close to—though never *at*—crossroads. Nothing was ever built at crossroads in South Fiellan, the hinterland of Rondé and always one of the last holdouts to sweeping change. It had been one of the last civilized holdouts of the old religion after the Conquest of Western Alinor, and it was one of the last holdouts of truly ardent Imperialism now. Other places might put churches at crossroads, but not us.

Crossroads were for murderers, suicides, traitors, and black magic. Waystones pinned magic into spells of protection and safety, the magic everyone had been most desperate to maintain even during the Interim.

The waystone at the Lady's Cross was split top to bottom and bound with black and white and golden cords tied in elaborate knots, which Dominus Gleason—who still kept them knotted and tied—said maintained the old Schooled enchantments and prevented those buried there from rising.

(And that, right there, was why Dominus Gleason was considered *not quite the thing* himself.)

I glanced past the hillock towards the crossroads. A few furlongs along the north road I could see the warm lantern-lights of the Green Dragon, beckoning any fools ready to part with their money into its welcoming fold. Well, one of the few ways I actually did take after my father was in my skill at games of chance; the ill luck of the rest of my life didn't follow me there.

The walnut tree I presumed Mr. Dart had meant was located on the southern side of the church, down the hill towards a little beck, in the ruins of the old priest-cote from back when the Little Church had had a priest of its own. The same stormy-night battle of magic that had split the waystone had seen the death of the last priest and the Baron's decision to build a new church on the north side of town, close to the Whiteroad Cross under which my father had been buried.

I nearly turned my ankle in a rabbit-hole, and decided to cut more closely to the church. I also dropped down to a walk. I did feel better, even if a quarter-hour run was nothing to my usual several-hour circuit.

Once off the main road the ground was plastered wet leaves, and it was getting dark enough that I couldn't see well. The sky itself was a peculiar light grey, not dark but certainly not permitting light down. After a moment I remembered from Mr. Shipston's cogswork that it was the new moon.

"House of the Dragon," I murmured aloud, hesitating before plunging between two thorn bushes.

Three months to the Winterturn Assizes. I just needed to keep my head down, refuse any particularly foolish suggestions of Mr. Dart's, and keep an even keel. Not make any more waves than those inevitably caused by my presence in town already. Be so meek and humble that everyone just accepted that I was Mrs. Etaris' new assistant, no threat to anyone—

Something moved in the shadows.

Three times a week we'd had compulsory self-defence at Morrowlea, but this was the first time I'd ever actually fought in earnest.

It was *entirely* different.

He was wiry and strong, and wore an oiled cloak, but my actions were clear and supple as water.

I got my leg between his, and we staggered backwards through the thorn bush. We rolled sideways across the bush again, the thorns gouging me in shoulder and side. Crashed up against the side of the church, and I pushed hard against it to break the stranger's grip on my shoulder.

I nearly had him, until he tripped over a stone and stumbled backwards. I tumbled after, like Jack after Jill in the nursery rhyme, and made sure each roll landed on him. We hit the edge of the slope, and somersaulted down in a messy tangle of limbs and cloth until we fetched up in a squelchy pile, panting and choking, near the beck. The calm in my mind evaporated.

In a sudden panic I rolled over to get out of the immediate way of my assailant, discovered his cloak was wrapped around my arm, and as I disentangled myself I realized I'd not only landed in nettles but also autumn-mildewy wild mint, and the combined dust and volatile oils made me start sneezing violently.

As I tried to suppress the sneezes I saw my assailant get up on his hands and knees. There was light glimmering off the burn, which caught a gleam off a dirk—my astonished intake of breath caught on my sneeze going out, and I started to choke in earnest.

Trying not to choke put all thoughts out of mind. I rolled over to get water from the stream, and lay there catching my breath for a good few minutes before it occurred to me that the person seemed to have thought better of his attack. I sat up again warily to see a shadowy Mr. Dart sitting on top of him.

He tossed me the dirk. "And here I thought I was going to be the one doing the entertaining tonight."

I caught the knife, got another whiff of nettles, and started to sneeze again, and this time Mr. Dart laughed. "Seriously, Jemis, don't you *ever* stop sneezing?"

The figure under him jerked, swore, and said, "Jemis! It *would* be you."

I got my sneezing under control, and said, cautiously, for I couldn't see the face, but that voice—I would always recognize that voice—

"Violet?"

Chapter Nine

SHE CURSED FLUENTLY.

Mr. Dart's mouth dropped open, the dim light reflecting on his teeth. I had to smile at his scandal. Then Violet said, "Jemis! What the hell are you doing here?"

"I'm from here! What are *you* doing here?"

"You're going to ruin—*Jemis.*" She spat another curse out, anatomically impossible to the point of hilarity. The pause afterwards was so awkward that I started involuntarily to laugh, and then started sneezing again, and finally I scrambled to my feet, followed more cautiously by Mr. Dart and Violet.

After another awkward pause she said: "So you're still alive, then."

I stopped laughing. "Didn't you think I would be?"

"You were remarkably ill this spring."

Her tone was off-hand and factual, as if it were all one to her whether I had lived or died. I certainly had not wished to see her again after the disastrous *viva voce* examinations, but I—well, I couldn't say I'd be indifferent to learning she or Lark were *dead.*

93

To give myself a moment to gather my thoughts, and also because I was uncomfortably damp and afraid the mildew would set
me off again, I said, "Perhaps we could get out of this muck?"

"Good thinking," Mr. Dart said, as one grasping at a straw of
sanity. We retreated up to the ruined priest-cote, where he'd left a
new-style oil lantern with the wick turned low. The old hermitage
had a table in half-way decent repair, but no benches or chairs. Violet and I seated ourselves gingerly on the table. Mr. Dart turned up
the wick before perching himself in the window embrasure where
he could look at us.

Violet was beautiful; everyone granted her that. Part-Shaian
ethnically, she had deep brown crinkled hair and deep brown limpid eyes, and skin that went from ivory to fawn over the course of
the year. In the lamplight she was golden, even with the streaks of
mud running across her face and the shadows from her hood. I
hesitated a moment and then offered her one of my extra handkerchiefs.

She took it with a twisted mouth and a sardonic imitation of
courtesy. "Thank you, Jemis. Always the gentleman."

I pressed my lips together. "Mr. Dart, did you—" but was interrupted by her lowering the handkerchief from a split lip and
laughing.

"So much for standing up against social injustice," she said,
and the disdain in her voice was so clear that Mr. Dart stopped admiring her and instead gawped incredulously before realizing what
he was doing and closing his mouth.

I found another handkerchief and dabbed at a scrape across my
palm. The dirk was heavy on my lap. It had a plain, useful look to
it; no decorative blade, this, but one meant to be used. Violet had

been one of the best knife-fighters in our sparring matches. One of the brightest and best in the whole university, in fact. Or indeed, the best and brightest; she'd been class valedictorian, and tipped to graduate First. I swallowed against furious acrimony. "There is a time and a place for courtesy, Violet."

"It's true you were very *polite* about it when you set about destroying Lark's life."

Mr. Dart said, "I say!"

"Didn't he tell you how he challenged one of the notable students in the year on the grounds that she was a sophist? I wouldn't have thought you so craven as not to admit it, Jemis. I thought you were proud of it. Standing up for the truth, you said. Protecting Morrowlea's reputation for promoting good scholarship and good thought, you said. Arguing that trite thinking, however beautifully presented, is still trite. Betraying—"

My voice burst out. "It was more than *trite*!"

"She was studying rhetoric! Of course it was supposed to be stylish. You betrayed her."

Expressions of horror, nobly-restrained humour, and concern were chasing themselves across Mr. Dart's face. I swallowed tautly. "She betrayed herself."

"She betrayed you, you mean! That's what this is about, isn't it?"

I sprang up, then sat down again when there was nowhere to go but to gesture with the dagger. At Mr. Dart's wary glance I set it carefully down on the table. "She betrayed all of us, Violet! Why didn't you stand up against her? Why are you still defending her now? You know as well as I do that her paper was all style and no substance, and not only that, it was cruel, pusillanimous, and *petty*."

"It was rhetorically perfect!"

"And intellectually bankrupt."

Mr. Dart said, "I say!" again, more faintly.

"You're just jealous—"

"Jealous?" I let loose an involuntary crow of laughter. "Why would I have been jealous of Lark? I loved her—I would have done anything for her."

Violet laughed bitterly. "Anything. Up to and including cutting her down before the whole school."

"Let us remember the whole school supported her." Something was fluttering in my throat, words I hadn't been able to say to myself, or to anyone—not even to Hal, certainly not to Mr. Dart. "Even you, Violet. Even you. The only person who stood behind me was Hal."

"Because you were destroying her reputation and her life! What do you think happens to someone who fails their final paper and barely scrapes a pass at Morrowlea?"

"Oh, I don't know," I said with heavy irony, thinking of how my own final term had been disastrous long before the *viva voce* examinations and the intense shaming by the rest of the school and the sight of my tutor solemnly and ceremoniously ripping my own final paper in half.

She held herself still for a moment, staring at me. "You didn't use to be so sarcastic, Jemis."

I was so disgusted I could barely look at her. I stared at the dirk in my hand instead. She didn't add anything else, and neither did Mr. Dart. I swallowed again, the tendons in my throat feeling as if they were about to snap from the tension. Finally I spoke.

"I suppose that was before the woman I loved betrayed my confidence, my trust, and her own honour. Before a woman I respected and admired for her courage and divine love of the truth was too cowardly to stand up for what she knew was right."

I paused, but she didn't say anything. I shuddered, my fingernails digging into the leather hilt. All the exhilaration from the brief run and the briefer fight was draining out of me, leaving me feeling shaky and tired. I glanced over at Violet, whose face was set.

"Perhaps I was more cheerful before all my friends but one looked away as the rest of the school turned against me. Before the faculty of a university so committed to the inherent equality of man they refuse external markings of wealth and honour let my fellow students *stone* me."

Before my uncle told me I ought to leave my home town, before Dominus Gleason propositioned me with something decidedly unpleasant, before Saya Etaris told me she was waiting for me to commit treason or suicide like my father. Before the Honourable Rag set me firmly into my new place, before Dame Talgarth cut me, before—I bit my lip and refused to say all those things. There were good things, too—Mr. Dart—Mrs. Etaris—my sisters—

"Before a former friend attacked me in the dark. Perhaps I am the tiniest bit cynical as a result."

There was a long and strained silence. I breathed stertorously, trying not to cry with tiredness and shame and fury and sheer disappointment. Mr. Dart fiddled with the oil lantern and tried not to look at me. Violet's face was pinched and pale, as if something I said had struck home.

I didn't know what else to say, but the words pushed out: "I am so disappointed in you, Violet. I really thought you were more than that."

It was her turn to swallow tautly. "Not Lark?"

I took a deep and unpleasantly noisy breath, wanted to hide behind my handkerchief again. Sighed. "Not when I saw what she wrote. The person I loved ... wasn't who I thought she was. As soon as I read what she'd written I knew she was just like it: superficially perfect and utterly hollow. It was as if all the lights came on. All I could see was the fact that not only had she betrayed my confidence in writing what she did, not only had she betrayed my belief in her, but that she always had. She always *did*, you know—I saw that so clearly."

Violet held herself very still, staring at me with an expression I couldn't quite read. Disapproval, dismay, disgust. I looked down again.

"All of a sudden I could see that she had spent all the time we were together manipulating me for her own amusement. She didn't care that I was sick and couldn't study—you were the one who convinced me to read our books aloud to you, who badgered me into writing my papers, who made me go to class. Lark always wanted me to skip class, to avoid work, to do *her* work when she wasn't well. Lark was using me the whole time. But you ... I really thought you were better than that."

I looked up at her, where she sat smaller than she had, tucked into herself, no longer coiled and ready to spring but deflated. I shook my head vigorously, trying to remind myself that she was a good actress, had played in the school performances. (I had, too, before Lark had said they took too much time away from her ...) I was savagely glad she seemed finally touched by my words.

"Lark betrayed me every moment, every day. She played me for a fool, and I fell for it. I suppose the fact that you were her best friend should have made me suspicious, but I never thought you knew what she was doing ... not until that moment at the end, when everyone turned against me and only Hal came down, and I looked at you—and you looked away. You looked away."

I hadn't realized until that moment how much that betrayal had hurt. There had been something about Lark, some fragility or conditionality to her love, that had always made me feel I had to make things up to her, that I had to be careful or else the glorious thing that we had would break—as indeed it had, in the end. Somehow I had always known with Lark that I had always to be hers, while she was only mine for a certain degree of *mine*. I was hers entire—but she was maddeningly partial.

At the time that had seemed a delicious prolongation of the joys of courtship, as if I had always to pursue her, to woo her, to shower her with my attention and devotion, while she bestowed her company as reward for that attention, that devotion, that blind adoration.

But Violet—Violet—Violet had been different.

Violet had been a very good friend, right up until she chose Lark over the truth.

"I suppose I ought to admire your loyalty to her," I added on that thought, trying very hard to keep my voice even.

Violet looked up, her eyes hooded from the shadow cast by the lantern. Smiled sadly. "Don't."

"Violet—"

Even I could hear that all I wanted was for her to make some apology. Her name hung in the air between us. She stood, her back straight and proud. For a moment I thought she wasn't going to say anything else at all, and then she said: "I ran away from an arranged marriage when I was fourteen. Lark's family took me in. I ... Jemis, you were right in the spring. You're right now. But don't admire my loyalty. Some things ought to be indefensible."

Everyone in town thought my father's reputation was indefensible, I thought, and swallowed. I was the only person who had truly believed him when he said the disgrace was calumny, and it was hard enough to keep standing up for that, over and over and over again.

If it had been someone else's reputation—would I have stood, as Hal had stood, to the challenge? It was only because it was my father that I had been able to stand up against Lark. My father, whose indefensible reputation I had been defending since his first death.

Would I have been able to say, *This is wrong,* for a complete stranger? For a story no one else knew or cared to know about? For an abstract ideal of the truth? Would I have looked in the face of my beloved and said, *This is wrong,* for anyone? Would I have found my voice if it had truly just been a matter of rhetorical sophistry?

I had thought Violet a better person than me, I realized. I'd thought that she would stand, where I wouldn't; thought that she would say, *For this truth I stand, and will die for it.* Thought she would cry foul for the sophistry, not needing to know it was also betrayal. Thought the fine words we university students all said were in her case no rhetoric, but pure belief. But only Hal had stood up.

I hadn't blamed Marcan that he hadn't.

"Violet," I said again, and she stayed in the act of lifting her hand to raise her hood against the wind and the rain howling past the door. She was wearing a long grey cloak buttoned tightly at her breast in defiance of fashion.

Grey cloak. I dropped my glance down. Long skirts.

Someone who glanced back at my cry and then ran when they saw me.

The words came unbidden: "You left the pie on the fountain."

She turned with her hand on the door, sharp as a whip, her face once again remote and dangerous. I stood up, conscious my hand was very close to the dagger, and also that Violet had almost always beaten me in hand-to-hand combat. "You knew I was here."

I wouldn't have thought it possible to be *more* disappointed in her, but as I fumbled through thoughts falling into place like crossword puzzle answers, I was. My voice came out a thin whisper, and I nearly did start to cry. "You attacked me on purpose."

"I say," said Mr. Dart again, even more faintly.

I felt as I had when I read Lark's essay, that rhetorically perfect piece about my father's treachery, taking everything I had told her about his return and disgrace and turning it into a savage attack on the few things people still admired him for, the small pieces of respect I could hold onto. People always talked about fury being hot, white-hot, but I found it cold, sliding into my veins and my heart and leaving me numb to all the fine bright passions. When I'd read Lark's essay all the fire was extinguished, dowsed in one moment with a hiss and a stench and a mess.

Now my stomach felt cold and slimy as if I had a bellyful of the muck we'd just fought in.

"I thought you were just not as strong as I believed you," I said. "But you're—what? A traitor?—"

Her expression went fixed, flat as a wooden mask. "Jemis."

"What?" I cried, forcing my hand not to reach for the dagger, not to raise this to violence, not to fall to the cold fire. "What do you want with me? Why are you *doing* this?"

"I didn't know it was you."

"I don't believe you!"

She turned suddenly, crossed the space between us more quickly than I could react, took my hand. "Jemis—"

Something about her touch made me think with horrifying clarity of Dominus Gleason, and my poor abused system revolted: I sneezed, pulling my hand automatically out of her grasp to cover my face. "Go," I said, between gasps. "Go."

Violet had been one of my closest friends for years; she knew where I kept clean handkerchiefs. Had been the one to help me make extra ones, trading hemming for poetry reading. She had been the one to keep my academics afloat when the hay fever made my attention skitter with every sneeze and Lark had merely laughed and told me not to worry, that soon I would be better and everything would be wonderful. Violet had followed behind Lark, picking up the pieces.

Violet reached into my clean handkerchief pocket and presented me with one of my spares. I took it automatically, with an automatic mutter of thanks, and blew my nose. She sat down beside me, and waited while I tried to compose myself. She smelled of sandalwood and mint. She didn't explain anything; she said, quietly, "The Lady bless you," as if she was completely and utterly certain the Lady would, and then she put her arm around me.

The touch was so unexpectedly comforting I started to cry, to my horror and Mr. Dart's. He said, "I say," yet another time, even more faintly, and I started to laugh. It turned to hiccoughs and I sat there, head bowed until my elbows were on my knees, Violet's hand resting on my back.

She spoke into the silence. "I didn't come here to hurt you,

Jemis. I didn't recognize you in the square through the rain. I didn't attack because I thought it was you."

I could see her out of the corner of my eye without turning or lifting my head. "Dare I ask why you did, then?"

She fiddled with a bracelet she wore on her left wrist, silver etched with fine geometric patterns that caught the lantern light. Girded herself as if to speak; then sighed. "I am investigating a mystery. I intended to continue my studies, and was travelling beforehand. The pie was a curiosity, nothing more."

I didn't believe her, but could see no good way to say so. "And you came to Ragnor Bella, why?"

"It has its little renown, you know, for being the dullest town in Rondé. The fish pie was a diversion, in a day otherwise of dispiriting ordinariness."

"So you went out for a walk in a rainstorm, at night, and assaulted a perfect stranger minding his own business ..."

"I thought you said—something untoward. It wasn't the best of ideas."

I sat up and frowned at her. That didn't sound like the Violet I knew, who wasn't impulsive and stupid. She looked at me and smiled sadly. "I suppose my thoughts on Ragnor Bella were coloured by Lark's essay, even if it was ... petty and—and pusillanimous. The phrases stuck in my mind."

They'd stuck in mine, too, especially in the black days of the early summer.

The hinterland of Fiellan, home to a people so dull their greatest pretension to interest lies in the traitor of Loe ... Jakory Greenwing, whose alleged valiancy in earlier campaigns was surely as much a trumpery courage as his treason was falsely brilliant. ... Deserving of all calumny and curses ... his treason was doubtless a major contributing factor to the Fall of Astandalas itself ...

"What was it about?" Mr. Dart asked, when she trailed off and I stared at the ground. "It was ... about Ragnor Bella?"

His incredulous tone said well enough that Lark was right enough that no one ever expected anything to be of interest in Ragnor Bella.

Violet glanced sidelong at me, but not with the expression that would have indicated she knew who I was. I braced myself for her account, which was mercifully brief. "It was the story of Jakory Greenwing, the hero of Orkaty and the traitor of Loe. He was from here, I understand."

Mr. Dart closed his eyes. "She wrote an essay about him?"

"She was a rhetorician ... she wrote a philippic, in the form of the goddess of Fame protesting History's attempt to introduce Jakory Greenwing into her halls." She paused a moment, and we listened to the wind howling around the priest-cote, a late moth buzzing around the lantern. I tried to shoo it away, but it kept buzzing back to butt its head against the glass chimney. Of course it did, I thought. "It was a magnificent piece of rhetoric, Jemis. But you're right: it was sophistry pure and simple."

"And slander," Mr. Dart said. Violet and I both looked up at him. The light caught her flawless profile, her eyes lined with kohl so she looked like something out of a First-Calligraphic period wall painting, with the streaks of mud glowing in the light like gold leaf. He glanced at me, then firmly at her.

"I studied late Astandalan history under Domina Black of Stoneybridge, and made a special focus of the Alinorel armies of the reigns of Eritanyr and Artorin. Moreover, I am a man of the barony of Ragnor in the duchy of Fiellan, and my father and my older brother both were good friends with the Greenwings, including Major Jakory Greenwing and his wife Lady Olive. I will gladly take you to my brother, I will show you the books I brought with me from Stoneybridge, and I will tell you this, Miss Violet, that all the supposed disgrace brought to Jakory Greenwing was due to mistaken identity and the fact that he was on a scouting mission when the fortress of Loe was lost to the Stone Speakers by the action of a different and unrelated Jakory Greenwing. He was decorated by both the Emperor and by the Lady of Alinor for his extraordinary courage and valour."

Violet spoke with grave formality. "I see. I can see why you were so ... exercised about it, Jemis, as a man of Ragnor Bella."

I jumped up and went to stand before the other window embrasure. The cool night air blowing through the broken panes was refreshing. My face felt hot and tight. Thankfully the priest-cote, though dusty and full of cobwebs, did not seem to be full of anything to make me sneeze uncontrollably. I tried not to clench the handkerchief too tightly.

Mr. Dart rolled his shoulders. "Now that we have settled that matter for the moment, let us turn our attention to the present day. Miss Violet: I am Mr. Dart of Dartington, lately, as I said, of Stoneybridge. I am afraid that while you and Mr.—uh, Jemis, are obviously well acquainted, I have not had the honour of your name?" Violet stared at him with much the same astonishment I felt. "Come," he said a touch impatiently, "we are a small town, and not on the road anywhere; we will be able to find out where you are staying if you do not tell us."

"If we were to enquire," I muttered, but my heart wasn't in it.

"I'm staying at the inn down the road," Violet said, after a long and thoughtful moment.

"The Ragglebridge?" I said, at the same time Mr. Dart said, "The Green Dragon?"

She picked up the dirk from the table and replaced it somewhere beneath the cloak, then stood, muscular and as tall—or as short—as me, with her crinkly brown hair braided back from her face and the hood puddled about her shoulders like a very old-fashioned yoke.

"Jemis," she said softly, "I am truly sorry I attacked you. I'm sorry about this spring. I'm sorry for ... everything. But I'm not ... in so many ways I'm not what you think I am. I don't think it wise we see each other again." She glanced at Mr. Dart. "I am sorry we met under such inauspicious circumstances, Mr. Dart. I don't expect to see you again, but I am ... I am staying at the Green Dragon."

"Even the Green Dragon would require a surname of some description."

She raised her eyebrows. "Very well: Miss Redshank."

He didn't say anything; neither did I. It wasn't a name of note that I could think of, though something about it rang a very faint bell of familiarity. Some story I had heard long ago, perhaps. Possibly a tale Mr. Dart had told me, his interest in history being well-established even when he was a boy and we sat at my father's knee begging for stories of adventure.

Violet lifted her hood again, then stopped again at the door to look back at me. "While we are being so formal ... Jemis, by what name should I remember you?"

I twisted my lips, but merely said, quite quietly, "Mr. Greenwing."

She froze, mouth parted, in almost comical surprise. I couldn't read whether it was faked or real; somehow didn't care. I didn't watch her go up the hill.

I suppose I should have mustered concern for a young woman walking alone at night—to the Green Dragon, no less—but she'd been the one to choose that house of mixed repute, not us, and ... I sighed.

Violet Redshank, even so.

Chapter Ten

"WHAT A CORKER!" said Mr. Dart as he came back to the table. "Frankly a bit terrifying."

I quirked a smile. "She is at that. She came First at Morrowlea."

There was a bit of a silence. I cast about for several things to say, then just gave up and said what I was thinking. "It was against the university statutes to give one's surname or home barony at Morrowlea. They wanted everyone to come in as equals. Everything was the same level for everyone, professors to freshmen."

"Radical," he said. "You must have loved that Lark woman, to tell her about your father."

I made a shrug to show I really didn't want to talk about it any further. "So. What's all this about picking mushrooms in the dark of the new moon?"

"Oh ... it's not that ..."

"Of course it's not. Come on, give. Are we going poaching, gambling, carousing, or cock-fighting?"

"A secret society is having a meeting in the woods tonight. I thought you might like to go with me."

"What, you belong to a secret society? What I missed by going on my walking tour of Rondé!"

"I can see why you didn't feel up to coming back right away," he muttered. "I don't belong to it, I just overheard people talking about it ..."

"Well, there wasn't much else to talk about. Before I came home, that is."

"True. Well, last month I was out—picking mushrooms—with an acquaintance of mine up the Rag, and ..."

"Come, come, Mr. Dart."

He leaned back on the table and grinned at me. "You're too suspicious by half, Mr. Greenwing. All right then, we were poaching salmon from the Baron's upper pools. As we were on our way back towards the Hall, we came up behind several men on their way home. We thought that they might be the Chief Constable's men, and, well, since we'd been reasonably successful in our fishing, we thought we'd best not draw attention to ourselves. We were close to the fork between Ragnor Bella and Dartington, and they stopped to make their adieus to each other there. One of them mentioned as to how he would be away for the next meeting, and a second said that they would see him at the new moon, then, and that they should meet the third at the crossroads—you know, where the old Astandalan road crosses the east highway, just before you get to Ragnor Parva—and they could go on together to the meeting-place at half past eight."

"What made you think it was a secret society, and not just an appointment for, say, mushroom picking?"

"They had a special sort of handshake and were discussing passwords."

"No! People don't actually."

"I shouldn't have thought young women of obvious good family would lay in wait for perfect strangers out of an alleged sense of boredom, but yet! Today has been far more educational than I expected. And here I was merely hoping for something exciting to come of the secret society when I decided to spend the weekend in town."

"Doesn't your brother need you? Isn't it harvest-home?"

"That's in a fortnight. Tor thinks I'm trying to avoid our local Corn Maiden's practice run."

I laughed. In the silence that followed I heard that the wind had picked up, and shifted to come round from the west: the bells of town were audible. I shook my head. "Only eight o'clock! It feels much later."

"It does at that," Mr. Dart said fervently. I was about to ask why he'd set our rendezvous for seven o'clock if his secret society members didn't have theirs until 8:30, but before I formulated the question he went on. "Is ... What do you think of Miss Redshank's story?"

I shifted position and winced as some bruises became evident. "Ugh. I'll be sore the morrow. Violet—well. She is a very loyal friend."

"I'll say. Violently so."

I chuckled wryly. "Yes. Um. Her account for why she was laying in wait for someone was perhaps ..."

"Absurd? Though I hesitate to give the lie to her."

"I'd not give the lie to Violet if you value your life."

Mr. Dart stared at me. "If you say so."

"She's one of the best blades in Morrowlea. And as you have

no doubt determined, she would also put loyalty over honesty any day."

"There are worse priorities." He hesitated again, no doubt realizing how that sounded.

I didn't have the energy to make a fuss of it. I was feeling battered from the sudden strange contretemps with Violet, whom I'd never thought—or hoped—to see again. And despite Mr. Dart's fine words, the reaction of everyone else in town to my return had made it clear how easy it was for Lark's and my uncle's view of things to be taken as historical truth. It had been a lot easier for her to argue for treason than for me to argue for honour; my only weapon had been the pitiful attempt to criticize her lack of generosity and thought.

And what had that won me? A lost degree, a stay in the hospital ward for a relapse of the illness (and bruises from the stones), and when an abashed Marcan had come to warn Hal and me that Lark had riled up the university even more, a hasty exit from Morrowlea for an unplanned walking tour of the kingdom. And the return to Ragnor Bella, where the only good things so far were Mr. Dart, Mrs. Buchance, and Mrs. Etaris.

I decided to just have it out. "Why did you ask me tonight? Really, Mr. Dart. Why me?"

He was turning down the lamp, and stopped with it just a glowing spark at the end of the wick. "Why wouldn't I ask you?"

"Because although Lark may have put the worst possible skew on my family history, nevertheless I am not properly of your class anymore, and outside of Morrowlea's experiments that matters."

I'd seen how much it mattered, as my remaining friends from Morrowlea added surnames and titles. Tover was a baker's son, and

Isoude a yeoman peasant's daughter. The rest ... Marcan the Count of Westmoor was not the only man of high estate. They had put loyalty over truth, too, not believing me about the disastrous *viva voce* examinations or why I'd been so dead-set against Lark—and I, as much a coward as Violet when it came to it, had not been able to tell them how much Lark had betrayed me, how ill she had used me, how thoroughly she had played me.

Once we left Morrowlea, Marcan and Hal were quick enough to forget Lark and her passions in favour of returning home with a high degree and the whiff of dangerous politics that brought acclaim and adoration. I'd been grateful for how easily they'd forgotten Lark—or pretended to—though of course they hadn't been the ones intending to marry her.

I made my thoughts go back to the current day. "The Baron will shun you for gallivanting about with me; so will the other gentry. Dame Talgarth's already given me the cut direct. Your brother won't like it."

"My brother," he said, turning down the lamp the rest of the way and starting to set it in its travel case, then burning his finger on the chimney and cursing slightly. "I love and respect my brother very much, Jemis, but I will not let him choose my friends for me! Besides, he was great friends with your father."

"My father shamed himself and us," I said sharply. "My mother was made a bigamist, my father's honours were stripped from him—his title, his fortune, his land. My mother's people disowned her, my father's people—oh! They continue to spread calumny, as if my father hadn't already died of shame and dishonour long ago. They dare suggest my mother had relations with Mr. Buchance while she was still married to my father—"

I stopped, shook my head. "Of course, she did, because my father was reported dead—twice over!—from the wars and she remarried before he came back to discover his disgrace. The Arguty Greenwings have been slighting me for years. You should have seen my uncle in town today—he told me outright I should leave. I can just imagine what ammunition they will have when they hear that I destroyed the reputation of a fair young lady of Morrowlea. I will be run out of town like my father, to commit suicide in penury and shame." I shuddered with frustration. "Perry, *Mr. Dart*, you should not be seeing me."

There was a pause. He said, "They *ran* your father out of town?"

"I am fortunate Mrs. Buchance is a kind woman, and that Mrs. Etaris is polite."

"Your father was a war hero!"

I tried not to laugh harshly, and sounded like Violet as a result. "Only in his first wars, Mr. Dart. Lark wasn't totally wrong about that part, alas."

He was arrested suddenly. "I mentioned at my aunt's that I'd seen you. ... Jemis ... she managed to insinuate that you came back so late after the funeral because ..." He looked down. I couldn't see his expression now that he'd turned down the lantern, but his voice was embarrassed and annoyed. "Because you were banned by Mr. Buchance from returning because of refusing to adopt his name."

"How dare she," I said frigidly.

"I'm just telling you what she insinuated. Jemis—"

"How *dare* she."

"You have to admit it's an odd situation."

"My life is one odd situation after another!"

"Jemis. I want to hear your side of the story. I'll be hanged if I'll be upstaged in loyalty by a woman calling herself Violet Redshank! The Emperor! There's more stinking here than that fish pie. Your uncle can't believe your father was actually disgraced—he's on the lists of distinction. What could he possibly gain for believing him dishonoured?"

"Only the entire estate."

There was a brief pause. Then Mr. Dart said, in a strangled voice, "I beg your pardon?"

I was glad he had turned out the lantern. It was easier, somehow, to speak in the dark. "Sir Vorel Greenwing is my father's younger brother. My grandfather, Sir Rinald Greenwing, had three sons and a daughter: Rinald the younger, my father Jakory, Vorel, and Jullanar who married the Honourable Lorkin."

"Yes, our Sir Hamish's parents."

I nodded. Sir Hamish, the painter, was Mr. Dart's brother's lover, though presumably he didn't know about all this mess to tell Mr. Dart about it. Or else he agreed with Sir Vorel about my father's disgrace, and thus Mr. Dart would not find a good reception of our friendship from that quarter, either.

"Sir Rinald the younger inherited the Greenwing estates when old Sir Rinald died. Jakory was my father, and joined the Astandalan army. Vorel married an heiress from west Fiellan. Jullanar's story you know. My father eloped with Lady Olive Noirell during one of his leaves, much to the disgruntlement of her people—and his, for although it was a good match, it was felt over-hasty. I was born while my father was away on campaign."

"The Voonran campaign."

"I ... yes, I suppose that would be the one." I sneezed uncomfortably. "When I was about ten he was called up to fight in the east

Alinorel campaign."

Mr. Dart shifted position, and I recalled he'd studied history. I went on. "I don't know all the details. I was ten, my mother was expecting another child, and the Greenwings were ... difficult, even then, especially when she lost the child."

"We used to run through their lands, you and Roald and I," said Mr. Dart.

"Yes. Until my uncle Rinald fell off his horse fox-hunting and broke his neck. Since he was without issue, my father should have inherited, except for the small matter that a few weeks before Sir Rinald's death, my mother had received a letter stating that my father was the traitor of Loe and had been shot running away from the court-martial."

"But then—"

I laughed roughly. "Oh, there's always a *but then* in my life. *But then* there came the next letter. The one stating that Jakory Greenwing had died in honourable circumstances while on a scouting mission, and awarding him the posthumous Medallion of the Lady's Grace as a result."

"Did your mother not write to the authorities?"

I shrugged; my shoulders felt painfully tight. As I moved a thorn pricked me. I extracted it from my waistcoat and started to play moodily with it. "I think she did. But then the Fall of Astandalas interfered ..."

"Your mother should have fought for you—you ought to have inherited the Greenwing estates. I hadn't realized."

The thorn slipped into my fingernail. I bit back a curse. "She had just lost a baby, been disgraced and made the scorn of the barony, lost her husband in dreadful and mysterious circumstances, and she wasn't a strong woman at the best of times. She ran through most of her inheritance keeping us alive during the Interim. When Mr. Buchance began to court her she was disowned by her people, but I think she desperately wanted someone to take care of her. She was that sort of woman. Mr. Buchance wasn't wealthy enough at that point to take on the Greenwings—not for a mere stepson. My mother looked forward, moved to town, and of course had Lauren the year after they married. I think she was sick of all the Greenwings by then."

"But then—" He coughed. I smiled wryly. He went on: "But then your father reappeared. Not having died either time—nor being the one who'd betrayed the Army, either, from what I've read in the history books."

I nodded assent, frowning at the shadows. How bewildered I had been—and how happy—not being old enough then to know that sometimes it is easier for the truth not to come out.

So much easier, sometimes, to sit back and let the sophists weave their nets.

"That was the talk of the barony," Mr. Dart said.

"Still is."

He made a gesture of wry acknowledgement. "How old were we? Thirteen? Fourteen?"

I swallowed. "Something like that. It was just before the end of the Interim. The arguments ... oh, Perry, the arguments. My father was not well, and there was so much that was strange about his story, why he'd disappeared for years, and Sir Vorel was putting it about that he'd *deserted* and that was why he hadn't come back before, and if he'd deserted then he still couldn't inherit. My father had brought back nothing—there wasn't any money for legal fees or anything."

Nothing but one book of poetry, my mother's marriage-gift to him, which he'd held onto through all his tribulations. That was in one of my inheritance chests, all by itself.

"I don't remember all this. My brother's not mentioned the legal wrangles."

"He might not have known about them. Wasn't he at university for his second degree while Sir Hamish was at court? And the Great Pestilence swept through about then. My father ... he was very ill, and the situation was so hard on my mother ... he did love her very much, I think, and wanted her to be happy, and here she was made a bigamist and the talk of the barony and shamed—and she was a shy woman—he went walking one day, and ... Sir Vorel's gameskeeper found him hanging in the woods, and ... and that was that. After the Pestilence had cleared, Sir Vorel was firmly ensconced in Arguty Manor, and my mother was ... she was happy to be Mrs. Buchance."

"How can Sir Vorel not acknowledge your claim?"

I smiled bitterly. "Easily enough, apparently. My mother died. I was a minor, and then went to Morrowlea, which runs year-round, and—you've studied history, Mr. Dart, you know people's memories are malleable, especially when it comes to disagreeable and inconvenient facts. Why doesn't Sir Hamish talk about this?"

"But to lie! They can't have a leg to stand on—your father was no deserter! His name is on the Roll of Distinction for *each* of his battles, including all six in the Seven Valleys. He was decorated by the Emperor's hand for saving General Halioren at East Orkaty, and by the Lady's fiat for the scouting missions at Loe. Don't you have those records?"

"No," I said, "I've never heard of them. My father died—or didn't die—what are you talking about?"

"You didn't study history? I thought you'd planned to."

"I had ..." I made a face, though he couldn't see it. "I started in the History of Magic, then ... after I became ... besotted with, with Lark, she convinced me to switch to Classical Literature. With a bit of History of Architecture thrown in. Ended up in Architectural Poetry."

"Besotted sounds about right!"

"Mr. Dart, look, I mean it—those honours aren't real. It's nice for you to say those things, but Sir Vorel's hardly going to back down for my saying so, and he has a lot more money than I do." I laughed a bit grimly. "Most people do."

"Mr. Buchance was rolling in it, though, didn't he leave you any? And your mother was an heiress—oh, you said her mother disowned her."

"Yes. As for Mr. Buchance ..." I sighed. "He told me he was leaving everything to his own children, which was right, though he'd see I had enough to live on. But that won't be available until after his will is read at the Winterturn Assizes, so I'm stuck here in Ragnor Bella keeping my head down until then."

"What are you going to do?"

"I suppose I should have gone to Inveragory and taken law, and then I might have a minute chance of not losing what little remains to me—which is my name. Not even a good name, I'm afraid, not after what happened at Morrowlea this spring, and not if people are suggesting I was disinherited by my stepfather—ugh!—What a tale of folly this is. Come, Mr. Dart, this is no good."

He finished wrapping the lantern. My eyes had finally adjusted to the dark. The clouds were still peculiarly light, and the shadows not as dark as they'd be on a full-moon night. An owl was hooting down by the stream. I realized the buttons on my coat had come undone in the fuss with Violet, and did them up again with hands that shook slightly. Getting cold, I thought.

Mr. Dart said, "Look, your father did win those honours. I came across them in my research. We can go to Kingsford and get copies made, if you want. We can certainly write to the Lady's re-cord-master at Nên Coravel."

"And how will that help? Perhaps Mr. Buchance left me enough to pay for the fees at Inveragory. Otherwise—"

"You came second in the duchy for the Entrance Examinations, you mustn't have done so ill at Morrowlea."

I laughed bitterly. "Didn't you hear Violet? Let us not discuss my tutor's comments on my final paper. And that was before what happened with Lark's."

"I find it hard to believe that they didn't—" He stopped. "They really let her get away with it?"

"I have no idea what Lark's final result was. But they certainly let the other students pelt me with everything that came to hand, up to and including the voting stones."

He gaped at me before catching himself again. "Jemis, that is unbelievable."

"Morrowlea can be a strange place."

"I thought that was just something Taran students said to make up for their jealousy of your architecture."

I had to smile. I'd never seen Tara, but the history of architec-ture books I had spent most of my second year reading made it clear that Morrowlea's campus was far finer.

"Mr. Dart, I am more grateful than I can say for your friendship. If tomorrow you decide against it—"

"Let's not start that again," he said firmly.

I stared at him, thinking belatedly that he had said *we* could go to Kingsford, *we* could write to Nên Corovel. *We* could do many things that I, Jemis Greenwing alone, could not.

Mr. Dart went on with deliberate levity. "I want to find this secret society, and find out what the hell is up with that Ghilousetten fish pie, and why your friend—"

I gave in. "Former friend—"

"Former friend Violet is giving herself a false name."

"I—what?"

"Redshank," he said impatiently. "As if anyone is actually called that! Seriously, I should have thought memorizing the works of Fitzroy Angursell would be all of a piece with Morrowlea's radical politics, haven't you read *Aurora* since we went away?"

"Well, of course—"

"Redshank's the name Aurora's serving-maid Tenebra uses when she goes undercover in Book Twelve. Your Miss Violet is not what she seems."

"Lady of Mercy," I said, "you're seeing conspiracies everywhere, Mr. Dart. Let's go find your secret society and a passel of other people as bored with Ragnor Bella's polite society as we are."

"Were."

"Were, then," I said, grinning, and we set off up along the side of the road with all the stealth an addiction to poaching could give and a much lighter heart than I'd expected.

Chapter Eleven

TO MY GREAT surprise, we arrived at the crossroads to find two men hanging about it. They were not trying to be particularly cagey about their presence; one was smoking a pipe, and the other was playing with his sword.

They were wearing fully hooded long grey cloaks and masks.

"A sword, no less," I murmured, to distract myself from superstitious unease at being at the crossroads. (Because, of course, certainly it was superstition.)

"Just don't sneeze," said Mr. Dart. "Please try not to."

"I always try not to," I replied in an indignant whisper. "What kind of secret society meeting is this, anyway? They're not even hiding."

"Shh," he said. "There's the third one coming."

A third figure in long cloak and mask hastened out of the dark along the north road. A couple of furlongs away a few lights shone at the Green Dragon. I had a brief moment wondering if it were possibly Violet, but the figure was shorter and substantially stockier than she.

The man with the pipe said, "Who comes to the cross-road?"

"One seeking wisdom," said the newcomer in a soft but masculine voice. "Who waits at the crossing?"

"One to protect," said the man with the sword, flourishing it.

"One to guide," said the man with the pipe, puffing mightily.

They shook hands. It did look like a complicated gesture, involving symbolic movements over their torsos and touching knuckles together. They all appeared to be wearing rings, or something that made a clacking noise when they touched each other. Then they stood, one on each road except for the one leading west to Ragnor Bella, and chanted:

"Over the sky and under the earth, west of east and east of west, by the stars and the stargazers and the watchers at the gate! We call upon the spirits of the old gods to guide us to our heart's desire."

Then they each made a threefold obeisance to each of the four directions. When the third one, the 'seeker of wisdom', had struggled to his feet—he was a portly man, and puffing with the exertion of kneeling and banging his head on the ground twelve times in short succession—the man with the pipe said, "Turn thrice and thrice and thrice again, and we shall guide you to the heart of desire. But as the Wisdom that you seek is secret, and the heart of desire a mystery of mysteries, it is meet and proper that your temporal eyes be covered that your spiritual eyes may be opened. O Seeker, prepare yourself."

Seeker stood still in the centre of the crossroads. The pipe-smoker clenched his pipe in his teeth and drew out a long sash or scarf from somewhere inside his cloak. He advanced on Seeker and blindfolded him, the sash long enough to go round his head several times. He backed up, puffing thoughtfully, then glanced at the sword-wielder, who said: "The way is clear, the seeker is pure, and the night awaits our passionate embraces. Hurry up, Guide, we're going to be late."

"Sorry, Guardian," said Seeker, his voice muffled. "I had difficulty getting away in time."

"We don't want to miss the opening, or we won't get anything to drink," Guardian said, dancing his feet a little.

Guide heaved a sigh we could hear, and said, with more solemnity, "Guardian, be thou most alert to the dangers on the path to wisdom! Seeker, be thou prepared in thy soul! Both of you, follow me!"

He grasped Seeker's hand and led the little party south down the old Astandalan road towards the Woods Noirell.

"Well," said Mr. Dart, when they had gone a little ahead, "I told you they were from a secret society."

"Sounds like a drinking society to me. Shall we follow on the road or in the woods?"

"Let's practice our stealth," said Mr. Dart, sounding as if he was grinning as much as I, and so we sneaked parallel and a bit behind the three men as they strode down the road.

***

AFTER ABOUT TWENTY minutes Guide stopped, ostentatiously turned Seeker around several times, and then led him off into the woods on the east side of the road. I tried to visualize where the path led. Down into the lower part of the Coombe, I thought, south of Ragnor Parva. I hadn't run this way the other morning, not wanting to get too close to the Woods Noirell.

"We're heading towards the South Rag," Mr. Dart whispered to me as we crept along behind the three men, who were going rather more slowly now that they were off the main road. The Astandalan highway was the best road in Fiellan, as smooth and wide and hard as when it had been built; this was a muddy bridleway, showing evidence of much passage in the mud churned ankle-deep. Mr. Dart and I, creeping through the damp leaves of the woods to the side, had an easier time of it. "This is getting close to Littlegarth and the springs."

"Perhaps they have their meetings at the Lady's Pools," I replied, but although the path was probably leading towards the hot springs and their shrine, our quarry turned off before we reached it.

We'd been going steeply downhill through a scanty mixed woodland, with fallen-over foxglove spires and miscellaneous fernery the main undergrowth, but as the path rounded a rocky outcropping and continued down to the Lady's Pools, a side trail split off and wound its way back uphill, along the other side of the outcropping and into a pine wood full of chest-high bracken.

We stopped to let them go ahead, because despite being wet from the day's rain, the bracken was still noisy. The three men hadn't spoken since they left the highway, but we could hear a sudden rise of voices in the near distance. No one was coming along behind us; they seemed to be the last of the society. "Look," Mr. Dart breathed, pointing, "firelight."

"Uphill or down?"

"Down," he said, after a moment. "They must be holding their meeting at that flat spot before the standing stone. There's an elder thicket between it and the upper pool, we should be able to see from there."

"I trust you haven't been picking mushrooms by the Lady's Pools."

He laughed softly. "No, no, just praying."

Which I supposed *was* possible.

***

MR. DART LED me down through the bracken out of the pines and into a stretch of mixed hardwood, much denser than higher up, and into the promised elder thicket. They were old shrubs, heavy with berries and a great deal of dead growth.

It was hard to see where we were going in the dark, and I wasn't sure how we were going to get through without snapping all the dead branches, but Mr. Dart clearly knew where he was going and led me onto a game trail. After a few yards he pushed my shoulder to indicate we should crawl the rest of the way.

"I thought you said you didn't come poaching up here," I whispered as I pushed my way through the leaf mould. It was damp and didn't rustle too much, but did feel unpleasantly slimy under my hands.

"Not for salmon in the Lady's Pools," he replied. "Pheasants, now ... they seem strangely attracted to Justice Talgarth's sweet peas this year. Can you contain your sneezes if we go close enough to see?"

"I'll do my best."

"You seem to have gotten much worse since you went away. Even since you visited me at Stoneybridge. Was that really two years ago?"

"Since I had a bad cold last winter," I agreed, and resolved not to sneeze though I should be desperate—though wishing had never helped prevent an attack in the past. I pulled my second handkerchief out of my pocket and stuffed it down my sleeve just in case. The strange unpleasant cat-piss scent of broken elders tickled my nose.

We eeled forward under the elders until we came to the edge of the thicket. It was awkward going, uphill, and we had to go through a patch of blackberries, but the noise of our passage was masked by a gentle wind soughing across us down the length of the valley, and by the rising babble of the secret society ahead of us.

I was gratified both that my sneaking skills hadn't entirely left me in my time at Morrowlea and that Mr. Dart clearly knew the area well, for when I came up beside him at last we were in a good position to see the gathering.

We lay beside another rocky outcropping at the lip of a small flat space scooped out of the hillside. To our right and left the hill was quite steep, rocky and tree-covered with a mixture of pines and some sort of hardwood I couldn't identify in the dark. The rocks formed a kind of bowl, with a shallow cave going back directly in front of us. Someone had lit a large bonfire in front of the cave, at the base of the old standing stone that guarded the main path down to the Lady's Pools.

The Ellery Stone, as it was called, was sacred to the old gods from pre-Astandalan days. Every boy (and probably girl) in the barony made their pilgrimage to it at one time or another, tracing the blurred carvings on the stone and adding their names to the cliff wall's graffiti. Older boys made fires in the hollow, and told ghost stories; the Honourable Rag, Mr. Dart, and I had done so in our day, scaring ourselves silly with tales about the sacred monsters that lived in the Lady's Pools and in the old drowned clay pits near the

Talgarths' house down where the Ladybeck met the Rag.

Clustered around the stone, mostly to the right side where the path came in, were a dozen or fifteen figures in the same heavy cloaks, hoods, and face masks as the three we'd followed from the crossroads. They were chatting and drinking and obviously having a good time. The masks meant they had to use straws, but careful experiments I had participated in at Morrowlea had determined that that was the quickest way to get drunk, so that was probably all right.

"I think we could have just walked up," I murmured, and Mr. Dart grinned.

After a few minutes someone starting banging a large gong, and the society members all hastily rearranged themselves into a semi-circle around the the bonfire, mostly along the edge of the cave, so they stood facing us across the level ground.

Mr. Dart said, "That's good, they won't be able to see us at all with the fire between us."

"You must have gotten up to some interesting things at Stoney-bridge."

"Shh ... the gonging is coming closer."

The well-trodden trail to the main road was to our right. The percussionist was banging the gong in threes—*dong dong dong—dong dong dong*—and as it neared we could hear it accompanied by some sort of rattle.

Then there was a pause, and then somebody cried out from the darkness: "Seekers after Wisdom! Guardians of the Truth! Guides along the Way! Sing forth your prayers!"

The assembled began to chant. It wasn't clear at first, then after a few moments the ragged chorus blended into solid words. It

didn't sound quite right. I frowned, and realized they were chanting in Old Shaian.

"*O Valdin, hear us. O Nestre, see us. O Ettin, know us. O Dark
Kings, embrace us. O gods of fire and blood, have mercy on us.*"

Mr. Dart's face was just visible to me in the light from the bonfire. "What are they saying?"

"*Truth, truth, truth.*"

"Uh ... it's Old Shaian," I whispered. "They're calling on the
old gods ... Valdin, Nestre, Ettin, the Dark Kings ..."

"They're not," he breathed, wide-eyed.

"*Chaos, strength, power, truth.*"

I felt as wide-eyed. The figures on the other side of the bonfire
were beginning to sway and stamp their feet. The gonging was doing
a double heart-beat now, and somebody had added a drum, coming
from the hillside above us so it echoed. I could feel the rhythm in
the ground under me, where my bones touched the earth. The secret society no longer looked quite so foolish.

"*Truth, truth, truth.*"

"They're asking for truth," I said.

"Not if they're calling on the Dark Kings."

I had come across a few references to the Dark Kings in my
History of Magic classes, although the Shaian lords of the Empire
had done their best to suppress the old religions of Alinor for being untidy and far too disorderly. I hadn't thought anyone did still
believe in the gods of the underworld and the ancestral flames and
the blood.

"*Truth, truth, truth.*"

Someone—a woman by the high pitch of her voice, though she
was as anonymous in her robes and mask as anyone else—started

to keen a high descant above the chanting. Her voice wailed across harmonics, not in tune and not intended to be, scraping the hairs up along the back of my neck. Mr. Dart shuddered.

"*Chaos, strength, power, truth.*"

The old gods of Alinor had been powerful, in their day, until the Empire came. Their worship had shrunk to the wild baronies and the nomads who refused Astandalas, sputtering rebellions breaking the Imperial peace. The early history of Alinorel magic was largely an account of the subduing of the old ways under the tightly-woven net of Astandalan Schooled magic.

"*Truth, truth, truth.*"

The stone shamans who had battled Imperial forces at Loe had worshipped the old gods; my father (or so he had told us, told me, that brief period after his return and before his suicide) had rescued General Duke Halioren from being sacrificed to raise them to the defence of their remnant worshippers.

I clutched at my handkerchief, though nothing about this was making me feel like sneezing. I wanted to bury my head in my hands. Mr. Dart had bitten his lip bloody when the woman started keening. I slowly brought the handkerchief in front of my face.

"*Truth, truth, truth.*"

Dong dong dong

"Aiiiiiee—aiaaaiiieee—aiaiaa—"

The noise stopped.

I clapped my hand across my mouth to stop from making a sound. Mr. Dart dropped his head down as if he'd been hit. We both breathed very shallowly.

The—cultists?—were standing utterly still. In their long cloaks they looked akin to the standing stone, faceless, flame-lit, silent.

They were rigidly expectant, staring, it seemed, directly at us.

Out of the darkness to our right came a small procession, and I breathed for the first time in what felt like hours, because it had not come swooping out of the thickets above us, or dripping wet out of the Lady's Pools to the left, where the old monsters were bound by the shrine to the new goddess.

First came a milk-white horned cow, her horns silvered, around her neck a chain of white asters. She walked forward on her own, neither wandering nor pushed. Her eyes were red in the firelight; or at least I hoped it was the firelight. She walked forward, and the suck of her hooves on a muddy spot was the only sound.

She walked up to the standing stone and stood next to it. The air was very still; the wind seemed to have died down while they were chanting. After the cow reached her place, I realized other figures had followed her: an ordinary-sized person in a shining white robe, a second, rather plumper, in solid black, and a third in a robe of shining silver. The third was extraordinarily tall and thin. In the silver robe he looked like a metal statue, like one of the automata the Ghilousettens were trying to build.

"That's Dominus Alvestone!" Mr. Dart hissed.

I dared not reply for fear of sneezing, but I felt my eyes straining wide, trying to reconcile the tall thin Scholar bending graciously over the Baron with this obscene masquerade.

All three priests—I was not going to call them avatars of the Dark Kings, even in my thoughts—wore masks, featureless ovals made of enamel or lacquer or metal: white, black, and silver polished so finely it caught reflections that were mirror-clear and horribly partial. One moment it caught the cow, and I saw the bovine face looking out from the human form, and I shuddered.

The white priest stepped to stand next to the cow. He was holding a knife made of whitened steel, with an edge I could see catching the light from here. He held it up, and the congregation surged down to their knees and up again, with a moan rising and falling like the wind.

The black priest stepped next to him. He held up a goblet made of smokey black quartz, and the congregation let out a louder moan and this time not only knelt but threw out their hands before them in a deeper obeisance, as I'd been taught as a child to do before the Emperor or the Lady, and did not get up.

The silver priest stood forward.

Dominus Alvestone? A Scholar—surely not—*surely not*—

He spoke in modern Shaian, his voice a throaty and compelling alto. "Children," he said, and I noticed that at his word the earth was starting to vibrate again, as if someone was drumming a very large gong very quickly and very low. "Seekers, Guardians, Guides. Why have you come hither?"

"*Truth*," moaned the crowd, heads on the ground, "*Strength. Power.*"

The silver priest spoke again. His hands were in his sleeves, holding who-knew-what. "And what will you pay for these things?"

"*Life*," they moaned. "*Blood. Power.*"

"Tonight," he said, "is the night of the Moon's treachery, when she turns her back on the Sun for her mortal lover. Tonight is a night sacred to the old gods, when we enter the house of the dragon that swallowed the seas. This is the third moon of our seeking, the fifth of our searching, the seventh of our longing. Tonight you shall taste what you desire. Tomorrow you shall see it. The third day you shall claim it."

The woman cried out in high exultation, like a wolf-howl in the mountains. The crowd drummed their feet.

"*Valdo, hear us. Ettin, see us. Nestre, know us,*" they moaned. "*O Dark Kings, embrace us. O gods of light and terror, renew us. O lords of shade and desire, speak to us. O shadow of the Moon, reform us.*"

"Good," the silver priest said, in an even deeper voice, and the low gonging rose up into a hugely loud thunder. "Begin the sacrifice."

The black priest made an imperious gesture to the cow. She stepped forward as if drawn on a lead, and at another of his gestures knelt at the white priest's feet. The silver priest stood between us and the scene, so I didn't see what he gestured nor could I hear what words he muttered, whether in Old Shaian or new.

The congregation rose to their heels and started to sway, their masks askew from their long obeisance, their voices groaning in the chant. The gong led them, and the woman keened.

The silver priest chanted and gestured. The white priest called out into pauses in the chanting, and the wind started to pick up here and there. It wasn't a real wind, up valley or down; it was plucking at different garments or leaves around the clearing, as if something invisible was moving about. I did not like that idea. I couldn't tear my attention from the sacrifice to see what Mr. Dart was thinking. I breathed through my mouth in the hopes I wouldn't sneeze.

The black priest knelt before the cow with his goblet below her throat. The silver priest cried out four words that pierced so strongly I forgot myself and clapped my hands to my ears—the white priest stabbed the cow with his knife—and all the noise again stopped.

The black priest caught the flow of blood in his goblet. The sound of the liquid hitting the stone was the only sound for a moment, and then the gong started its solemn double heartbeat again, and the congregation arose slowly like the wave of the wind and began to stamp and sway in its rhythm.

When they were all moving in unison the silver priest said, "Prepare yourselves for the fire and the knife and the blood, my children, and come to me. Drink deep, for tonight we enter the next stage of the mystery."

The black priest stood next to the Ellery Stone. The white priest had blood all the way down his front, and held the wicked long knife—red and white now, and dripping. The silver priest pulled out a handful of something from his robes. When he threw it on the fire it sparked and sputtered black and white and silver, and sent up a billow of blood-scarlet smoke.

The congregation slipped out of their hooded cloaks, and I saw they were naked below their masks.

"Come!" cried the silver priest, and the fire flared up in a gout of silver and black sparks. "Come see your doom!"

He raised his hands to show that he held a glimmering stone, white and silver and black, about the size of his hands and polished as brightly as his mask.

The congregation let out a moan in unison, dropping down into the full obeisance, hands flat and outstretched, while the silver priest cried, "The Heart of the Moon and the treasure of the Dark Kings! Come! Come under the knife and the fire and the blood, and worship."

One of the naked men cried out in a guttural voice and flung himself into the fire, standing there, letting the flames writhe around him, his mask burning off, his face in a rictus, and when he came out wreathed in smoke his body shone white and silver and black, his face red and unrecognizable. He grovelled before the black priest, who poured blood into his mouth, and then knelt before the white priest, who made three swift shallow cuts across his torso, and then he flung himself down again into the obeisance before the silver priest.

The silver priest dipped the stone into the man's own blood and used it to draw patterns across his body, muttering all the while, his left hand dribbling bits of some sort of powder as he did so, so the man glittered in the firelight with blood and with reflective glints.

The stone did not seem to be getting bloody, or perhaps it was absorbing the blood as it painted, for when the man's body was wholly disguised—his face red and his hair plastered bloody—the silver priest let him kiss the stone. I saw the expression on the man's face, and it was unholy ecstasy.

The congregation howled in triumph, and the silver priest said, "Glorified is he who came first! Come! Children, come to your desire! Come under the knife and the fire and the blood, make your offering, and worship!"

The first man stumbled off back to the congregation, who gave him wide space except for a few who ran up, ululating, bearing flagons, and poured wine across him. He smeared it across himself and howled, his arousal evident, his face ecstatic, those around him clamouring and pressing close to lick and kiss him.

I turned my head to keep from retching and saw Mr. Dart looking as flabbergasted as I felt. He gripped my arm tightly as another man let out an animal cry and leaped into the fire. "I'm sure that's—" He stopped abruptly.

I swallowed. Blood in my mouth from biting my tongue made me gag. I coughed. "More of a cult than a secret society," I managed after a moment.

"The, the wind's turning," he said.

I turned back at a particularly loud cry to see that the mad cult-ists were starting to act on their arousal, and also to get a face full of the most appalling stench as a gust of wind hit me.

My whole body seized. I jerked backwards helplessly, brittle stems cracking under my convulsions.

"Jemis, you're—be *quiet*."

I wrapped my arms about myself, half bent, nose and eyes streaming, knee squelching in my own mess, trying not to sob from the sheer disgustingness of it all. My body felt like it had that night in the outhouse after the wireweed, as if my stomach was trying to reject its lining. Except that on that occasion I'd been safe from everything except drug-induced dysphoria, and on this—

The wind had turned, and waves of smoke and blood were washing over us. I knew intellectually it wasn't real blood, that the wet warmth was my own sweat and snot and vomit, but it didn't matter, for as I tried to gulp clean air the wind brought smoke and magical incense, and I couldn't control myself any longer, and sneezed and sneezed and sneezed until my vision dissolved utterly into sparks and I couldn't hear anything until at last I stopped, and in the ringing silence heard Mr. Dart's faint and horrified whisper:

"They heard you."

Chapter Twelve

I WAS STILL holding my handkerchief.

This seemed incredibly important. I clutched it tight to my face, body seizing as waves of nausea and sneezing surged through me. My ribs—head—nose—jaw—sides—ringing—hurt. The handkerchief was my only safeguard.

Ages later, I finally felt able to uncurl from about my knees. I fell forward under yet another sneezing fit, and my arms plunged up to my shoulders in frigid water.

Water?

I pushed myself out of the muck and onto rocks, and this time managed to keep my balance. My eyes were watering, and it took a few more minutes of panicked breathing before I could squinny them to look for Mr. Dart. He was sitting next to the pond clutching his arm and gulping.

Pond. Pool. Yes. We'd gone down the hill—away from the cultists—tripped over something—fallen face first off a cliff into the uppermost of the Lady's Pools. Fallen in. Sat up. Started sneezing again.

I started sneezing again at the mere thought, but it was the merest echo of a wheeze compared to earlier. I dabbed at my nose and pulled out another handkerchief and finally felt as if I could muster enough breath.

"I don't know that I'm cut out for espionage," I panted eventually.

Mr. Dart spat out an expostulation, face twisted in a grimace as if he'd bitten something sour as an unripe persimmon. "The Lady! What the hell was that?"

Just as I thought it odd I could see his face so clearly, someone laughed. I lifted my head gingerly.

The Lady's Pools were a set of spring-fed ponds, each perhaps ten or twelve feet across. We'd come to the top one, which was surrounded by a lip made of black marble. Their water was usually very still apart from the bubbles breaking the surface, and very dark, even in the daytime, even in the summer. At night, on a cloudy no-moon night, they were a limpid black like the pupil of an eye.

In the middle of the pool there was another standing stone, at its base a flat stone that people used for certain holy-day rituals that had everything to do with preventing the sort of thing that was going on up at the Ellery Stone.

I remembered when the whole town turned out for them, and we went in procession around the barony boundaries, shaking rattles, ringing bells, singing hymns, and witnessing the priests and the duchy Grand Magister performing the Schooled magic. That was before the Fall, of course. I don't know what happened to Fiellan's Grand Magister in the Interim, but he hadn't been by since, and Beating the Bounds had turned into a military procession where the local nobles ride their horses and show off their weapons.

That lapse might have something to do with why there was a cult meeting up the hill. It almost certainly explained why there was a woman in the middle of the pond.

Woman was perhaps not the right word. She had a human body and face, dark and luminous and beautiful, her hair a smoky black halo with a netting of tiny diamonds scattered through it. Her eyes were dark as the pools, and gleamed.

I could see her perfectly clearly because she was robed in golden light.

For a brief moment Mr. Dart and I stared in astonishment. She was laughing, merry as a summer afternoon, and the air was full of the scent of honeysuckle. We stared—I lowered my handkerchief slowly—Mr. Dart opened his mouth—and then she made a broad open-palmed gesture and disappeared in a shower of light and perfume.

I was all set for collapsing into a combination of sneezes and worship, but Mr. Dart was made of sterner or at least more pragmatic and less allopathic stuff, and instead of falling down he grabbed my arm, pulled me upright, and propelled me down the path.

We stumbled along cursing, eyes squinting blindly in the dark, the sudden vision as incomprehensible as the cultic activities preceding it. The crashing noises grew louder and started to echo off the rocky sides of the valley. I pushed faster, tripping over roots, brushing up against prickly growth alongside the path.

I hadn't been this way for years; I couldn't remember what way the path went below the lowest of the Lady's Pools, where the Ladybeck split into several streams to go around the Talgarths' house before flowing into the Rag. Littlegarth was just upriver from the confluence, so we should hit it first, I thought. The Garden Hut was the public house in Littlegarth. They'd be open till midnight—

"Left, damn you," Mr. Dart hissed. "Not *into* the Lady's Pools again."

The Lady—surely we had just seen the Lady—

I ricocheted off a boulder and went nearly headlong into a thicket. Mr. Dart grabbed my collar and pulled me back upright, then pushed me on again. I tried to hold my breath, but kept having to release it in explosive puffs as we jerked and jagged around obstacles. I had no idea where we were or where Mr. Dart thought we were going, and only hoped he wasn't leading us blindly in circles.

I twisted my ankle in a little hollow. Careening back the other direction, I launched straight into Mr. Dart, who gripped me until I stopped moving. "Hush."

I couldn't hear anything past the sound of my own breathing and blood.

Blood—an honest-to-goodness cult to the Dark Kings—who were certainly neither honest nor good—Mr. Dart whispered in my ear, so close his beard tickled against my jaw, "I'm afraid they're—"

A voice rose up—not in shouts of triumph but in eerie ululations. Male or female I couldn't tell; but it made all my hair stand up in pure reaction. Mr. Dart flinched.

The sound held us still, him with his hands gripping my arms, me straining to see into the shadows. Metallic and wild, the ululation went sailing across the registers. It was like being trapped inside a bell with a cricket.

Perhaps they've gone past us, I was about to say, when I realized that the falling darkness was a rising mist, and that the mist was shrouding figures naked and masked and wearing long grey robes like Violet had been wearing.

O Lady, I moaned inwardly, my breath catching in my throat. If only she would come *now*—

The figures were not running. They were not howling, except for the one whose keening cut through the air like a knife. They did not even seem to be walking. They were coming nearer.

I felt a sick fascination rising in my stomach. Some part of me was responding against my reason, responding to something in the air, in the wind swirling the mist, in the ululations. My reason said *run*; my reason said *this is wrong*; my reason said *flee*.

My heart said *listen*.

I listened; I had to. Mr. Dart was gripping my arms. The more I tried to hear something else, the more the wailing filled my mind; the more I tried to penetrate the shadows, the more the mist held my eyes. My reason whimpered, *Where is the Lady in all this?* My reason said, *She showed herself for a purpose.* My reason said, *This is not right.*

My heart said, *Yes!*

Unfortunately the majority of my time at Morrowlea had been devoted to the heart.

Out of the darkness a gleaming figure took shape, collecting all the light into silver, face blank and robes like fish scales, shimmering like the herring burnished by fire, the whole thing sinuous, shining, deceptively fascinating.

The silver priest floated towards us, glowing now in the mist, face brilliant, almost coming into focus. My heart was thudding high and hard.

I leaned into it, as I'd leaned into running, as I'd leaned into Lark, when she filled my heart and mind and life like the first sunlight of spring, like a long drink of water.

My heart had been withered and empty all summer, as dead as the leaves falling around us. This was the spring of life, the water, the sunlight, the food for my hunger.

So said my heart.

My reason said: *No no no no no this is not right not right not right*

Mr. Dart was gripping my arms like iron bands.

The silver king was turning toward us, the mist behind him shaping a retinue of shadows. I leaned forward, pressing hard against the force binding my arms, reason calling faint as Mr. Dart's words, some hunger in my heart turning unerring to the silver king turning toward us.

The ululation changed its rhythm, rising and falling faster now, falling into recognizable notes, the pattern key of a spell we'd learned as boys.

Once the commonest of sounds, the whistle to summon light.

Dol-fa-ti-ti-dol

Whistle a few notes and anyone could call light into a dark room, mage or no, before the Empire fell.

In the Interim it had called ... other things.

Dol-fa-ti-ti-dol came the high wail.

The silver king turned towards us, glided towards us. He raised up his arms and the light left all the faint glimmering reflections and ran home to his embrace. The shadows behind him swirled grey on black, smoke on black velvet. The wind promised me that it would fill the dark hole left by Lark—

Oh, Lark, I thought, how I had loved her—

Dol-fa-ti-ti-do-o-o-ol

The light gathered into a ball, a great armful of silver fire. All around us the forest was so utterly silent, and dark, and all I could see now was the light and the silver face and my heart thundered in my chest as it expanded trying to grab all the fullness it could and the light started to expand, silver light that frosted everything it touched, cold light turning each leaf and twig and bracken frond into silver gilt.

My chest ached to expand along with the light expanding outward towards us, my ribcage aching with the blood pounding through my veins, my head throbbing, the forest in my vision darkening as the wave of silver came gliding sliding towards us, and all I could hear was the wailing, and all I could feel was my heart pummelling at my breast as if it were a caged beast hurling itself desperately to freedom—

Mr. Dart took one deliberate step forward, and as I twisted away from his grip he let go of one of my arms, reached his arm back deliberately so that for the barest moment it was illuminated by the frothy edge of the silver tide, and while I was consumed with a tyrant wave of jealousy that he could heed the call while I was yet immobile—flipped my coat up over my head, and while I fought with the sudden dazzle-darkness, shoved me into the night.

I eventually flailed my arms and head free, buttons popping everywhere, and was able to glare at him, or in the direction I thought he was in, since I couldn't see more than blurs.

When I cursed him he shoved me again. This time I lurched through a cobweb and flinched sideways into him. He stopped abruptly. "Can you still hear them?" he asked in a hoarse whisper.

I held my breath. The woods were eerily quiet, with a heavy close feeling to them. I couldn't hear the keening. I felt like keening myself, just to relieve the internal pressure. I hadn't realized how much of a hole there was in me until I saw the light gathering.

I started to pull against Mr. Dart again, preparing to run back towards the silver king, to throw myself into the cool silver light. But each motion pushed me into cobwebs and hanging vines; I kept stopping in horror at their touch. Some late flower was aggravatingly scented, and my nose's reflexive twitching kept distracting me.

I flinched away again from another netting of spiderwebs, and stepped on something soft and moving. As I gagged in horror it exploded up under my feet.

Mr. Dart is no poltroon, but even as I was thinking, *pheasant*, he exclaimed sharply and ran forward. I followed into a face-full of mildewed leaves, and lost both reason and heart in favour of base physical reaction, alternately tugged and tugging as I sneezed or held it back.

He led me into more cobwebs of appalling thickness. My shoulder crashed into something sturdy holding up the webs, sending a mass of dried seedpods clacking wildly. I reeled away towards Mr. Dart, through a hideous mass of vines shrouded with spidersilk.

The musty, mildewy leaves, damp and slimy with the rain, wrapped about in spiders, were bad enough—I was already sneezing enough to alert every auditor in half the county—but then as I tripped over something I went face-first into a spray of lingering blossoms of something that were not so much intensely fragrant as violently so.

Not even the wireweed-laced tobacco—not even the smoke from the cultists' sacrifice—not even the Lady's perfume—had gone so immediately against my system as did those flowers. I took half a breath in and my head exploded.

Mr. Dart did his best to catch me, but I was incapable of con-trolling my limbs. We staggered a few steps backwards, got out of the twining plants, lost our balance on the edge of a bank, and both of us pitched straight into icy water with a large and alarming splash.

Chapter Thirteen

THE SHOCK OF the cold water released the first convulsions—and the spell.

I broke the surface gasping gratefully, unable to concentrate on anything but getting away from the flowers and onto the bank where I could breathe, and Silver Priest be damned—as he most certainly was, to invoke the Dark Kings as he had. I tried to explain that I was fine, that I wouldn't go running again, but Mr. Dart shoved me the other direction, into a stand of bulrushes.

I went sideways under again, got an earful of muck, realized we weren't in deep water, and got my feet under me. Before I could stand upright, Mr. Dart pulled my sodden clothes down sharply.

I sat down hard into the water and stared at him. "Shh!" he said in my ear, as softly as any poacher my father would have admired. "Hide."

From what? I wanted to ask, but then I saw the lantern swinging towards us.

It was a strange red light, and I frowned at it for a good few seconds until it resolved into an old-fashioned werelight. I hadn't seen one of *those* in proper use since before the Fall of Astandalas—even at Morrowlea no one's used them since the Interim, when good intentions made for some very strange results for things done under magical light.

"What was that?" asked a nervous voice: feminine, breathy, high-pitched. "They aren't coming here, are they?"

"They won't come past the boundaries, domina," another woman's voice replied, this one deeper, melodious, and controlled. "Never fret. They're under control."

Something about the way she said *control* sent a shiver down my spine. The first woman sounded only partially convinced. "They seemed very wild, crashing through the woods like that, howling and drinking and ... other things."

The other woman sounded very satisfied with herself when she replied. "They are devotees of the old gods, domina. That is how they worship. Do not fret yourself."

"I wish we hadn't had to come out the same night."

"The rain delayed our harvest, but it'll be the stronger for being picked tonight, domina. The moon is in the House of the Dragon, and that means increased vigour in seed of all sorts."

"You're certain they can't come in here?"

The second woman's voice was nearly a purr. "Not past my boundaries, domina."

"Then what was that noise in the moat?"

Moat? I frowned at the dim red light, which had paused a few yards away from us, further down the bank. It barely illuminated anything but a wavering circle on the grass, and the lower half of the speakers. The Baron's manse had a moat, but that was on the northern side of Ragnor Bella, nowhere near Littlegarth and the

Lady's Pools. The Talgarths' house was built on the river, but that was hardly a *moat* ...

Mr. Dart gripped me tightly. I sank my mouth down below the level of the water, to make sure as much of me as possible was covered. The speakers came a few steps closer. I could see that there were actually three of them, the two speakers in long cloaks and the third a servant of some sort, far enough back that I couldn't make out age or role, only that he was wearing trousers and carrying something quite large, perhaps the size of a money chest. A basket, I realized, for whatever they were harvesting.

Harvesting?

"I will look for you, domina. I do not expect it is anything more than an animal."

The one holding the werelight paced closer to the water. She was clearly looking into the reeds and water plants to see what had made the noise. I held my breath, but could feel the sneezes rising up behind my nose, through the ravaged back of my throat. I was miserably sure I would give us away.

Mr. Dart poked me in the side with something stiff. Using the slowest movements I could manage, I turned to look at him. He passed me a broken length of hollow reed, then sank out of sight amidst the arrowleaf plants next to him.

There didn't seem to be anything else for it, so I imitated him, putting the foul-tasting reed in my mouth and sinking slowly under the water, clutching at the slimy bases of the plants before me to anchor my position.

I could barely breathe through the reed, my throat thick and sore, but with my nose below the surface I seemed at last free of the need to sneeze. That was joy enough to keep me under.

The werelight was clearly visible on the surface of the water, swinging back and forth over the bank. Mr. Dart was a dark shape next to me. I pressed myself down into the cold muck. All the muscles in my back and neck ached with trying not to float.

We held ourselves like that until the light was well gone. I waited after Mr. Dart rose slowly in a cloud of bubbles, fearful I'd start sneezing as soon as I broke the surface. Eventually he pulled at my collar and I rose.

I managed to suppress the immediate outburst, at least enough that I only made a continuous whuffling kind of noise with occasional snorts mixed in, like nasal hiccoughs.

The bank was not all that high, but it was steep, we were waist deep in the water, hands cold and unresponsive, and our sodden clothes extremely heavy, and Mr. Dart seemed to have hurt his arm.

I kept freezing in place in the attempt to prevent explosive sneezing—and, well, several minutes of increasingly disastrous attempts added the effort to keep from laughing to our exertions.

Eventually we gave up on that part of the bank and pushed into deeper water to see if we could swim to a better landing. Light from a house window passed through a screen of cedars to illuminate a stretch to one side, so we swam the other direction.

We snaked our way through a patch of water lilies with some difficulty, the stems slimy and uncooperative, before I clunked my shoulder on a large branch sticking out into the river. It was smeared with algae and moss and bird droppings, but provided enough leverage for us to finally roll to a soggy and relieved halt on a stretch of closely-cropped lawn.

There were lights above us. I blinked away the bright specks brought on by the exertion under low breath. They were still there.

Rolling to a more upright position, I discovered that we'd clambered out on the wrong bank, and were now on the greensward below the Talgarths' house.

"Ugh," Mr. Dart said softly. "I've just put my hand in goose shit."

I caught my breath carefully. "I suppose you'd be able to tell the difference from duck."

"Ha ha. The Talgarths only have geese. And sweet peas."

I pushed back against the wall of the house and with great difficulty got out of my wet coat. Geese ... and when had the Talgarths diverted part of the Ladybeck to form a moat around their house? *Why?* "What are they hiding?"

"Old-fashioned immorality," he replied, scooting himself next to me. "And magic, obviously."

"Everyone already thought that."

"True."

"What do you think they're harvesting?"

"Justice Talgarth's sweet peas."

I wheezed into my wet and squelchy handkerchief, somewhere between sneezes, laughter, and hiccoughs. The breeze kept bringing wafts of the intense flower-smell, fortunately somewhat diluted by distance. I was so wet that the drips from my hair were making splashing noises as they fell onto my shirt.

I rubbed at the bridge of my nose, trying to wipe away snot and water and goodness knows what else. "Thank you for breaking the enchantment back there, Mr. Dart."

"Oh, my pleasure, Mr. Greenwing."

"Did you touch that silver light?"

He was moving his hand back and forth as if trying to stretch

out a kink in his wrist. I winced at the thought of how much my stupid staring at an obvious evil wizard had nearly cost us. He shook
his head. "No, just wrenched it, I think, when we fell in the Lady's
Pool."

I tried not to sneeze as I let out my breath over-hastily in relief.
"Thank the Lady for that."

"Indeed." He leant back against the wall with a sigh. "I've been
invited to supper here tomorrow. I don't think Dame Talgarth
would be overly pleased to find me out here tonight."

"Impolite," I managed between quiet explosions.

"Quite."

Another pause. I tried to come up with something useful. "Do
we go back across the moat or look for a bridge? I haven't been here
since they diverted the stream."

"That was two years ago, after the bank started to go at the old
clay pits."

I was grateful he hadn't suggested exploring them tonight,
something we'd done a couple of times as boys, to see what might
be hidden in the caves along the Ladybeck's confluence with the
Rag. What with cults and the Lady and magic going on at the Talgarths, it could be almost anything.

Mr. Dart sounded as placidly thoughtful as when discussing
the merits of Mrs. Landry's cheese soufflé over lunch. "They've
got a drawbridge, but it'll be up. Justice Talgarth is very concerned
about the Good Neighbours in the Woods Noirell, the brigands in
the Arguty Forest, and the ruffians on the roads everywhere."

"When clearly he should be worried about the cultists in his
back yard."

"Those women must belong to the house. I think the nervous

one was Domina Ringley, Dame Talgarth's sister. I wonder what she's doing out-and-about at midnight. Harvesting something sinister? And that wasn't Dame Talgarth with her."

I listened to his tone of voice with a sinking heart. "Now, Mr. Dart—"

"They're not part of the cult, surely. Domina Ringley was worried about them coming in."

"And they knew about it, how?"

"Come now, Mr. Greenwing, where's your sense of adventure? Are you not your father's son?"

I gave in. "They wouldn't have swum the moat."

"Good thinking," he replied, and so we made our squelching way around the perimeter of the house, foiled at looking inside by tightly-drawn curtains and some modern shutters on what were presumably the kitchen windows.

Unfortunately, the drawbridge was up, the little boat was fastened to the other bank, and the geese were wide awake and vigilant.

They were white blobs against the grey grass. The first one gobbled at us, the second hissed, the third raised its wings and lunged, and the fourth took off with a high cackle for Mr. Dart. I kicked the one nearest me, connecting the one foot with a satisfying thunk but skidding the other on loose droppings. I windmilled wildly.

Mr. Dart cried: "Lights!" and plunged into the water.

The wild cackling and hissing and imprecations, together with the threat of imminent discovery, made me turn and dive into the moat after him.

"Hurry up," he said, sounding rather like the geese as he hissed and pushed me into the boat. "That might be Dame Talgarth!"

"We can't have her finding us," I agreed solemnly, hauling him up after me. The geese were causing enough of a ruckus on the other bank that whoever was at the door seemed to be leaning out to glare at their milling chaos.

"Lie flat," I added, pushing him down and following him with a strangled sneeze. "Curse this bloody hay fever."

"Shh!"

"Now who's not much of a rebel at home?"

"Radical, you dolt."

I risked a glance over the rim of the boat. Someone in light-coloured clothing was standing at the house door cursing the geese for being het up to no purpose. I started to relax, but as I lowered my head saw a red light bobbing along the bank towards us.

"We haven't even been *drinking*," Mr. Dart said mournfully.

I shoved him. "Out, out!"

"Hell!" said he, starting to laugh. "Get away, you oaf."

"The domina's coming back. Hurry."

I sniffed mightily, a mistake as I got another waft of the intense perfume. Held my breath as we tumbled onto the bank, pulled each other up, and set off at a lumbering run towards the shrubbery looming darkly ahead of us.

We were both so wet and tired that we couldn't move very fast. I was marginally faster, my runs finally coming into some use, and got to the safety of the shadows just in time to look back, see Mr. Dart pass me—and be nearly hit by something red shooting towards us at head-height.

I flung myself across Mr. Dart, landing us both awkwardly and painfully into some spiny shrub. The thing hit a tree ahead of us with a loud *crack* and a singed smell.

"What in the nine worlds is that?" I hissed at him.

He started to crawl away from the house on his belly, towards the tree. I followed him with a wary eye on the way the trunk was emitting sparks and a bad smell of such a rotten-egg intensity that I retched and sneezed at the same time.

"Your father was the soldier," he hissed back. "Shh."

We both listened. I gulped, face against the cool moist ground, breathing in the earthiness, nose twitching like a mad rabbit. Several more *cracks* exploded above us, but over to our right, a bit away from where Mr. Dart was aiming.

I wondered how often his poaching trips had led him to this part of the Coombe. The rotten-egg smell grew stronger and stronger, mixed with a gust of wind bringing the sickly intense flower-perfume. I gripped myself hard, hands clamped across my mouth and nose, retching soundlessly (and fruitlessly, by this point), and was sure my body should just shut down from over-stimulation. Alas, this did not happen.

"Stop sneezing, will you?"

I grimaced into the dirt. "If only I could."

He started forward, pushing carefully through the undergrowth. The wet leaves slapped at my face, but I kept close beside him, determined not to lose him in the darkness. We were going slightly uphill, but I knew enough about dark woods to know that one's sense of direction could be totally off in the dark—especially when one's head was ringing dizzily from lack of air and over-exertion.

My breathing settled down into the fast-paced nasal hiccoughs again, as if I was hyperventilating under hysteria. This annoyed me considerably, as the only reason to panic was the fact I was making enough noise to alert anybody to our presence. I kept holding my breath and then having to release it with a soft explosion when I could no longer manage.

After an interminable time, during which the *cracks* got less frequent and somewhat more distant, Mr. Dart said, "Didn't your father teach you anything worth know—*elp!*"

The exclamation came a moment too late for me to avoid tipping over the sudden short cliff he'd just rolled off. We tumbled to a halt at the bottom in a tangle of limbs and bracken, breath heaving and bones rattled, but I didn't think I'd done more than jar myself.

"Right ho, Mr. Dart?" I murmured when I could form words.

"Right ho, Mr. Greenwing."

Neither of us made a move to disentangle ourselves. We listened, instead, me to my breathing, my gradually slowing heart rate, and the noises of the woods around us. The wizard appeared satisfied, or at any rate didn't pursue us down the cliff. Other sounds were less comprehensible but could have been pheasants or boars or the like. Theoretically, at least.

It was increasingly cold and the rain, of course, chose that moment to begin falling again.

"He taught me how to gamble," I said after another few minutes. "Which I thought would be of more use tonight, to be honest."

"I am sorry, Mr. Greenwing, that the evening's entertainment did not go as planned."

I moved my head out of the way of a particularly obnoxious rock. "It's certainly given me a new appreciation for the hazards involved in picking mushrooms."

He chuckled a little too loudly, for we heard an exclamation and the unwelcome sound of purposeful movement through the woods—and not the woods above the cliff.

That's below us, I thought, moving slowly and carefully to a sitting position and helping Mr. Dart get out of the pile of bracken he'd landed on. The bracken was wet enough to not be supremely noisy, but I didn't get far before I froze at the sight of a purple light floating disembodied through the air.

Mr. Dart clamped his hand over my face.

Indignation warred with horror; horror won. The light moved this way and that, leisurely, too high for ordinary human height. The Silver Priest had been abnormally tall, I thought, and unconsciously tried to catch my breath.

Tried—choked—Mr. Dart had perforce to remove his hand—I screwed up my face and pinched my noise and clenched my gut—just as the light seemed to be leaving I could hold it in no longer.

"Oh, Jemis," Mr. Dart said sadly—there's really no noise so unmistakable as a sneeze—and a voice out of the dark cried: "Well, well, well, if it isn't my old runabouts. Mr. Greenwing and Mr. Dart."

Chapter Fourteen

MIRACULOUSLY—ALTHOUGH I hesitate to use that word—I wasn't late for work. The market bell was still ringing as I dragged myself into the store with as fair a pretence at nonchalance as I could manage.

Mrs. Etaris turned from the counter, where she had been opening a crate of *New Salons*. "The young men used to call it 'catching the night worms' when I was young. Though that was in Fiella-by-the-Sea; possibly they've always said 'picking mushrooms' here in Ragnor Bella."

"Uh," I said, and blew my nose.

The Honourable Rag had, so he claimed, been out collecting worms, the marshy forest below the Ladybeck being the best location for it, as surely we well remembered from our boyhood forays into fishing. As he bore a wriggling bag of nightcrawlers and a small trowel for good measure, neither Mr. Dart nor I could well argue with this statement, utterly incredible as it seemed.

Not having provided ourselves with such accoutrements, we pretended to have been poaching salmon and that I had fallen into the Ladybeck and dragged Mr. Dart in after me. With equal bonhomie the Honourable Rag agreed that it was a very bad turn of luck, goddess wot, and I should be careful not to catch my death of cold. He didn't seem to feel Mr. Dart was in any danger.

The whole situation made me think of a particularly bad hand in the card game of Poacher I'd once used to win against Violet's Salmon of Wisdom by sheer ability to tell a plausible tall tale. Sadly in this case I did not think we had come even to a draw, cheerfully blasé as Mr. Dart was. It was only the fact that we'd seen the Honourable Rag's purple werelight, I was certain, that provided him with an equivalent concern for us keeping our stories and our thoughts to ourselves.

There was no sign of any companions, nor, more fortunately, of wizards, cultists, or other strangers. The Honourable Rag seemed to bear a field of sheer bland normalcy with him, almost as disconcerting in its way as the silliness of the secret society members turning into a serious cult.

We squelched slowly up the hill towards the road, past the turn-off to the Garden Hut and past the crossroads, where even the Green Dragon had blown out its lanterns. The Honourable Rag managed all the while to keep up a continuous stream of inconsequential gossip about people I neither knew nor cared about. I focussed on keeping one foot in front of the other and not sneezing too horribly, while Mr. Dart asked bright questions about the gossip and the Honourable Rag kept laughing.

We got to the Ragglebridge just after sunrise. At the sight of the two fishermen at their posts (the larger one grinned into his beard, no doubt at how dishevelled the growing light revealed us as), I roused myself to say my adieus. Mr. Dart started to say something, but the Honourable Rag clapped me on the back hard enough to stagger.

"Off to work you go, good lad! We're off for a hunter's breakfast at the Arms."

So off they went, with Mr. Dart casting me one final would-be-eloquent look I couldn't decipher. I turned down the back way to Mrs. Buchance's for a hasty wash, shave, and very welcome change of clothes before running to Elderflower Books before the market bell had quite finished ringing.

Catching the night worms, indeed.

Before either of us said anything further, Mrs. Landry came in. She greeted her sister amiably, nodded at me, and asked for a copy of this week's *New Salon*. I hastily went to the counter—the market-day delivery of the *New Salon* was my sole assigned task so far—and undid the string tying the bundle. While she waited for me, Mrs. Landry smiled archly at her sister. "Have you found out anything more about that herring pie of yours?"

"Of Mr. Greenwing's, rather," Mrs. Etaris replied.

Mrs. Landry looked at me. I didn't feel up to a polite smile, so just nodded my head awkwardly. "I see," she said, with an air of the greatest significance. "And what do you make of it, Mr. Greenwing?"

"Nothing," I replied immediately and truthfully.

"Nothing?" she replied even more archly, as deliberately oblivious to subtle verbal cues as the Honourable Rag.

My thoughts flashed to the ring, which—I realized, heart sinking—I'd entirely forgotten to tell Mr. Dart about. At least I hadn't lost it in all the night's excitements; I'd found it still in my waistcoat pocket this morning.

"Oh," I faltered, when she kept staring at me, as much at a loss as when attempting to prevaricate in front of Mr. Fogerty the fishmonger—and then I decided on the *other* strategy from Poacher, which was the truth. "To be honest, I haven't thought about it much this morning."

Mrs. Landry looked disappointed.

Mrs. Etaris chuckled. "Now, my dear—be sure if we find anything out I shall keep out the juiciest gossip for you."

I would have taken that an insult, but Mrs. Landry responded with another arch smile. "Do be careful not to step on your husband's toes—he's the investigator in Ragnor Bella!"

Mrs. Etaris frowned at her. "I should be disappointed indeed were private curiosity become a crime. It would be a sign of great woe for Alinor."

"You've been reading too many old romances again, dear. I suppose you know your business best. Mind, the town's abuzz that there might be highwaymen in the Arguty Forest."

Mrs. Etaris neatened the stack of books on the shelf beside her. "There are always rumours of highwaymen in the Arguty Forest. Have you finished with that, Mr. Greenwing?"

"Your paper, Mrs. Landry," I replied, and exchanged it for a handful of coin. She nodded, the feathers on her hat bobbing as she went out the door.

In the hopes that there would be something to calm my throbbing head, I went to the back room for a glass, and found jugs of both water and coffee. After swallowing a hasty glass of water, I poured a cup of coffee for each of us and took them out to the front room, where Mrs. Etaris was now arranging a stack of brightly-coloured historical romances on the front table. I wondered which ones Mrs. Landry thought she'd been reading too much of. *The Passion of Madame Anastasiya? The Underwriters of Li Shan Do? Black Tulip?* Fitzroy Angursell's utterly illegal (and certainly not—well, *almost* certainly—surely Mrs. Etaris wouldn't dare keep it in stock) comic epic *Aurora?*

Mrs. Etaris smiled. "Thank you, Mr. Greenwing. And thank you for arranging the cookery books yesterday."

I glanced at the shelf, and had to blow my nose again. "You're welcome, Mrs. Etaris."

The market-bell rang, and I straightened up as a rush of people came in for their *New Salons* and a handful of other things, books of poetry and practical gardening and the grammars of obscure languages, and obvious intent to gawk at me.

I was too busy for a while to do more than handle the cash and try not to sniff too unpleasantly, with a bare few mouthfuls of coffee here and there. Mrs. Etaris welcomed most of her customers by name, smiled at them all, and helped them find what they sought—and in several cases, what they didn't know they wanted.

She had a gentle encouraging manner that was hard to resist, and to my extreme if inarticulate gratitude turned away the pointed questions about why I'd missed my stepfather's funeral and how long I was planning to be in town and why I was working there and how generally peaky I looked.

After the glut thinned, I went into the back to clear my nose as best I could in privacy. When I came back, Mrs. Etaris had found a book for me to look at: *Exchanges and Excellencies: Magical Systems of Northwest Alinor*, by one Magister Aube of Kingsford. "Thank you," I said, "but why give me this? I don't think I've mentioned that I studied History of Magic, have I?—Or at least, that I began with that?"

"Did you indeed?" she said, with a heartening smile. "No, I don't believe you have. I thought you might find Chapter Three of interest—oh, Mrs. Buchance, how lovely you look this morning."

I pushed the book aside and tried to smile at Mrs. Buchance, who was wearing a a pale grey walking dress and did indeed look particularly fetching despite her mourning. She was holding my tricorner hat in her hand and a folded garment over her arm. "You were in such a hurry this morning," she said. "I thought you might like your hat and coat for later, Mr. Greenwing."

"Oh ... thank you, Mrs. Buchance."

It was my summer-weight coat, not the one I'd—hell. Not the one I'd abandoned somewhere in the woods last night. Please, I thought, say the suspicion I'd left it beside the Talgarths' moat was wrong.

"Mrs. Inglesides is taking the girls with her boys for a picnic down by the Point, so I thought I'd spend the afternoon going through Mr. Buchance's paperwork in his offices here in town. His business partner has written to ask me for some records, and I haven't had much opportunity to find them."

"Must the Charese portion of his business wait for the Winter-turn Assizes, too?" I asked.

Mrs. Buchance hesitated. I flushed at how impertinent that had sounded. "I didn't mean—It's none of my business—"

But she was smiling sadly. "No, they have a different system. It is nearly through their period of probation ... once I can get the Chief Justice to sign off on the documents, as witness to my status as his widow, I will be able to access them. But he's not back yet from the summer course he was teaching in Ormington."

I remembered what Dame Talgarth had said in the bakery. "He's expected soon, I heard."

She nodded patiently, and I thought, of course she'd know much more about such news than I. "So my brother said." She passed me my hat, which I put next to the book, and then when I sneezed seemed struck with something, and added, "Have you found out anything about that ring we found in the pie?"

Mrs. Etaris said, "You found a ring? Did you *eat* the pie?"

"No!" I said, a bit too strongly, and moreover sneezed emphatically; both women laughed. "One of my sisters knocked it off the counter, and it broke on the floor. While we were cleaning it up, Mrs. Buchance found a ring had been cooked into it."

"How curious. Do you have the ring with you?"

It had, quite miraculously, not been lost—despite the scuffles, secret societies, and at least seven different tumbles. Unlike several of my handkerchiefs, which had not fared so well: I'd started out with six, but by the time I came to transfer my pockets to my second waistcoat this morning, I only had three. Well, at least they weren't embroidered with anything more incriminating than the Old Shaian ideograph for *Racer*, Violet's idea of a good pun on my horse-derived name and my affinity for running.

Before I could do more than place the ring on the counter, someone came in for a book of riddles. Mrs. Buchance took her farewells and left politely while Mrs. Etaris saw to the transaction. I poked at the ring and sighed at how clumsy I was.

Mrs. Etaris examined it carefully when she was finished, but seemed to find no answers in the flower pattern of red garnets or the heavy gold, either.

"It makes me think of a sigil of the Lady of Alinor," I said hesitantly, looking around at the shelves for a book on emblems, and not knowing where to start.

"Heraldry is in the third room," Mrs. Etaris said. I blinked at her, and she smiled. "It's closed due to a slight mishap we had there after the last Embroidery Circle meeting. I daresay you'll have time next week to start clearing it out."

She sipped her coffee, frowning at the ring. "You may be right about the Lady, though I wonder if I haven't seen something like it more recently ... We shall have to consider."

I nodded and tried to look intelligent, though I felt even peakier than earlier, and probably looked it, too, as Roald Garsom had indicated when he'd come in for a picture book ("the one where the knight ends up like you!"). I might look pretty bad, I thought, after last night; but it still seemed somehow unfair that the town fool felt emboldened to say so.

Mrs. Etaris pushed the book of Alinorel magic at me. "Now, as for this book, Mr. Greenwing—Lady bless you!" She waited until I'd gotten myself under control, and then said, "You seem to be sneezing worse than yesterday, Mr. Greenwing. Did you catch a cold while you were out, ah, picking mushrooms?"

"Oh, probably, given everything else that happened."

"They say that Morrowlea breeds idealists. You seem to be of the cynical variety."

I grinned reluctantly. "I do my best, Mrs. Etaris."

"I'm sure you do, Mr. Greenwing."

A few more customers came in, seeking a guide book to the Farry March, a collection of harp music from the Inner Reaches, and a three-volume work on *Trees of the Western Forests*, which put paid to our conversation until they'd all cleared out. The search for the guide book had disarrayed several shelves, so while Mrs. Etaris remedied that, I flipped through the book she'd given me. Chapter Three was titled, "Identifying Proclivities to Magic and the Seven Magical Senses."

Mrs. Etaris poured us both some more coffee, though the jug was nearly tepid, alas. When I looked up at her in befuddlement she said, "It has been exercising my imagination how you can be so very sensitive to scents that—to be frank—no one else notices. I had wondered if it had something to do with magic, but of course it is not an easy thing to find anyone able or willing to test—nor is it something I imagine you wish much spoken of in town, when you already have your little train of rumours."

"But ... magic doesn't run in my family."

She raised her eyebrows at me. "Not in the Greenwings, perhaps, but the Noirells were well known for their skills in the days before the Fall."

"I see," I said, and not for the first time wished the Noirells had not disowned my mother. But before I could go further, the door opened, and Violet walked in.

She was dressed in the most elegant height of fashion for a young man of the coastal city-states, in a knee-length ivory and crimson coat over black pantaloons and waistcoat. She wore a gilt-handled rapier at her belt. She did not appear to be hiding her sex; her hat was a dashing deep-brimmed tricorner with ostrich feathers tumbling down, and exquisitely feminine. The autumn style, I supposed.

Mrs. Etaris turned to greet her affably, and paused for the briefest possible moment of astonishment before catching herself. Violet looked at me with a quirk of her lips, the old familiar smile from when we'd been friends. I swallowed against my immediate, foolish, probably disastrous desire to smile back. Mrs. Etaris returned the grin. "Is there anything we can help you with?"

"I have come to make my apologies," Violet declared, turning to me and drawing her sword.

Only the most tenuous remnants of self control prevented me from saying "I say!" like Mr. Dart.

Still holding the sword, she sank down to her knees in the formal supplication. "Jemis, I am sorry for my behaviour this spring. I am sorry for what I did not say, that I did not stand behind you, that I did not prevent that travesty of scholarship from happening in the first place. I am sorry for attacking you last night—" Mrs. Etaris' eyebrow lifted, but she said nothing—"and I am more sorry than I can say to learn the sad tale of your family history, into which I enquired at the Green Dragon last night. For all these things I apologize."

And she bowed right down to kiss my boots.

I glanced at Mrs. Etaris, whose mouth was open in surprise, and then realized my own was gaping as badly. After a few astounded moments my heart started to beat too fast and I bent down. "Violet—"

She resisted, sitting firmly on her knees while I tried to pull her up. "Do you accept my apology, sir?"

"Violet! This is absurd."

She met my eyes with a solemn and serious intensity. "You accused me last night of dishonour: and though my anger forbade responding as I ought, I say now, you are correct." With a grand gesture she threw her rapier down on the floor between us.

I stepped back hastily, bumping into Mrs. Etaris, who steadied me without betraying a hint of alarm.

Violet went on: "I am dishonoured. I should carry no sword. I beg you to accept my apology." And down she went again.

My study of Classical Shaian Literature had focussed on architectural puzzle poetry, but I had read enough of Violet's beloved epics to know what I ought to do, silly and old-fashioned and uncomfortable as it seemed.

I didn't want to carry a grudge along with my snivels. Not when I knew—had realized last night—that there was a lot more going on in the world than my tired feud with Lark.

I tried to blow my nose discreetly, and to put myself into some properly epic state of mind, but although a few lines from *Aurora* came to mind, I decided not to try Mrs. Etaris' patience that much and instead stuck with plain prose. "Violet, I accept your apology. You did what anyone would do in the circumstances. Take back your sword and—and bear it with honour and valour in—in service of the truth."

This time she let me lift her up, using my left hand; with my right I picked up the sword by the blade and offered it back to her. She stared at me intently, and I thought inconsequentially how pretty her eyes were, and then I flushed and turned my head in embarrassment to where Mrs. Etaris was no longer gaping but was instead smiling. I cleared my throat.

"Mrs. Etaris. May I present to you my, er, friend, Miss Violet Redshank, lately of Morrowlea? Miss Redshank, Mrs. Etaris, Ragnor Bella's bookmistress. And my employer."

Violet bowed. Mrs. Etaris curtsied very slightly. There was a pause, and then Mrs. Etaris said, "How delightful a colour your coat is, Miss Redshank."

"Thank you, Mrs. Etaris," replied Violet, her voice demure. "I was most pleased to find it in a store in Laketon this summer."

I snorted, but that was a bad idea, and it took me a moment to recover my breath.

"Poor Jemis. You seem to have caught a cold since last night."

"Oh, it's possible. Mr. Dart and I fell into the Talgarths' moat after—Please, never mind that."

She and Mrs. Etaris both raised their eyebrows again. Violet, shrugging, continued. "Very well then. Well. I did not tell you the entire story of my being here—nor why I was interested in the star-gazy pie—" Mrs. Etaris narrowed her eyes, then smiled in some satisfaction, though why I didn't know. "Jemis, Mr. Greenwing that is, I am looking for my—my cousin, who was kidnapped this summer."

I started. "Kidnapped!"

"Yes. I have been following her trail. She is a gifted cook. I believe—I'm sure she made that pie."

I didn't know quite what to say, so said what first came into my mind: "How did it get to be on the fountain?"

"You seemed to know something of it. That's why I've come to ask your assistance. If you will let bygones be bygones."

I found that grandiose apologies or not, I was still a bit indignant at her behaviour. "You tried to kill me last night!"

"Oh, well, that was before I learned the truth," Violet said, her hand touching her sword hilt.

Mrs. Etaris had a slightly fixed expression on her face. "Now, Mr. Greenwing, I believe—"

And she stopped, as the door banged opened hard enough to shake the glass in the windows.

Mr. Dart thundered in with pallid cheeks and a glitter in his eyes, clutching his arm as if he'd hurt it. "Mr. Greenwing!" he cried. "The Lady's curse is come upon me!"

He held out his left arm, folding back his sleeve with trembling fingers, and showed to us a hand that shone white and smooth as polished marble.

Chapter Fifteen

MRS. ETARIS LOOKED from Mr. Dart to Violet to me, frowned, and then said: "Mr. Greenwing, would you fetch some fresh coffee from Mr. Inglesides, and then we will be able to discuss your clearly quite remarkable evening's activities in comfort."

"Yes, Mrs. Etaris," I said, and hastened out before thinking to myself there was no reason at all to include Mrs. Etaris in the discussions, except that—well, except that she seemed to be thoroughly in the thick of things, and she was protecting me against her husband and my uncle—and to be honest, I liked her.

The square was full of booths and market-day strangers. The Honourable Rag was in the midst of a crowd of fainting admirers near the fountain; he seemed to be flirting with some dairymaids as big and blond as he. (That sounded as if it ought to be a ballad. ...)

I ducked into the bakery, where a crowd of people were picking out bread and buns and market-day specialties. I exchanged greetings with them all, though I was struck, at sight of a man with a nick across his chin, by the realization that any one of them might have belonged to the cult performing blood magic to the Dark Kings.

It was a disquieting thought and I was distracted buying coffee (and trying very hard to suppress an attack of sneezes all the while in the interests of hygiene), and ended up with a whole loaf of gingerbread and a frown from Mr. Inglesides as a result. He was short and hasty with the business of the day, and it wasn't until I was back outside again that I realized I had probably offended him with my brusqueness.

Mrs. Etaris had put a notice on the front door of Elderflower Books stating that the store was closed for half an hour due to a private collector's arrival; the curtains were drawn to provide some protection against curious eyes, which a closure on market-day was sure to attract. When I entered, I saw that she'd pulled up an extra chair from the back room, so that Violet, Mr. Dart, and she could all sit down. I set my purchases on the counter and perched myself on the stepladder.

"Will people not wonder about the store being closed?" I asked.

"Yes, of course," Mrs. Etaris said, "but your affairs, apart from being quite interesting, seem of an urgent nature. People will have noticed Miss Redshank's arrival, and assume she is the noble collector who desires privacy for her purchases. Did you say anything at the bakery?"

"No, Mr. Inglesides was busy and I was ... distracted."

"Indeed. Let us, therefore, confabulate. Who would like to go first? Miss Redshank, you spoke of a kidnapping; Mr. Dart, of a curse; and Mr. Greenwing, of violence, the Talgarths' moat, and a ring that may appertain to the Lady of Alinor—or perhaps to the Honourable Master Ragnor, if Mr. Dart is correct."

I stirred, but she merely smiled and continued: "And, of course, we have a mysterious pie of Ghilousetten origin found abandoned in the middle of Ragnor Bella, which may or may not have anything to do with the rest."

"There's also the Lady," said Mr. Dart.

I cleared my throat reluctantly. "Not to mention the cult."

Mrs. Etaris closed her eyes but couldn't quite control her face. "Of course there is, Mr. Greenwing. Who shall begin?"

"The lady first," said Mr. Dart, with a glance of outright admiration for Violet. I wondered what had passed while I was in the bakery for his distrust to melt so thoroughly. Mine seemed to have gone the way of the Empire of Astandalas, and be left to relics and wistful ruins.

Violet's eyes had widened at Mrs. Etaris' calm account of the curiosities before us, but she nodded, and folded her hands in her lap, her posture as erect as Mrs. Etaris'. "Thank you, Mr. Dart." She took a breath. "After convocating from Morrowlea this spring, I went to visit my aunt in Newbury, in Ghilousette."

"One moment, Miss Redshank," said Mrs. Etaris. "Are you yourself from Ghilousette? Your accent does not seem to be Rondelan."

"No, I'm not from Rondé. My aunt married a ship's captain when he came to the port where she lived, and returned with him to his own land. She was an aunt I much admired, and since I had the opportunity I went to see her and my cousin Daphne—Miss Carlin, as you would say here. I arrived there in the first days of summer, and to my surprise found that my cousin had gone missing on her way home from university and my aunt and uncle were utterly distraught."

"How unfortunate."

"Yes." Violet hesitated for a moment. In the quiet monosyllable I read a host of painful memories, and felt my anger at Violet dissipate even further. It was hard to keep annoyed with her; it wasn't her fault that Lark had been so manipulative. And it *had* been a very grand apology.

I wondered what it would take to make my uncle kiss my boots.

Serious enchantments and probably drugs—or at the very least a concussion—after I'd personally and at the greatest peril saved the kingdom from the hordes of evil, I thought, and tried not to smile.

Violet went on: "My uncle was due to set sail shortly after my arrival. My aunt and I investigated the matter as best we could, but were hampered because—well, you know that in Ghilousette magic is banned?"

We nodded. She picked her words with evident care. "There are those who believe whole-heartedly in the law, and those who would prefer the old ways but understand the reasons and are loyal to the Duke, and those who prefer the old ways and practice them in secret, with great threat of danger. And then there are those ..."

"Anywhere something desirable is banned," Mrs. Etaris said thoughtfully, "there are those who make it their business to supply it, with ruinous prices and great danger to all involved."

How was that the way Mrs. Etaris' mind worked? It must be all the romances. I frowned at *Black Tulip* and *The Underwriters of Li Shan Do*. It had to be one of those; I'd read *The Passion of Madame Anastasiya*.

Mr. Dart nodded. "Do people smuggle magic in Ghilousette? How?"

Violet shrugged. "I don't know how it's done, but I am quite certain my cousin was stolen by those trafficking in illegal magic. Her baked goods were evidently magical to any who tasted them."

"What led you to Ragnor Bella?" Mrs. Etaris asked.

"There's a Ghilousetten exile here who is involved in the trafficking. I've spent the summer tracking leads, and I had thought this trafficker another dead end, until I saw in the square yesterday morning the pie. A stargazy pie. A Ghilousetten pie, and ... I believe it was my cousin's."

"Was it magical?" Mr. Dart asked skeptically. "I can't say I wanted to eat it in the slightest."

"I sneezed at it."

"You sneeze at everything, though, it's hardly indicative."

"Mrs. Etaris has a theory that my sneezes are a sensitivity to magic."

Both Violet and Mr. Dart were unable to contain their mirth at this suggestion. Mrs. Etaris waited until they had done laughing, sipping her coffee with great equanimity, before concisely explaining her reasoning. It seemed unfortunately sound. I ate some gingerbread and tried not to snuffle in an aggrieved fashion.

Mrs. Etaris set down her cup. "We have, then, a theory of the *origin* of the pie, but not of its arrival in Ragnor Bella's town square or of its full significance. Now, Mr. Greenwing—with the gallant assistance of Mr. Dart—has determined that herrings were bought this week by Dominus Gleason, Mr. Shipston, Baron Ragnor's household, the Talgarths, and Mrs. Landry."

I nodded. "So Mr. Kim said."

"Mrs. Landry is my sister and I can vouch for both the herring—which she made into a dish from Fiella-by-the-Sea, much to the disgust of her husband and children—and for the fact that the only persons to join her household since last winter were a new kitchen-boy, aged ten, and Mr. Landry's second cousin once removed from Kingsford-Below, who is assisting her in her parlour café. Miss Featherhaugh is not, I think, your cousin."

Mr. Dart smirked. "No; Mr. Greenwing didn't sneeze on her at all when we had lunch there yesterday."

I glanced at him dourly. "Thank you, Mr. Dart."

"I'm sure you will be able to turn a nose for magic into a useful thing, like a bloodhound, as soon as you can control it. You will have to be careful, though, or you will lose your growing reputation as the most fashionable—if also most disaster-prone—young man in Ragnor Bella."

"Thank you, Mr. Dart."

Mrs. Etaris poured us each more coffee. Violet sipped hers, her earlier smiles more serious now. Mrs. Etaris bit her lip thoughtfully. "We can, I think, leave aside the Landries. My sister has never been inclined towards breaking the law, while Mr. Landry is a staunch liberal, and believes in general philanthropy and hard work. Neither of them would have any truck with anything illegal, and even less anything so unfashionable."

"We haven't discussed the ring," Mr. Dart said. "It's the Honourable Rag's, I'm almost certain. And we know his house bought herring."

Violet nibbled at her lip. "Do you think he would be party to smuggling?"

"He went to Tara," I put in.

"That doesn't *necessarily* mean he's fallen in with criminal gangs, Mr. Greenwing."

"Thank you, Mr. Dart." I decided not to say that I knew well that the Honourable Rag played high and freely, and that deep as the Baron's pockets were, the gaming-houses of Orio were infamous. I temporized. "I don't know what he thinks about practicing magic—but he was certainly sneaking around last night, night crawlers or no night crawlers."

Violet gave me a curious glance. I shrugged.

Mr. Dart shook his head. "I don't know about his actual views, but I think even he would be careful not to tread on his father's toes. His father would disinherit him if he found him playing with magic."

I looked at him, remembering the purple werelight in the woods.

Mr. Dart frowned, obviously thinking the same, then went on firmly. "Why, the Baron refused the Earl of the Farry March's offer for the Honourable Miss, though she wanted to accept it, because the Farry March is too taken-up with magic and the Baron thinks Fiellan should follow Ghilousette."

"You run in his circles," I said, trying not to sound envious.

"Moreover," Mr. Dart said, ignoring this, "the Honourable Rag has gone over entirely to manly sports and virtues. He would never be party to something so underhanded as enslavement. If this involved a daring raid across a border, perhaps, though I'm not sure the drinking societies of Tara left him enough wits for planning that."

"But the ring—"

"I think we are getting side-tracked," Violet interrupted. "I don't see we have have enough information to know what to make of the ring. Will you pass it to me, Mr. Dart?"

"Yes," he said, and slid it across the table to her. He moved awkwardly, using his left hand; his right lay heavily in his lap where he'd placed it. "Here."

Violet examined it carefully. "I see why you thought it might be an emblem of the Lady, Mr. Greenwing, from the red flower. Hmm. Yet you believe it this Master Ragnor's, Mr. Dart?"

"I've seen him wear it this summer." At my puzzled glance he added, "Mrs. Etaris showed it to us when you were at the bakery getting gingerbread."

"Mm," I said, and remembered to eat some. Violet smiled impishly at me. I bit my lip to keep from snorting.

Mrs. Etaris tapped her fingers on the table. "Hmm. Let us set that aside until we can decide on our course of action. Certainly it is suggestive; perhaps too much so. Miss Redshank, have you any questions?"

Violet was smiling with a strange curl to her lip. She shook her head, setting the ring next to the coffee pot. "No. What of the others who bought herring?"

"We have only been able to speak to Mr. Shipston. He is a Ghilousetten physicker, who claims to have been a metal-wizard, now in exile, though given that Mr. Greenwing was affected only by the cogswork on his wall, perhaps not much of one. He was most distressed at the sight of the pie, and threw us out of his house." She paused. "He also mentioned a woman in his household by the name of Miranda, whom none of us had ever heard tell of before."

"Daphne!"

"Perhaps. It is certainly most suggestive. But Dominus Gleason claims to be out of town, when he is not. Mr. Greenwing spoke to him yesterday, and my daughter saw him this morning rushing along the river-path when she was collecting the eggs. He is clearly keeping something a secret."

We all took a break to eat gingerbread. The sounds of the market came through the front wall, muffled but pleasant. All those people out there with their own lives, in quiet backwater Ragnor Bella—the dullest town in Rondé—and some of them were certainly cultists. I shuddered at the sudden vision of bloody sacrifice and orgiastic dancing.

"You shiver, Mr. Greenwing," Mrs. Etaris said. "You do seem to have picked up a cold last night."

"It's not that. Mr. Dart and I saw something ... very disagreeable last night."

He snorted, and stroked his marble hand awkwardly. "The Lady knows."

"If it was the Lady."

"It was," he replied firmly.

Mrs. Etaris stared at him. "Whatever were you doing last night? Not simply carousing at the Green Dragon, as I had presumed?"

"Well, no." Mr. Dart said, flushing behind his beard. "I'd invited Mr. Greenwing to go out with me to observe the meeting of what I thought would be a secret society. It turned out, when we got there—"

"One moment, Mr. Dart. How did you know about this secret society?"

"I overheard people speaking of it, and was curious, since nothing much else seemed to be happening this month in the barony. My mistake! Mr. Greenwing and I met up, had an, er, encounter, with Miss Redshank here, and then after she returned to her lodgings, followed some men to the Ellery Stone, where they ... turned out to be a cult giving sacrifice to the Dark Kings."

Even Violet looked astonished and impressed. Mrs. Etaris froze. "What did they sacrifice? And to what? How do you know it was to the Dark Kings?"

"I didn't understand what they were saying—Mr. Greenwing did."

"I took Old Shaian at Morrowlea," I said when they all looked at me; Violet nodded. "They were calling on the Dark Kings. And there was a white priest, a black priest, and a silver priest. That's in the old histories of pre-conquest Alinor. Mr. Dart thinks the silver priest was Dominus Alvestone."

"Really?" asked Mrs. Etaris, with apparent surprise. "He didn't seem utterly depraved when he came in last week for a book on Fiellanese folklore, but I suppose it doesn't always show."

Mr. Dart and I exchanged mildly confused glances. Violet said, "What did they do?"

We explained, picking around the most disgusting parts of it, trying not to be too crude—not that Violet would have minded, but Mrs. Etaris' expression grew more and more set as we fumbled through the story.

"Then," Mr. Dart concluded, "just as they were getting well into the, the frenzy, the wind turned and Mr. Greenwing started sneezing violently. We, uh, hastened out of the thicket, went down to the Lady's Pools, and, er, saw the Lady." His voice changed, and he added, with a faraway look, and another touch of his marble arm. "She was beautiful."

"I'm not sure it was the Lady."

"Who else would have been there, at the holy stones?"

"Any of the other wizards out-and-about, perhaps?"

Violet frowned. "Did she say anything?"

"I don't think so," I replied uncertainly. "She laughed ..."

"He was sneezing too much."

"Thank you, Mr. Dart. The cultists came down the hill after she disappeared, and we, er, decided to get out of their way. In the dark we mistook ourselves, and ended up toppling into the Talgarths' moat. Someone's doing illegal magic *there*."

"At the Talgarths'?" Mrs. Etaris shook her head. "They're most loyal to the Lady."

Violet spoke thoughtfully. "That doesn't mean they're definitely against magic. Elsewhere the Lady's devotees continue to use Schooled wizardry."

"That's what I thought," Mr. Dart put in. "Jemis said he was sure they were doing illegal magic."

I sneezed, then sighed in exasperation. "They were attacking us with bolts of magic. Violet, you read about that—"

"I'm not sure I'd call Dame Talgarth a devotee of anything except dinner parties," Mr. Dart said, with an abrupt chuckle, overtop of Violet's protest that she hadn't done more than glance at offensive magic for a paper. "And Justice Talgarth's obsessed with his sweet peas."

I sneezed vigorously at the mere thought. "They were awfully strongly scented."

"Really, Mr. Greenwing, your nose is appallingly sensitive. Though I will grant they were perhaps somewhat ripe."

"Thank you, Mr. Dart."

Mrs. Etaris tipped her cup around on her plate so the thick syrupy dregs swirled mesmerizingly. When she spoke I felt a faint jar, as of a thin line snapping.

"Mr. Dart, do you know who cursed you? The woman at the fountain?"

"You mentioned the Lady's curse?" Violet asked.

"That was something that happened in the Interim," I said, remembering the strange creeping paralysis that had affected those who poked around some formerly magical places. "Around the broken waystones. People called it that even though it wasn't really the Lady so much as everything else. And it stopped when the Interim finished."

Mr. Dart nodded. "It was surely not the Lady. Unless it was for presuming to look upon her beauty ... there was magic in the woods, though. The cult—"

I snorted, or tried ineffectually to. "—Domina Ringley's companion, who was throwing bolts of magic at us—"

"We don't know that was her. That could have been one of the dark priests."

"I suppose so. You did put your arm into that silver light when, er ... when you breaking the fascination the Silver Priest cast on me."

Violet looked sharply at me. "You were caught by a fascination?"

"Some sort of spell, anyway," I said, embarrassed to admit it. "The priest was using the old lighting spell, but it made this silver light, and I couldn't look away."

Mr. Dart nodded. "You were enthralled. He was ahead of me," he added to Violet and Mrs. Etaris. "I wasn't in the direct line."

"How did you break it?" Mrs. Etaris asked.

He blushed again. "Flipped his coat over his head, and pulled him down the path until we got caught up in the sweet peas. Probably it was all the sneezing when you ran into the flowers."

"Falling into the moat broke it," I said thoughtfully, remembering the shock of the cold water, and shivering. "He is a powerful wizard."

"The Dark Kings were reputed to be very powerful," Violet said. "I remember you telling me about them, Jemis, when you were reading that history of Schooled magic on Alinor."

I shuddered again. "I'm not sure I believe that the gods are walking, do you?"

Mrs. Etaris tipped her coffee cup thoughtfully again. "They say an angel was seen in Ragnor Parva when a boy was born at the end of the Interim, but I must confess I had not given much credence to their claims of the boy being a saint. I should think it much more likely you saw the Lady of Alinor than the White or Green Lady Herself."

"If it is the Lady of Alinor," Mr. Dart said, slowly at first but with increasing eagerness, "then the service she might desire is not—oh!" and he stopped, blushed behind his auburn beard, and said no more. The White Lady required celibacy of her priests; the Green Lady, the opposite; as for the Lady Jessamine ... well. She was human.

Violet and I exchanged sardonic glances, and Mrs. Etaris said, "I see we have several puzzles. First, we have the mystery of Miss Redshank's cousin, which appears to be most personally grievous and of urgency, and apparently is connected to the mystery of the stargazy pie. Second, we have the problem of the curse laid upon Mr. Dart; but despite its obvious urgency we shall have to think further on it. And third, we have this very disquieting news of a resurgence of the worship of the Dark Kings by blood sacrifice. They are contenting themselves with cows and shallow cuts now, but they will not remain there long, not now that they have tasted blood from the black goblet."

Violet looked at the cookery books beside her, pulling out *Fifth Imperial Decadent Style Dinner Parties* from where I'd shoved it in awry.

Mrs. Etaris watched her smooth out a corner of the cover inattentively, frowning at her thoughts. She spoke half-inattentively. "Nor do I like the sound of this stone they have found. The Heart of the Moon, you say the silver priest called it? There are old Shaian rituals to do with the Moon that would not be well mixed with the Dark Kings. And it's only the second day of the Transit of the Dragon, as they'd call it. Something shall have to be done about this, if we can figure out where to start."

"With the Talgarths?" I suggested.

"I'm going there for dinner tomorrow," Mr. Dart said. "I can investigate."

Violet turned the book about the table with slow, pensive movements. I watched the ivory lace and rich wine-coloured cloth of her sleeve, and wondered again just where she was from, and who her family was, and why she was investigating the disappearance of her cousin all alone in a foreign land. The following thought that she was not *completely* alone gave me a certain pleasure.

Then she said, "I wonder if I didn't see the Silver Priest as I was coming into town. A very tall man with abnormally large hands and feet, did you say?" Mr. Dart and I nodded uncomfortably, my mind, at least, swarming with unpleasant visions of the silver light and the gleaming mask coming out of the shadows. Violet nodded. "He was dressed in Scholar's robes and talking to a strapping young lord with Beaufort curls."

I was all set to go find the Honourable Rag and pummel him into confession right then, dairymaids or no dairymaids, but Mrs.

Etaris gestured me down firmly. "No, Mr. Greenwing. We must consider a sensible course of action. It would be most rude to go accuse a guest of our barony of being a priest of the Dark Kings—a matter far more than unfashionable—and it would, moreover, be most foolish to suggest the Honourable Master Roald is associating with them. Worship of the Dark Kings was outlawed before the Conquest because of the violence associated with the cult."

"All the more reason to stop them. He was hanging around the woods that night—"

"He's the *Baron's son*," said Mr. Dart.

"He's a right prat, that's what he is—"

"What about my cousin?" Violet asked hastily. "What would you suggest we do, Mrs. Etaris?"

Mrs. Etaris frowned at her coffee cup for several minutes. We fidgeted in silence, Mr. Dart touching his petrified hand and Violet glancing at the wall of books beside her. I picked up the ring and examined it for any further clues. It told me nothing; no useful inscription; just the floral emblem and the heavy weight of it. I couldn't think of anything useful to do.

Confronting the Silver Priest appealed to part of me; confronting the Honourable Rag rather more so, though I knew he could take me in any fight, especially given how tired I was and how weak still after the spring. I sighed. I was tired, but also knotted with anxious energy. I wanted to go for a *run*.

Finally Mrs. Etaris stirred. We all looked at her eagerly. "It seems to me," she began, "that we need more information. We need to find out whether this is indeed the Honourable Master Ragnor's ring, and what account he gives of it—and whether we believe him, of course. Though I have never heard of him being called a deceitful young man."

"He'd thump anyone who dared give him the lie," Mr. Dart said. Violet looked approving.

"I daresay he would. At any rate, perhaps you and Mr. Greenwing—or perhaps just you, Mr. Dart—could ask him about the ring later today. I shall take Miss Redshank to call upon Mr. Shipston, on pretence of showing her his marvellous cogswork, and see if we cannot find out who this Miranda of his is. As for the Silver Priest—he certainly sounds of the same description as Dominus Alvestone."

Mr. Dart made a baffled gesture with his left arm; his right moved a bit in his lap but not far. I felt a bit sick, looking at it. I couldn't think why I wasn't equally losing some function to the indiscriminate offensive magics last night. "Even in the robes and mask you could see his proportions. I'm sure he was Dominus Alvestone. The blackguard!"

"Would you recognize any of the other participants?"

Mr. Dart looked at me, and blushed. "Not ... not in their clothes."

"I don't think the Honourable Rag could have been one of the cultists—he didn't seem to be drunk enough."

"He never seems drunk enough," Mr. Dart said. "I think that's all he did at Tara—that and go hunting, apparently."

"But how would he have gotten to the other side of the Talgarths' house so quickly? Without everyone else following?"

"Other people *were* following, though. And I'm not sure we were all that fast. We spent quite a while in the water when those women were looking for us."

Violet covered her mouth with her hand to suppress a smile.

Mrs. Etaris paused a moment, into which silence there came a sudden jangle from the doorbell as the door was flung open.

I jumped up in reaction, but the words of alarm died in my mouth when I realized the woman before me was Domina Ringley.

She looked transfigured, her eyes alight, her face exalted, her whole being thrumming with energy and bubbling delight. Something in me belled in response, and I stepped forward, as if she was a fire at which I could warm my hands.

My foot caught on the edge of the rug, and I looked down instinctively; looked away; and sneezed.

"Jemis," Violet whispered, as I caught my breath.

I forced my hands back to my sides. "Is, is there anything we can help you with, Domina Ringley?"

Her eyes were wide and shining, pupils wide as if she'd dropped belladonna into them, skin no longer sallow but golden. She met my gaze with delight, smiling so cheerfully I couldn't help but respond, though I was trying hard, my fingernails digging into the palm of my hand. No one else seemed to be moving. In the far distance outside I could hear a voice cutting in and out through the noise of the market, but couldn't make out the words.

Then Domina Ringley stumbled forward as someone pushed in behind her. "I say!" I said in protest when the Scholar fell on top of me, catching her with some difficulty.

"Unhand my sister!" Dame Talgarth said in a fearful voice.

"Dame Talgarth," I began, "Domina Ringley is—"

Dame Talgarth actually spat on the floor, and while I was still staring at it grabbed her sister's arm and propelled her backwards out of the room. "You *disgusting* young man. *Unhand her.*"

Chapter Sixteen

"WELL," I SAID, with an attempt at sangfroid. "I don't think I'll be going to any of Dame Talgarth's dinner parties any time soon."

"What is Domina Ringley *taking*?" Mr. Dart said. "She looked ... I don't even know ..."

Violet shook her head slowly, not in denial but in concern. "Jemis, she looks like you did when you were high on wireweed."

"You tried wireweed?" Mr. Dart asked in astonishment.

"Not on purpose," I replied, closing the door again and trying to avoid meeting anyone in the market's eye. I looked back to see that Mr. Dart and Mrs. Etaris were both frowning mightily at me, while Violet looked distressed.

The courage of one's convictions, I thought, and to say the truth ... I sighed and crumpled my handkerchief in my hand. "It was when I tried smoking a pipe ... it turned out someone had laced the tobacco with wireweed."

Outside in the market square people were going about their business, carefully not looking at where Dame Talgarth and her sister were arguing between the statue of the Emperor Artorin and the memorial to the Fall. I'm sure they were all, however, paying *close* attention.

"What did it feel like?" Mr. Dart asked curiously. "People say it's the most extraordinary feeling, all centred and focussed and utterly sure of oneself and exhilarated at the same time."

"Maybe if you don't take it with tobacco," I said. "It was awful. I was sick for days."

"You didn't feel anything? *She* looked exhilarated. Exalted."

I thought of the cold outhouse, the vomiting, the weak days in bed. Lark coming to see me, smiling at me, falling in love. That had been the exaltation, the transfiguration, the exhilaration. I swallowed against bile. "I am sorry to disappoint you, Mr. Dart."

"Why take it, then?"

I shook my head, looking at a woman pushing through the crowd towards Dame Talgarth and Domina Ringley. Tall, stout, regal in her bearing, wearing a fashionable dress in this year's colours, strong nose and cold blue eyes—yes, I thought, that could be the wizard attendant, hastening past us, nearly catching her skirts in the iron railing at the base of the Memorial—in which case—

"They say," began Violet. The breeze swirled by and I sneezed; and was left shaking my head in mystification and annoyance that the thought I'd nearly had had slipped away in a sneeze, again.

"The Lady's blessing upon you," Violet said. She had been known to come up with the best benedictions to my sneezing of anybody but Hal, but her mind appeared now to be on other matters; when I turned to her she was frowning at her hands.

She continued: "They say that taking wireweed opens one to the spirit realms. Lark said—" She cast an apologetic glance at me. I shrugged, a bit despondently, and she continued. "Lark said that it's used in some religions to forge a connection. Between the taker and the earth, or between two individuals if they take it together, or magically in some circumstances—and it augments certain types of magic, though of course no one would talk about that—and she said people get addicted to the sense of, of purpose and connection and love, and the incredible heights of emotion it inspires—"

She faltered. I frowned at her, about to say I'd felt nothing of the sort, when something about Violet's expression made me think of the circumstances of when I'd taken it. It was right after I'd met Lark, the same Yule ball. *How* I'd met Lark, actually.

I'd come with Hal and a few others. We were standing by the punch bowls and eyeing the women across the room, like many another clutch of young men in many another university. I was trying to get up the nerve to ask Violet to dance; I'd been admiring her from afar through several classes by that point.

Before I had done so Lark had pulled out an elegant ivory pipe and filled it with tobacco, and I'd been so struck by the beautiful woman with the smoke wreathing her, her eyes brilliant, watching me, that I'd gone over without waiting for an introduction—that she was Violet's friend was enough—and she'd laughed when I approached and offered me her pipe—how had we all forgotten that she'd been the one smoking it first?—and before I'd taken two mouthfuls of the smoke she'd kissed me and I was—hers.

"I only smoked it once," I said numbly. "But Lark ..."

Lark smoked all the time.

I had a rush of visions, of Lark with that elegant ivory pipe, blowing smoke rings over me, laughing when I sneezed. Lark coming to see me in the hospital wing with her apologies, kissing me better—until I *was* better, until I was as exhilarated with what I thought was love as Domina Ringley was with wireweed.

Lark, encouraging me away from History of Magic to Classical Literature. Lark, kissing me until I felt as high on love (and purpose, and connection) as if I had spent a year and a half smoking the wireweed directly.Lark, the glory of the university—

Lark, the liar, user, and cheat.

Lark, who made sure I was utterly hers, while she played with anyone she pleased.

Violet, who was her closest and best friend. Violet, who wore a grey cloak the night of a cult full of grey-cloaked figures. Violet, who had attacked me—and whom I trusted without reason, without sense, because of a friendship founded on Lark's—

"Jemis," said Violet, her voice breaking, as I stared in horror at her. "Jemis, please—"

"No," I said, backing up, trying to think through the crashing of my thoughts, feeling as if my heart was breaking all over again. "No."

"Jemis," said Mr. Dart, standing up with his left hand raised as if to grab Violet, who wasn't moving.

"No," I said violently, shaking my head, hand on the doorknob, needing to go, needing to *run*—

"Jemis," Violet whispered, but her voice was drowned out by a sudden clamour as the market bell pealed forth the fire alarm.

I jumped, jerked at the door, prepared at last to act, but my hands were sweaty and slipped while I fought with the handle. Mrs. Etaris grabbed my collar and halted me roughly before I could exit. "No, Mr. Greenwing," she said firmly. "You don't know where to go."

Someone in the square cried out: "It's Mr. Shipston's! Form a bucket chain from the fountain!"

"There," I said, trying to twist out of her grip.

"Mr. Greenwing, you must not be over-hasty."

I stopped, staring in astonishment, to see that she was serious. Behind her Violet was frowning, pinching her hat so the feather crushed, so incongruously I thought: no, wait, that's not what Lark's Violet would do—that's what *my* Violet is like—

"I—" I began, faltering on everything.

"No," Mrs. Etaris said again. "Think about where his house is. We shall help better via the river. This way."

"I can't help with a bucket," Mr. Dart said in agony, "I can barely move my arm."

The first impulse ran out of me; now I followed dumbly behind Mrs. Etaris. She led us quickly through the back streets, including a couple narrow alleys I hadn't realized were there. Violet stayed close behind her, with Mr. Dart and me following at the rear. As we wound past the backs, I suddenly had a face full of smoke and ash. The others all started to cough; I, naturally, sneezed.

"Jemis," Mr. Dart said hoarsely, "do you have any extra handkerchiefs?"

"I always have extra handkerchiefs," I said with faint indignation, and pulled three out. Mr. Dart took one and clapped it to his mouth with a muttered thanks. Mrs. Etaris dipped hers into a puddle at her feet, then bound hers about her nose with quick knots. I emulated her, having rather more trouble with the knots.

"This is the problem with being a man," Violet said in a low voice, having tied hers as easily as Mrs. Etaris, and helped Mr. Dart. We went down another side alley. "You don't learn anything useful to do with needlework."

"I'm sure your sailor uncle knows his knots," I retorted auto-matically, and at her baffled look realized—started to realize—was trying to realize something when Mrs. Etaris stopped, and I saw what lay before us.

Several people had come out to gawk from the nearest houses to Mr. Shipston's. The physicker's house was gouting black smoke from its street side. Mrs. Etaris glanced sharply around the scene. From here we could see that there was indeed a water-wheel on the river side of the house, groaning as it spun in the quick stream of the Raggle.

"It looks like they should have been able to get out," Mr. Dart began in relief, but just then a second-floor window exploded into fire with a sound that was eerily human.

"That sounds—You there!" Mrs. Etaris shouted at the nearest bystander. "Fetch buckets from inside and form a bucket chain from the river. Mr. Dart, you go to the front and see if everyone has come out. There are at least three people in the household, Mr. Shipston, his man, and a maid."

"There's a cook, too," a woman said. She was grinning, and seemed to be enjoying herself. Mr. Dart nodded and pushed through the crowd, using his petrified arm as a kind of club to knock people out of the way.

"It could spread," Mrs. Etaris said frigidly, and half the crowd scattered under the force of her frown. They reappeared quickly with pots and buckets and quickly formed a bucket chain under the bookseller's direction. Violet and I were pushed out of the way, closer towards the house.

Violet said, suddenly, "Is that a *person* in there?" She pointed up at a window on the first floor, at the opposite end to the one spouting fire, where a human shape was hammering fists against the glass.

I don't know what madness seized me, except that perhaps I was fed up with being considered the foolish son of a disgraced war hero, or drugged by the woman I'd loved, or bewitched by what I'd thought a good friend, or being the risibly sneezing young Mr. Greenwing, or what—without thinking further I threw myself shoulder-first through the glass of the ground-floor conservatory, and into the house.

Chapter Seventeen

THE FIRE MUST have started on the other side of the house, for there was little smoke or sense of danger on this end. With the wet cloth over my nose and mouth I found myself breathing almost easily. I had no inclination to sneeze. I felt no fear, only a clear sense of purpose. I moved quickly but without haste, knowing from some deep place that carelessness would kill me faster than anything else.

I'd only been into the house the once. What had I seen from the entry-way? A hallway leading straight to a flight of stairs; rooms on either side; another pair of rooms on each side of the flight on the upper floors. A typical pre-Fall Fiellanese townhouse, in short, though as this was the old mill there were extra rooms on the river side.

If this was the conservatory, and I'd come in the back side of the house, then the kitchen would be to the right, and the servant stairs between them and the front, running up next to the shrines where Astandalan rituals used to be performed.

I opened doors as I went to be sure not to miss anyone. The last before the stairs contained a shrine in obvious use; and I recalled that Mr. Shipston claimed to be a magician.

I held my breath but felt no need to sneeze. Of course; everyone knew the rituals were empty, and had been empty since the Interim (when they had been anything but empty of power, but not the power anyone wanted or expected). The next door over should be the stairs—and it was.

Now I heard the fire, roaring down the stairwell like a monster. And over it a wailing sob that sounded so like the woman keening over the drums of the Dark Kings that I hesitated.

Violet said in my ear, "You're making a chimney. The fire will grow—"

I jumped and leaped up the stairs. She was right, the roaring above was changing tone, growing hungrier, furious. Violet behind me leaped up with the door slamming behind her, no skirts to trip her, even as the stairs spiralled up in the smallest possible space. I panted through my thick nose and the handkerchief. On the last turn to the first floor I skidded to a halt, Violet thumping into me. The fire was above us; the cracks between the floorboards were glowing scarlet. To our left ash was sifting down.

The wailing had come from the river side. I'd gotten turned around on the spiral, and hoped the right was still the right direction. I launched myself through door after door, Violet slamming them shut behind us.

A sitting room full of pieces of clockwork; a bedroom all in green; a room of blue drapery with nothing in it but a single standing harp taller than me and an incongruous claw-foot bathtub set beside it.

That was the end of the house. I stopped at the window and flailed around. Violet was standing on the other side of the harp, staring at me, her eyes wide over the handkerchief.

"The sound came from here," she said. The air seemed to be getting thin. I couldn't hear much beside the thundering fire over us. The plaster in the room was crumbling. "We must—"

The harp shuddered in a deafening jangle of notes, and toppled over on its side. I jumped towards the window as a piece of the ceiling fell in. Violet crashed over beside me, and reached to open a door I hadn't seen, half-hidden in the wainscoting.

Inside a narrow closet was a long grey hooded cloak, with dark stains about its hem.

"Violet," I said uncertainly, and then something broke above us and in the cracking of the house my own reserve snapped, and I turned to her in fury.

"Did you *know* the whole time? About Lark giving me wireweed?"

She said, "Jemis, the house is *on fire*."

"Violet." I glared at her, the closet door trembling in my hand, my eyes stinging. "Tell me."

She met my gaze, eyes wide and kohl-smudged over the white handkerchief. I could hear the fire roaring above us, but I didn't move, the need to know far more urgent than the physical danger.

(A thought came distantly: that I had believed, last night, that physical danger would always outweigh other concerns.)

I could see her give in.

"Yes. I knew. I knew from the start. It wasn't the first time."

I couldn't even formulate words to reply. Violet reached out and grabbed my hand from the closet door. "Jemis, please believe me. I am only telling you this because we are in a burning house. She was punishing me for liking you. I did my best to stop you from being ruined," she added, a touch more softly.

I thought of the spring, and laughed bitterly, but the laughter turned to choking as something fell with a crash from the ceiling behind us.

Violet grabbed my arm. "Three rooms—but there were four windows on this floor—"

She was right. "Four—there must be a bathroom—" I thumped along the wainscoting, looking for another hidden door, and a foot or two from the closet found a hollow noise.

"There's no handle," I said urgently.

"Jemis—" Violet pushed me aside. I felt light-headed from lack of air. She was scrabbling at the wood with her dirk. There was a howling noise coming from inside the wall. *How horrible*, I thought, *how horrible how horrible how*

"Push, Jemis—shoulder it—it's stuck."

Violet's voice was calm, rational, focused. I took a few steps back into the room. The house seemed to be tilting. I didn't like to think what that meant. I took as deep a breath as I could manage, then held my breath against coughing and sneezing and all that. I can run, I thought; I had run, and run, and run, all this year. Run away from my illness and my failure at Morrowlea and the strange twisted relationship with Lark, whom I had thought I loved.

Violet cried, "Run!"

I launched myself straight at the wall with all my speed, and the door to the old bathroom splintered under my weight.

The pre-Fall fixture bath, the size of a bed, was full of water, full of light from the fire on one side and the light streaming in the window on the other, and full also of a howling naked woman with a fish's tail who had fallen half out of it in a desperate attempt to get to the window.

Violet and I didn't wait to blink twice—or not thrice, anyway. As if we'd planned it, I went to the window and used the ewer from the washstand to break open the window. Violet went to the mermaid and gave her a very sympathetic smile.

"We're on the river side," I said, my voice weirdly insouciant.

"True."

We looked at each other and then at the mermaid. "Ma'am," I said, "the river is below. The house is on fire. We shall have to jump holding you."

The mermaid closed her mouth on the horrible screaming. Looked startled. Then, in an accented voice, said, "Yes."

So Violet and I each took one of her arms. Violet used her dagger to push out the rest of the broken glass, I clambered out onto the sill, and we hauled the mermaid up between us. And then, since one glance behind me to see that Violet had made it to a teetering balance on the windowsill also served to demonstrate that the bucket chain had not succeeded in putting out the fire at all, without more than the briefest, "Ready?" we jumped into the Raggle.

***

I DON'T EVEN want to think about that period in the river.

The Raggle is smaller than the Rag—either of the Rags—but in spate it's still quite large enough. I bumped my knee against the old bridge pilings hard enough for it to register through my panic.

There seemed to be a lot of shouting, and muddy brown water, and tugs this way and that, and then I was sneezing and retching and sneezing some more on the bank a bit downstream of the Ragglebridge while someone pounded me between my shoulder blades.

"Violet?" I gasped, and then thought: *I'm so confused.*

"Here," she replied weakly. I rubbed my face to get the water out of my eyes and my hair out of my face. I'd lost all my handkerchiefs except one, which was sopping wet. Someone helped me get to my feet and struggle out of my coat.

There went my second-best coat after the first, I thought inconsequentially.

"Oh," I said, and, "thank you."

It was the bearded fisherman from the morning. His companion was down further at the bank, looking earnestly and worriedly downstream. With the first's assistance I tottered down to him.

"Thank you," I managed, before coughing again. "Is there—"

"There's someone else in the water, but I can't see where she got to," he said. He was wet to his chest and had a rope tied to his waist. I looked at it dumbly.

The bearded fisherman said, "We heard the cries from upstream that people were in the river. We got ourselves tied to the mooring post and waded in to rescue you and the lady. But the other lady—"

"The other lady is a mermaid."

They looked at me in astonished disbelief. I blushed. "I think she'll want to stay in the river."

From under a cascade of brambles and vines that swayed in a tangle of leaves in the water, a voice spoke petulantly. "There is *nothing* I want more than to get out of the river."

The fishermen looked very doubtful. The second one said, "There aren't any mermaids on Alinor."

"I am an abomination."

"Surely not!" said Violet, splashing over to us.

"Are you—are you Miranda?" I asked, trying to grasp at some straw of sense.

"Who told you my name?"

"We want to help you," I said, trying to be as soothing and reasonable as Mr. Dart or Mrs. Etaris, though rather spoiled in the effect by another emphatic fit of sneezing. "Please. Are you—are you—" my brief glimpse of her had not made it clear how old she was. Older than me, I thought. "Are you Mrs. Shipston?"

"Miss," spat the voice. "I returned to my maiden name after my husband abandoned me, the traitor. My brother took me in."

"He wasn't keeping you prisoner in that tub?" Violet asked, looking about as fascinated and horrified as I felt.

"My *defilement* kept me there."

"Oh. Right," she said, and started to sneeze.

I, of course, immediately followed suit. The bearded fisherman had undone the rope, and was coiling it back around the mooring post. "Um," I said to him, "I'm afraid I don't know your name? I've seen you of a morning."

"Clegger," he said gruffly, with a twinkle; "he's Ned."

"Thank you kindly, Mr. Clegger, Mr. Ned. I'm Jemis Greenwing."

Mr. Ned was a thinner man than his friend, the one who usually touched his cap with one finger and said nothing. He touched his cap with one finger, grinning. "Me first name's Jemis, after your granther's horse, too, belike. Me father lost a bet."

I sighed, but I couldn't help but smile. "Mine, too."

Violet giggled through her sneezes, and a woman who'd been hovering behind us took the opportunity to bustle forward and throw a blanket over her. "Now, miss," she said firmly. I recognized her belatedly as the innwife. "You just come in and dry yourself off. My Julie's much of a size of you, and you won't mind a dress, will you, if it's dry? As for you, Mr. Greenwing, whatever were you thinking to take a woman into the river after a mermaid? Wanting to be in a folk tale, you boys are, half the time."

"We jumped out of a burning house," I said lamely.

"And what were you doing in there? Something foolish, no doubt. Come away and have a nice hot pot of wine, my dear." She bent a worried face towards the vines. "And—Miss Shipston, was it? Would you like some hot wine?"

There was a pause, and then the vines parted, and a woman peered out. She might have been pretty at one point, but lines of grief and woe had etched her face hard and angular. Her hair was a grey-streaked dark brown, braided up in a kind of coronet much as I'd seen in Ghilousette, where the women wore lace caps. Her voice wavered as she said, "Thank you kindly, goodwife. I ... I haven't been so well used in many a day."

The innwife nodded and bundled Violet away, with a call over her shoulder to me: "When you're ready, Mr. Greenwing, come in and dry off."

I sneezed again. "She makes it sound as if I did this every week."

Mr. Clegger said, "Perhaps 'un should let people know you didn't burn yourselves in the fire."

"I'll go," said a youth, who'd been watching all this agog (and with an utter fascination for Miss Shipston the mermaid). "Whose house was it?"

I coughed. "Mr. Shipston the physicker's. Tell Mrs. Etaris the bookmistress."

"Ooer!" he said, and dashed off through the crowd that was peering at the tangle where Miss Shipston had once again retreated.

"Perhaps," I suggested to Clegger and Ned, "we could give Miss Shipston her privacy?"

Clegger nodded. Ned glanced around, with a slow movement, and then cried out in a voice that startled me considerably. "Away with ye! The lady's had her troubles, and don't need you gawping at her like a bear in a zoo! Go to, the news'll be round the town soon enow."

"Mr. Ned," I said in amazement, watching the crowd scatter with much good-natured laughing and chatter, "you have a remark-able voice."

"Och, I was town crier in Sowter's Circle for many a year till I retired, and I still win the barony hollering contests, let me tell you."

I started sneezing, and barely managed to form the words to thank them again before being firmly pointed inside. There I dis-covered that my sneezing was not only due to the magic surely sur-rounding Miss Shipston, but also to the much more ordinary cause of multiple immersions in cold water.

The innwife—from a sign above the parlour bar I saw that the innkeepers were the Callouns—was nowhere to be seen, but Mr. Calloun came out immediately. "My word," he said, "you'd think my wife had never seen a woman in trousers before, she was that taken by the lady, and clear forgot that you'd be chilled through from your ducking as well. Now then, Mr. Greenwing, you have this pot of wine, and take it with you to the back room where the fire's good and hot, and get yourself out of your wet clothes while I send the girl for a change."

***

DRY, WARM, AND in clothes that were—well, dry and warm, and never once fashionable in all their years of sturdy existence—I made my way back into the front parlour to find Violet coming down in a thick woollen dress, well cinched in at her waist with a sash, that had been modelled on a style once fashionable, in the last years before the Fall. It was a washy blue that looked just fine with her complexion. She pirouetted on seeing me, short corkscrew curls bouncing about her cheeks. "Well, Mr. Greenwing?"

"Well, Miss Redshank," I said, with as courtly a bow as I could invent—and I did take the hand she'd extended for balance and give it a kiss, much to the snickering amusement of the youth who'd been sent as a runner.

Then I dropped her hand, remembering. Her face fell.

"Gents f'r you," the boy said laconically, and took himself off at a cry of "Nedling!" from what I took to be the kitchen. Violet and I went back outside to where Mrs. Etaris, Mr. Dart, and Mr. Shipston were now standing with the Callouns and the fishermen. Miss Shipston had not yet, it appeared, been willing to leave her hiding place.

Mrs. Etaris turned. "Mr. Greenwing, Miss Redshank, I am very glad to see you well. Now—"

"Jemis, you idiot!" interrupted Mr. Dart, hitting me on the shoulder. "What made you run into a house on fire?"

"There was someone inside," Violet said. "What would you have us do, abandon her?"

"Not kill yourselves! And then you jumped in a flooding river! Where you might easily have drowned!"

I remembered abruptly that Mr. Dart's mother had drowned during the Interim, and I forestalled Violet's next retort by saying, "You're right, it was a bit stupid. Although, we did have a mermaid with us by the time we got into the river."

"A ... mermaid?" said Mr. Dart, and we all turned to the water.

Mr. Shipston suddenly teetered, and Mr. Clegger helped him sit down on the bench that ran along the edge of the dock for the convenience of boaters. I looked at Mrs. Etaris, who was frowning at the river.

Violet caught my eye as I looked around helplessly. "Miss Shipston?" she called. "Will you come out to talk to us?"

There was a moment's silence. Mrs. Calloun shook her head briskly and said to her husband, "I should go in and see to the meat. You bring them in for hot wine afterwards!" She frowned at me. "Especially the two young'uns who went in."

"I'm not that young," I said, but not very loudly, so only Mrs. Etaris, who was standing close, heard; she smiled but didn't say anything, for as Mrs. Calloun stumped up the stairs to the inn, the vines parted and the sleek damp head of Miranda Shipston peeked out at us.

Chapter Eighteen

"I AM AN abomination."

She said it plainly, as a fact, as something she had mostly come to terms with. Mr. Shipston moved his head, bringing his neckerchief up to cover his mouth. He looked old, tired, worried, but there was an edge of relief to his bearing. Not having to hide, I thought. His safe house had burned down, and yet ... his secret was uncovered.

"I was not always this way. I was never beautiful, but I was human, and I had a good dowry." She looked at her brother. "I married the year of the Fall. His name was Deinge." She paused, the water swirling about her, her hands clutching tight to the edge of the dock. The next words came out in a fierce burst. "I do not go by his name. It was his doing I am this way."

"What happened?" Mrs. Etaris asked, her voice gentle. She leaned slightly forward, but did not step closer, I saw.

"We had hoped for a child ... He had yearned for a child. I had wanted one, terribly had I wanted a child of my own, but in the Interim ... I do not know how it was here in Fiellan. In Ghilousette when the lights went out ..."

I looked around. Mr. Shipston had his eyes closed, his face grey. Mr. Dart was stroking his stone hand, frowning, his eyes on the river, and I thought he must be remembering, as I was, *when the lights went out*. We had been very lucky in Fiellan. The roads failed, the magic failed, the lights went out—and yet. Our food had spoiled, but the crops when we planted them grew into the things we expected. All livestock and human births failed at first, but when later infants had come they were what they were supposed to be.

I had studied enough History of Magic at Morrowlea to know this had not been the case in other lands. In the Farry Marches people had in desperation turned to the Good Neighbours; in Ghilousette they had forbidden magic. There were no mages left in Hastowel, it was said, because at the Fall each had caught fire and burned for a year and a day, a living flame, and after the first child born with magic afterwards had done the same at puberty, anyone born with magic was killed before they met that fate. In the Lesser Arcady, all were born with magic; but the orders of living creatures had blended, and those born were only half human. Half tree, half bird, half horse, half goat. Sometimes it was not physically evident which half was which.

Mrs. Etaris' face was set, her posture as erect as ever, her eyes on the distant horizon. Mr. Calloun was rubbing his moustache, trying not to look at where the water around Miss Shipston was bubbling as if her tail was thrashing in agony. Violet's face was completely blank, and I realized again I did not know where she came from, what horrors she might have seen.

I deliberately looked straight at Miss Shipston, and for the rest of the conversation she stared at me, and I couldn't see anyone else's reaction. Her eyes were pale blue and small and moved restlessly, but always back to me. I couldn't bear to look away from the pain and the fear and the self-loathing in them.

"In Ghilousette we had delighted in the contrivances one can make with hands. Cogswork and steam—fire and steel were our loves, as a people. Even before the Fall we did not look much to magic, except that we used it, as all the Empire used it. When the lights went out we did not look to our witches to save us.

"But when I could not bear a child ... my husband, he was not the only one to be a little ... unhinged, by what happened. We had delighted in our contrivances. We did not use witches, we of Ghilousette! In the city of Newbury, we said, there were no witches! The Astandalan wizards set up their anchor stones and their leys, and our engineers turned their magic into steel, into fire, into steam, into built things.

"In the Interim, the magic left the buildings and entered people. The dreams ... We no longer desire to dream, in Ghilousette. We do not speak of such things. We turned outside. When you cut the bread and it screams, when you draw the water and it is blood, when you must wrestle with the wood to give it to the fire—when the world is mad, a madman seems sane."

She laughed, high and wild, and I remembered how in Ghilousette this summer no one had spoken of art, of music, of poetry. I had asked why there was no music, and been told it had gone from the fashion. No one spoke of anything but money, or the newest contrivance, or the doings of the Ducal court, or the new play from Kingsford that was safely historical.

I had been so heartbroken and so miserably sick that I had thought this more appropriate than strange. Been so overwhelm-

ingly revolted by the endless enthusiasm for *Three Years Gone* I'd
been pathetically grateful the Ghilousetten audience had been so
focused on the lead actor's looks and figure they'd barely mentioned the plot.

"Slowly things settled down, and the engineers wrested sanity
into the world. The lights came on—candles and lanterns now. Magic no longer. Never magic. We had already rejected all magic when
the Duke banned it officially. I do not even like to say the word,"
she added, her mouth twisting, her eyes twisting into me. "It is an
obscenity. But I am an abomination, and the defilement of my
mouth does not matter."

She knocked a piece of wood away from her, with a rough awkward gesture that nearly sent her spinning out into the river. As
she clawed back to her hold on the dock, I saw her tail break the
surface, silvery scales flashing like the herring.

"My husband was convinced we were due a child. That was how
he talked. He spoke as if we had missed a package in the post, that
the delivery had gone astray during the Interim. It was a monoma-
nia for him. After the Interim, we were well-off—he was a builder of
clocks, and once they worked again, he was in demand. There are
many other things requiring such cogswork. But he could not rest,
he would wind the clocks, and he would say: It is late, it is late, it is
late. Over and over. Late. Late. Late."

Her voice rose up again. From the corner of my eye I saw Mr.
Shipston shaking, and I wondered how many times he had heard
that high wail from his sister.

"I thought it too late. I did not want to bring a child into a
world that was broken. He wore me down. Over and over again.
When will he come? He is late. He was sure we were due a son.

Perhaps he had dreams. We all had dreams."

We were all silent, and I did not want to look at anyone, especially not her. I closed my eyes. We might have been spared much, but in Fiellan all of us had had dreams, too. Mr. Dart's mother had run into the river at Dartington in the grip of one of the dreams, crying that she could see her dead family floating down, screaming that the dead were coming down the river, that we had to save them. I had dreamed ... well. One had come true.

"He found one of the old witches in the country. She claimed that because she followed the old ways, she had not lost her magic like the scholar wizards had. She claimed she could do the old magic. He took me to her. I did not want to go. I never liked magic, even before. And the old ways were banned long before. Dead, I thought. But my husband insisted, he was so certain our son was waiting to be summoned, had been misplaced, had not been able to find us because of the Interim. He begged me. I relented.

"The witch was very old. She said the old ways demanded a price, not in coin like the honest wizards before the Fall, but in blood and promises. She said that the old ways are strongest when they deal in birth and in death, but that the prices then are highest. My husband offered her gold, iron, steel. She took the money for herself, but said no, for the magic to work, the sacrifice had to be worth the asking. The Dark Kings would do the choosing, if we did the asking."

I thought Mrs. Etaris made a movement, like shaking her head, but when I broke Miss Shipston's intense gaze for a moment to look, she was standing very still, and her face was sober and serious.

"I did not understand. My husband did not, either. He said of course, we were there to ask for a son. We would give anything for a son, he said. The old witch said, good, and—"

Miss Shipston broke off suddenly, made a high cry of agony like I heard her make in terror of the fire. I jumped, and saw that Mr. Dart tried to cover his ears, his right hand falling heavily and hitting the bollard behind him with an audible clunk. I bit my lip and Miss Shipston again held my gaze with her pale eyes.

"She put me naked in a circle. Lit the blue fire around. Put horrible things in the cauldron. Sacrificed a white cock and a black hen and a silver-laced capon. Performed the old sacrifices. The old ways! She poured the blood over me, and made my husband take me there like an animal. And an animal I became for the abomination of our deed. The Dark Kings did not come, or if they came they did not answer, or if they answered they did not care. We did not know. We paid our promises and our gold to the old witch, and when we came back to the city we thought we were done."

She kept her voice from trailing up into hysteria again, but her breath came fast and short. I wondered if Mr. Dart was hearing the drums as I was, seeing the naked people dancing in their blood and fire, summoning the Dark Kings for power. He had picked up his right hand with his left and stuck it carefully into his waistcoat pocket, so it looked nearly normal. Miss Shipston's eyes looked totally mad.

"I grew sick. We thought with child, and my husband rejoiced. He did not care about my sickness, only the son that was coming. I did not think it odd, he had been so strange, it was all so strange. I found myself forgetting things. Little things at first, like where I had left a book or where my latch-key was. Then bigger things. My way about the city. Where my brother lived. Things I had studied. How to read."

We were all dead silent. Every Alinorel child learns to read; it is our pride, even in the Interim no one would have let that requirement go. Mr. Kim the fishmonger's barrow-boy read travellers' tales from the southern reaches. Garsom the town fool asked for his picture-books on holidays. To lose the ability to read? I shuddered.

Her voice was flat now. "My husband lost other things. His love of me, for one. His patience. His clocks. All he cared about was our son, our son, our son. I grew bigger. The witch had ordered us to return to her for the birth, because the Dark Kings come for birth and death, she said. I did not want to go. I wanted to stay in the city, with the physickers, with my brother who would know best. My husband did not care, he cared only that his son be born. We went back to the secret place where the witch met us.

"She said that the child was breech within me, that we would have to offer more to the Dark Kings for the child to be born safely. My husband did not care, he said all that mattered was his son be born. He promised whatever they asked. I was terrified, but the pains were so great that I said I would give anything so long as it stopped hurting and I forgot nothing more.

"The child was born: a boy, red-haired as a Colquine, his father's delight. For a moment I was able to rejoice: and then my husband looked at me and recoiled, tore my son from my arms, and backed away in horror. I did not know what to do, cried out, sobbed to him to come back, but he covered our son's eyes that he would not see me. I called to him that I was his wife, even if he had not loved me, and he shook his head and said, I do not know you, I do not know your name, you are nothing to me. I said, I am the mother of your son! And he said, *No*, and he ran. I tried to stand to follow, and that was when I realized I was ... changed."

She curved her tail out of the water briefly, and shuddered with horror at herself. "I demanded redress from the old witch, but she just laughed and laughed and laughed, and said the old gods took what they willed as payment for what was asked. No more would I hurt below, she said, no more forget, as I had asked. She left me there, in the middle of the woods, alone. I do not forget. I remember that night, and every night since.

"Two days I lay there. I did not know where we were. I had come in the carriage with the curtains drawn. I wanted to die. Then—"

Her voice softened for the first time, only a very small amount, but enough that I was able to take a deep breath. I felt as if I had been holding it for the whole length of her speech, as if I were the one drowning in pain and grief and bitter, bitter anger.

"Two days later my brother came. He told me he had gone to see my husband, been rebuffed from seeing me. Been told I was no more my husband's wife. Been told I had died. Gone mad. Been put away. Different stories, they made no sense to him. My husband was not a good liar, but he was wealthy, and hired people to keep my brother away from the house. My brother was a physicker, he knew people in the city, he asked.

"Finally my husband's coachman came to him, he was uneasy in himself. My husband had first told him I was to stay with the witch to heal, that I had wanted to stay, and then the next day he told the coachman to go pick me up and take me to the Knockermanstone, because the Silent Council knew about the business in the woods. The coachman did not want party to that abomination, he came to my brother, they rescued me.

"We could not go back to Newbury, not with the Silent Council, nor go to our family in Ghilousette if the Knockermen were alerted, so my brother fled with me here to Fiellan, and here we have stayed. Until we were marked by the Grey Ones, and the fire sent at last to cleanse me."

She looked fiercely at me. "You should have let me die. I would be cleansed. I would be clean. I would be *clean*."

Chapter Nineteen

MISS SHIPSTON FINALLY looked away from me, slipping back under the vines, as if she couldn't bear to let us see her any longer.

I started sneezing.

"Oh, Jemis."

"It's—not—on—purpose—Violet."

Mrs. Etaris walked over to the bank and knelt beside the tangled growth. "Miss Shipston, thank you for telling us your story. It must have been very difficult for you."

There was silence. Mr. Shipston made a moaning noise. We looked at him; he was shaking. "What am I to do? My poor Miranda, and my house is destroyed. Where can we go? What can we do? What *is* there to do?"

Mr. Dart looked suddenly round at me, touched my arm. I let him push me a few steps away, trying not to sniffle too loudly. "The Lady," he whispered.

I stopped sneezing and coughed instead. "I'm still not convinced that was the Lady."

"How can you be so doubtful? She is—"

"Your arm—"

"My arm is immaterial."

"It is precisely not, and that's the problem!" I sneezed violently several times in a row, and gasped out the rest, angry and humiliated and frustrated with my sneezing, with a sudden wash of exhaustion, and with helplessness at what to do. "And if I didn't have this bloody stupid sneezing—"

"It was my fault for taking you in the first place."

"I told you you would regret it!"

"Don't start in again on how inferior you feel—"

"It's not a feeling, it's the truth."

"Mr. Greenwing! Mr. Dart!"

Mrs. Etaris' sharp voice recollected me to my surroundings. Mr. Dart was breathing hard, his colour up and his left hand raised as if to hit me. He dropped it slowly, rubbing his other hand where it was weighing down his waistcoat.

As soon as I stopped shouting I started to sneeze again. I walked a few yards away, regretting the loss of my handkerchiefs. There was a rag in the borrowed coat's pocket, but it was not very big and not much use. No one said anything, so far as I could tell, until I composed myself and returned to the group.

Mrs. Etaris looked hard at me as if to make certain I wouldn't start arguing again. "Now," she said briskly. "We should go in before you and Miss Redshank catch cold, but we cannot leave Miss Shipston to fend for herself. You seemed to have a suggestion as to what to do, Mr. Dart?"

He didn't say anything, glaring instead at me. I swallowed a sigh. "We believe we encountered the Lady at the Lady's Pools, Miss Shipston. Mr. Dart thinks she might, er, return for a petitioner."

"I am a monster. What are these pools?"

"Hot springs," Mrs. Etaris said. "They were where the Astan-dalan rites took place, and are sacred to the Lady of Summer and Winter."

There was a long pause. I looked around cautiously. Violet was gazing at the fishermen, who were listening to all this with an air of polite incredulity; Mr. Calloun looked as if he wanted desperately to leave and be doing something else; and Mr. Shipston seemed about to faint. Only Mrs. Etaris smiled when she caught my eye. I did my best to smile back, but wavered in the face of Mr. Dart's scowl.

"How would I get there?" Miss Shipston said from her hid-ing-space. "In a wagon?"

"No, no," said Mr. Shipston. "We can't risk it, Miranda."

Mr. Clegger cleared his throat, and then flushed in embarrass-ment when we all looked at him. Mrs. Etaris smiled kindly. "Have you an idea, Mr. Clegger?"

"This here river's the Raggle," he said. "The South Rag what runs through the Coombe joins it north of the city, and there's a weir, but if Miss Shipston was able to swim the distance, she could go down to the confluence and then up the South Rag, and from the Talgarths' there's the Ladybeck to the Pools. There's been rain enough she should be able to swim the beck, even, if she's willing. It must be five or six miles by the rivers, but."

"I've never swum very far," said Miss Shipston.

"I could walk along the shore with you," Mr. Clegger said. "Show you where to go. Make sure you don't get swept anywhere. The area around Littlegarth can be confusing, what with the old clay pits and the new embankments."

"Corindel," she said plaintively, and we all looked around until Mr. Shipston heaved himself to his feet, grabbing Mr. Clegger's shoulder for balance, and said, "Miranda, dearest, of course I'll come along with you."

***

BACK INSIDE THE Ragglebridge, Mr. Calloun deposited us in the side parlour, where a fire was burning hot and cheerful. He left us with mutterings about more hot wine and food. I managed to bring my sneezes into quieter sniffles, and sat down across the table from Mrs. Etaris, next to Mr. Dart.

Mr. Dart's stone hand fell out of his pocket and thumped uncannily against the table. I shuddered, and of course started sneezing again, and was still recovering over by the fireplace when the door burst open to reveal Mr. Calloun with his promised and long-delayed pot of mulled wine, accompanied by the rather well-dressed and certainly well-lit-up figure of the Honourable Rag.

"Hulloo-oo-oo," he called, flinging himself into the room and my vacated chair with all assurance. "Glad to see the reports of floods and fire and wild magic are completely wrong!—Although, I say, Mr. Greenwing, what's this I hear about you charging into burning—Gadsbrook! Miss Indrilline!"

We all turned to look at Violet. She gazed at the Honourable Rag with a composed expression. "I'm sorry, sir, but you are mistaken. I am Violet Redshank, lately of Morrowlea."

The Honourable Rag seemed to have read *Aurora* recently enough to recognize the name, for he choked. Mr. Calloun busied himself passing out cups of hot wine and didn't betray any illegal reading. I tried to remember where I'd heard the name *Indrilline* before. Something I'd read in History of Magic? Or perhaps Archi-tecture? Was there an architect named Indrilline ... ?

The Honourable Rag grinned, his initial surprise fading now into a luxurious and exquisitely presented boredom. "Are you now? Come to see our Mr. Greenwing, have you?"

She gave me a cool glance. I took a gulp of wine, still feeling shivery and snively, which was infuriating, and stepped a bit closer to the fireplace.

"No. I am seeking my cousin."

"Alone? A lady of *your* quality should hardly be travelling on her own."

Violet ran her hands down her borrowed dress and raised her eyebrows at the Honourable Rag. "You are very free with your as-sumptions, given that we have never met before."

"Oh, that's what we learned at Tara. Assumptions, assurance, asininity, you name it. I'm the baron's son. Roald Ragnor."

She curtsied with devastating calculation. He smiled fatuously while she removed a golden ring I realized belatedly was the one from the pie. Dropping my gaze, I saw he wore none. Violet spoke seriously. "Do you know this, sir?"

I had known the Honourable Rag well, four years before. I knew where to look when he told a lie, how the corners of his eyes would crinkle at the inner joke (prevarication always was a joke for him, no matter how serious the circumstances were to Mr. Dart or me or anyone else), how he would flick his fingers off his thumb when he was about to tell a whopper.

He didn't flick his fingers, but his eyes crinkled before he tipped his head back and roared with laughter.

"Gadsbrook, I thought you'd ask me some impossible thing out of the old riddle-books of Morrowlea. Do they keep them still? At Tara we always laughed about 'the old riddle-books of Morrowlea, kept under strictest lock and key, that none but the proctors see, in case of truth and verity ...'"

He tossed the ring up in the air, caught it, and slid it easily onto his signet finger. "Of course I recognize it, it's my very own ring, and I didn't think to see it again. I lost it at a—" He aimed a grin in Mrs. Etaris' direction. "I lost it at the Green Dragon, where I'd gone for a pint on my way out catching worms. But stay! How did you come by it?"

"That is my own business, Master Ragnor. When did you *lose* it?"

"Does it matter so to you?" He frowned at her, looked up her up and down twice with something between appreciation and a connoisseur's disinterestedness. One finger flicked, then another, down his right hand. "This Monday past, Miss Redshank. Now, I have answered you, tell me true how it came to you?"

I'd forgotten his penchant for doggerel verse. I gritted my teeth and drank my wine and was relieved only a bit to see that Violet seemed immune to his charm—though perhaps that was because she seemed to suspect he'd been involved in the disappearance of her cousin. "I found it in a herring pie."

I would have sworn his astonishment was genuine, for the moment before he flung himself back into the chair again and laughed even more heartily.

"Not that fish pie of Mr. Greenwing's! By th' Emperor, the town is gone mad for fish! I had my dear father demanding herring and only north coastal herring for his new cat, which is a persnickety beast from the coastlands, and turns up her nose at a good piece of rabbit that any other cat would be glad of. Give me a dog any day," he added expansively, "a grey courser, a setter, a pointer, an otter hound—" he grinned at me, eyes crinkling—"a falcon and a boar-spear, and I am happy. Cats! Only good for mice. Fish pie, indeed. Were you at the Green Dragon on your night off, Mr. Greenwing?"

"Master Ragnor," Mrs. Etaris said calmly, as I twisted my hands firmly in the too-long sleeves of my borrowed shirt, and did not lunge across the intervening space to punch the baron's son, however dearly I wanted to. "You say you lost this ring on Monday past?"

"Did I say that? I think it was Monday. It might have been Tuesday. Or Wednesday. Not a lot going on," he added to Violet. "What with the weather as foul as it was this week, the good boys were at work and the bad boys at play—inside. Albeit—Mr. Dart—where were you this Tuesday past?"

"Threshing grain in my brother's barn."

"Another good boy." He laughed again, pushed himself back, ready to leave. "Any more interrogations for me, Miss Redshank? Mrs. Etaris? Mr. Greenwing? Now that you're finally back to scandalize the good gentry, life should be much more interesting. Fire, mermaids, herring pies, gossip, and half the town jammed with fools debating the folly of the rest, and all of them talking about you. I'm delighted you're back."

I decided I had best not say anything. Mr. Dart pursed his lips, but said nothing, either. Violet said, "Do you know anything of the Legendarium, Master Roald?"

There was a pause, which I thought suspicious, before he grinned. "No, why? Yon mad rumours of mermaids?"

"The Knockermen," she said evenly.

He gave another great shout of laughter. I thought it made him look a right ass indeed. "You'll be asking about goblins and ghouls in the Woods Noirell next, won't you? Keep to the coast, Miss Redshank, and leave Mr. Greenwing to his family bugbears. Lady wot he has enough of 'em." He stood up, with a careless nod to Mrs. Etaris, and bounced out the door.

"Well," Mrs. Etaris began, but the Honourable Rag bounded back in the door and interrupted her.

"I say, Miss Redshank, tomorrow evening Dame Talgarth's having a do, and Dominus Alvestone's invited. He's studying botanical folklore of south Fiellan, he might well know something of your Knockermen. Do come with me. Dame Talgarth won't mind in the least."

Mrs. Etaris coughed; Violet gave him a cool frown. "Thank you for the invitation, Master Roald, but I'm afraid I have other plans for tomorrow."

"Suit yourself, but you'll miss out," he said cheerfully, then winked at me. "It bodes to be full of gossip this week."

When the door shut behind him Mr. Dart said, "Miss Indrilline?"

"I have no idea what he was talking about," said Violet, and I wondered again where I'd heard the name before.

I tried to rally my thoughts, rubbing my throat absently. It felt raw from all the shouting. "We should have asked Miss Shipston about these Knockermen."

Mrs. Etaris raised her eyebrows at me. "That would hardly have been either kind or discreet."

Mr. Dart frowned at his arm. "I'm going to the Talgarths tomorrow. I could ask Dominus Alvestone."

"Do you think that's a good idea?" I asked, the silver light and the howling cultists coming violently to mind. I shuddered and reached for more wine to cover up the movement. "If he is the Silver Priest ..."

"Good point," Mr. Dart said, with suspicious haste.

Violet fiddled with a dangling thread on her sleeve. "Jemis—Mr. Greenwing, that is, do you know anything about the Knockermen from when you read History of Magic?"

I sat down again, shivering harder than ever, but determined not to show it. "It sounds a bit familiar, but I can't think exactly. They might be one of the kinds of Good Neighbours. But I didn't read much about them."

Mrs. Etaris said, "The person who would know about the Good Neighbours is Dominus Gleason."

"He bought some herring, too," I said, sneezing. "Ugh. This is *worse* than last winter."

"I think I'd rather have a stone arm than your perpetual cold," Mr. Dart said. "Though of course it would be preferable to have neither."

"Perhaps we should make a sling for your arm, Mr. Dart, before we go," Mrs. Etaris said. "Miss Redshank, Dominus Gleason—properly he would be Magister Gleason, but he chooses not to parade his talents—is a professor emeritus from Fiella-by-the-Sea. The university there once had a fair school of magic, but they closed that faculty after the Interim and Dominus Gleason retired here. It occurs to me, Mr. Greenwing, that Dominus Gleason might be able to determine whether my suspicions about your sensitivity are correct."

It would have to be Dominus Gleason, I thought, but was hesitant to try to put my deep reluctance to become obligated to him into words. It wasn't as if I had anything besides him being disturbing to accuse him of. I swallowed a few gulps of wine, and tried to come up with a better excuse.

"I'd rather wait till we find out if he's in league with Knocker-men, whatever they are, before asking him if I have an undeveloped talent for sniffing out magic."

"I love how emphatic your sneezes can be," said Violet, with a sudden bright smile, and for a brief deceptive moment I felt warm.

***

THE HONOURABLE RAG'S comment about the difficulty of getting through town was spot-on. We started up the main street from the Ragglebridge towards the square, only to be blocked by a crush of wagons and carts coming down both the main street and the first northern crossroads. One of the out-of-town farmers hailed Mr. Dart.

"Mr. Linkett," Mr. Dart said. "Whatever has caused the jumble here? And why are you trying to get out of town this way?"

Mr. Linkett, who was in his mid-forties, it looked like (and dressed rather like I was, in a rough green wool tunic and leather leggings, with the addition of a flat woollen cap), rolled his eyes. "Well, Mr. Dart, it's like this. The market-bell rang the fire alarm a couple of hours ago, so all the marketers between the fountain and the easter side moved their stalls to help with the water chain. Then just as that seemed to be calming down and we're wondering if we might get some custom after all, the hue and cry sets off from the souther side that someone's herd of pigs has gotten loose and is heading for the river through the poulterers, and by the time we'd caught the hens back—well, it's just as well you hadn't brought any of your ducks in, Mr. Dart."

Mr. Dart declined to comment. I tried not to laugh. Mr. Linkett chortled.

"I decided it was about time to head home, and was blessing my stars that I was heading north, given that the easter and the souther sides were such a jumble. But when I got towards the gate I found the north road blocked something wicked. It seems Justice Talgarth's man was coming back ahead with the luggage when something went awry with the carriage and it lost a wheel coming over the bridge, then the horses freaked out because of that and the smoke coming up, and the carriage turned over at the bridge, and of course they was bringing all the Justice's books from a summer away, and there were a bunch of people crowding round asking the carter for the news—so you can think what a mess *that* was. So I got my wagon turned around and decided to go the long route round by the Ragglebridge and up the old highway, but so did half the market, and not to mention that all the townsfolk are worried about the fire catching, and want gossip of the Justice's travels, and in the middle of all this—"

"There's more?"

"Aye! In the middle of all this, the Chief Constable," and Mr. Linkett bobbed his head awkwardly at Mrs. Etaris, "the Chief Constable came out all in a pother from the constable-house—the rest of the constables were helping with the market crowd already, o' course—to find Lady Flora rushing up to him, and they bumped into each other, and then just as they were starting to talk the Baron's son comes riding up on that red-bay hunter of his, with Dominus Gleason in tow behind him, and says that the Scholar said his house had been burgled while he was away. So the Chief Constable asks what had been taken, and the Scholar won't say, because it's magic most like, and they're having an argument about what to do, and the Chief Constable says there've been a whole lot of strangers in town, and wants to go looking for them, and Lady Flora mentioned Mr. Jemis, because o' course she's got a nose for gossip. But then—"

"Yet more?"

"Oh, aye, Mr. Dart, what a market-day it's been in town! So they're talking, and the Baron's son is all over the place blocking everyone from moving with his horse fidgeting. I stood where I was, a cause I'd been shoved up under the stairs of the Court House while everyone was to-ing and fro-ing in the square. And then this woman I don't know came out of the Court House, looking like she'd seen a ghost, and she went up to Lady Flora and slapped her on the face, and then when we were all still staring, walked off."

"Someone *slapped* Lady Flora?"

"Oh, aye! The Chief Constable about had apoplexy. We market-folk were all staring, and then what should happen but one of the constables comes running up, yelling his head off that he's seen a mermaid in the Raggle, and welladay was he ever going to follow her to kingdom come—and half the town with him. So I thought I'd best come home before something else happened and my cart ended up catching fire or something, and here I am. But I'd be sure cautious goin' into town today, Mr. Dart, it's half mad. Come along with me, if you like."

"Thank you, Mr. Linkett, but I'd better ... I'd best find Cartwright and, well, we have some other things to do. Will you send a message to my brother once you're back in Dartington telling him that I think I'll be in town another night?"

Mr. Linkett nodded slowly, and took up the reins of his big draught horse, which had been waiting with its eyes closed and a hoof cocked up as if all these troubles and trials were nothing to it. "Aye, Mr. Dart, I'm sure all the county'll be at the Broken Arrow lookin' to hear the news from town tonight, and Master Dart with them." The farmer geed his horse and set off at a slow clop in the wake of the other marketers, who had cleared out somewhat while we'd been talking.

"What a day in town indeed!" Mrs. Etaris said. "Let us go to Dominus Gleason's the back way. Fortunately we have no horses to delay us."

Indeed, horses couldn't have gone the route she took us by. I was once again amazed at Mrs. Etaris' knowledge of the back alleys and little gaps between houses, but was too busy trying not to let waves of dizziness overwhelm me to say anything. Mr. Dart, who had managed with Mrs. Calloun's assistance to outfit himself with a sling, did say, as we turned onto Dominus Gleason's cul-de-sac after edging along a narrow path between raspberry canes and a stone wall, "How do you know all these back ways, Mrs. Etaris?"

She smiled at us as she stepped aside to let me ring the bell at the door. "Oh, I've always enjoyed exploring places, Mr. Dart. Don't you?"

I had to hold onto the doorframe for balance; I hoped it was unobtrusively. Mr. Dart rearranged the knot of his sling and didn't reply. I gulped, throat raw and thick-feeling.

The ancient butler opened the door. He was frowning even more severely than the day before. The air that wafted out of the house was even stronger—I fainted.

***

A LITTLE LATER I came to myself on a couch in a sitting room of such fantastic appearance that I thought I was hallucinating. It looked like the inside of the Lady's cathedral I'd seen in Kingsford, elaborate vaulting with medallions and moulded fruit and grains and things. All of them brightly painted stone—except that it didn't smell like stone—

"It's all right," Mrs. Etaris said calmly. I felt pressure on the back of my neck, and bent down obediently until my head was between my knees. "Breathe through your mouth. Once. Twice. Again.—Thank you, Mr. Whilt. Here, eat this, Mr. Greenwing."

I accepted what she handed me, some sort of sweet dry biscuit. I chewed slowly, swallowed, and after another few minutes my brain stopped whirling in my head, and I felt as if I could manage to sit up. I did so cautiously. Mrs. Etaris leaned close under pretext of placing her cool hand on my forehead, and murmured into my ear, "That was perfect; he wouldn't have let us in otherwise. Is that better, Mr. Greenwing?"

"Yes," I said, stopping my nod halfway through as I started to feel odd again. The sneezes were threatening to recur. I breathed shallowly in the hopes that I might be able to prevent them from overwhelming me again. The whole house smelled musty, papery, dusty, and there was that strange edge of corruption—or glue?

"I really didn't want visitors," Dominus Gleason said in a high, whiny sort of voice. I blinked away the water in my eyes. I'd never been into any room in the old Gleason place but for sneaking visits into the library. We were in what seemed to be some sort of drawing room or personal chapel. The furniture was old and heavy, and

Mr. Dart and Violet both sat uncomfortably on the edges of their seats.

"I'm very sorry to trouble you," Mrs. Etaris said, "but I think Mr. Greenwing will need to sit for a few minutes longer before he will be able to continue."

"What's wrong with him, anyway? Ugh. Strange for a young man to faint like that."

"He must have breathed in too much smoke when most valiantly rescuing someone trapped in Mr. Shipston's house earlier. It has been a trying day for everyone, I'm afraid. I understand you told the Chief Constable you'd had a burglary?"

I hoped they were watching Dominus Gleason's face. I closed my eyes against the riotous colour of the room, and concentrated on not retching from the waves of dizziness that seemed still to be coming at me. Someone pushed a glass into my hands, and I sipped the cool water gratefully, wondering how it was that Mrs. Etaris managed to imply so easily that her husband had told her about the burglary.

"I'm glad he's treating it more seriously than he implied earlier," Dominus Gleason replied. His voice did sound thin and—what was the word?—querulous, that was it. "I was to be out of town for a few days, Mrs. Etaris, as Whilt told you yesterday when you called. Ugh. When I came home I discovered that someone had broken in and stolen some of my books."

"Infamous! Have you any idea who might have been interested? What manner of books were they?"

He coughed, a hacking sort of thing that sounded painfully congested, and recurred in a kind of hiccoughing effect through his speeches. "Ugh. I've long had problems with boys breaking into my library. Ugh. I don't practice magic any longer, of course, Mrs. Etaris, but I could hardly destroy my books, could I? Ugh. It may be that magic comes back into favour in future."

"That is quite possible, indeed. It seems likely this is more of the same, does it not?"

"That's what the Chief Constable said. He doesn't like me—no sense shaking your head, Mrs. Etaris, your husband has never liked me, it goes back before the Fall when ... well. Ugh. I used to be outspoken about some changes I thought would be worth seeing happen, and he disagreed. And of course he disapproves mightily that I chose to retire here. Ugh. It's my family home, Mrs. Etaris, where else would I go? I have no family left, this house is all to me. Ugh. And I am outraged, yes, outraged, Mrs. Etaris, that someone would break in and damage my library looking for—"

He stopped abruptly. I thought back to when Mr. Dart and the Honourable Rag and I were the boys breaking in. Everyone had known how easy it was to get into Dominus Gleason's library; he regularly left one of the windows unlocked. Everyone thought he was trying to foment rebellion and support for the Red Company. The rumours ran clear that if one wanted to know about Fitzroy Angursell's poetry—or, after the Fall, about that so-unfashionable magic—you never asked directly, but Dominus Gleason's was where you went.

"It doesn't matter," he added. "I will report it properly to the Chief Constable. Ugh."

"Of course. The constabulary is the appropriate recourse for theft. Nevertheless, if you decide otherwise, and give me the titles, I can make discreet enquiries among my fellow booksellers to see if they come on the market. We do try to keep limits on the trade in stolen books, Dominus Gleason."

"Erm, yes. Ugh. Now Mrs. Etaris, you came yesterday and again today, you obviously have a question for me?"

He spoke too hastily, I thought, and knew Mrs. Etaris would have noticed too—and Violet as well, she was always alert to what people were not saying. Except for Lark, lying Lark—I rested the cool glass against my forehead. I'd been doing so well trying not to think about Lark.

"Oh, yes, of course. I was distracted by Mr. Greenwing. I had two questions for you. The first is that I understand you acquired some herring from Mr. Fogerty this week, and I was wondering whether you had perhaps a recipe for herring pie? I was feeling somewhat homesick for a taste of Fiella-by-the-Sea, but my sister did not have the recipe, and it occurred to me you might."

"Herring pie? I ... That's the dish with all the cream, isn't it? I suppose Mrs. Whilt might have a recipe for that, if you ask her."

The old man sounded nonplussed at the question. He paused, then added, "I feel I must explain to you, Mrs. Etaris, that I am not a well man. Ugh. I have been consulting with a noted physicker of Inghail who has been researching in the barony this year, and he had recommended I eat more fish—and that most plainly.

"I hate fish," he added plaintively. "Ugh. I was away yesterday for meditation—that is another aspect of his practice, which does not follow the Rondelan method. Mr. Greenwing might do well to consult with him, as clearly his running cold does not answer to Fiellanese physicking, either, and Mr. Shipston will be in no good position to give Ghilousetten potions again any time soon."

He made his hacking cough again, and I realized it was a form of laughter.

Once he subsided Mr. Dart said thoughtfully, "Would the physicker of Inghail be Dominus Alvestone? He consulted with my brother's library in the summer."

"Yes, yes, Mr. Dart, Dominus Alvestone is most well known for his work with—well, with the sort of ailments that those of my profession have faced since the Fall. Ugh. He has been most intrigued by the stability and general health of Fiellan, and especially in our barony. Ugh. We're notable for being one of the least affected regions in all of Alinor, did you know that? But no one knows why."

"How curious," Mrs. Etaris said. "Mr. Greenwing, are you feeling somewhat recovered?"

I opened my eyes and set my jaw against the swirling sense of wrongness. "I think so. Thank you, Dominus Gleason, for your aid."

"Not at all, not at all," he said. "Is there anything else I can do for you?"

I caught a glance from Mrs. Etaris, and so despite my reluctance, I said, "As it happens, I had a question for you myself, sir."

"Oh?" He hacked into a handkerchief. He did look unwell, I thought, with dark circles under his eyes, and a way of holding himself as if his skin hurt. He was smiling at me with an odd gleam in his eyes. I swallowed hard. I really didn't want to be in his obligation.

"I came across mention of something called the Knockermen in Ghilousette, and I was wondering if you might know whom I should consult to find out more."

There was a strained silence, and then Dominus Gleason sank back into his seat. "I think you had better sit down again, and tell me what is really going on, Mr. Greenwing."

Chapter Twenty

I GLANCED AROUND helplessly, the waves of dizziness throwing my wits off.

Mrs. Etaris said, "Perhaps I can summarize—I think Mr. Greenwing is not yet feeling quite himself. Mr. Shipston mentioned that he had moved away from Ghilousette with some fear for the Knockermen. This seemed to have some relation to a question that had brought Mr. Greenwing's friend from Morrowlea, Miss Redshank, here to Ragnor Bella."

"Miss Redshank, eh?" he said, with more hacking, and a determined leer that got my back up. Violet smiled at him coolly and I realized she probably had to fend off those sorts of leers frequently. No wonder she'd worked so hard with weapons in the Morrowlea salles. "Seeking the Knockermen instead of the Longworths, are you?"

The Longworths were the family of assassins that the disguised Tenebra went seeking in *Aurora*. I risked a glance at Mrs. Etaris, who looked politely bewildered. Violet smiled at Dominus Gleason with almost exactly the same expression she'd given the Honourable Rag when he'd asked her if she was one of the Misses Indril-line.

"I seek information," she said. "Mr. Greenwing has offered his assistance."

"He could sniff them out, assuming they don't come for him first," he said with a disturbingly lascivious glance at me. I started to sneeze again in discomfort, and he hacked. "Didn't you realize you're shedding magic like dandruff? Fool boy. They'll be coming for you next, if they're in Fiellan. Ugh. They could make good use of someone who can smell magic. Ugh. But my offer still stands, Mr. Greenwing."

"What are they?" Mr. Dart said, casting me a worried glance.

"The Knockermen? Ugh. In the Legendarium, they're one of the bands of the Good Neighbours. They're to be found in mines—they knock, hence the name. You don't want to stay in a mine after the Knockermen start knocking, because it means they're doing their mining. They follow human workings to harvest magic—from people and from places. We don't have mines in Fiellan, so it's no surprise you don't hear much of them. The heart of their realm was in the Kilromby Islands, in the tin mines."

"Ghilousette has a lot of mines," Mr. Dart said.

I already thought I knew the answer to that, and shook my head. Dominus Gleason nodded in approval. I tried not to recoil obviously.

"Iron and salt mines. Ugh. The Good Neighbours don't like iron and salt, Mr. Dart. Or the ban on magic. Fools! The Duke will find that ban will come back to bite him."

"Have they left their mines?" Mrs. Etaris asked. "Is that what you mean about Mr. Greenwing perhaps being in danger?"

Dominus Gleason hacked long enough that his butler came up with a glass of water into which he stirred a pale pink powder. I sneezed heartily at a sudden blast of lilac as he approached, and everyone looked sidelong at me. Dominus Gleason slurped his medicine, which seemed to soothe his chest but make his watery eyes yet more glittery.

"I am still in communication with many of my old colleagues," he said. "Over the past few years there have been those looking for the old books. Ugh. The Legendarium. The old ways. I am a Scholar, I have my standards. Some of my colleagues ... Ugh. Not everywhere is as accommodating as Ragnor Bella. They take what they can."

"And the Knockermen?"

"I have been hearing," he said, "only hearing, and I tell you this because I know you are discreet, Mrs. Etaris, because Mr. Green-wing has his own problems, and Mr. Dart I know your heart is high and brave." He didn't mention Violet, but then of course, I thought, he would presume from her choice of name that she was a kindred spirit—which I supposed she was.

"Ghilousette is not the only place where magic is banned, nor is it the only place where people yet are born with magic or still desire what can be done with it. Ugh. The Knockermen in the Legendarium mine for magic. The new Knockermen have learned ways to steal magic for their own purposes."

Violet spoke tensely. "Are there Knockermen in Ragnor Bella?"

Dominus Gleason cackled. "Miss Redshank, if I knew that, do you think I would still be here? They would not leave me to speak. I am old, but I still have my magic, and I have many books of power. No, they have not come to Fiellan yet. This is a rumour in Ghilousette, in Tifou, in Tarkin, and of course in Kilromby. Nowhere that people still keep some of the old ways alive. Magic in Fiellan is unfashionable, but it is not banned; unspoken of, but still practised. Ugh. Ragnor Bella has always been most conservative. I have some respect still, from those who understand the ways of things. I have my knots on the waystones. And I have my students, you may be sure." He hacked again, and looked very meaningfully at me. "When the student is ready the master comes. Ugh."

O Lady, I thought passionately, let *anyone* else come.

Mrs. Etaris spoke quietly. "Which of your books were stolen, Dominus Gleason?"

He hesitated again, then shrugged unconvincingly. "Ugh. Nothing of this sort. Ugh. History of religion."

"Ah," she said, and looked around at us. "I think we've probably taken up too much of your time already. Mr. Greenwing, if you're feeling well enough, shall we go see what havoc has been wreaked in the market square in our absences?"

"Mm," I said, and we all stood up. Violet came up beside me and laced her arm through mine, as if for politeness' sake. I smiled gratefully at her.

Dominus Gleason walked us to the door. His eyes looked even more glittery, and I wondered what exactly had been in his medicine. He smelled of camphor and lilacs and something else that made me sneeze. Violet squeezed my arm as I tried to cover the noise with my pitiful handkerchief.

"Mr. Greenwing," the Scholar said, stepping far too close to me so he could speak. I didn't trust my body to reply, as I was clenching my lips shut in the hopes I wouldn't retch or sneeze, so raised my eyebrows. "Mr. Greenwing. Come see me when you are ready."

I bowed curtly, hoping it merely looked like I was trying not to be sick again rather than insult him. He made his hacking laughter again, then plucked at his loose shirt. I wondered abruptly whether there were many light cuts across his torso that made him so uncomfortable in sitting, and so admiring in his talk of the old ways, and swallowed against revulsion.

"I hope," Violet said after we had followed Mrs. Etaris and Mr. Dart down the street a ways, "that there are other teachers of magic in Ragnor Bella."

***

WE PICKED OUR way back through town to Elderflower Books. The market square was empty but full of more litter than usual. Pinger and Garsom were mooching around picking up the scraps of paper, vegetables, cloth, and so on; they were paid by the town council to keep things tidy. Mrs. Etaris waved at them as she unlocked the store. Its blinds were still drawn, the chairs left akimbo.

"Would anyone like some coffee before we start?" Mr. Dart asked. "And food?"

"Oh, that is a good idea, Mr. Dart. Miss Redshank, will you go with Mr. Greenwing to help carry?"

Violet linked her arm in mine again as we crossed the square to the bakery. Mr. Inglesides was in the process of closing up for the afternoon. "Mr. Greenwing!" he said, smiling, as I entered, and then gaped at Violet. "Er, hello, miss."

"This is Miss Redshank, a friend of mine from Morrowlea," I said, and from his tiny frown of recognition knew he definitely had read *Aurora*. "We had a bit of an accident earlier and ended up in the river. Do you possibly have any coffee left, Mr. Inglesides? And

I see you have some buns—could we get those?"

"You can have the whole lot," he said, putting aside the broom and going to rinse his hands in the basin and ewer set behind the counter. "I'm closing early today after the fuss in the market. Miss Pilker—my assistant, Miss Redshank—lives down the same street as Mr. Shipston whose house caught fire, so I sent her home early." He shook his head as he put the remaining sweet buns into a paper bag. "She fusses so, it seemed a hardship to make her stay. That was before all the madness started in the square. The bookstore's been closed since this morning, though—anything wrong there?"

"Miss Redshank is a collector," I said, "so Mrs. Etaris thought to close the store to permit her some privacy in her decisions."

"Oh?" Mr. Inglesides looked askance at Violet's peasant dress. She smiled at him with slow mischief, and he melted. "Oh, I see. How ... how much coffee you do want, Mr. Greenwing?"

"Enough for four, please, Mr. Inglesides."

After the flustered baker passed us the goods, and in a sudden access of geniality refused any payment, gaping the while at Violet, we went back out. Pinger and Garsom were still picking through the litter, but Pinger ambled over as I adjusted my grip on the hot jug. I nodded at them. "Good afternoon, Mr. Pinger."

He looked a bit gratified at the address, and dashed off his cap to make a sort of bow (complete with heel-click, I was half-embarrassed to see). "Mr. Greenwing."

He paused. Violet was looking mystified but polite. I wondered what he wanted, but also knew he did not respond well to prodding—he'd been an old soldier before the Fall, and in the Interim had been muddled a bit by the magic, and now tended to wildly elliptical pronouncements. His friend Garsom treated him as something like a prophet, calling out 'Hear ye! Hear ye!' whenever Pinger had something to say.

"Mr. Greenwing," Pinger said again, and sighed heavily. He looked up at the sky, scratched his nose, looked at Violet with an intense and somewhat accusatory stare, scratched his ear—his tics always made me start to feel horribly itchy—and finally he said, "Justice Talgarth was asking about you."

"Really? He's not back yet, I thought? Who—whom was he asking?"

"The Old Gods," Pinger said ominously, not quite spoiling the effect by tapping his nose meaningfully.

"What a strange man," Violet murmured as he trundled back across to where Garsom was carefully piling things next to the fountain. I tipped my head back at a waft of fresh air, seeing that the earlier sun had clouded over again. Mrs. Landry cut across the far corner of the square, frowning at the two men and then waving at us before heading towards the hotel. "Does everyone know you in town?"

I opened the door to Elderflower Books for her. "What do you mean?"

"Just that everyone seems to know you by name."

Mr. Dart looked up from where he was sitting at the table, examining his stone arm. "Oh, everyone knows our Mr. Greenwing. His family affairs were the most exciting thing to happen in Ragnor Bella before this confounded stargazy pie."

"And no doubt they'll continue to excite comment long after," I said, trying not to sound sour or depressed at the thought, depositing coffee and bakery treasures on the table before him. "Pinger wanted to tell me that Justice Talgarth was asking the Old Gods after me. Because of course that's just want I wanted to hear."

"Not much we can do if the Justice is part of that cult."

"You don't reckon—" I began, and then stopped. Mrs. Etaris had come out of the back with her hands full of mugs. She looked, as ever, proper: upright carriage, perfectly unexceptionable gown with reasonable corseting, her ginger-mouse hair done up in the soft twists appropriate to a middle-aged matron. But there was something in the set of her chin and the glint in her eyes that made me wonder, suddenly, why she'd hired me.

"Please do sit down, Miss Redshank. Will you fetch the cream and sugar, Mr. Greenwing?"

"Yes," I said, and while fetching these and a stack of side plates (the back room was well stocked against visitors to tea and Embroidery Circle meetings) tried to recapture what I had begun to say. When I came out again I took a bun to nibble.

"You were about to say something?" Mr. Dart said while I tried not to scarf the bun down. It had suddenly occurred to me that apart from half a piece of gingerbread I hadn't eaten since breakfast—no wonder I'd been feeling dizzy. My throat felt unaccountably sore. Getting sick again was just what I needed.

"I don't know ... I think I've lost it. Go ahead."

"Six households bought herring," Mrs. Etaris said. "The Baron, the Talgarths, Dominus Gleason, Mr. Shipston, and Mrs. Landry." I watched her tick them off on her fingers, and recalled the Honourable Rag doing the same while he lied to us. Mr. Dart and I used to tease him for his easy tells—did he remember that?

"I believe we can disregard my sister. I know she has no extra person in her house besides Miss Featherhaugh, and given Mr. Landry's staunch belief in all things conventional, I think we can absolve him of trucking in magic. Mr. Shipston, as we have seen, most certainly does truck in magic. However, since he is afraid the Knockermen are after his sister, I doubt he has done anything more than try to lie low."

"And have his house burn down," I said, sneezing reflexively.

"I think we may have to leave that to the Chief Constable to investigate," Mrs. Etaris said, with an expression suggesting that what the Chief Constable investigated was largely determined by her. I looked inquiringly; she added, "My husband is not likely to, ah, press too hard if his investigations should point towards our town's leading citizens."

Violet stirred. "I have reason to believe someone—and I think it must have been either Mr. Shipston or Dominus Gleason—both of them previously *Magister*, is that not so?—is in frequent contact with some rather unsavoury people in Ghilousette. That was what brought me to Ragnor Bella in the first place."

Mrs. Etaris looked judicious again. "Dominus Gleason certainly was once Magister Gleason, but I don't believe Mr. Shipston ever taught in a university—he claims to have been an alchemist and then a physicker in Newbury, and his appropriate title would therefore have been Learned. But of course it would be improper now to call them by anything other than their desired titles. How someone introduces himself—or herself—is the final consideration, Miss Redshank."

Violet quirked her mouth. "Yes, I see. Thank you, Mrs. Etaris."

"Now, Dominus Gleason might well have been deliberately misleading us. However, since we have no proof of such—"

"Besides how creepy he is," put in Mr. Dart, casting me another worried glance. "I'm not asking him about my arm. Lady knows what he'd suggest I do about it."

"Mm. Fortunately or unfortunately, we cannot assume that means he is guilty, Mr. Dart. Let us go forward under the assumption that Dominus Gleason told us the truth, and that he himself has nothing to do with the Knockermen or Miss Redshank's cousin. Or Mr. Dart's arm."

Mr. Dart did not seem to think that a foregone conclusion; neither did I, but then again both of us had been away, and Mrs. Etaris presumably knew Dominus Gleason better than we did. I tried to think. "That leaves, then, Baron Ragnor and the Talgarths."

"The Honourable Rag was definitely lying about something," Mr. Dart said, "but I'm not sure if it was anything more than that he was gambling at the Green Dragon and didn't want to say so directly."

"Would his father be so concerned about what he fed a cat?" Violet asked doubtfully. "It seems very odd."

"Our beloved baron is decidedly odd," I said, remembering some particularly eccentric occasions at the Manor. "But he is also vehemently against magic—or he was."

Mr. Dart and Mrs. Etaris both shook their heads. Mr. Dart said, "If anything, it's worse than ever. But then again, we did see the Honourable Rag—Master Roald, that is," he corrected hastily, "out-and-about."

"With a werelight," I mentioned.

"Mmm, yes, that's true. But the Honourable Rag doesn't—or didn't, anyway—hate magic to that extent."

"He doesn't hate anything to any extent."

"That's true." I frowned at the table. "He did go to Tara ..."

"That doesn't necessarily mean he's gone to the bad, Mr.

Greenwing."

Violet snorted. I smiled reluctantly. I wanted to say that the Honourable Rag could easily have fallen afoul of bad company while at Tara, as the university was on one horn of the headland comprising the city of Orio, but before I could formulate a way to say so that did not break confidences from before we went to university, Mrs. Etaris knocked her hand on the table.

I started, and looked guiltily at her. She smiled. "While this gossip is no doubt entertaining to you both, I believe it is more important that we determine what we can of Miss Redshank's cousin. Since we began our enquiries about the pie so openly, those who are responsible may well be alerted. We must make haste before any changes occur."

We nodded. I drank some coffee too quickly, coughed, and then said: "What about the Talgarths?"

Mrs. Etaris sighed. "Yes. What about the Talgarths? We have not been able to make any enquiries of them. They do not, so far as I know, have any connection whatsoever with Ghilousette."

"They're known for keeping pre-Fall standards in their house," Mr. Dart said. "Lights, hot water, cold boxes, everything. Always think it must cost them Dame Talgarth's fortune to keep it all running."

"They're definitely using magic, and at the least hosting a wizard. Who may very well be Domina Ringley's attendant."

"The one who was running after her through the market this morning?" Violet asked.

I nodded. "They're doing something secretive, to build a moat around their house."

"That was because they kept getting flooded," Mr. Dart protested. "They mightn't have been doing anything nefarious."

"They were creeping around at midnight."

"So were we," he said, and we both laughed. "Nevertheless, we weren't intending to be there—it was quite by accident, Mrs. Etaris, I assure you."

"I am entirely reassured."

"They couldn't have been out by chance," I said. "They had a werelight and a servant with them. And they mentioned the cultists. And a harvest."

"That doesn't seem to lead us towards Ghilousette," Mrs. Etaris said thoughtfully. "Justice Talgarth's hobby is breeding perennial sweet peas, and Dame Talgarth's interests are almost entirely in maintaining her social position by judicious dinner parties."

"I thought sweet peas were annuals," I said, blowing my nose again at the mere thought of the ones we'd run into. "They were my mother's favourite flower," I added when they looked at me.

Violet smiled. "They're one of my favourites, too."

"I believe the Justice has been crossing them with some of the perennial vetches to see if he can't breed a new species." Mrs. Etaris took a few sips of coffee. "Miss Redshank, could you tell me a little of your cousin? When was she taken?"

Violet rubbed her fingers free from crumbs. "Daphne Carlin. She's, ah, younger than I, but because I had not gone immediately to university after the Entrance Examinations, we were in the same year at university. She'd written to invite me to Newbury on my way home from Morrowlea, but when I arrived at my aunt's I found she hadn't arrived. She never did come, so I began my search to find out what had happened."

I tried to remind myself I oughtn't to trust Violet. Somehow I kept forgetting and going back to how things had been before the spring.

Mr. Dart said, "I can't imagine how the Talgarths could be keeping someone captive in their house—Dame Talgarth hosts a dinner every week, and a larger party once a month. Never any expense spared. Pity you two aren't coming. Are you sure you don't want to, Miss Redshank?"

"I'm meeting an acquaintance from home tomorrow," she said, and I thought: You said you ran away from home at fourteen. Who can this be?

And then I thought: Do I trust what she says now, or what she said in a burning house when no one at all could hear us?

Violet added, "And I'm surprised at you, Mr. Dart, inviting me to someone else's house."

"Yes, but I already know you can't go," he replied, smiling, "so don't think my manners are as easy as Roald Ragnor's."

"Easy's one word for it," Violet murmured.

"He looked more than a little foxed," I pointed out. "But it was almost as rude as when Dame Talgarth gave me the cut direct in the bakery yesterday.—Oh!"

"What is it?"

"Mrs. Talgarth's sister. She's a Scholar, and she's from Kilromby, and she's—" I frowned. "No, I've lost it again."

"Kilromby. She wouldn't have any connection to Ghilousette, either," Mr. Dart said.

I stifled a sneeze. "Kilromby was one of the places Dominus Gleason mentioned as having to do with the Knockermen."

"The ones in the Legendarium," he objected. "It sounded as if the new Knockermen are all to do with Ghilousette." He frowned.

"Mrs. Etaris, do you know anyone who went to Kilromby from Ragnor Bella? We could ask around to see what reputation Domina Ringley has."

"I don't think anyone has gone to Kilromby of late," Mrs. Etaris said thoughtfully. "Not since the troubles began there; no one has wanted to take ships."

Violet said, "My cousin did."

Mr. Dart and I were both starting to speak, and we stumbled into quiet. Violet flushed, I think in annoyance that we hadn't been listening to her. "My cousin went to Kilromby."

"The Talgarths," said Mr. Dart. "But how ..."

"Yes, Mr. Dart?" asked Mrs. Etaris.

"Surely Justice Talgarth wouldn't be party to blood magic."

"Perhaps he doesn't know," Violet said. "Didn't you say he'd been away?"

"Alisoun," I said abruptly.

"Alisoun?" Violet asked sharply; both Mr. Dart and Mrs. Etaris looked politely baffled.

"That's it. I think it was her half day yesterday. Mr. Kim mentioned it."

Mr. Dart frowned again. "Mr. Kim—not Fogerty the Fish's barrow-boy?"

"Yes, I saw him at Mrs. Jarnem's sweetshop after work yesterday. He's courting Alisoun Artquist, who is from Kilromby originally—and who is working for the Talgarths! And it was her half day yesterday."

"Are you feeling dizzy again?" Violet asked solicitously. "I don't see how she could be related."

I glared at her. "Don't you see? She could have brought the pie into town."

Mr. Dart shook his head doubtfully. "If Miss Carlin's there, and if this Alisoun has anything to do with her, and if—how did the Honourable Rag's ring get into the pie, anyhow?"

I sneezed. "I have no idea. We could ask Mr. Kim what he knows about Alisoun's situation."

Mrs. Etaris nodded. "That's a fair idea, Mr. Greenwing. Perhaps you could—why, Mrs. Buchance, whatever is the matter?"

The door had slammed open to reveal Mrs. Buchance, bonnet askew and eyes wide. She started forward to grab my hands as I instinctively rose and reached out to her.

"Oh, Mr. Greenwing, I'm so glad you aren't arrested!"

Chapter Twenty-One

"I BEG YOUR pardon?" I said, sinking back against the ladder. "Why should I have been arrested today?"

"Someone found the carcass of a cow in a bonfire with the bones all silvered, and it's known you and Mr. Dart were out-and-about last night."

"Oh, I say," said Mr. Dart, sounding very like the Honourable Rag. "We saw the cultists, but were not party to them."

"I never thought you would be," Mrs. Buchance replied. "I am most distressed at the mere rumour, and feelings are running high in town today."

"Do sit down, Mrs. Buchance," Mrs. Etaris said. "Your own feelings appear somewhat high, if I may say so. Will you have coffee?"

Mrs. Buchance hesitated in the act of taking off her coat, glancing from me to Violet. I tried to compose my whirling thoughts and emotions while I performed the introductions. "Mrs. Buchance, this is Miss Redshank, a friend of mine from Morrowlea here on family business. Miss Redshank, this is Mrs. Buchance, my late stepfather's second wife."

Violet blinked, but stood away from the table that she might perform a curtsey. Mrs. Buchance returned it with bare politeness, and without blinking twice at the name; indeed, Violet looked rather more surprised at hearing her relation to me. I sighed and sneezed and felt miserable despite the coffee and buns.

"Now then, Mrs. Buchance," Mrs. Etaris said. "What brings you to my door? Certainly not only that there are wild rumours flying about Mr. Dart and Mr. Greenwing having a bit of youthful fun."

Mrs. Buchance smiled wearily. "It's a good thing you were with Mr. Dart, Mr. Greenwing. No one would suspect him of any ill magic."

I tried not to respond, but couldn't hold it back. "I've been back in town *three days*."

"Mr. Greenwing," Mr. Dart said. "I'm sure she didn't mean—"

"What?" I said, more angrily than I meant, and flushed, but couldn't quite stop myself, as all the week's snubs suddenly crystallized. "What am I supposed to say? I know what people are saying: they have been generously open. I am a traitor's son, and obviously I am going to betray all confidences anyone places in me. Why bother finding out anything about me? It will no doubt merely accord with what they've already decided, which is that I'm a craven ingrate leeching off my stepfather's wife and destroying the very fabric of society. I'm surprised no one's suggested presenting *Three Years Gone: the Tragicomedy of the Traitor of Loe* as the Winterturn festival play, but that's probably only because it hasn't made it here from Ronderell yet."

There was silence. Then Mr. Dart said, "Your father wasn't a traitor."

"You try telling people that; they might listen to you."

He swallowed and sat back, and I felt savagely satisfied. I turned to Mrs. Etaris. "I'm sorry, Mrs. Etaris. I am grateful for your offer of a job, but I don't see how this can possibly work out for you. My uncle hates me, the Baron will ... agree with the Talgarths, and your husband is beholden to them for his position. You spent the better half of this morning dealing with people asking about me. Dame Talgarth is going to boycott you. All the gentry will, except perhaps Master Dart and Sir Hamish, and I don't know about them when the rest of the town is against it. Lady knows about everyone else, but I can't see it being a good idea to stay."

Mrs. Etaris didn't say anything. I turned to Mrs. Buchance, who was sitting with her hands wrapped around her coffee-cup, her eyes filling with tears. I tried to sound mature rather than plaintive. "I can't stay here if all I'm doing is destroying everyone else's reputation. Mine is ... what it is, but if I'm not here people will forget your connection to me, Mrs. Buchance. My sisters will be far better off if they're not considered relations to me. It's not as if I have anything to offer them." I shook my head as she seemed about to say something. "I will come back for the Winterturn Assizes, so Mr. Buchance's will can be read, and once it has been I can leave you to it."

"What about your inheritance?" Mr. Dart asked.

I had to laugh, and gestured grandly at the square. "My inheritance? I have what I have from my father. The three chests from my mother will be easy enough to go through."

"You should be the squire of Arguty Manor."

"And not having gone to Inveragory for Law, and not having

taken Rhetoric at Morrowlea, I'm hardly going to be able to argue my uncle out of it, nor do I have the money to hire anyone else. Perhaps I will go to Nên Corovel and give my services to the Lady, and that will be that. I can tell her about Miss Shipston while I'm about it."

"Will you not inherit anything from your stepfather?" Violet asked cautiously.

I glanced at Mrs. Buchance, who had tears streaking down her face. I tried to speak as temperately as possible. "No, it's going to my sisters. He said there'd be a small competence, but I'm not expecting anything much. We talked about it. I kept my father's name, and I keep my father's patrimony."

"But that would be enough," Violet said, and when I looked at her in genuine confusion she added, "to go to Inveragory, if you wanted, for another degree."

"How? I could pay my living, possibly, but hardly tuition on top of it."

Mrs. Etaris said gently, "They do offer scholarships for second-degree students, Mr. Greenwing."

"And if I were Violet and had come First at Morrowlea, then they'd probably give me one. Since I *failed*—"

"I didn't come First," Violet interrupted.

I stared at her, and for a moment thought she meant—and then realized. I sank down on the ladder again. "You don't mean they gave it to Lark, after all that? They couldn't have. They couldn't have."

Violet took a deep breath. "No, Jemis. They gave it to you."

"Weren't you there for the graduation ceremony?" Mr. Dart asked. "I thought that was why your first letters were so late."

I thought of the disastrous *viva voce* examinations. How I'd spent the next several days in the hospital wing, and how Hal and Marcan and Tover had packed up my belongings for me and smuggled me out against the fury and fervour of the rest of the students. I glanced at Violet. "No. Things were so bad after Lark's ... I was so sick ... I ruined my degree. Dominus Nidry ripped my final paper in half. I never even presented it. I *failed*."

Coming off an unwitting wireweed addiction. Heartbroken in so many different ways. Bruised physically and emotionally and mentally by my fellow students.

An utter failure, with only Hal proven to stand behind me, when it came down to it.

Violet spoke with great precision. "At the graduation ceremony the Chancellor of Morrowlea stated that your courage to argue for the truth against the strongest personal and public disinclinations was what the university at its best stood for, and that you exemplified not only excellence of scholarship and academic achievement but the far greater excellence of character that it takes to stand against lies and calumny, no matter the consequences."

I stared at her. She smiled sadly, apologetically, wistfully. It took me a moment to think why she was so apologetic: and then I thought of her high words, her angry defense of Lark, her attacking me. She was a superb actress: though whether she was acting now, or had been acting before when she attacked me, I had no idea.

She added, "They must have sent your degree astray, if you haven't gotten it."

"They probably sent it to your uncle," Mr. Dart said. "That's where anything misdirected to Greenwing would go."

I sank down until I was finally sitting properly. To my deep shame now I was crying. I couldn't look at anyone. Thought of the coolly elegant Chancellor of Morrowlea, an expert in the nature of lightning, the founder of the radical movement from her own time as a student there. I covered my face with my hands. "She can't have. She can't have. I *failed.*"

"Jemis, she did. I'm not making this up. You came First in the year at Morrowlea. You can go wherever you like."

"I'm sorry," I said, trying to control myself. "I'm sorry. I thought I failed. I was sure I failed. The way they looked at me ..."

"They were looking at their own failure," Violet said, and the words hung there for a long moment. Then she added: "I was. We all were. The only one who didn't was Hal. He stood with you. But you stood up first."

I started to shake, somewhere between sobs and laughter and sneezes.

"Mr. Greenwing has had a trying day," said Mrs. Etaris to no one in particular.

Mrs. Buchance spoke hesitantly. "Mr. Greenwing ... if you want to go to Inveragory, or Nên Corovel, or, or, wherever, you may of course. But don't think ... you said Mr. Buchance spoke to you about his will?"

I scrubbed my face and sat up to try to compose myself. Mr. Dart passed me a handkerchief, one of his own; it smelled like violets, but not in a sneeze-inducing kind of way. I swallowed painfully. "When he came last winter. We spoke about what I was planning on doing after graduation. At the time I was ... was courting someone, and expected to be going to her family afterwards. That was before the examinations, of course."

There was another pause. Violet said, "Did Lark tell you about her family?"

"No, but I told her about mine," I said tiredly. "That was what started the whole thing. It always does, as you've probably gathered." I glanced briefly at Mrs. Etaris and Mrs. Buchance. "She wrote a rhetorical piece against my father. I couldn't stomach it."

"The final papers are free to be read by the other students as well as the faculty," Violet explained, to my gratitude. "Most of the time no one bothers, or they only have easy questions at the oral examinations. Usually there aren't any serious challenges except from a couple of the professors, and people read their paper and that's it. Jemis challenged Lark on hers as being intellectually trite and morally bankrupt and wholly unworthy of a Morrowlea student. Which it was. He couldn't say it was personal slander ... but he didn't need to. It wasn't a very nice atmosphere, in the end."

"Oh," said Mrs. Buchance faintly.

"This was the young woman who was giving you drugs against your knowledge?" Mrs. Etaris said, and when I looked up at her in shock she actually smiled. "My dear, you have had a most difficult time. Now, I don't know about what Mrs. Buchance thinks about matters, but you've missed the autumn entrance for Inveragory, and it seems to me there are some mysteries still to be cleared up in Ragnor Bella."

"But your reputations—"

"Mr. Greenwing, I had more people come into my store—and buy things!—yesterday than I had most of the rest of the month. Sir Vorel compelled my husband to lay false charges against my former assistant, out of pure bigotry against a quite lovely young man, and both of them know very well that if they try anything of the sort again I will make public allegations against them both. Dame Talgarth buys no books from me as it is; Sir Hamish sent me a letter by one of his marketers saying that he was delighted I had hired you; and I am no serf of the Baron's. As for Mrs. Buchance ... let her say her piece."

"You didn't see Mr. Buchance's will, did you?" she asked.

I closed my eyes and rubbed my forehead. "No. He was going to revise it on his return to Ragnor Bella, he said. That was why he was telling me about his plans."

"He was sounding you out."

"I know," I replied tiredly. "He wanted me to adopt his name and take over his business. But I couldn't—my father—"

"He understood," she said gently, reaching forward to take my hands, which she gripped tightly while staring earnestly at me. "Please don't think you need to leave because of what people are saying."

"Oh," I said, my voice breaking.

"Come on," Mr. Dart said, "there's a cult afoot! I need you to help me find out what's going on. Not to mention what on earth I'm going to do about my arm."

I stared at them. My face felt hot and stretched, my throat tight and sore, my eyes sandy. "But—"

"I think you should go to bed," Violet said briskly. "We can't do much more tonight, can we? We'll have to see what Mr. Dart finds out at this dinner party tomorrow."

"But ..."

"Come now," Mrs. Etaris said. "Make no decisions in haste. Things will look different in the morning once you've slept. And don't worry, I shall make certain my husband's thoughts do not turn to you when considering the silvered cow. Or the stolen books from Dominus Gleason."

I tried to speak lightly. "Or the fire at Mr. Shipston's."

She smiled. "Well, I think it's quite reasonable to put it about that you were the one to go in to rescue Miss Shipston, don't you? Let us put something delightful into the mouths of the gossips for once."

Chapter Twenty-Two

THE LAST TIME I saw my stepfather was just after the first day of spring in my final year at Morrowlea.

Mr. Buchance had come, as was his wont, on his way back from Highthwaite in Chare, where his partner managed more and more of their business affairs as Mr. Buchance's new family grew. He had taken me out for lunch at the Morrowlea Arms in the little village down the hill from the university, a place usually off-limits to students.

We'd had the usual awkward conversation, him asking me stiff questions about my studies and me asking him equally stiff questions about his business, his second wife, and my sisters, until we came to the dessert and he sighed, pushed away his custard, and said: "Jemis, what are we going to do with you?"

I looked at him.

He looked very serious. "I'll see you won't starve. I can keep on with the allowance until you decide what to do. It's just that—"

"I understand, sir," I said, and I did. My mother's money had disappeared into the task of keeping us alive after the news had come of my father's disgrace and death, and given the Fall of Astandalas in the middle of this, even after my father had come home alive and claiming the disgrace was a mistake, there was no Empire to claim an Army pension from, and no money to contest the slander, if slander it was when all we had were the two sets of official documents, one cataloguing the extent of my father's treachery— and the other his heroism. I'd believed his story of the mistakes involved; few others had.

I had already received my inheritance. Three boxes full of my mother's belongings. My surname, and all the rumours and gleeful expectations of those who were waiting for me to turn out even worse than my notorious father and poor deluded bigamous mother, whose own family had disowned her so completely that when I had written to my grandmother to tell her of my mother's death the only reply was My *daughter has been dead these five years since.*

Mr. Buchance had told me before I went to university that if I wanted to take over his business and be a wealthy man through mercantile trade I would have to adopt his name. It was Charese law that a business could only pass father to son without being bought for the full price, and though that was not the law in Fiellan, despite his emigration he remained a Charese merchant through and through.

I might have accepted a formal adoption by Mr. Buchance, if my father hadn't come home.

"I understand," I said again. "I'll be one-and-twenty this month—time for me to be making my own way in the world. You will pass on my love to my sisters?"

"Of course," replied Mr. Buchance, and we talked about Lauren and Sela and Zangora and Elinor and the quick growth of Lamissa until it was time to leave, and I knew without him ever saying it how desperately he wanted a son to take over his business and carry on his name and do all the things I was so stubbornly and unsuccessfully trying to do for another man.

As I walked back up the hill towards the university Lark met me. She'd been working in the carpentry sheds and was dressed in something I couldn't remember, apart from the dramatic sun hat she was wearing against the spring sun, and how very beautiful she was.

The memory was jewel-like, one of the most exquisitely preserved moments of my life, as sharp-edged as when I opened the door of Mr. Buchance's house, one winter's afternoon, aged fourteen and a half, and found standing on the step my dead father.

The clear spring afternoon light, her smiling up at me from under the wide brim of her hat, kissing my frowns away. The way that my worries and frustrations and guilt dissolved and floated away with the smoke rings she blew from her ivory pipe, how she laughed merrily when I sneezed, how that didn't break the spell.

Every step we took up the hill made me feel better. How lucky I was, I remembered thinking, to have found love so searing and beautiful and true as this. Why worry about the future, when I had Lark, who loved to plan and organize and arrange and always had such glorious ideas.

It didn't matter that we'd obeyed all the university's rules, had never spoken of our families or ranks or fortunes or even where we were from, that we wore the uniform robes and participated in all the work that built the university, from the stool Lark had made in the carpentry shop to the work cataloguing the library that I had been doing that morning—that didn't matter, not at all in the light of the smile she gave me.

Our life together stretched ahead, as shining as the splendid city of knowledge raising its golden battlements above us, as unshadowed as the day, as glorious as the swift flight of a falcon piercing the sky from right to left as we walked, as magnificent as the high white clouds building against the blue.

So when Lark said, "Let us be rebels, Jemis my love. Tell me all about your family."

—Well. I did.

***

WHEN I WOKE the next morning it was to a silent house. I turned onto my back, looking at the canopy over my bed. The first three days in town I'd woken to shrill cries and to one or other little girl launching herself through the curtains to bounce me awake, my sisters still finding my presence at home exciting. The first day of work, being a special occasion, I'd found Sela, Lauren, and Elinor all piling up—Lamissa and Zangora were still too little to participate in the sororal ritual.

This morning, though, they'd left me alone. I opened the curtains to see a dull grey morning, of the sort that made it nearly impossible to tell the time from the light. I felt much better, but still lay there languidly until morning necessities impelled me to the privy.

Much nicer than the outhouse at the old house, I thought, remembering the cold trudge down the garden in the morning with the chamberpot. Mr. Buchance had spared no expense on the new house, putting in a cistern and pipes in the new fashion for running water both hot and cold. I ran a bath for myself, as hot as I could stand, and while I floated happily it occurred to me that it must be very late indeed and Mrs. Buchance had taken the girls to the holy-day service.

I found a note from Mrs. Buchance in the kitchen, stating that they had indeed gone to church and would moreover be going to the Inglesides' for lunch, and I was welcome to join them there if I didn't have other plans with Mr. Dart and my friend from Morrowlea, and that Mrs. Etaris had sent along a book. I studied this note while eating lukewarm porridge from the pot at the back of the stove.

Mrs. Buchance had gone to the local kingschool, and her hand-writing was almost as elegant as Mrs. Etaris'. Once I moved the paper I realized the book from Mrs. Etaris was underneath it, and since I hadn't brought anything else down with me to read, naturally I opened it.

It was the book on Alinorel magic. I was still feeling a bit unwell, not inclined to reading solidly, so I flipped through it, reading a few sentences here and there. There were convoluted diagrams comparing the five primary Schools of Astandalan Magic and a discussion of the fourfold and threefold paths of traditional Alinorel magic, though nothing on the Dark Kings, as I saw when I checked the index out of curiosity.

There was, however, an entry for *Drugs, Magical Use of. See also: Wireweed.*

Under *Wireweed* all it said was: *A kind of perennial legume native to the north Kilromby Islands. As a drug, illegal in every country of Oriole and the New Reaches, and with good reason.*

Under *Drugs, Magical Use of,* however, were three pages of explanations for what, exactly, Lark had been doing to me.

Chapter Twenty-Three

I WAS READING this passage over for the fourth time when the doorbell rang. I nearly jumped out of my skin at the huge solemn clank, and spent a few moments trying not to choke on my last mouthful of coffee before I was able to go see who it was.

"Good morning, Mr. Greenwing," said Mr. Dart, with a bow. "Might I come in?"

"With pleasure, Mr. Dart," I replied, with a bow of my own.

I shut the door behind him and he burst out laughing. "Oh, Jemis, what have we got ourselves into?"

"Come have some coffee in the kitchen."

"Quite the house," he said, following me down the hallway and gesturing at the wallpaper, which ran heavily to maroon. "Just needs a few more oil paintings to be properly starchy with the best of them."

"Don't give Mrs. Buchance ideas. She thinks I need to improve my taste in frivolities."

"Like your hat?"

My hat was lying on the table next to my book. I patted it. "My hat is the height of fashion, I'll have you know."

"If you insist." He flung himself into the seat next to where I'd been sitting. "Once you go to Inveragory, you can be first in the styles."

I stopped with my hand on the coffeepot. "The Emperor."

"What, hadn't you thought through what coming First at Morrowlea meant?"

"I had not," I said. "I came home and fell asleep, and woke up half an hour ago."

"I always find myself thinking best in the bath."

"Have a bun, Mr. Dart. I was thinking about other things."

"Oh, indeed?" I turned to the ice box to fetch some cream for the coffee, and he laughed again. "Fine, I won't tease you. We have too much to speak of."

"Go to, then."

He picked up a bun and frowned at it. "Is this onion? Not from Mr. Inglesides, is it?"

"Mrs. Buchance made it."

"In that case ..." and he swallowed half of it whole with evident pleasure. "I don't see why the Ragnor Arms doesn't have better breakfasts. Cartwright told me it was my own fault for sleeping through the service, but he's sanctimonious that way. He's been a brick about having to help me with my clothes and things, since my arm's off, so I had to let him make his comments."

"Clearly whatever it is you want to say is a little difficult to articulate."

"You're in fine form this morning!" He made a face and left off poking his stone arm. He was wearing clothes that rivalled even the Honourable Rag's—or Violet Redshank's—for elegance, black breeches and a plum waistcoat with a plum-and-silver knee-length coat above it. I almost asked him if only wore plum, but decided he was far more likely to run with the digression than with whatever he actually felt burdened to say.

"Mr. Dart."

"Because you are always so to-the-point! Fine. Mr. Greenwing: I have been thinking."

"A most dangerous propensity."

He bowed in his chair, though the effect was spoiled by the crumbs caught in his beard. I debated whether I should mention them or not. "Thank you. Jemis, I'm a little worried about your friend Violet."

"I don't think she's addicted to wireweed," I said, my thoughts still running on the book.

"What?"

"Sorry, that's what I've been thinking about. What do you mean, then?"

"Why—" He glanced down at the book on the table, which had fallen open on a page of complicated diagrams about substitution- ary magic as practised in the Outer Reaches. "What *is* that?"

"The book Mrs. Etaris gave me yesterday. I have no idea what that's about, I've only read a couple pages. It's very relevant to figur- ing out what might be going on with Miss Carlin, however."

"That's just it," he said eagerly. "How do we know what's going on with Miss Carlin?"

I sat back in my chair. "I beg your pardon?"

He gestured wildly. "What do we know about this situation? What Miss Redshank has told us. We don't even know if there *is* a Miss Carlin."

"There's the pie," I said.

"And the only person we know for certain had access to it is—Miss Redshank. Look, Mr. Greenwing, I've been thinking hard about this since I woke up. There was no evidence of anyone else coming to the Little Church for a meeting—just us. And we did make our rendezvous where someone could hear it—do you remember you thought you heard someone?"

I frowned, casting back to the day before last, as I'd seen him out of the store on his way to his aunt's. "I ... yes, I suppose so."

"A lot's happened since then," he admitted, a touch condescendingly.

I raised my eyebrows at him. "But she would have recognized me from that conversation. Why attack me later?"

"Unless she intended to attack you, all along. You have to admit her explanation for why she assaulted you was very peculiar. Then there's the fact that she's definitely lying about her name, refuses to say where she's from, and chooses to stay at the Green Dragon."

"People who aren't from the area wouldn't know about the Green Dragon."

He gave me a withering glance. "Didn't you get out of your university, ever? You just need to walk in the door of a place like the Green Dragon—hell, half the time you don't even need to go *in* the door of a place like that—to know exactly what you'll find. Places aren't called the Green something-or-other if they're not offering the special services to the Lady of Summer!"

"Well—"

"So this woman with a false name *claims* she had no idea you were here, except that she knows you're broken-hearted after her best friend's betrayal. She *claims* her cousin has been kidnapped on

her way back from Kilromby to Ghilousette, and that this has something to do with magic trafficking out of Ghilousette into Ragnor
Bella. She *claims* the pie was made by her cousin."

"But—"

He overrode me. "We don't have any proof for any of it! All
we have is her word—and your trust, which is obviously a bit ... I
mean, there are reasons against her, aren't there? What if she's the
one trying to catch this Miss Carlin? What if she's trying to ruin
you utterly—crying publicly that the Talgarths are party to stealing
magic will mean social ruin for you if you're wrong, no matter that
you're not disinherited from the Buchance fortune. Or that you
came First at Morrowlea—and congratulations on that, by the way."

"Why don't you think she's lying about that, then?"

"Don't sound so offended!"

"Pshaw!"

He ignored this, and fished in the pocket of his waistcoat with
his left hand until he could pull out a letter. "Because it occurred to
me the other place Morrowlea might have sent something was your
old house, so I stopped by this morning, and asked if there was a
letter for you, and here it is."

I took it from him and unfolded it slowly. It was a very of-
ficial-looking letter, dripping with wax seals and gilded lettering,
and in the ancient ideographic script of chancellery and university
documents it did, indeed, state that I, Jemis Greenwing of Ragnor
Bella, Fiellan, had come First in the university, on account of my
'courageous defence of the truth and good scholarship in the face
of much outrage and intellectual, moral, and social peril'.

I stroked the document flat. My heart eased a tiny amount. I
had this, if nothing else. Too much had happened yesterday, but

this, oh this ... I had been so angry that my drugged—and, as I had learned this morning, ensorcelled—infatuation with Lark had caused me to ruin my university career ... this was something they couldn't take away from me, not if the university had given it to me for the reasons they had.

My father would be proud of me for this, I thought, and on that thought smiled at Mr. Dart.

"What about the rest of it? We saw the cult with our own eyes— and Mr. Shipston and his sister were definitely scared of the pie, and Dominus Gleason—"

"I'd be scared of my shadow too if my sister had been turned into a mermaid by black magic! We found out things about the pie, and like fools said so. Miss Redshank merely had to claim it as a sign from her cousin. Why would her cousin make a stargazy pie? *How* could she, if she is being held by the Talgarths—even with Alisoun Artquist to bring it into the middle of town? If Miss Carlin is being held captive so her magic can be stolen, how on earth did she make a pie, anyway? In fact: how do we know Miss Carlin even exists?"

I opened my mouth to rebut all this, and then thought of the pages I'd been reading over and over again, how Lark had very clearly been stealing my unknown gift at magic and using it to make herself as charismatic and attractive as possible. Everybody had fallen for Lark—just as everybody was falling for Violet. Except, evidently, Mr. Dart, but his distrust was a new development.

A sudden spasm of sneezes reminded me that I'd been sneezing more or less constantly since I met her, though I'd put that down to logical causes—hell! I always put my sneezing down to logical causes, despite how obviously unnatural my predilection was—and Violet seemed to have lost her anger remarkably quickly—and all it had taken was a smile for me to make friends with her.

"Fine, then. And your explanation for why the Honourable Rag called her Miss Indrilline? Which I admit I thought was strange, but I can't remember where I've heard the name before. But she really has been at Morrowlea with me for the past three years, and we're not like the schools that have long summer holidays, so she couldn't have been doing anything very nefarious."

I bit my lip, Lark's definitely nefarious behaviour coming again to mind, plus the serious hole in my logic that there'd been months since the spring convocation where she could have been doing anything—not to mention she'd claimed (hell! that word again) to have spent a year doing other things—what other things?—before starting at Morrowlea.

"Mind you, I can't think what the Honourable Rag was playing at by naming her. It seems rash even for him."

I stared at him meaningfully.

"Cartwright remembered better than I," Mr. Dart admitted. "He collects broadsides from half of Oriole. He reminded me that *The King's Gazette* had done a special a couple of years ago on all those revenge killings in Tarvenol."

"Hell."

The Indrillines were the criminal kings of the Western Sea.

Chapter Twenty-Four

WHEN I ASKED at the Green Dragon for 'Miss Redshank', I was greeted with deafening guffaws and several offers of drinks while I waited.

I soon found myself ensconced in the back corner, behind a handful of dangerous-looking louts. It being a holy-day, the drinking was moderate and the gambling kept mostly out of sight. I watched people going in and out of the back room, dressed in a range of clothing from the middle heights of fashion on down to the worst lack of it, and wondered where all these people came from. Up and down the highway, I supposed. It no longer went to Astandalas, but the main road (such as it was) from South Fiellan to the Farry March branched off the fine old road just on the other side of the Woods Noirell.

I pulled out the book on Alinorel magic and read it with what concentration I could muster. The two lines about wireweed were next to useless, but the accounts of "The Magical Uses of Drugs" were cross-referenced to a brief discussion of the old religion's use of a dried lilac concoction to promote 'insight'.

I'd not brought anything with which to make notes, but I sat with my drink and read the chapter over and over again, trying to fit together Dominus Gleason and Domina Ringley, the wizard attendant and Miss Shipston, Violet's stories and the cult. And something odd was definitely afoot with the Honourable Rag.

I was sure I was missing something important. I was also worried about Mr. Dart going to the Talgarths' alone, but there didn't seem to be any way for me to get there that wouldn't cause more problems than it solved.

Especially since we still weren't entirely certain what the problems *were*, let alone how to solve them.

The saloon grew increasingly noisy. I was in a corner away from the main entrance, fairly near the kitchen, where the door banged open and shut regularly. Perry was the tipple of choice, with a shot of pearjack to stiffen it up. *Persiflage*, they called it there. Light banter, with an edge.

I sipped mine as best I could—I'm not a hardened drinker, and despite my morning indolence and slow progress out to the Green Dragon it was only the middle of the afternoon—but the stuff was so fierce and raw that I had to swallow quickly to get it down.

Of course I should have known better.

***

AFTER ABOUT AN hour, it occurred to me that Violet had still not come back from wherever she'd gone to. I was about to get up and go home—I was just sober enough to think that was a better idea than more pearjack—when someone slid into the seat across from me.

I eyed him a bit warily. He was not from the respectable end of town. He wore an earring like a sailor or a Traveller, crinkled hair done up in a messy queue, rough clothes more than several steps down from mine. He grinned, showing a gold tooth. *Definitely* not from the respectable end of town.

He laid a gaming tube on the table. "Up for Twelve?"

Now, my father, in the brief period of time between his second and third tours of duty, had decided that I—at the age of nine—needed to learn something of a soldier's life. We had, accordingly, spent a glorious long summer fencing, wrestling, swearing, and gambling. (He did mention a number of the finer points of drinking but left the practical experience for a later period of my life.)

I wasn't all that keen on gambling as a regular thing, but I was drunk and distressed by my thoughts, so I said, "Sure," and proceeded to clean him out of five wheatears, a bee, four silvertuns, and a handful of copper pennies before he gave up and went back to the bar, muttering.

Remembering some words of wisdom my father had also passed on to me that summer, I used one of the wheatears to buy everyone in the Green Dragon a round, which ameliorated things rather.

I was feeling mellow and quite right with the world when another stranger sat down in the chair across from me, dislodging Red Bess and her friend. The two women had been sizing me up since I'd started winning. I was a bit regretful that I'd been so absorbed in the account of the waxing and waning power of magical drugs in synchrony with the moon that I hadn't noticed Red Bess until she sat down, so I couldn't decide if she or Mrs. Etaris were in fact the shorter.

Unlike the first gambler, who'd looked like a raffish layabout farmhand, this stranger was well-dressed in Tarvenmoor fashion, doublet, tights, codpiece, and all. He was perhaps in his forties, pale-skinned, lean and with duelling scars on his cheeks. He was easily the most dangerous-looking person I had ever seen in my life. I smiled very cautiously as he slid another glass across the table to me.

I sneezed a little, though there mustn't have been much magic at the Green Dragon that night (or possibly the persiflage had something to do with it), for I'd not gone through two handkerchiefs yet.

His hat was not quite so excellent as my own, being a beaver of unexceptionable quality and last year's style of brim. He'd made it up to look more of the mode with a grosgrain ribbon in dark garnet red, which matched his doublet. My hat was much the same, though my waistcoat was watery blue, and I was wearing my summer-weight coat, more or less back to normal after its time in the river thanks to Mrs. Buchance's skill.

"Good even to you."

He probably had more weapons in his doublet than I had handled in my entire life.

"And to you," I replied with an attempt at carelessness, with a nod for the two glasses. Both contained a beautifully made classic persiflage, rich golden perry with the pearjack a deeper amber teardrop in the centre. I was quite seriously impressed that he'd made it over from the bar without stirring the contents, and drunk enough that I said so out loud.

He smiled slowly. "You've quite the hand at Twelve. D'you know Poacher?"

Aside from the accent, his voice was unmemorable, his features barely more so—if one excepted the scars slashed across his cheeks.

In my effort not to be entirely unnerved by the scars, the red waist-coat and ribband kept distracting my glance. I tried not to stutter when I replied. "Learned to cast at my father's knee."

He pulled out a deck of cards. His were old but of high quality, hand-painted instead of cheap prints. Poacher's more involved than Twelve or Lotto or most of the other bawdy-house gambling games, involving strategy and general wit to 'land' the fish—the desired high card—without entangling in the other's 'lines'. Three suits, Trout, Salmon, and Happenstance. Quite a lot of moves.

There are several rules, which I won't go into at the moment (but anyone is welcome to come over for a game any time ...). It's an old tradition that both players drink down their first glass in unison before acquiring a second, more serious round, and that the bets are made *after* the first hand is drawn.

We drank our persiflages—my second, more than enough for me—and Red Bess, with a kiss to my cheek that smelled of carnations, slid out of her seat to go the bar and order us the next round. While we awaited her return, together with a few other onlookers, the stranger said, "D'you read the *New Salon* much?"

"Every week," I replied inattentively, distracted by Red Bess, who was admittedly a respected master of the art of distraction. Her working outfit was a sight to behold. The fashion would have passed muster at Dame Talgarth's dinner party, being a Second Imperial Decadent gown in sheer pink muslin bound with complicated red ribbons to accent the shape of her bodice. It was both utterly modest and completely lewd at the same time, and even Mr. Dart's brother would probably have cast an admiring eye over it.

"Read the *Letters to the Editor* often?"

I recalled my attention to my smiling opponent, taking the cards for my turn shuffling. Made myself shrug. "On occasion. You?"

"I prefer the *Etiquette Questions Answered* column."

"It is generally entertaining, and occasionally educational."

He laughed, a short barking kind of laugh, while I divvied the cards into their two piles, Happenstance and Fish. "So it is. But I find the Crossword most instructive."

I sneezed briefly as someone crossed behind me, sending a gust of wet air and sharp citrus (citrus?) over me, and spent some time pushing the handkerchief into my dirty handkerchief pocket, and had to answer at random since I'd mostly forgotten what he'd said by that point, except that it was about the *New Salon*. "It is diverting on a dull day."

"Exactly," he said with apparent satisfaction. Red Bess set down the glasses before draping herself over the stranger's lap from the seat next to him. He did not appear to find this unsatisfactory. I thought the pink muslin and red ribbons looked very nice next to his red doublet with the white gashes, even though the reds didn't quite match. Red Bess seemed to find the scars rather alluring.

I dealt the Fish, and he the Happenstance cards, and we fell briefly silent to consider our hands and the bets that would come next.

From the Happenstance cards I drew Book, Dog, and Friend with Lunch, which was a reasonable set of affairs, a good place to begin from. Then I fanned the Fish cards in my hand and tried hard not to gasp. I had the three Rainbow Trout cards and the high Salmon, and with a perfect Net in my hand had to spend the rest of the game pretending I didn't have it.

How to bet, I wondered frantically for a moment. I wasn't worried about the money—not with my winnings from earlier sitting in my pocket—but I had a certain familial pride to live up to. No one had mentioned that they recognized me, but then the Green Dragon was the sort of place where they might, or they might not, depending on circumstances.

(The Happenstance cards for Poacher include Bailiffs, Laird Dogs, and Banditos—any of which might conceivably enter into the Green Dragon—though probably not War Parties or Fire Dragons, which are also to be found in the card game but not, fortunately, very often in Ragnor Bella.)

I took a sip of the new persiflage, nearly gagging at yet more alcohol. This was well past my limit. My father would be distressed. Mr. Dart as well, very like.

Then again, my father would be distressed that I was betting by the cards, and not the man. I felt sloshy and slow, and not at all up to dealing with a Tarvenmoor duellist at the Green Dragon for almost-certainly-nefarious purposes probably involving brigandage.

I blinked up to see the stranger gazing steadily at me. He was smiling, and not looking at his cards, and I thought, with cold abruptness: this is not about the game.

By the Emperor, I thought a moment later, when he laid a ring down on the table, and said: "Challengers first. I bet this golden ring."

By the Emperor, this is another secret society, and I've somehow given the passcode. Bloody *hell*.

"Uh ... the Summer Queen," I said, putting a wheatear and a bee down where the coins glinted gold and silver next to the ring.

He'd set the ring with its signet facing me. It bore the same five-petalled flower picked out in tiny garnets as the ring the Honourable Rag had worn, and which the pie had contained, and which meant ... what?

He nodded acceptance of my ante, and drew a Happenstance and two Fish, laying down one of his first draws of the latter.

I realized that the Honourable Rag could easily have lost the ring again in a game of chance earlier that day, or indeed the evening before—Mr. Dart said he seemed to have become a most hardened gambler in his time at Tara, which everyone was turning a blind eye towards because, well, the Ragnor holdings were vast and the Honourable Rag well able to take care of himself in a fight with the kinds of thugs one was likely to get in Ragnor Bella.

My Tarvenmoor gentleman was a cut far above the usual sort, however, and I wouldn't have liked to see even Violet sparring seriously with him. Though admittedly Violet sometimes had much the same cool appraising look in her eyes as the duellist did looking at me. Which was disconcerting in quite another way.

I played a few hands with my Happenstance cards alone, shuffling out Dog for first A Fish Eagle, which was no good, except it was a Red Card and therefore required me to pick up two Happenstances to replace it, and which led me to A Boat and A Second Friend with Urgent Needs, and just as I was debating how best to go about the necessary transmigration of cards—for one was only to draw from the same pile two hands in a row—there was a sudden sharp tinkle of a small silver bell hung over the bar.

I sneezed immediately and strongly, and dropped my cards so I could cover my face rather than spray across the table at Red Bess and the duellist.

When I recovered myself (and pulled out my third handkerchief, which was a bit stuck), I saw that all signs of illegal activity had disappeared, including the cards, the persiflage, and the stranger.

The ring still sat next to my two coins. I eyed it warily, weighing whether it was due to some sense of honour—he had undoubtedly seen my perfect Net and the plausible Tall Tale encapsulated in Boat, Book, Friend with Lunch, and Second Friend with Urgent Needs, which readily beat most hands unless he had the Wise Salmon, Holy Quest, and Grail cards—or some deeper, more sinister, reasoning.

I was still weighing my odds in this rather less straightforward gamble when the front door burst open and the Ragnor Constabulary burst in, truncheons waving and whistles shrilling, and looking for blood.

Some other long-ago lesson made me grab book, ring, and coins, drop to the floor, and while the Constabulary were busy with the bartender and five ruffians who hadn't been quick enough to get all the accoutrements of Hixhen off the table before them, crawled behind the tables and through the back door.

I stood up in the deserted kitchen to brush myself off. The floor of the Green Dragon was not the most salubrious of surfaces; the second Mrs. Buchance wouldn't have tolerated it in her disused outdoor privy, let alone inside an eating establishment. Not that people usually came to the Green Dragon for its quality of food.

A tray of stuffed rolls that had not been on the bill of fare lay cooling on the side, and I hesitated approximately five seconds before laying some coppers next to the tray and taking three. It was hard to juggle the ring and the hot pastries at the same time, so I slipped the ring on, my earlier concerns forgotten. It was a bit loose but didn't seem entirely likely to fall off. I didn't sneeze when I waved it experimentally in my face, so whatever it signified, it presumably wasn't a deleterious enchantment.

Yes, I know.

***

I WENT OUTSIDE to find that everyone appeared to have slunk off into the barn—or at least that's where I could hear low voices—but I thought that surely the Constabulary would think to look there—they were stupid, but surely not *that* stupid—so I turned up my collar and turned my steps to the road home. Rather to my surprise, it was getting dark. Well, hours pass quickly when drinking and reading, even without friends to chat with. I wondered what had happened to Violet—and what everyone else was up to.

On their way to dinner at the Talgarths', I recalled triumphantly, though only briefly because despite the pastries I was still drunk enough to feel maudlin and sad at the thought that all my friends would be enjoying a Fifth Imperial Decadent style dinner party—possibly complete with flute-girls and acrobats—while I was walking down the road in the dark, and the rain, alone, towards a crossroads no doubt under the power of the Dark Kings and the cultists.

I know.

When I got to the crossroads, I spent a few moment regarding the the waystone. After a few minutes I realized I was leaning up against the stone, no doubt doing something awful to Dominus Gleason's careful spells, not to mention the discourtesy to the dead laid there.

I wouldn't like someone leaning up against the waystone under which my father was buried.

I was drunk, I realized. I did not want the unquiet dead rising. But I still stood there, looking at the cords binding the broken stone and shivering. Then I heard hooves and the creak of wheels.

I lowered my head as the vehicles approached, and devoutly hoped no one recognized me.

Two carriages went past without slowing except to make the turn: the Woodhills' and one I didn't recognize. The third, solidly black except for a stylized white moon painted on the coat of arms, pulled to a creaking halt. Naturally, if against my better judgment, I looked up.

Someone inside leaned out and looked at me. I regarded him thoughtfully. It wasn't quite dark, and we were out of the woods; dull shadowless light illuminated everything. We could see each other fairly well. Or I could see that he was a plump man wearing black robes and a black hood and a well-polished black mask.

He spoke in a low and hoarse voice. "A young man waiting at a crossroads at sunset on the third evening of the Moon's transit through the House of the Dragon. Dear me. I hadn't thought they taught anything worth learning in Ragnor Bella."

"I've been away," I replied, as suavely as I could.

There was a kind of smile in the voice. "Well indeed. The pay's the standard: your heart's desire."

I paused a few heartbeats, but he seemed entirely serious; well, he would. "And the work?"

His turn to pause, and then he chuckled low and sinister. "Easy as serving a pie."

And that was how *I* ended up at the Talgarths' that evening.

Chapter Twenty-Five

TO MY SURPRISE, the Black Priest's nefarious plan quite simply *did* consist of having me serve pie to the diners. Or rather, doctoring dessert with a special liquid, which he gave to me in a phial, and serving it to the diners.

He stared at me intensely the whole while he was explaining his plan, which took the entirety of the twenty-minute carriage ride from the crossroads to the Talgarths'. I stared back in a half-pretended semi-stupor, wondering why exactly he was rambling so very much in his explanations.

Nevertheless, I nodded at what seemed appropriate times, and wondered just how likely it would have been for someone else to have been there, ready and willing to do something obviously both illegal and dangerous for such a vaguely-worded and dreamy future reward.

(*Stargazing* was the word that came to mind, in the *Encylopedicon*'s terminology.)

The Black Priest didn't seem to suspect anything, which worried me. It also worried me how I was to avoid being recognized once inside the Talgarths'.

We pulled off the main highway onto the equally smooth carriageway leading to the Talgarths' house. The Black Priest continued to stare at me, and I continued to pretend I was more drunk than I was. The golden ring felt cool and heavy on my finger. The phial was transparent black glass, heavy for its size, with some sort of iridescent liquid sloshing heavily around inside it.

"Mrs. Figgery is expecting you," he said, finishing up the fifth iteration of his instructions as we clunked over the drawbridge, turned onto gravel and crunched to a halt. "Go to the back door and tell her your name is Potts, and she'll set you right."

I nodded and set the phial into my pocket, and got out of the carriage. His stare felt tangible on the back of my neck. I first straightened, then slouched, thinking that I was supposed to be some middle-class layabout, and that it would be better not to carry myself and speak like a young man of consequence—which was what I was trained to be, if not in practice. My hair felt straggly and coming out of its queue; I'd lost my hat at the Green Dragon. Well, I probably had a slightly better chance of recovering it tomorrow from the tavern than I would from the Talgarths'.

It was sifting rain. I had perhaps a hundred yards to walk between where the carriage had stopped, in the shadows of a group of pines, and the house. The Talgarths had spared no expense—even the back was brightly illuminated with mage lights set in coloured glass, showing off the fanciful turrets and domes of the pile.

The Grange had been built by Justice Talgarth's father in the heyday of Emperor Eritanyr's reign, which was called in architectural history the Fifth Imperial Decadent Period. Northwestern Oriolese interpretations of this style were called Bastard Decadent, a fact which had always amused me tremendously.

White-washed brick (the usual building material in south Fiel-lan), copper tiles like a snakeskin roof, round windows and moon doors of all sizes and inconvenient locations, and the multi-co-loured werelights showing off the carved plaster ornaments. And that was just the outside.

It was perhaps the rain, and that the wind was at my back, but I got to the door without having to sneeze more than once. I took a deep breath of the cool night air before knocking, and resolved that whatever else I did that night, not doctoring the desert was something I could count on.

Not sneezing was a fainter hope, but I gripped my third hand-kerchief tightly and resolved to do my level best.

Not being in the same room with people I knew—that was prob-ably the best plan, too.

Otherwise, I was going to wing it—and hope that Mr. Dart was in fact there and I could speak to him out of notice of anyone else.

I nodded to myself, That seemed a reasonable plan: don't sneeze, don't draw attention, don't try to mingle, don't poison or enchant or drug anyone, and try to talk to Mr. Dart alone and unnoticed.

I knocked on the door, and while I waited—why is it that one rarely stares at the door? It seems rude, somehow; I always end up looking around aimlessly—I noticed the carriage disappearing not back down the drive, but around the corner of the house to the front where the guests would be entering.

Hell, I thought, and the door opened.

***

BEFORE LETTING ME in, Mrs. Figgery the housekeeper called Mr. Benson the majordomo, a tall fat man who rubbed his fingers with glee when he saw me—and the ring I wasn't quite able to keep hidden by my handkerchief. I was not sneezing near as much as I expected, but could feel the ticklish need to do so bubbling in the back of my nose.

"We've lost half a dozen footmen to that cursed woman's experiments," he said to the housekeeper.

"He'll look right enough," she said coolly; "at least she's replacing them."

"True," he said, then barked at me: "Name?"

I jumped, nearly said my own, managed to squeak out, "Mr. Potts."

He rolled his eyes. "Aping your betters, are you? Of course it is. Name, boy."

I tried not to show an obvious hesitation, though my mind was whirling. I hoped it was confusion but feared I wasn't yet sober. Jemis was too uncommon, the only other person I'd ever met who was called it was Mr. Ned the fisherman. My father had found it funny—my father—"Jakory."

"Jack it is," Mr. Benson said, and Mrs. Figgery said, "The dressing bell has gone, Mr. Benson."

"Damn!" he said, and grabbed my arm.

I had to scurry to keep up, as he led me down a series of back corridors to a hidden staircase, then hastily up five flights without a pause. I was breathing hard by the time we got to the top; despite his bulk, Mr. Benson appeared unmoved.

"In here," he said, thrusting me into a room full of steam and coppers and laughing men in various states of undress. "This is Jack," he boomed into the noise. "Get him ready, he's taking Hink's place."

"What, another one?" someone said out of the steam. I waved my hand in front of my face. The air was heavy with some type of perfume that appeared a mixture of lilac and lavender. I sneezed a couple of times, but lightly, and relaxed at the thought that we'd been wrong about the magic used indoors. It seemed the Talgarths kept all the display for the public areas.

"Aye," Mr. Benson said, and pushed me forward until I stumbled against a scalding-hot copper. I tripped over myself trying to back away, and landed with a thump on the floor.

Someone laughed and two others grabbed hold of my boots and pulled, and before I knew it I was as naked as the others and being thoroughly bathed in as fine a bath chamber as any I'd ever seen. It matched even the one at Morrowlea reserved for high-ranking guests, which I'd drawn on cleaning detail one winter's day, and gotten into trouble for using first. Another one of Lark's bright ideas that had landed me in the soup.

I couldn't see any of the other servants very clearly through the steam. My remaining inebriation didn't seem to be a huge problem, or indeed an isolated incident—there were flasks of something cool being passed around, though I did retain enough of a head to feign taking my turn instead of actually drinking. My clothes had disappeared, which didn't bother me until someone said, "Oho, Jack's brought his own drink!"

I pulled myself out of the bath, accepted a towel someone thrust at me, and said in the general direction of the voice, "It's uh, not for drinking."

"What's the good of it, then? Fancy bottle."

"Uh, it's a ..." I paused, then something I'd read once floated to mind, and I added: "It helps your innards go, if you must know."

The room roared with laughter, and I heard a clink as if a stopper was being replaced, and breathed a sigh of relief. Someone—the speaker or another, I had no idea—emerged out of the steam, wrapped in a towel, and passed me the phial with a suggestive leer.

The glass clinked against my ring (which I'd managed not to lose, though the soapy bath had nearly removed it half a dozen times) and he dropped his gaze down and then up, and then he grinned, draped his arm over my shoulders, and led me out of the bathroom and into a dressing room that felt like an icebox in comparison.

The room was nearly empty, but clothes were laid out on various stands, with accessories in shallow baskets lined up along a table, shoes below and ribbons above.

I looked at my companion. He had jet-black hair, bright blue eyes, and pale freckled skin, like a Kilromby islander. He was thinner and less muscular than I, but had the reach on me, and besides, I had no idea where in the house I was, what exactly I was meant to be doing, how serious any of this was, or what.

"Is there a Miss Carlin here?" I asked at random, and he tipped back his head and laughed. "Good one, man, good one! Miss Carlin. Hoo boy." He reached out to a smaller table next to a rack of pink satin I hoped we were not putting on, and drank a good long slug of a silver flask before passing it to me with a wink.

"Just to loosen up any nerves before the night's work."

"Is it hard work?" I temporized, accepting the flask but not lifting it to my mouth.

He grinned again. He was definitely foxed or worse, his pupils dilated wide. "Jack, my lad, they're old-fashioned and *we're* the servants. Hard work." He wiped his mouth and winked. "Hard, but hardly work—especially not once they get to dessert."

***

DURING THE EMPIRE, only the very wealthiest and most important had actual human servants; everyone else made do with magic. (The poorest, of course, who couldn't afford even magic, had therefore to make do with their own labour and tedium.)

I remembered, as a boy, how my father's house had all the little luxuries everyone took for granted: the hot and cold running water, the privies, the lights, the cold boxes (that did not need ice to stay cold), the way that dust and grime simply wafted away in the light breeze that was really, well, whatever it was that the Imperial wizards bound to be the cleaners.

But a dinner party, where one was trying to impress one's guests? Oh, that's when the money was spent. Servants, as many as possible—as well-trained as possible, too, of course, but the exceptionally well-trained were very expensive and in very great demand indeed, so people made do with as many as well-dressed as possible. Like the resplendent furniture and dishes, the servants were to be seen and admired—though also like the furniture and cutlery, not to be considered as anything other than useful objects in the house. Individuality was not encouraged.

While Mr. Benson went through the order of service, I only half-listened, for surprisingly enough I did know what to do. The Refector of Morrowlea had been a noble family's Master of Etiquette before the Fall and insisted that every student in the university know all the points of a formal dinner party, from the various perspectives of the host, guests (of many ranks, since the university held that anyone, of however humble a beginning, could rise to any position by their intellectual merits and personal accomplishments), and servants of all stripes. On two occasions I'd been a footman, and on one of them the Duke and Duchess of Erlingale had come to visit the Chancellor of Morrowlea, so I was well prepared, all things considered.

I was rather more concerned that my garb be put on properly and sufficiently thickly to disguise me. Since I was still not sneezing more than anyone else at all the powder and perfume in the room, I had tentative hopes that even though the first step of my plan was already foiled, the rest of it would proceed acceptably.

Thus it was that an hour later six footmen stood in a row across from six maids in matching garments, ready for a ballad or a period painting or what I sincerely hoped was not going to turn out to be a Late Bastard Decadent style orgy. I surveyed my reflection in the long mirror set in the hall outside the main dining room, and was both deeply satisfied and utterly horrified.

We footmen were wearing well-polished ankle-high black shoes with golden buckles, and above them tights in a shimmery gold silk, tied with black velvet ribbons just below the knee. Above these, the breeches were pink satin with gold stripes down the outside seams. The fitted jacket with wide rolled-back cuffs was also pink satin, with black and gold piping and buttons, the inside of the cuffs black and gold striped satin. White gloves—which hid the ring I had managed not to be divested of. Best of all, a thoroughly powdered and rouged face, topped off with an elaborately shaped white periwig adorned with pink, gold, and black ribbons.

The women were wearing black satin gowns with pink aprons, gold ribbons, powdered and rouged faces, and beehive periwigs powdered with gold dust. Their gloves were white and their shoes polished black, their waists cinched tight in corsets.

I blinked at the row, wondering if any were Alisoun Artquist, but I could barely tell one apart from another by height and physique, let alone identify one from an inarticulate lover's description. Then one of them tilted her head just slightly at a word from her neighbour, and as I saw the motion I thought—

Violet.

Chapter Twenty-Six

"BUT WHERE IS your brother, Mr. Dart?" a strange woman in eye-watering yellow and blue clothing was saying. "His absence is quite throwing off the table."

We were lining up against the inner wall with our libations—I was holding the black-lacquer and gilt decanter of golden wine that would be used for the invocation to the Emperor—and as we shuffled into position I lost track of which of the pink maids was Violet.

What the hell is she doing here? I asked myself; and then thought: well ... the same thing as me? Except—what game was she playing? What was she *doing*?

This is a game of Poacher, I told myself. You're good at Poacher, Jemis; you're your father's son.

"Oh," Mr. Dart replied, "the river's in spate from all the rain. He had to attend to some matters at home, Mrs. Figheldean. Since I sprained my wrist I couldn't be of much use." He gestured vaguely at his stone arm, which he'd outfitted with a rich aubergine sling to match the rest of his clothes (aubergine and cream and gold; I resolved to mock his purples), which went rather better with the room (which we servants matched, featuring as it did an awful lot of pink, black, and gold) than did Mrs. Figheldean's egg-yolk and blue caftan.

"And the Justice is still away, and my poor dear brother-in-law Sir Vorel in bed with a catarrh ..." Mrs. Figheldean surveyed the group. I blinked and followed her lead. I knew everyone but for a strange young woman, pleasant-featured but sickly-looking, whom I took to be her daughter.

Unfortunately the only certain ally I had was Mr. Dart; depending, of course, on what game Violet was playing.

Mrs. Figheldean smiled coyly. "You ought to have brought your friend from Stoneybridge."

"I beg your pardon?"

"Who's that very elegant young man you've been gallivanting around with this week? A friend of yours from Stoneybridge, I'm sure."

Mr. Dart smiled, a touch mischievously. "No, that's Mr. Greenwing. Major Greenwing and Lady Olive Noirell's son. He's just come back from Morrowlea."

Mrs. Figheldean attempted, not very well, to hide her surprise. "*That's* Jemis Greenwing?"

"In the flesh."

"Not quite as I'd heard him described ... He's filled out well," she added hastily. "I met his father once, years ago. He doesn't favour him. I hadn't thought he'd return to town, though."

"Whyever not, Mrs. Figheldean?"

"Oh, he isn't *quite* ..." She trailed off delicately. "All that fuss with his father ... his grandfather gambling away the holdings before dear Sir Vorel could redeem them ..."

Mr. Dart looked properly scandalized and interested, but, alas, she was interrupted by Mr. Benson entering with a silver bell to ring the libations to the Emperor and the Lady. These were done in due course, with luxurious slowness and slightly excessive fervour about the Emperor, and everyone sat down.

The invocation to the Lady passed without incident, although I saw that one of the maids heaved a great sigh of relief when Dame Talgarth finished the prayer. It might have been Violet—but then again it might not have been. Dominus Alvestone looked smug.

As was to be expected, the Talgarths had a Bastard Decadent table, a vast rectangle of mirror-polished black marble, the stone just visible between the three pieces of pink-and-gold brocade running lengthwise down it. They had compromised with chairs rather than the reclining couches that would have been used in the central Empire (and which, I'd learned after a Central style dinner party at Morrowlea, were excruciatingly uncomfortable for those of us unused to them).

The centre was decorated with gilt epergnes laden with various glass fruit and sweet pea blossoms, illuminated with Collian fretwork mage-lamps. In every other household in the barony those would have been wrapped away for when magic became socially acceptable again, but here they had pride of place.

I realized I'd been breathing normally for the entire service so far. I frowned. They were definitely mage-lamps, the light gleaming pink, green, gold. The sweet peas kept distracting my glance; they looked subtly wrong. Dark pink and white, pale mauve and a deeper crimson, clustered in loose globes of blossoms, scent sharp and piercing as a nail. Yet I wasn't sneezing, when in the open air of the garden I'd near perished from convulsions.

Miss Figheldean was placed beside Mr. Dart; the Honourable Miss Ragnor was on his other side, across from Miss Woodhill and the Honourable Rag. Lady Flora, Domina Ringley, a woman in purple and green I took to be the wizard attendant, Mrs. Figheldean, and Dominus Alvestone rounded out the top of the table, with Dame Talgarth at the head.

It was rather imbalanced, even for a Bastard Decadent table, which generally ought to have more women than men, at least according to the book. No Master Dart nor Sir Hamish, nor Sir Vorel, nor Baron Ragnor. Nor me, of course.

Dame Talgarth looked a little displeased by something, but as she was glaring at her sister it was perhaps that Domina Ringley had insisted on being seated next to her attendant.

I had plenty of time to observe, but little to listen, for in short order I was too busy with serving the many small dishes of the first courses to do more than catch snippets of conversation, little of which was interesting.

Dominus Alvestone, with a predatory gleam to his eye (though that might have been my own doubting vision), asked the Honourable Rag about the quality of deer hunting this autumn. The Honourable Rag said he preferred boars.

I served rabbit in sorrel and cream, blackberries adorned with borage flowers, fried dumplings, and then a bowl of water scented with the same floating blossoms as filled the epergnes on the table. Domina Ringley's attendant spent most of her time staring at the wall opposite her and playing with her emerald pendant necklace.

Conversation centred mostly on the weather, my reprobate character, Dominus Alvestone's researches (which apparently were on riverside plants), and rumours of illegal distilling in the Arguty

Forest. At one point Mrs. Figheldean suggested I might be behind the distilling, which started a round of discussion about my grandfather's love of whiskey, horses, and gambling, my father's ill-fated career, my mysterious absence over the summer, and speculation about whether Mr. Buchance had in fact disowned me or not.

Mr. Dart gallantly defended my character, supported—to my surprise—by the Honourable Rag, who kept giving backhanded compliments about Morrowlea. I did my best not to dump food onto anyone.

Somewhere in the middle of the fourth course Domina Ringley's attendant stopped me in the process of removing an empty platter with a hand on my arm.

I leaned over her courteously, trying not to look her in the eyes. She drew me close, close enough for me to smell the rich floral perfume she wore and see the fine wrinkles hidden by a smooth powder on her face. She wore kohl around her eyes, which were the same green as her pendant. Her voice was low and controlled, the same one I'd heard in the gardens the other night.

"I'm expecting a messenger," she breathed into my ear, her hand sliding off my arm to follow the line of my tunic to my satin breeches. She smiled as I tried to edge away from the touch, evidently enjoying my discomfort as her hand wandered. "Go to the sally door and let in the one who comes."

I glanced towards Dame Talgarth, but she was talking loudly to Miss Figheldean, and the wizard slipped her hand a little further over. I crouched lower in embarrassment at my instinctive response. "He will give you a gift," she said, and began fondling my ear with her tongue.

Out of the corner of my eye I saw Domina Ringley smiling at

me; no one else seemed to notice what the wizard was doing. After a few damp and ticklish moments she added, "Take it."

She released me and I stumbled out the door and down the main stairs before realizing I should be going by the serving passages, but I didn't know the house and couldn't find any of the hidden doors. I tried to straighten my garments with shaking hands, but it didn't help.

I ended up outside the kitchen, where the magisterial Mrs. Figgery materialized in front of me. "What are you doing down here?" she asked disapprovingly. "It's not time for the fish."

"Uh, the, the, Domina Ringley's attendant asked me to meet her messenger at the, the sally port. Ma'am."

Mrs. Figgery gave me a long look. Behind the rouge and powder I was flaming scarlet, I was quite sure. I stuttered out, "D-dame Talgarth didn't say anything."

"She wouldn't," Mrs. Figgery said dryly, then nodded her head at a plain wooden door down the hall. "Best get it over with. The Black Dog's been coming these six months past, and there's nought we can do about it now."

I went through the door, puzzling over her words. The door led to a plain whitewashed hallway with plain wooden doors along it. At the end was a flight of stairs leading into a cold stone room with a barred wooden door.

I opened the door, and there before me was the Black Priest, and behind him a silver mist rising.

He stepped across the threshold and kissed me.

***

SOMEWHERE BETWEEN THE sixth and seventh courses another

footman and I were sent down to the kitchen to ferry up the ninth course, an enormous whole sturgeon stuffed with all sorts of things I didn't even try to determine under the sauce. It was a full seven feet long from snout to tail, which looked disquietingly like Miss Shipston's.

I frowned around the kitchen. The cook was sprinkling chopped herbs over the sauce and arranging some frills of purple and green kale decoratively around the edge of the silver platter. My mind felt as if it was splintering. I had been down here—no, I hadn't been in the kitchen—I'd gone—

"Hey," said the other footman, who was the same black haired Kilromby islander who had dressed me. "You look like you need some refreshment."

"No," I said, my voice coming out squeakily, and I cursed under my breath and coughed. He laughed genially, and took the bottle one of giggling kitchen-maids passed him. I said, "No, no, I'm fine."

"Don't be silly," he said, and waved aside my hands and my protests to pour a good slug of whatever-it-was down my throat.

It was thick and sweet and tasted like perfume. The footman, obviously an expert in the matter, tipped my head back until I had perforce to swallow or choke. I swallowed.

"Oh, well done, Corwil!" said a kitchen-maid, and everyone started giggling madly. I smiled foolishly back at them.

"Good lad," he said, and pulled out a little pot of rouge to fix my appearance. I could feel the thick sweet potion working its way down and along my veins.

The ring was blocking the magic, I thought muzzily, and then Corwil's kitchen-maid came up to peer at me, and without a moment's thought I kissed her heartily.

"There we are," said Corwil, while the kitchen-maid giggled again and pulled her friend over for a repeat. "There's your Miss Carlin for you."

I blinked at him. He nodded meaningfully at the undercook, a sallow-faced young woman with sharp eyes who was not joining in the merriment. The sallowness didn't bother me—probably she had to spend most of her days in the kitchen, poor woman, cooking the elaborate Astandalan meals the Talgarths demanded, which even on an ordinary day would run to several courses more than anyone else served. Her features were pretty enough, or could have been, if it were not for the sly expression and the pinched mouth and the fact that her fingernails were dirty.

I kept staring at her hands, unable to help myself once I'd noticed the dirt. Her hands looked as if they belonged to a different person, with loose skin and freckles that looked unfortunately like liver-spots.

Corwil took a long slug from the same bottle he'd given me. He seemed very pleased with himself. "I hear she's got more dirt on the mistress than on her hands."

"Mm," I said. My mind and my body seemed to be moving at two different speeds, or perhaps it was directions. My thoughts were plodding down the track of *drugs ... sweet peas ... wireweed from Kilromby ... Knockermen knocking at the door ... cult ... drugs ...* My body was interested in other matters.

Another one of the kitchen-maids came up, and again without thinking about it I reached out and swung her around and kissed her. She giggled and shoved me pleasantly away. I bumped into Corwil, who was setting down his refreshment again, and in the absence of a kitchen-maid kissed him.

Since I'd told Mr. Dart the truth, that my interests didn't run to men, this was actually the first time I'd ever kissed (or been kissed by) one. Except that like the kitchen, it felt unaccountably familiar.

The cook turned around, saw us, and gave us a thorough chiding that sounded so pat I wondered what exactly went on at the Talgarths' on a regular basis. No one seemed to find the potions or the kissing or the magic at all strange.

It *was* strange, wasn't it? I thought doubtfully as Corwil and I met two other footmen at the kitchen door and carried the huge platter upstairs. It was strange that there was so much magic around. That no one minded that we started kissing in the kitchen. That no one had blinked when the wizard started to fondle me.

I clutched at my corner of the platter. That's right. She had been trying to—had sent me down—I had been sent down to the kitchen for the sturgeon—

No, I thought, trying to make my mind behave. First of all I had been sent down to *open* the *door*—

"Come along, Jack," Corwil cried, "we're nearly at dessert!"

We got to the butler's pantry, and Mr. Benson, there to preside over the grand entrance of the sturgeon, found that I'd let my gloved fingers slip into the sauce.

"Go and get another pair of gloves," he said in aggravation, and my mind scattered again. He called the next footman out with an exasperated whisper. "I'm disappointed in you, Jack. You were doing so well."

I nodded shortly and hastened down the hall at his gesture. I only stopped once through the doors when I realized I hadn't a clue how to get back to the servants' dressing hall—and that I

needn't feel quite so chastened as all that, as now I had the opportunity snoop around the house at will. Or I thought maybe I should
feel chastened, though actually it was very difficult to think, or feel
anything but the heat and a nearly irrepressible desire to giggle.

The doors swung shut behind me. Upstairs, I thought; it was
up on the fifth floor, and the dining room was on the second. One
of the things about Bastard Decadent architecture is that unless
the staircases are very grand, they're hidden. Servant staircases are,
obviously, not very grand at all. In a bigger house, even the serving
halls would be hidden—it was said that the King's palace in Kingsford was honeycombed with passageways, and that the Palace of
Stars in Astandalas had walls of triple thickness so that servants
could come and go with no one ever the wiser.

The Talgarths were not quite so rich as that, so they'd made
do by hiding the doors. I giggled and clapped my hands over my
mouth to stop the noise.

I peered at the painted wooden panels on the corridor walls,
trying to figure out which was a door, and was therefore very close
to the wall when one of the panels swung open nearly into my face.
I stepped back hastily, hands still across my face, and was about to
call out eagerly when I saw that the panel did not open into the
stair, but rather into the dining room itself.

A rush of clatter and rich air rushed out. I stepped back a bit
more, holding my breath for fear the magic-laden air would overwhelm me with sneezes. It didn't, but that mystery was overrid-
den by the fact that the person exiting was none other than the
Honourable Rag. He closed the door behind himself very quietly,
and crept off down the hallway without even noticing me standing
there behind him.

After a moment I decided to follow him. He went unhesitatingly through several more panels, up and down two staircases, and through an empty room full of cushions, until I was completely lost and more than a bit surprised to find myself in a privy, fully visible in the large mirror facing the door. At that point he turned around and said, "Why the hell are you following me?"

He clearly didn't recognize me, by the supercilious tone and annoyed glare. He was every inch an aggravated lord. "Uh," I began, tugging at my gloves with no thought other than embarrassment. "Master Roald, I had wondered if—"

"Yes?"

I glanced helplessly from resplendent baron's son in scarlet to the pink and gold froufrou footman in the mirror. The soiled glove was stuck on my finger and I tugged it viciously. "I need your help," I blurted, as the glove popped free and the gold ring I'd been given at the Green Dragon came with it. The ring sailed across the room and hit the mirror beside the Honourable Rag's head with a crunch of breaking glass, which I, however, barely noticed because that's when I finally began to sneeze.

Ribs aching, I sank against the wall, using the soiled glove as a handkerchief for lack of anything better. After a moment I heard the Honourable Rag laughing, and that set me off, so that between the sneezes and the laughter I couldn't breathe, and started to choke.

Finally he tugged me across to the sink, where I gulped water and scrabbled around for the ring until I could jam it back on my finger. I heaved an immediate clear breath, and in the space of three heartbeats realized that I'd been quietly succumbing to the magic.

"Greenwing, you dog, you never told me you'd joined Crimson Lake. What's been up with all the suspicious looks and elaborate obsequiousness?"

I wanted to protest this description but he pummelled me roughly on the shoulder. "No, wait, I do actually need to piss."

While he attended to that I did my best to straighten up my disguise. I'd wiped away a fair amount of rouge and powder, but with a bit of water on the glove I repaired the damage as best I could. I still looked like the man playing Barleycorn in a troupe of players, but at least I didn't look too much like myself.

I twisted the ring on my finger. Crimson Lake, eh? A secret society that a random stranger—or surely not *that* random, since he'd clearly picked me out on purpose—in the Green Dragon dropped me into, of which the Honourable Rag also happened to be a member. A ring that, while not in itself apparently magic, blocked my sneezes. I twisted it again so the garnets were in the right position. That was worth quite a bit, in my estimation. I hadn't been able to breathe so clearly in ages.

But it didn't do everything, I reminded myself, trying to hold onto the thought that the wizard had sent me to let the Black Priest in, that I had done so, and that whatever 'gift' the Black Priest had given me had also blanked my memory of the encounter. I swallowed against nausea.

"Now then, Greenwing," the Honourable Rag said, washing his hands with the care that his hygiene-mad father had instilled, before perching himself on the edge of the marble washstand. "What did you actually follow me here for? Actually, why are you here?" He gave me another once-over. "That's a brilliant disguise, by the bye. Where did you learn to serve so faultlessly? Everyone noticed that the service had improved since the last dinner-party, which I assume you weren't also secretly serving at?"

I collected my thoughts. He was smiling, the corners of his eyes crinkled. Secrets and shenanigans, and I still hadn't an idea of who to trust in this mess of secret societies and cults. Except that I was fairly certain the Honourable Rag had had nothing to do with the cult. Though I still wasn't sure about the pie—or his secret society—or why he mocked me to my face and defended me behind my back—

"No, just tonight," I replied. "The egalitarianism at Morrowlea extended to teaching everyone how to behave in any position at a formal dinner, from lower footman—my esteemed position tonight—to royal host. The faculty took the view that any of their students might well end up in either role."

"And having taken the role of Barleycorn tonight, will you be playing the King of Autumn at the Dartington Harvest-Home in a fortnight?"

"Given that Mr. Dart keeps running away from their Corn-maiden, I imagine not."

He laughed. "Well then?"

"I've been given to understand that there may be a young woman of Ghilousette being kept here under some duress."

He quirked his eyebrows. "By whom?"

"Violet."

"Oh yes, your inestimable Miss Redshank."

"Why did you ask if she was one of the Indrillines?"

"I used to see them in Orio. One of the cousins was in my year at Tara."

Pause, while I wondered if there were other reasons he'd seen them. The Indrillines were the criminal kings of the Western Sea: they ran the undercity of Orio, and if he'd not heeded my warnings about gambling (and given the fight we'd had on the subject, he likely had not), he could easily have fallen afoul of them.

Then Violet's words floated back to me: *Lark's family took me in. I am indebted to them.* And instead of worrying about the Honourable Rag's possible connections I thought about her. Lark, who had access to wireweed, who flouted the rules, who thought nothing of using me, of stealing my magic and my heart and my mind—O Lady, I thought, but surely Violet wasn't—

"I thought I'd seen your Miss Redshank in the company."

I shook my head, rejecting the idea that Violet could deliberately belong to the gang (though a small, distant, unhappy part of me had no trouble at all believing Lark was one of them), scrabbling at some excuse. There were such things as blackmail—I swallowed, thinking of Violet in the dark outside the Little Church. "She's been at Morrowlea with me."

He shrugged. "If you say so. You're looking for a young woman of Ghilousette—name and occupation?"

"Name of Miss Daphne Carlin, occupation ..." I paused, wondering how far I could go. Wondering now if Mr. Dart was right, and there was no Miss Carlin at all. (Then who was the one in the kitchen? Were Corwil and I even talking about the same thing? He was on drugs; I was drunk ...) "She's a baker of uncommon talent, I gather."

"So uncommon that in Ghilousette she might attract the wrong sort of attentions?"

"Something like that."

"Hmm." He frowned at himself in the mirror, pulling out an

ivory comb from his coat pocket and using it to restyle his curls. "It's the wine break—oh, of course you'd know that, wouldn't you? Dame Talgarth's sister is doing the entertainment."

"What do you mean, doing?"

"She's an illusionist, I gather."

"An academic illusionist entertaining people at her sister's dinner party? In Ragnor Bella?"

He grinned at me through his reflection, patting his head with satisfaction before stowing the comb away again. "Don't you sound all scandalized and proper, now, Mr. Greenwing. No one else seems to care at all, and my father's not here."

No one else, I reflected, was wearing the magic-suppressing rings; or at least not as far as I knew. "Hmm," I said. "What do you think we should do?"

"Go back in; what else is there to do?" he said, sounding surprised. "We'll have to see what's toward with this Miss Carlin, and I'm quite intrigued with what Domina Ringley might come up with. I'd thought the Kilromby illusionists had stopped practicing after the Interim."

I made a noise of mild agreement, an emotion I didn't really feel, and followed him out of the washroom, wondering whether it was just wealth, and handsomeness, and carriage, and rank, that made me follow him so easily against my own inclination. But I didn't have anything else to do—or I didn't, until I heard the knocking.

The Honourable Rag tilted his head. "D'ye reckon the entertainment's begun already?"

I swallowed dryly. "The Knockermen."

"The what? Folk tales scaring you now?"

I glared a little peevishly at him. "It's the name of another secret society." Well, criminal gangs presumably were fairly secretive.

"No need to sound so haughty, dear Mr.—"

"Potts."

"Potts? Really? Where did that come from?"

"It's a long story." I pressed my hand against a likely looking panel on the appropriate side of the hall, and a door swung open. The knocking came through loud and clear, echoing through the half-finished passage thus revealed. "Will you come?"

"Has this to do with the damsel in distress?"

"It might."

He stared at me consideringly for a moment, weighing I don't know what, eyes crinkled with a lazy amusement. I tried to match him for insouciance, not that he could probably tell under my disguise. "Welladay," he said finally, "what are you waiting for?" and plunged into the passage with a *sotto voce* whoop.

Chapter Twenty-Seven

AS I COBBLED together later from the disjointed account of Mr. Dart, while the Honourable Rag and I were creeping through the increasingly strange corridors of the Talgarths' house trying to find the source of the knocking, the diners were under siege.

It started, I gather, innocently enough. While Mr. Benson was carving up the sturgeon, it began to snow.

They took this, as one might, to be part of the evening's entertainment, which to be honest had been rather tame. Despite what I'd been led to believe ought to be appropriate entertainment for a Late Bastard Decadent dinner party, there had been no acrobats, no dancing girls (or boys), and (despite the wizard attendant's wandering hands) no orgies. There was music from a gallery to one side of the room, where a quartet of musicians were playing chamber music of the sort that was far more traditional Fiellanese than anything you would have heard in the central provinces.

The musicians switched to another song, this one an instrumental version of a folk melody, according to Miss Woodhill from West Daverary, and Dame Talgarth said to her sister: "Now we shall see what you have done."

Now, I'd noticed that Domina Ringley appeared far less drug-addled than she had before, and was sticking rather grimly to drinking the fizzy water that was one of the many little luxuries on offer. Dame Talgarth, on the other hand, had been drinking heavily; Mr. Benson, who was acting as Wine Steward, had been refilling her glass with rare frequency. It was her house, Mr. Dart and I both supposed, and no one could naysay her with the Justice still out of town.

And then, between the lemon sorbets and the sturgeon, between one note and another, the snow.

The musicians kept playing, Mrs. Figheldean, Dominus Alvestone, and Domina Ringley kept talking about me, and Miss Woodhill, Miss Figheldean, and Mr. Dart sat politely wondering what would happen next, and watching the wizard attendant fiddling with her necklace and fondling the staff. Mr. Dart ate a bit of the snow along with his last spoonful of sorbet; he said it tasted like peppermint oil.

Mr. Dart (channelling Mrs. Etaris rather than the Honourable Rag this time) turned to Mr. Benson, who was passing behind him with the wine, and said: "Is it not yet time for the Lady?"

And Mr. Benson, with what Mr. Dart described as a glint in his eye and a rumbling kind of tone to his voice, said, "After the fish course, sir."

"My mistake," said Mr. Dart, and the musicians played on.

***

THE HONOURABLE RAG and I were lost.

Of course, I'd been lost since I left the dining room area. The

Honourable Rag had clearly known how to find the washroom, but equally clearly was now opening doors at random. I twisted the ring on my finger, the soiled glove flapping loose in my other hand, and trailed behind him like an assiduous servant. I kept trying to tell myself that that was a perfectly respectable thing to be. I have to say it's much easier to argue for the essential equality of all men and their trades when it's entirely theoretical.

The Honourable Rag stopped eventually in an octagonal room with four doors in it. The one we'd entered by swung shut behind us. He turned to look around at me. The four walls lacking doors were adorned with tall mirrors in elaborate gilt-plaster frames. It was abundantly clear in our reflections that the Honourable Rag had not only about a foot of height on me but also considerable breadth of muscle. I sighed.

"Any ideas, Greenwing?"

I brushed at a loose curl falling down from my periwig. "There's always the old stone-skipping rhyme."

He grinned and started to twirl around while he chanted. "Bother, pother, tother, and truth: here's a stone for the duchess and one for the duke, one for the king and one for the fluke, silver gold copper and tin, turn-round-quickly-and-let-the-next-one-IN—I think that's the door we came in by."

"I'm not one to dismiss tradition just because it's traditional," I said stoutly, and opened the door behind me. And perhaps it was the same one we'd just gone through, but that didn't matter much, because it was snowing here, too, and, moreover we could see who was doing the knocking: one of the cultists—or at least (the voice of my Morrowlea tutor suddenly thundering critically into my mind) someone dressed as one.

The Honourable Rag cried, "Oy!" and set off down the hall at a brisk pace. He was wearing fancy shoes, however, and almost immediately slipped on the snowy marble, did a spectacular somersault, and cracked his head on the floor hard enough to stun himself. The figure hammering at the wall looked back—it was wearing a dark mask—and lit off to the right.

The footman's dressy ankle shoes had poor grips, but though I skidded a bit I got safely to Roald's side. He was out cold. I bit my lip, trying to think what was best to do. Eventually I took off my periwig and laid it under his head, and then decided that since there's not a lot else one can do immediately for a concussion besides rest, I'd do better finding someone else.

Still being entirely lost, however, I thought I might as well find out what was going on with Grey Cloak. The thought of the hammer that Grey Cloak had been holding made me take the Honourable Rag's carbuncle-hilted dagger. It was just as nice as I'd suspected when I first saw it.

It was still snowing and I kept thinking how absurdly cold my head felt without the periwig, worrying about what other effects the various drugs, drinks, ensorcellments, and near-ensorcellments might be having on me, and suddenly stopping dead as I recalled, and then lost, some no-doubt-vital piece of information.

Violet is here! I let the Black Priest in! The wizard attendant is in league with the Black Priest!

(*Seemingly*, my tutor's voice said again: *do not be so hasty about jumping to conclusions!*)

Grey Cloak disappeared around two corners, but one benefit of indoor snow was that its footsteps were utterly clear. The trail led me securely along several hallways of increasing impressiveness until they set off up a grand staircase that I realized must be in the centre of the house. The snow was falling more thickly in the lower reaches, obscuring the ground floor. Going up I kept one hand on the railing to avoid the Honourable Rag's fate, the dagger clutched in the other.

About halfway up the stair, the footsteps turned sideways into a large painting. I hesitated a moment, wondering if this was a very good idea (magic! Violet! the Knockermen! the cult!), and in that moment a voice cried out in pain and alarm and Grey Cloak came tumbling out backwards on top of me.

I picked myself up, pushed Grey Cloak down again as he tried to get up, and then jerked off the mask.

It was Mr. Dart.

"Mr. Dart!" I cried, astonished.

"You can't hide in there," he said earnestly, getting up and tugging at my hand. "There's already someone in there." He tugged me insistently towards the stairs. I followed, trying to hide the dagger.

"Why would we be hiding?"

"We're playing Capture the Castle," he said very seriously. "I've captured you, you're my prisoner until the game is over."

We started down into the snow. "Come," he said, "she said we had to hide until the horn blows."

I realized, somewhat belatedly, that he must have been enchanted, and instead of protesting merely said: "Perhaps we should go outside?"

He looked scandalized. "*They're* outside!"

"Who are they?" I asked cautiously, and in the pause heard the knocking begin again.

"Them. The ones who are coming to capture us. The game's

afoot, we must hide."

I gave up trying to make sense of what was going on in his head, and guided him instead back along our footprints, thinking that perhaps we could rescue the Honourable Rag and hide him from danger. The knocking continued, echoes falling into echoes and making it impossible to discern where anything was coming from.

But as we came to one of the cross hallways, I realized that there were, indeed, other people loose in the house, for not only were there multiple sets of footprints, but there were people down the ends of the halls.

All of them were wearing dark grey cloaks. They seemed busy knocking on walls, and I thought perhaps we could get out of sight without being noticed, but Mr. Dart called out gaily: "I've got a prisoner! Carry on, men! *I've* got a prisoner!"

They looked over. I decided not to wait.

I picked a door at random and ran through it, Mr. Dart giggling and protesting along behind me, but though his left hand was surprisingly strong he was no match for me. The knocking continued, no longer completely erratic but increasingly synchronous, an effect that grew more and more alarming the more pronounced it became. I bounced off walls, the noise a muffled protest to the rhythm, bashing through doors as I came to them without any idea at all of where we were going. Down stairs when we fell on them, through doors when they lurched up before us, the dagger in front of me and Mr. Dart bobbing along behind. The ring on my hand seemed warm, and my blood was thudding in my ears.

That I looked undoubtedly like a man run amok entirely escaped me until I crashed through a pair of elegant doors in the Calligraphic style and nearly knocked Mrs. Etaris into the moat.

Chapter Twenty-Eight

"I BEG YOUR pardon," I said, catching hold of her shoulder and arm with a tight grip unfortunately rendered even more awkward by the knife. Mrs. Etaris regained her balance, and frowned quizzically at me.

"Please," she replied, with a vague gesture at the knife point just touching her jugular. "Don't let me detain you."

"Mrs. Etaris!" I hastily removed the knife and stepped back, bumping Mr. Dart, who was peering out the doorway beside us. Mrs. Etaris did not look in the least bit at a disadvantage, or even flustered, unless you count a sparkling eye and wispy hair escaping tight braids as *flustered*.

She peered a second time at me, and covered her face with a gloved hand. "Mr. Greenwing, as I live and breathe." When she lowered her hand she hadn't fully stopped smiling. "What a clever disguise. However did you come to think of it?"

It was my turn to frown quizzically. She was wearing an ordinary dark blue dress, nothing of the disguise or the costume about it. The fine leather gloves she wore ... well, it was cool this evening, colder than the night before. The same probably went for the dark wool scarf that had slipped from around her head and which she now rearranged to cover her mouth and hair.

"Uh ... by happy coincidence, I suppose you could say."

She nodded vigorously. "Serendipity. Always increases when there's adventure afoot and magic in the air—although you're not sneezing, Mr. Greenwing. I'd hardly have recognized you!"

I flushed and held up my hand, ring glinting in the werelights illuminating the house like a fairy palace.

"Is that not Master Roald's ring?"

"No." I explained, as concisely as I could, my encounter in the Green Dragon.

"I'm glad the constabulary didn't catch you there," was her slightly distracted response; she had caught sight of Mr. Dart, who was now crouched down looking at the moat and making tender quacking sounds. "He's under an enchantment," I said. "I believe."

Mrs. Etaris looked at me with such a sarcastic eye I wanted to sink down next to him. "Indeed." She took the knife from my lax grip and examined it in the next patch of yellow light. "This *is* Master Roald's, is it not?"

"Yes ..." Wincing, I explained the rest of my evening so far, or at least up to my arrival at the Talgarths', Mrs. Etaris nodding thoughtfully all the while and bouncing the dagger from one palm to another. She looked as if she did it all the time.

Rather disconcerted, I launched into an account of the odd conversation in the kitchen, but before I could expand on my surmises of what was going on, or on the various even-more-confusing elements of it, I was interrupted by a door banging on the other side of the nearest shrub.

Mrs. Etaris lit up with what I considered misplaced excitement. She raised a finger to her lips to silence me, and set off towards the noise. She kept close to the house wall and moved branches with care. I crept behind her, reflecting that I was wearing bright pink and gold satin and no amount of caution was going to make me inconspicuous, and that Mr. Dart was protesting leaving his birds despite my efforts to shush him.

On the other side of the shrub one of the kitchen-maids was arguing with a parlour maid in pink. I recognized Violet's voice immediately.

"... Why did you start already?"

The kitchen-maid shrank back. "You said when the strangeness started—"

"If they complete the incantation now, the whole effort will be for naught! Alisoun, you only had *three* tasks!"

"I'm sorry," she wailed.

This was Alisoun Artquist? And Violet *knew* her? Well enough to set her tasks? I glanced at Mrs. Etaris, who was regarding the two women with a pleased, indeed nearly smug, expression. I frowned painfully. Surely I hadn't just missed that part of some conversation?

"I did the first two right enough, and it wasnae easy getting the Cook to—what's that?"

I shrank back into the dubious cover of the shrub, but they were looking at the water near their feet. "A goose, maybe," Violet said cautiously, but then something large and smooth and glistening broke the surface in a silent arc, and Alisoun cried shrilly. "It's the Lady-monster! I knew this was impious and wrong, I knew it wasnae right to trust you, I knew it, I knew—"

"Hush," said Violet firmly, and, looking after the ripples, saw us.

Mrs. Etaris lowered her scarf from around her face and stepped forward with as pleasant a smile as if we'd met on her shop step. I trailed behind like an assiduous footman again. Somehow it didn't bother me so much when it was Mrs. Etaris rather than the Honourable Rag I was following.

I tugged Mr. Dart along to where Mrs. Etaris had stopped near the bank. "Miss Redshank, how ... serendipitous. Miss Artquist, I presume? And—Miss Shipston?"

Miranda Shipston rose dripping from the amidst the arrowroot plants and rushes, looking like some Calligrapher's painting of a Collian legend.

I wished I had a handkerchief to worry—and a clue to explain everything. Perhaps the ring suppressed only my sneezes, and this was all an elaborate hallucination brought on by far too much persiflage and an empty stomach. I clutched the soiled glove.

"I found it," the mermaid said happily. "Right where you thought it would be, Mrs. Etaris." She held up the shining black stone the Silver Priest had called the Heart of the Moon.

I sneezed.

Violet immediately swung round, eyes narrowed beneath the rouge and powder. "Jemis?"

I caught my breath. "I'm honoured you recognize my sneezes so immediately."

"I've listened to them this past twelvemonth and more, they become distinctive."

Alisoun twisted her hands in her apron. "Miss," she said beseechingly, "I'm going to get in sore trouble. You dinnae know the

Cook. She's nae good woman, she'll tell the Mistress on me."

Mrs. Etaris considered her for a long moment. "Why don't you go inside, Alisoun? We have some things to discuss out here, and I'm sure Miss Redshank will be able to fill us in on your involvement."

"I'm nae involved, Miss, I swear I had nae to do with any of it but passing the messages! There didnae seem no harm in it, not but my Gilbert is going to be sure mad, and if he won't marry me after he finds out these carryings-on I don't know what I'll do, miss, I'm sure I don't."

"Never cry for the future before it's happened, my dear," Mrs. Etaris said soothingly. "We shall do our best to see it all sorted out properly."

"I hate it here, I hate it!" Alisoun said, looking around at us and at the gaudy lights up the building. "All this magic, and people drunk or drugged or worse half the time, and the Cook ..." She shuddered. "It's nae right, what's been going on, that's that. The Justice wouldnae like it. When he was here it wasnae like this."

"The Justice will be here soon, tomorrow, I expect," Mrs. Etaris said matter-of-factly. "Go in, Alisoun, and get back to work."

Alisoun protested a few times, until Violet nodded sharply at her, whereupon she gulped back her tears, opened the nearly-hidden door beside her, and slipped inside. Violet, Mrs. Etaris, Miss Shipston, and I all looked at each other. Mr. Dart sat down in the grass and leaned his head against my leg.

"I have to admit," I said presently, when it appeared no one else was going to say anything, "that I am somewhat puzzled."

"Why is that, Mr. Greenwing?" Mrs. Etaris asked.

So many questions rushed to mind I stumbled on which to

ask first, and finally blurted out the last: "I still don't understand what's going on with the pie!"

Mrs. Etaris and Violet broke eye off staring at each other so they could look instead at me and laugh merrily.

"My dear Mr. Greenwing," Mrs. Etaris said presently, "I must admit I have yet to answer that question to my own satisfaction. Nor indeed what Domina Ringley thinks she's playing at. Unless you can shed further light on either of those matters, Miss Redshank? For I believe you have been looking for this stone."

Violet shook her head slowly. There was another silence, broken only by the sound of Miss Shipston swishing her tail in the water and some raucous merrymaking coming from a window high above us. Mrs. Etaris smiled expectantly at Violet, without any appearance of awkwardness or disappointment or anything besides mild expectation. I frowned so hard my forehead hurt. My head really was absurdly cold without the wig on.

Finally a timid voice from the water said, "I don't understand why you're wearing serving garb, Mr. Greenwing. Do you work here?"

I looked down at Miss Shipston. She looked significantly happier than she had earlier, though not much saner, her pale blue eyes still far too fixed and intense. "It was serendipity that I was brought in as a servant, but I wanted to be here because I was worried about Mr. Dart coming to dinner here."

"Were you?" Violet asked in surprise. "You didn't seem to be earlier."

"That was before I got hired as a servant by the Black Priest because I was hanging around the crossroads at sunset on the night of the new moon and sent to go serve a phial of suspicious liquid to the guests at Dame Talgarth's dinner party."

"What happened to the phial?" Mrs. Etaris asked curiously.

I drew it out of one of the gores in the doublet, where it had been pressing coldly and malevolently against my waist. The black liquid caught the werelights with disquieting iridescence. "I rather forgot about it," I added, "because I think I figured out one part of things—or I thought I had, until you turned up with Miss Shipston and the stone and Violet turns out to know Alisoun Artquist and—and, well, I really didn't think Miss Carlin existed—"

"She doesn't," Violet said, sighing.

"But she does. Or at least ..."

"What did you figure out, Mr. Greenwing?" Mrs. Etaris asked.

"I think ... well, I don't know how it fits in with anything now."

"Never mind that, dear. We all appear to have pieces of the puzzle—it's time to lay them out and work together."

That was presumably directed at Violet, who didn't seem inclined to comment, so I cleared my throat and rallied my thoughts and tried to ignore the trills of laughter and flute music coming from upstairs. Some of the laughter was unmistakably lascivious; maybe Dame Talgarth had found dancing girls from somewhere after all.

Or perhaps this was the *hard work after dessert* my fellow footman had winked at me about. O Lady, I thought, glad Mr. Dart was down here with me, if none the wiser. I cleared my throat again. "You see ... I mentioned that sweet peas were my mother's favourite flower."

Mrs. Etaris twirled the dagger around one finger in the hand not holding the stone. She looked as if she did *that* all the time, too. She was still gazing at Violet, who was staring at the knife; Mrs.

Etaris' voice was again abstracted. "Yes ..."

I gestured at the darkness on the other side of the moat. "When Mr. Dart and I were blundering through Justice Talgarth's sweet peas the other night, I didn't notice it, because I was sneezing too hard, but when I saw the sweet pea blossoms on the table, I realized they weren't exactly right. I mean, they're obviously related, but they're the wrong shape."

"Sweet peas come in all sorts of colours," Violet said. "And all the pea family has the same sort of flower. Beans, too."

"So does clover, but it doesn't look like a pea blossom unless you look at the individual florets. And that was what these are like—they're not a spray of blossoms like sweet peas or garden peas or runner beans—"

"I'm *so* glad you know your vegetables," Mrs. Etaris murmured.

"Uh, thank you," I said. "We took turns in the gardens at Morrowlea. That's why it went all year round. ... Anyhow, the flowers in the table are like giant clover heads. The same way a cowslip is like a primrose, but in a cluster."

"Fascinating," Violet said flatly.

I flushed, grateful (marginally) for the rouge. "It got me thinking why that would be, and I remembered—that book you lent me, Mrs. Etaris, only talked briefly about wireweed, but it did mention it's a legume. From Kilromby. And Mr. Dart was worried about the plants washing down again because the cows were getting the staggers and jags from them."

Everyone looked at Mr. Dart, who said dreamily, "Dame Talgarth sat in the fish."

"Ah," said Mrs. Etaris, as if everything fell into place for her.

Miss Shipston still looked confused, and Violet pensive, and there didn't seem to be anything to do about Mr. Dart, who was now humming, so I continued.

"Justice Talgarth has been breeding sweet peas for years. You told me, Mrs. Etaris, that he's been trying to breed for a perennial type. The book said that wireweed comes from Kilromby ... where Domina Ringley has a position. We saw that she's taking wireweed, and is clearly under the control of her attendant—Mr. Dart and I saw them out here in the middle of the night, talking about how the rainy weather had delayed them, and how they needed to harvest something before the new moon. Domina Ringley could well have been passing wireweed seeds to Justice Talgarth to use in his breeding regimen for years, but I don't know about that. It seems risky, unless he's in deeper than I imagine."

"And this year?" Violet asked.

"This year the Justice spent the entire summer in Ormington teaching a course. Domina Ringley had a sabbatical, so came to keep her sister company for the summer, keep an eye on the gardens—and if she planted wireweed instead of sweet peas, who would know besides Justice Talgarth?"

"His gardener, presumably."

Mrs. Etaris shook her head. "Except that he does all the sweet pea trials himself. Mr. Greenwing is quite correct that no one would suspect anything if Domina Ringley made the argument that she was trialling a new species for the Justice to consider on his return, and planting a large number of plants. That's what one does to domesticate a wild species, one plants a good number in order to see the natural variety of the species. Well, well, well."

"I suppose that means," I added, with a sinking feeling as I considered the warren of hidden stairs and corridors in the house behind me, "that there are boxes and boxes of the stuff hidden in there."

"That seems quite likely," Mrs. Etaris said. "Good work, Mr. Greenwing. ... Miss Redshank, do you have any thoughts?"

There was a long pause. Miss Shipston swished her tail some more. Violet frowned at the stone in Mrs. Etaris' right hand. I leaned against the wall, heedless of my pink satin, and listened to the faint music above us. Mrs. Etaris continued to smile expectantly and look utterly normal, apart from the dagger in her hand.

Violet sighed. "Jemis, Mr. Greenwing, why did you say you thought you were wrong about Miss Carlin?"

"Oh ... the reactions of the other footmen when I asked if there was a Miss Carlin working here."

"You actually *asked* if she were there?" Violet sounded aghast.

Mrs. Etaris sounded as if she were trying not to laugh. "It has the merit of directness."

"I don't have your evident experience with espionage," I retorted. "I thought it was worth a try."

"Dinnae fash yourself," Violet said with a fair imitation of Alisoun Artquist's Kilromby accent. "What did they say?"

"The footman just laughed at me and said 'good one,' but when we were down in the kitchen he pointed out the undercook, a sallow woman with dirty fingernails, and said she was Miss Carlin."

"The things you notice."

"She's a cook, Violet. Her hands should be clean."

"The things you care about."

Mrs. Etaris interrupted gently. "Are you sure he said she was Miss Carlin? Did he say so directly? What were his exact words?"

I cast my thoughts back with some difficulty. Back through

the hallways—past the Honourable Rag—hell, I'd left the Honoru-able Rag on the floor in the snow!—and there were cultists on the loose!—through the dining hall—the footman flirting with the kitch-en maid—the potion—the Black Priest!—Corwil winking at me and saying ... I spoke the last aloud: "'She's your Miss Carlin.' That's what he said."

"Could be *she is* or ..."

"Or *she has*," Mrs. Etaris finished for Violet. She tapped the dagger hilt against her cheek. The carbuncles glittered in the were-lights. "If it is the code word for wireweed, which is at least possible ..."

"You don't seem to think Miss Carlin exists, either?"

Mrs. Etaris looked with surprise at Violet. "Miss Redshank, it was a nicely plausible reason for your coming to Ragnor Bella, but I believe events have outpaced it."

"I'm so confused," Miss Shipston said plaintively, just beating me to it. Mr. Dart started to snore.

Violet opened her mouth, closed it, frowned, and finally said: "Perhaps you could explain why you think I'm here looking for this stone?"

Mrs. Etaris nodded placidly. "Indeed. There are two explana-tions, I think I can say. First of all, I was thinking about your name, Miss Redshank, and that of your alleged cousin, Daphne Carlin. Mr. Dart expressed some worries to Mr. Greenwing and myself that we didn't, after all, know much about you; he seemed to feel you had further motives for being in Ragnor Bella than your stated in-tention. On reflection, I agreed with him, since I had noticed a few oddities of your behaviour myself."

Violet spoke with composure. "What were those, Mrs. Etaris?"

"As I mentioned to Mr. Greenwing and Mr. Dart, Redshank is a name common to Eastern Oriole, to Pfaschen, Obforlen, the Little Kingdoms. I went to university in Galderon, and as I have always had an interest in folklore and rural legends, I happened to remember songs I heard there about a certain baker of prodigious magic named Daphne, and her shepherd lover, who was named a variety of things, but often Carling or Carlend or, indeed, Carlin. So for you to have as a cousin a baker of magical pastries named Daphne Carlin, well, my suspicions were aroused."

Galderon, I thought: not a well-known university, and far away from Fiellan. It had something to do with revolutionary politics ... and architecture and plumbing magic ... And had Mrs. Etaris in her younger years studied any of those things?

Mrs. Etaris went on, to my increasing astonishment, describing all sorts of little details that I had missed or entirely misinterpreted: Violet's reaction to my mentioning Alisoun Artquist and her immediate suggestion I was over-tired, her distracting us from Domina Ringley's attendant—and finding Dominus Alvestone—when we were in the market-place—her judicious explanation of the effects of wireweed, so that we all focussed on that question. When at last she stopped, Violet didn't say anything.

I said, "Mrs. Etaris, that was utterly fantastic."

Mrs. Etaris turned to me and grinned, looking abruptly young. "Wasn't it? Pity it's entirely fabricated. The second, and rather more genuine reason, Miss Redshank, is that I heard you discuss the situation with the Honourable Master Ragnor's man down the back of the Raggle. The stepping stones come out near my back garden, and I happened to be down the bottom of the garden very early this morning when you went by."

She tossed the stone at Violet, who caught it with an astounded air and quick grace.

"Now," Mrs. Etaris continued, "I think it's your turn to explain yourself."

Chapter Twenty-Nine

VIOLET LOOKED AT me, almost apologetically, then kept her attention on the shining stone in her hand. She spoke with a certain relief, as if glad not to be lying any longer.

"I have no cousin named Daphne Carlin. I picked it out of a folk song—you're quite right about that, Mrs. Etaris—I needed an excuse to be looking around Ragnor Bella, and that was the story I'd made up. I wasn't expecting Jemis to be here—Jemis, I really wasn't. I had no idea where you were from. I truly didn't know you were the son of Jakory Greenwing. Lark never said."

I didn't say anything. Mrs. Etaris said, "Why *did* you come, Miss Redshank?"

"I came ... I was sent to look for ... two things. There have long been rumours that there is a source of clean magic somewhere in southern Rondé. *Clean* magic, untouched by the Fall, powerful good magic. We need that, where I'm from." She looked down at Miss Shipston. "I'm sure you can understand that. When I was at Morrowlea I was able to look around, enough to know it wasn't in that part of Erlingale. But when I heard the stories of Fiellan—for

Lark did do some research into the area, Jemis, she didn't just rely on your story—"

I couldn't help myself; I snorted.

"Anyhow, it wasn't in Morrowlea or southern Erlingale. The area was too restless, at any rate, for what we'd been hearing. There's a sense of unrest, of urgency, of pain, growing in the hinterlands, Mrs. Etaris—not just Ghilousette and the Farry March, but Erlingale and even the farther parts of Ronderell are growing tense. Only Fiellan seems to be keeping calm and peaceful. I went back to ... where Lark is from, with her. I told you, Jemis, I owe her family a great deal."

Could Violet be in the Indrillines' power? It seemed incredible. But it had seemed incredible that she hadn't stood up to Lark in the spring, too. "Go to," I said stiffly.

She winced, then looked at Mrs. Etaris. "I ran away from an arranged marriage at fourteen. Lark's family took me in. I couldn't just ... not ... I am obligated to them. *Deeply* obligated."

"I understand," Mrs. Etaris said, with a strange note to her voice.

Violet paused, then closed her eyes and nodded. "I heard someone talking about Ragnor Bella, how it was the dullest town in all Fiellan—all Rondé, someone else said—all of Oriole! a third person claimed—and it drew my interest. A dull town? Peaceful, prosperous, where the only interesting thing ever to have happened was the infamous Jakory Greenwing's return from the wars? I thought this might well be the hiding place for the stone. When I reported back the—the family asked me to look into this."

"So the whole story about Ghilousetten trading in magic and the Knockermen is entirely false?" I asked, too incredulous to be outraged—yet.

"No—yes—no—" Violet stopped, took a deep breath. "Look, I can't tell you everything, Jemis. It's not kind to you."

I laughed harshly. "The things that matter to you."

"I'm trying not to implicate you further!" she said intensely, but with a low voice. "Jemis, use the brain you were given. I cannot tell you where I am from. I cannot tell you who sent me. The *family* is not known for liking tattletales. I was sent to look for what could be the source of Fiellan's relative stability and prosperity since the Fall. I have certain resources and connections from the family, and was also asked to look into certain of their business interests. These, together with other indications—such as those I told you before about the Ghilousetten connection—drew me to Ragnor Bella and, eventually, here to the Talgarths'."

I swallowed an exclamation, and managed cautiously: "Am I correct about Domina Ringley?"

Violet shook her head in what appeared relieved exasperation. "I don't know her story, but I'm sure ... you see, the Knockermen—the ones not in the Legendarium—run the largest smuggling operation this side of the Ord, and I ..."

"You can't get too close to them?"

"Everyone should be careful around them," she replied gravely. "I won't say I wasn't asked to notice details if I could. The more I looked into it, the more I realized that the stone was the key—after your and Mr. Dart's story about the cult, I was sure it had to be it." She looked at the stone in her hand. "It is very alluring."

"I don't see how it could be a source of clean magic," I said, "given what the cult priests were doing with it. It was absorbing blood and all sorts of things."

Violet withdrew her finger from touching a bit of the stone between the folds of the handkerchief. "What is it, then?"

"And where did Miss Shipston find it?" I added, relieved to let my mind turn from revelations of Violet's—what could I call it? Perfidy? Betrayal? Secret life?—to this piece of the puzzle. We both turned to Mrs. Etaris, who was smiling and seemed not a whit disconcerted by Violet's story.

"Ah," she said, "perhaps this is where Miss Carlin comes in to the tale again. Miss Shipston, if you would?"

We looked down, but Miss Shipston was nowhere to be seen. "How odd," Mrs. Etaris said calmly, but I noticed that she spun the dagger in her hand until she was holding the hilt properly. "Well, I can tell you that—the Lady bless you, Mr. Greenwing."

I sneezed again, and a third time, and gulped back cool air in the hopes that it would help. "The ring was *working*," I said, and felt abruptly near tears, as the familiar phlegm began to fill my airways. I scrubbed at my face with the soiled glove. "Excuse me."

"But the stone is no source of magic," Mrs. Etaris said, "not unless Magistra Bellamy is entirely—Miss Shipston!"

"Run!" the mermaid gasped, breaking the water in a sudden flash of water droplets. "They are coming, the Dark Kings are coming!"

"I beg your pardon?" Mrs. Etaris said.

"Over the drawbridge, they are coming, they are going within."

Violet and I looked at the shining stone in her hand. I said, "The Black Priest brought me here. The stone was here. Dominus Alvestone is here. The wizard attendant sent me to open the door to the Black Priest—I forgot to mention it—I keep forgetting it—he cast something on me—I don't understand why—"

"You just said it," Mrs. Etaris said: "The house is full of wire-weed."

Violet shook her head in admiration. "What a brilliant cover. A cult of the Old Gods to cover the Knockermen's crimes ..."

"The cult is criminal as well," I said, trying discreetly to wake Mr. Dart up. He didn't seem inclined to move, except that his stone arm slid out of its sling and weighed down my foot. It was really quite heavy; my heart contracted that he had been bearing it so quietly.

"But it sounded as if there were protections against the cult," I said, and then the penny dropped again. "But that's because the attendant is part of it. May even be the ringleader."

"Last night there might have been protections," Mrs. Etaris said thoughtfully, "but tonight there is a dinner party, and Dame Talgarth does follow the old conventions."

"Meaning?"

Violet put her hand within her conical bodice and drew out the small book of *Fifth Imperial Decadent Dinner Parties: A Handbook.* I blinked at her. "Did you *steal* that?"

"You sound remarkably aghast for someone who has been sneaking around someone else's house on false pretences all night."

"That's from *our* store."

"A day and a half!" Mr. Dart said suddenly, leaping bolt upright.

I staggered away from him and nearly went into the moat. Violet caught me, and I floundered upright, only to see the door swinging behind Mr. Dart.

"He's gone back inside!"

"Thank you for that statement of the obvious," Violet said,

with a delicious mockery of our tutor's manner. "And Mrs. Etaris has gone off around the corner."

I shook my head. "What ... I am so confused ... what did she mean?"

Violet shoved the book at me. "I think she means that Dame Talgarth will be having an illusionist as the finale of the dinner party—that's the appropriate ritual ending for the first New Moon after the autumn equinox."

"The Honourable Rag thought Domina Ringley would be providing illusions."

"There you are." She flipped the pages, frowning as her high periwig cast a shadow on the page from the werelight behind her. I moved to stand next to her where I could see the text. "The problem is that—"

"The orgy is supposed to come first. Dame Talgarth *surely* isn't—"

"Not just that, but you let the Black Priest across the threshold. And the Dark Kings come at the beginning and the end."

Sex and death, that meant. I swallowed. "Hell."

We stared at each other. "I shouldn't trust you," I said.

"No."

"You keep lying to me."

"Yes."

"You're never going to tell me the truth, are you?"

"Probably not."

There didn't seem to be much I could do about that. I straightened my shoulders. "Well," I said, trying to drawl in imitation of how I'd always imagined the debonair Fitzroy Angursell to have spoken on the eve of some grand adventure. "It looks as if we might be staging a rescue."

Violet smiled slowly at me. My heart beat faster. The drugs and the magic, of course; except that it wasn't, of course. She slipped the book back into her bodice, lifted her freed hand, and I thought for a moment—but then she shook her head. "You can't possibly go back inside like that. And what happened to your periwig?"

I blinked. "I left the Honourable Rag lying on it. He slipped and knocked himself out."

"Men. I'll do my best with the powder." She pulled out a small round tin from down her bodice. I barely refrained from commenting on how much room she appeared to have down there, which on a hasty second thought was a distinctly ungentlemanly sort of thing to notice.

She flicked it open to reveal a quantity of grey powder and a small sponge, with which she quickly and thoroughly repaired the damage running, sneezing, wiping my face, and so forth had done to my make-up, and then proceeded to dump most of the rest of it on my head.

"Your hair is so silky," she murmured, using her fingers to twist it back into a tidy queue. She pulled out one of the ribbons from her own ensemble and tied it. "There. Not perfect, but I expect by this stage of the evening no one will care. I regret to say I asked Alisoun to spike the wine before I realized what exactly was going to be going on with the dinner party."

"Dare I ask with what?"

"—This is all very civilized and delightful," Mrs. Etaris burst in, rushing back at us like a dark blue sheepdog herding her flock, "but I'm afraid we really should be going inside if we don't want our friends and neighbours to be sacrificed to the Dark Kings. Especially since it would be a botched sacrifice given that Miss Redshank is in possession of their ritual stone."

"I think on the whole, I'd prefer not to lose my one close friend in Ragnor Bella to their machinations."

"Don't be melodramatic, dear Mr. Greenwing, you have many friends."

"In Ragnor Bella, I said, Violet."

"Hush," said Mrs. Etaris, her eyes bright and flashing behind the scarf, which she'd arranged to cover the lower half of her face. "Are you ready?"

"You're certain this isn't truly magic?" Violet asked, folding the handkerchief more completely around the stone.

"Magistra Bellamy—I have no time to explain—no, it's a piece of polished obsidian from Kaphyrn, which is why it has magical resonances, but it is not in itself a source of magic, and according to Magistra Bellamy is purely a conduit."

"Very well, then," said Violet, and tucked it down her bodice as well. I tried hard not to stare. Morrowlea fashions had run to much looser stays and flowing Arcadian-style gowns in pale colours. Surely even a tight corset didn't make that much of a difference to the shape of a woman's bosom?

I was still trying to work out how Violet could possibly have that much room down her maid's outfit when we went through the door to find ourselves at the tail end of a mass of cultists in full bacchic fervour.

Chapter Thirty

EVEN MRS. ETARIS halted before launching into the mass.

She looked up and down the hall, as if counting. Violet—I don't know what Violet was assessing, but she looked calculating and thoughtful. I imitated them to very little purpose, except for finding one of the hidden doors near us.

Mrs. Etaris whispered, "They seem to know the house well. They're splitting, I would guess one portion to collect the wireweed and the other to the sacrifice. Now ... we must get upstairs to the dining hall before things go utterly awry ..."

"Up here!" I said, glad to be of help, and pushed open the door to reveal one of the serving stairs.

I had to stop at the top of the third flight of stairs to catch my breath, my throat sore. I didn't sneeze, but did cough at the dusty air kicked up by our arrival. Violet raised her eyebrows deprecatingly at me. "You need to find some stairs to run up for practice."

"I don't really intend to make a habit of this."

"No? It's ever so much fun."

"I'll look for a fencing partner instead."

"Because Ragnor Bella runs *so* much to sword fighting."

Mrs. Etaris was breathing a little heavily as she joined us. She wrapped her scarf again around her face, tucking the ends securely under. Violet assisted her to arrange a fold to cover her mousy-auburn hair.

"There. No one should recognize you."

"I wouldn't expect them to," Mrs. Etaris said, eyes crinkling in a merry smile. "They have no reason to expect me here, and, of course, they will be both drunk and half-enchanted by this stage of the evening, I should think."

"And drugged with ardmoor, I'm afraid," Violet added.

Ardmoor. That was what I'd drunk down in the kitchen, the famous aphrodisiac of Orio. Albeit habit-forming, at least it was not reputed to be quite as dire in its addictive side effects as wireweed.

"Mm, I see." Mrs. Etaris opened the door before us a crack, and peered out carefully. "Right. This opens into the next room over from the hall, the wine steward's pantry ... and oh my word." She let the door slide carefully shut as she started to chuckle.

"What is it?" I asked, more nervously than I quite liked. Violet glanced at me deprecatingly again.

"Oh ... Mr. Benson appears to be in ... cahoots ... with Domina Ringley's attendant."

I edged forward to peer through the crack, and stifled a snort. "Is that what you call it, Mrs. Etaris?"

Mrs. Etaris might have been blushing behind her scarf; she sounded very prim. "It's one name for it."

Mr. Benson and the lady in green and purple were sprawled up against the wine steward's table. The decanters were pushed inelegantly against the wall; one crystal decanter had already fallen off under their movements and another was near to toppling. Viscous ruby port spilled across the white marble floor, making me for a moment fearful of blood before I saw the shards.

"I think we might pass quickly behind them and into the dining chamber," Mrs. Etaris said. "They seem most preoccupied, don't you think, Mr. Greenwing?"

"Oh, I expect so," I said, and backed away. "I'm not certain ... I'm surprised Mr. Benson would be party to this. He seemed like the Proctor at Morrowlea, Violet, entirely concerned with the proper arrangement of the evening."

"From that book, this sounds very much part of the proper arrangements." She took her turn with the crack. "He also looks as if he's the one being seduced."

"How do you reckon that?"

Violet and Mrs. Etaris both looked at me, then exchanged glances, and then Mrs. Etaris said gently, "Never mind that, Mr. Greenwing. Now, shall we go see what is happening with the dinner party?"

"I think that's a good idea, Mrs. Etaris," Violet said, and from a pocket in her skirts drew forth a long silver dagger. I was merely grateful she didn't have that down her bodice as well, and was a bit late realizing that both the women were armed and I wasn't.

Mrs. Etaris and Violet had already gone into the room, ducking down below the line of the lady's dubious attention. I was trying to watch both of them and tripped on a rucked-up piece of carpeting laid to muffle the sounds of shoes on marble. I tumbled right up against Mr. Benson's feet and knocked him and the wizard off the table with a crash from the remaining decanters.

Mr. Benson let out a shriek as he landed on the floor, curling up around himself. I winced in strong sympathetic reaction. The wizard did not appear hurt, though she was very angry. She jumped to her feet with balletic grace and glared at me.

The venom in her expression held me fixed. I caught my breath.

There was an odd feeling to the air, thunderstormy and airless. My throat was closing, my nose filling again with mucus. I wasn't sneezing but unable to look around, to speak, to think clearly.

I raised my hand to my mouth automatically, trying to cover my nose and mouth with the glove I was still clenching. The ring knocked against my teeth and the constriction eased enough for me to gasp several breaths. *Magic.*

Her eyes narrowed. One hand lifted to the emerald pendant, gripping the stone with white fingers. I stared at her hands, fighting again for breath. Her fingernails were dirty. The ring seemed to be buzzing weirdly. Perhaps that was my head. I felt dizzy with lack of air. The port wine and dust from the passage-way and the fine powder Violet had dumped on my head were combining to choke me. My hand felt heavy. I wanted to drop it down, drop myself down, lie down at her feet next to Mr. Benson.

Her lips turned up into a smile with nothing of merriment or courtesy in it. My head drooped away from her intense eyes, pale as Miss Shipston's and even less sane. Her fingernails were really remarkably dirty. Her nails were painted a glossy lacquer, pale silver like a fish scale. Against her sallow skin they looked like the herring scales from the stargazy pie. The emerald seemed almost to be glowing between her fingers.

Miss Carlin down in the kitchen had fingernails like that, I thought. She wasn't wearing green and purple, wasn't dressed as a lady, but she had been—

"That's it," the woman before me said, her voice soft and caressing. "Step closer, darling."

I tried to shake my head, tried to step back. Mr. Benson was at my feet. I couldn't step onto him. Stepped forward to get away from his legs.

"One more," she murmured, hand massaging the stone. "You'd do that for me, wouldn't you?"

With great effort I raised my eyes from her hand to her face, trying to muster the air to repudiate her, reject her, but as soon as I lifted my head I was caught again in her sharp pale glittering intensity. The air felt close and thick around me, ears echoing thunderously and field of vision narrowed onto her face. I held the ring pressed against my lip, the metal throbbing with my blood. I was so dizzy. Her eyes were so much like Miss Shipston's—her hands like the undercook Miss Carlin's—her fingernails like fish scales—

"My darling," she said, her melodious voice cutting through my racing heartbeat like fish underwater. I gasped silently, shallowly. The air was so thick. "Give me your hand. That's it. That's it."

She spoke as if I were a child, I thought with faint indignation, but not coherently enough to prevent myself from dropping my hand from my mouth.

As I slowly extended it she smiled deeply at me, reached out with her fish-scale fingers to caress my hand, draw off the soiled glove. I perforce stepped closer, until I could smell the intense lilac-and-sweet-pea perfume she wore, a smell that seemed to go straight to some place behind my eyes. I tried to tug my hand away from hers, but she merely drew me closer.

And then, as seductively as Lark had ever made love to me, she kissed me deeply—and pulled off the ring.

Chapter Thirty-One

I'M NOT SURE I can say I sneezed so much as I exploded.

All the pent-up reaction to all the magic in the Talgarths' house, the enchantments the wizard had been trying to wrap me in, the wireweed and the illusions and the lights and the talcum powder and the dust and the port wine and the sweet peas and the lilac—

I don't think I shall ever forget her expression.

She didn't resist when I grabbed the ring from her hand and shoved it back on my finger. She didn't protest when I grabbed the emerald pendant from around her neck, breaking the chain and no doubt bruising her neck. She was still shuddering, one hand touching the moisture on her face with little revolted motions, when I bent down to retrieve the largest piece of decanter from the floor.

Mr. Benson was out cold, under what spell or distress I didn't know. I pulled off his decorative sash and used it to bind the wizard's hands, and then, remembering a few comments in my early History of Magic classes, gagged her with my decorative cuff of Orchpoint lace, which ripped off handily with the assistance of the jagged shard. She finally opened her eyes when I pulled the knot tight, glaring at me. I hastily picked up the shard again, and she swallowed hard.

I hesitated then, prisoner in one hand and makeshift knife in the other, stuffed up but no longer sneezing, awkwardly half-aroused despite myself and half-disgusted by everything. I turned the wizard around, shoving her towards the door into the dining chamber. It was designed to open when prodded with a foot (further evidence of the Talgarths' cost-cutting measures, as in a proper Astandalan house the doors would have opened by magic), but I had to really kick it to get it open.

The reason for this was evident as soon as I did get it open, for one of the chairs was thrown across the door. I kicked this out of the way, propelled my prisoner inside, and stopped in the doorway in astonishment.

The great sturgeon lay dismembered in the middle of the table. It looked so thoroughly dismembered, in fact, I wondered for an incredulous moment whether someone had sat in it. When I saw the backside of Dame Talgarth's dress, with the saffron sauce streaking her from floor to waist, I didn't know what to think.

Dame Talgarth was in the process of throwing herself at Dominus Alvestone, fists raised and punching wildly. Mr. Dart was trying to pull her off, hampered by only being able to use one of his arms. One of the maids and two of the footmen were having hysterics in the corner. All three of them were in dishevelled states of undress, with food and wine stains liberally evident. The other footmen did not seem in evidence.

I looked around. Miss Figheldean was bent over a puddle of pale lavender in the corner I took to be Miss Woodhill. Mrs. Figheldean was nowhere in sight, nor was the Honourable Rag, nor Mrs.

Etaris nor Violet nor the rest of the servers. Nor any cultists.

There was Domina Ringley, the only one to notice our arrival. She stood on the table, one foot on the sturgeon's head and her hands full of the clover-like wireweed blossoms. The room was full of thick scent and heavy magic, and I sneezed. The wizard shook horribly in my grasp.

Domina Ringley lifted the flowers in her hand like an offering to the gods. She took a deep breath, preparing to say something, staring fearsomely at us. I held my breath in astonishment. The wizard shook again, and I realized that she wasn't shuddering with horror but with laughter.

I did the only thing I could think of, and hurled the decanter at Domina Ringley. She ducked away from it, slipped in the sturgeon, and landed breathless full length on the table. One remaining epergne went sailing off onto the marble floor with a tinny ringing sound.

"Silver plate," Mr. Dart said, turning his head at the sound. "Oh—hallo—Domina Ringley's down—"

I'd had to release one hand from the wizard to throw the decanter, and now she twisted fully out of my grasp and ran towards the table. I let out an exclamation and set out after her, but Mr. Dart was faster, and clubbed her with his stone arm. I slipped on something, gasped, and skidded against the wall. I tipped through another doorway and landed hard several steps down, on top of someone who said, "Ooof," with great feeling.

"Mrs. Etaris?" I said hesitantly, catching my breath.

"You keep arriving so unexpectedly, Mr. Greenwing," said she, setting me upright with sturdy movements.

"What just happened?"

"I could ask you that, except I can smell the perfume on you and I heard the sneezing, so I suspect a partial ensorcellment."

"Yes, but—"

"Violet and I entered the dining chamber to find that Domina Ringley was beginning the sacrifice to the Dark Kings under cover of her fake illusions."

"What—Domina Ringley—fake illusions?"

"Do keep up, Mr. Greenwing. Of course Domina Ringley is involved with the cult. You were the one to say so."

"Really?" I said, as she set off at a good pace down the hallway. "Uh—where are we going?"

"The drawbridge, of course."

"Oh, of course." I stumbled on a shallow stair. "Could you explain a bit more about what's happening, please?"

She made a turn without hesitation, as sure-footed as when going through Ragnor Bella's back alleys. Her next words pushed my curiosity about that out of mind.

"Very well, then. Your friend Violet is clearly acting as an Indrilline agent, though I must admit I don't believe all of her tale on that front. You gave me the clue, Mr. Greenwing, when you said you thought Domina Ringley was growing wireweed under pretence of growing out new species of vetch for Justice Talgarth's sweet pea breeding programme. Watch your step here."

I rebounded off the wall and followed her more circumspectly, rubbing my nose. The passageway was dim and narrow, but not dusty; I found I could breathe much better. "I'm afraid I'm not following you."

"This part is straight-forward," she said critically, looking both ways before opening a door onto a brightly lit passageway, scurrying across what I realized belatedly was the main public hall of the Talgarths' house, and into another dark passage on the other side. "Essentially, I was thinking over what I'd heard from Magistra Bellamy about the stone, your Miss Redshank's reaction when I gave it to her, and her reaction again when I told her it was not the source of magic, and—Mr. Greenwing, are you all right?"

"No, I feel dizzy," I said. "I'm sorry, Mrs. Etaris. I find the air here hard to breathe."

"Of course you do," she said in a much more sympathetic voice. "I should have remembered. We're nearly there, at any rate."

"Why the drawbridge?"

"Shh!" We stopped before a closed door so she could press her ear to it and listen. I watched her in puzzlement before something I'd studied in Architecture finally made it through the fog in my brain, and I pushed the small square of wood covering a peephole open.

Mrs. Etaris smiled gratefully and peered through it.

"There's Master Roald," she whispered. "Hush now."

I wasn't saying anything, so I tried to breathe more quietly. I found another peephole and stooped to look through it. The Honourable Rag was sitting on the floor on top of my periwig, brushing himself down, but just as I focussed on him he turned, paused, and then smiled in greeting.

"Miss Redshank, I believe. I see why you rejected my invitation. A most fetching outfit."

Violet stopped before him. "Master Roald."

"You received my message, then."

"You need to be more careful; it was nearly lost."

"Nearly is only a problem when it's on the other side."

Violet tilted her head to look at him with that cool consideration, the look of the Tarvenmoor duellist—or an Indrilline agent. (The Standard, I thought, inadequately and unhappily. Why did I fall for women like this?)

The Honourable Rag smiled, leaning back on his hands. The golden ring glinted as he moved. "I've paid my year's dues, I hope you see that."

"You are a fool if you think it stops here," she replied.

"Is that how you were caught? Being foolish? Or is that only what happened when you met Jemis Greenwing?"

There was a pause, and then Violet walked forward two steps and slapped him across the face. He blinked at her, smirk finally gone, eyes dangerous.

Violet spoke with a low and vicious intensity. "Your business is mine because your folly has made it so. My business remains my own. Be the big man in your little backwater, and never let it be known what you did in the back rooms of Orio, and hope to the Emperor that you learn no more of blackmail than you have tasted this summer."

His voice was shaky, but I did have to admire the fact that he did continue on: "And Mr. Greenwing?"

"Perhaps you might try learning from him what honour means," she said. "Go to: tell everyone you've rescued them from the cult. They'll believe you, I'm sure."

And off she strode, leaving the Honourable Rag sitting there on the floor staring after her, until he finally shook his head and stood up, and smiled, and said to the air, "Now *there* is a woman," and stalked off the other direction, riffling his curls with one hand as he went.

***

WE HASTENED ACROSS the hallway, me retrieving my periwig as we passed it, with jumbled thoughts and sentiments, and in due course arrived at a small square room with a window and a large windlass in it. Mrs. Etaris nodded in satisfaction. "I was quite certain they wouldn't be leaving *this* to contemporary magic," she said. "Mr. Greenwing, will you look out the window and tell me what you see?"

The window was rather too high for her to see out of. I stretched up to my full height, such as it is, and peered out into the night.

"It's nearly dawn," I said in surprise.

"Yes, it's been quite the night. Do you see anyone?"

I frowned at the moat, calm and quiet in the soft grey light coming from the left. The Talgarths' front door faced southward, of course. This orientation had originally led across a lawn to the river, but had necessitated the drawbridge after they diverted the Ladybeck for their moat.

"I don't see Miss Shipston anywhere."

"No?"

"The lady wizard upstairs had eyes like hers," I said with a shiver, "all pale and mad."

"Did they indeed? The road, Mr. Greenwing."

I looked up into the mists on the other side of the river. "There are riders coming—banners—" My mind flashed to the game of Poacher, and my thoughts about how the Green Dragon wouldn't be witness to—"Mrs. Etaris, it can't be one of the southern barons revolting, surely not? Those look like—I can't see the standards—"

"I'd forgotten you'd been on the edge of all that unrest across the border in West Erlingale," Mrs. Etaris said. "No, it's not a war party. It's Justice Talgarth come home and, if I do not mistake myself, an ambassador of the Lady sent for Miss Shipston. Wind down the windlass, Mr. Greenwing, if you would."

"Why would—"

"Your Miss Redshank is not the only one able to communicate outside the barony," she said demurely.

The riders, half a dozen or so of them, halted on the other side of the moat. One rider, corpulent and empurpled, waved them back. Justice Talgarth in his official cape, indicating the distance the drawbridge came down. One of the banners caught the wind: a white unicorn on blue and green spun out, catching the first rays of the sun.

I sighed with relief at the sight of the Lady's flag and set my hand to the windlass. The handle turned easily, the drawbridge coming down smoothly. The horses stamped a bit, and one neighed, but the riders were good and kept control. Once it was down Mrs. Etaris nodded decisively.

"Do we go to meet them?" I asked uncertainly, looking around the little room to see another door, this one undoubtedly leading to the antechamber to the hall where the butler might stand awaiting his master's return.

"What are they doing?"

I looked through the window again. Justice Talgarth was speaking to the other riders, all of whom dismounted. They left one of their number to watch the horses and the rest followed the Justice across the drawbridge. They were about halfway across when the main house door boomed open with a satisfying crash. They stopped.

The Honourable Master Roald strode out, the gagged and bound wizard in tow.

Mrs. Etaris opened the door to the antechamber between the windlass room and the front entry, found a wooden chair, and placed it where she could stand and look out the window with me. I discovered the window opened, and slid the pane across.

"Justice Talgarth," said the Honourable Rag, in a clear and carrying voice. The morning breeze tossed his blond curls back so they caught the sunlight. In his scarlet and gold he looked like a prince. Two of the Lady's people were women; one eyed him most favourably. (The other, who was dressed in a Scholar's long black robes, hood lined with Fallowven blue, was focused on the wizard.)

"Master Roald," replied the Justice. "Dare I ask what has occurred? I had an urgent post from the Chief Constable saying that my wife was under threat from a renegade wizard and that a mermaid was involved!"

I glanced at Mrs. Etaris, who grinned at me. Her scarf had slipped down again, so I could see her delight. "You didn't ..."

"Shh," she whispered, "our voices will carry."

I frowned and turned back to the party on the bridge. The Honourable Rag had gathered himself up for a spot of oratory.

"Justice Talgarth, I feel I am greatly to blame. I encouraged Dame Talgarth to have one final dinner party of the summer, and under the blandishments of Domina Ringley encouraged her moreover to make it a traditional late Astandalan style one, such as she loves but does not often mount in these lesser days."

"I am relieved," I murmured. Mrs. Etaris suppressed a giggle.

"I did not realize what temptation the occasion would prove to the false nurse attending Domina Ringley—"

"My sister-in-law has been ill with a lingering chest complaint for several years," Justice Talgarth said to the chief legate, a short man in silvered mail overlaid with a rich surcoat bearing the Lady's crest. He had short curly black hair and beard and a strong nose, perhaps hailing from the south of the Western Sea.

"I see," said the legate, exchanging a glance with the woman not wearing Scholar's robes. She nodded thoughtfully.

"That may be so," said the Honourable Rag, "but she was abusing that position of trust, and your wife's hospitality, to rendezvous with another renegade wizard, this one pretending to be a Scholar of Inghail here researching in the barony libraries, but instead inciting some of the local rabble to a trumped-up cult of the old gods."

He pushed the wizard forward a step so she glared at him. "This is the false nurse. As near as I can make out, she learned you were returning home this weekend, and decided that not only would she and her accomplice complete their run of theft from the local country houses—for I have learned that these two renegades were plying their wicked deceptions in Yellem and Garmont before coming here to Ragnor!"

"Infamous!" said Justice Talgarth.

"Indeed, sir," said the Honourable Rag. "The false Dominus Alvestone and Madame Harcourt, here, arranged for their cultist followers to invade the Garth and despoil the house, while she used her magic to subdue the diners and staff. Domina Ringley had asked her assistant to perform an illusion as a favour to her sister and an honour to the Lady on this autumnal feast, but Madame Harcourt used the opportunity instead to enchant and confound us."

"How did you spite her?" the legate asked, with a doubtful look at Madame Harcourt, who was sagging now against the Honourable Rag's hands. With a glance at the Scholar, the Honourable Rag set her down on the drawbridge, where she slumped inattentive to her surroundings. Or apparently so. I frowned at the way she slid her hand slowly across the boards towards the Honourable Rag's foot.

"It was only thanks to Mr. Dart of Dartington's quick work, and the assistance of two of the servants here, that we managed to foil their evil. I escaped the worst of the enchantment only fortuitously, having left to visit the privy before the wizard began her work. But this, of course, left the diners alone to face their peril."

Mrs. Etaris snorted. My respect for her went up yet another notch.

"Mr. Dart was the first to realize something was amiss. He took it upon himself to break Madame Harcourt's concentration, and thus prevent the full completion of the ensorcellment, though with some grievous result to himself. Without his prompt action I don't know how we should have managed. He was quickly attacked by Dominus Alvestone, who had seen what was going on—but while Mr. Dart subdued Dominus Alvestone and his attendant, your butler, Benson, had forced Madame Harcourt into the butler's pantry and was immobilizing her. He managed to bind her with the assistance of one of the footmen, but alas, he was injured in the struggle."

"And the footman?"

"The footman ran away, because at that point the cultists Dominus Alvestone and Madame Harcourt had ordered to come had arrived, and I was engaged in full battle with them." The Honourable Rag held up his arm so everyone could admire his tattered scarlet coat. "Two of your maidservants, Justice Talgarth, are of remarkable courage, for they bound the fallen with rags and sashes after I had disarmed them."

"How many are there?"

"Some two dozen," the Honourable Rag said off-handedly, to surprised and impressed murmurs. I looked sidelong at Mrs. Etaris, who rolled her eyes. When I looked back at the bridge, I thought I saw movement from Madame Harcourt, but on second glance she was still, crumpled into herself, and the movement was in the water. Miss Shipston, no doubt, listening in.

"They are all bound and locked into one of the rooms," the Honourable Rag assured his audience, with audible self-satisfaction. "Once I had finished rounding them up, I sent the maidservants to clean up and returned to the dining hall, which I found as I have said. Mr. Dart filled me in on what I had missed, and just as we were debating what to do with Madame Harcourt—Dominus Alvestone is unconscious and bound within—one of the servants rushed in to tell us riders were approaching. Down I came with my prisoner, therefore, to tell you of what has befallen."

"I—I'm not quite sure what to say," began Justice Talgarth, whose face was nearly as purple as his cape at this point. "I must thank you, Master Roald, for your decisive work."

"It is nothing but what I felt called to do," he said, most pomp-ously, "and Mr. Dart and your servants were of great help."

"Ware!" cried the Scholar-mage suddenly, in a thick accent. "The wizard—"

We all looked at the wizard. The Honourable Rag moved his foot back hastily as the dress suddenly collapsed into itself and a thick silvery smoke rose up. While they all backed away, coughing, the water below roiled and a sleek grey tail flashed in the air—and

Miss Shipston rose up with a wriggling figure clenched tight in her hands. The Scholar mage chanted a string of words that set a series of flashes in the air, bright sparkly things like Winterturn fireworks, and the wriggling thing turned back into the body of a woman.

Miss Shipston sank under the weight. She bobbed upright a moment later, flexing her tail to get to the bank, where the envoy's men had hastily gathered to collect the wizard in.

Then they all stared at Miss Shipston, until the envoy said: "Thank you. Lady Antoinette?"

The second woman walked away from the group to talk to the mermaid. "Miss Shipston? I have been sent by Lady Jessamine to speak to you."

Miss Shipston stared. "M-me? What do you mean? How does the Lady know my name?"

"She has her ways," said Lady Antoinette, and sat down on the drawbridge heedless of her dress, the better to talk. I felt more puzzled than anything, but relieved that someone, at least, would be there to help the poor woman.

The rest went inside and upstairs, leaving Lady Antoinette and a guardsman with the horses. Mrs. Etaris got off the chair, groaning as she straightened from kneeling on the hard wood, and promptly sat down again. I slid down to the floor.

"I guess we can't go home just yet."

"I expect we'll be able to go presently," Mrs. Etaris said. "Fortunately I don't open the store the Monday after market-day."

"Mm."

"That was a good story of Master Roald's, wasn't it?"

"Mm."

"Come now, Mr. Greenwing, surely you didn't want credit? I

think Miss Redshank and Mr. Dart fabricated a delightful tale for him to say. It has the merits of being mostly true, avoiding all mention of wireweed smuggling or the Indrillines or the Knockermen—or you—and yet explaining almost all of what went on tonight. And I daresay the accomplishment of Madame Harcourt and Dominus Alvestone with respect to the cult is quite correct."

I thought back to Madame Harcourt's voice, general size, and motions. "She could well have been the White Priest."

"Indeed, in the old days that would have gone to a woman. The white priest is female, the black priest male, and the silver priest an androgyne of one sort or another. I shouldn't be surprised if Dominus Alvestone turned out to have once been Domina."

"But ... it certainly seemed to be a real cult ..."

"That it was being used as cover for the Indrillines' harvest of wireweed does not prevent that, Mr. Greenwing. Things are not always simple, you know."

I sighed. "I still don't know how you knew where the stone was, nor why Violet—"

Mrs. Etaris patted my hand. "Once we'd realized that Dominus Alvestone was staying here, and that he was the Silver Priest, I thought about where *I* would hide such a precious fake, and came up with the old clay pits along the Ladybeck. They're easy enough to get to from a boat, and I'd heard from Madame Bellamy, when I went to enquire about what kind of stone they might be using, that Dominus Alvestone had been seen punting along the Ladybeck and the Raggle at all hours, claiming to be a botanist looking for rare night-blooming plants."

"A botanist ..."

"Yes, I expect he, Domina Ringley, and Madame Harcourt were

all three of them in it, more or less deeply. I don't suppose we'll ever know the depths of it, unless your friend Miss Redshank finds out from her connections and chooses to tell us. Madame Bellamy's house is along the Rag, not far from here, so when I had thought of the clay pits I followed the riverside path until I found Mr. Shipston, Mr. Clegger, and Miss Shipston herself. She was quite willing to assist me in finding it, and I was able to send Mr. Clegger to the posting-house to send an urgent message on to Justice Talgarth."

"And the Lady's embassy?"

"You and Mr. Dart met the Lady the night before last," Mrs. Etaris said, smiling down at me. "She might well have known by her magic that there was enchantment here. And if not … perhaps Miss Redshank's messages from the Green Dragon are not going only to the Indrillines on their way to the Western Sea."

I nodded, mind whirling. We sat in silence for a while, listening to feet tromp back and forth over the drawbridge. "What do you think I should do about Violet, Mrs. Etaris?"

"Do?" I looked at her, and she smiled gently. "My dear Mr. Greenwing, there is little to be done."

"Oh," I said glumly, and sat there frowning at my pink breeches. "And Mr. Dart?"

"Magistra Bellamy is going to do some research on his behalf. Very discreetly. I believe neither of you will want to involve Dominus Gleason if at all possible."

I looked at her, but she was examining her gloves to see if she'd torn or stained them. "Oh." I was finding it hard to focus. I was so hungry, I thought, I would have been willing to eat even the stargazy pie. "Wait—what about the pie?"

"Oh," said Violet, flinging herself into the room and grinning at how she startled us. "I'm sorry, Jemis."

"*You* made it!"

She shrugged apologetically. "No. It was a message for me."

"From—"

"From someone up to their ears in Lark's family's business," she said, "and most desirous of no one finding out."

"Roald," I said, things coming together. "He's been gambling far too high, hasn't he?"

Violet shook her head, smiling. "You'll do well at Inveragory, Jemis."

"Violet—"

She paused, hand on the door, much the same way she had paused at the door to the priest-cote. This time I was no longer angry, though perhaps I ought to have been. My head was hurting, my nose itchy. Overall I felt half itchy and half bruised, and altogether befuddled, and generally—

I wanted to ask her if I could write to her. But instead I said, "Violet ... go with the Lady."

"And you, Jemis," she replied thickly, and turned away hastily, but not so hastily that I didn't see the tears forming. And that, as they say, was that.

Or nearly.

***

MRS. ETARIS AND I walked back to Ragnor Bella together. We were quiet most of the way, until as we crested the rise by the Little Church Mrs. Etaris said, "We never do know the full stories to things, you know."

I was startled out of my reverie. "I beg your pardon?"

"On adventures. We never do find out everything."

"Oh," I said.

She tucked her arm into mine. "Nor do the right people ever get the credit."

"Oh," I said again.

The morning light shone from behind us, catching the blue smoke rising from the town, and a grey glitter on the sweep of the Rag to the north.

The wrong sort of herring. A cult, two secret societies, Violet certainly-not-Redshank, Mr. Dart, the Honourable Rag, Mrs. Buchance, a university result I hadn't dared hope for, an affinity for magic I hadn't dreamed of, a life that was not at all what I had expected six months ago—

A life that I might very easily have lost, if Lark was an Indrilline and had gotten her own way. A job I once wouldn't have been able to admit liking.

I sauntered along, enjoying the morning, Mrs. Etaris' hand light on my arm.

Mrs. Etaris chuckled lightly at her thoughts, and when I glanced at her, said, "But then again, Mr. Greenwing, it would hardly *do* for us to get the credit for saving a dinner party to which neither of us were invited."

She smiled mischievously. I smiled back.

The Etiquette Mistress, I tell you.

Note

Stargazy Pie *is the first book of Greenwing & Dart. Book Two,* Bee Sting Cake, *carries on the adventures of Mr. Greenwing and Mr. Dart (not to mention the Honourable Rag) as Jemis tries to establish a place for himself in Ragnor Bella, Mr. Dart tries to persuade him to more adventures, and all the neighbourhood, including an errant dragon, is eagerly preparing for the much-anticipated baking contest at the Dartington Harvest Fair.*

Bee Sting Cake *is now available.*

Please visit the author's website, www.victoriagoddard.ca, for the opportunity to join her newsletter, to be informed about new releases and to receive a free short story, "Stone Speaks to Stone," the true tale of what happend to Major Jakory Greenwing at Loe.

Made in the USA
Las Vegas, NV
28 February 2024

86432435R00218